MISSION IN MALMÖ

Torquil MacLeod

McNIDDER & GRACE CRIME

Published by McNidder & Grace
21 Bridge Street
Carmarthen SA31 3JS
Wales, United Kingdom
www.mcnidderandgrace.com

Original paperback first published 2023

A catalogue record for this work is available from the British Library.

ISBN: 9780857162380

Designed by JS Typesetting Ltd, Porthcawl
Printed and bound in the Czech Republic by Finidr

To the late Bill Foster. Much missed.

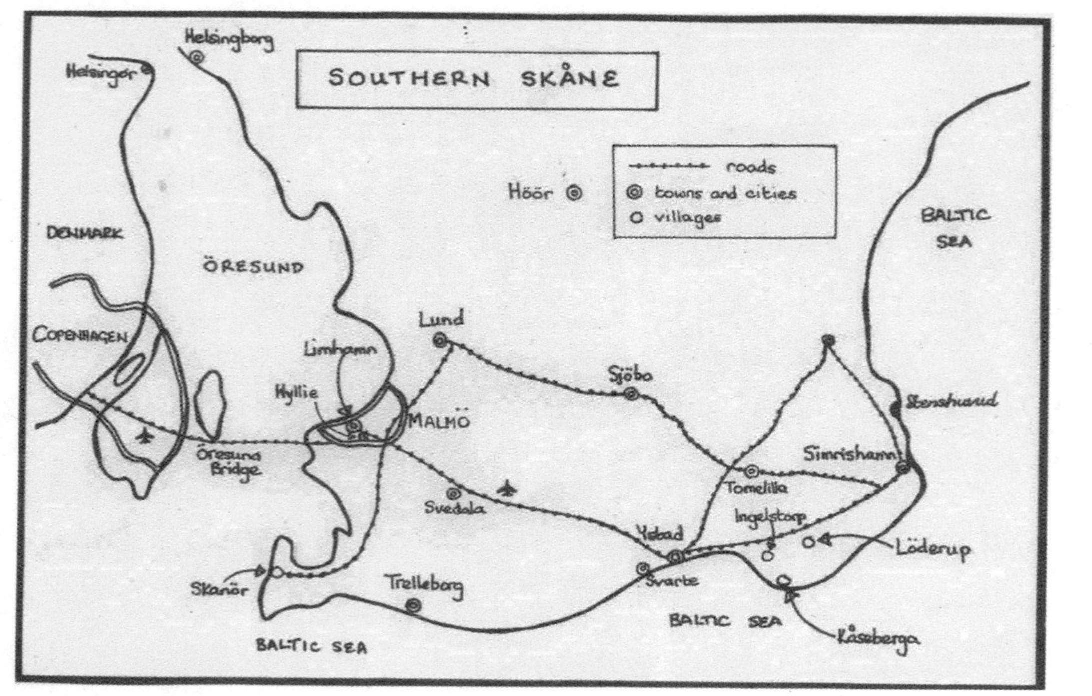
SOUTHERN SKÅNE
roads
towns and cities
villages
Helsingborg
Helsingør
DENMARK
ÖRESUND
COPENHAGEN
Öresund Bridge
Limhamn
Hyllie
MALMÖ
Lund
Höör
Sjöbo
Svedala
Skanör
Trelleborg
Ystad
Svarte
Tomelilla
Simrishamn
Stenshuvud
Ingelstorp
Löderup
Kåseberga
BALTIC SEA
BALTIC SEA
BALTIC SEA

PROLOGUE

Six months ago.

'I want the Swede found!'

Salvatore Baresi gave the Boss a warning look.

Some solemn heads had turned to look at the imposing, silver-haired man in the expensive dark coat and the gleaming handmade shoes. He was standing, straight and taut, next to Baresi, who thought that the dark glasses were an affectation too far; the Boss was scary enough without them. There were nervous glances from the other mourners. The beefy, unsmiling pallbearers slowly lowered the coffin into the ground as the priest muttered the expected religious platitudes on death.

The weak, wintry sun bathed the scene in a ghostly pale light as a woman began to moan loudly. Baresi knew it was the Boss's daughter, Antonella. It was her fool of a husband who was heading towards the Pearly Gates. If St. Peter had any sense, he wouldn't open them. Matteo was no great loss, but the Boss had taken his death personally. He was kin; for Italians like him, that counted for a lot. But the strong bond of the familial unit had been stretched to the limit in Matteo's case; the guy was a handicap.

The widow slumped against a supportive shoulder as her ten-year-old son threw some dirt into the hole. It rattled as it dispersed over the top of the wooden coffin. Then she was steered through the same manoeuvre. This only produced more wailing. Baresi could sense the Boss's teeth gnashing, and his eyes were glinting. The man might be nearly eighty, but you could see he looked after himself, unlike many of his contemporaries who hadn't made old bones. He was lean – just like his operation. After cutting his teeth on the blood and brutality of the archetypal Chicago gangland scene, he had adapted to the modern realities of their business. He didn't suffer fools gladly – unless they married into the family, and even then, they had to work hard to gain his trust. Yet the Swede had won him over. Even Baresi, by his own highly sceptical standards, had been taken in.

And then it had all gone wrong. The Swede had fooled them all. But how had the FBI found out? And why the fuck had he wasted cocky, dumbass Matteo?

The gathering parted as the Boss went to the graveside and added his earthy contribution. He gave his daughter a valedictory nod and returned to Baresi.

'Enough.'

He began to walk briskly along the wide path through the Mount Carmel Catholic Cemetery, and Baresi followed.

'Any word?'

'We've had the boys out in Andersonville. Plenty of fucking Swedes, but no sign of ours.'

They were surrounded by two hundred acres of aging tombstones and gaudy family mausolea. Beneath all this petrified ostentation lay generations of holy men and hoodlums – cardinals and archbishops rubbing skeletal shoulders with the likes of Al Capone, the Genna brothers and Sam Giancana. The place was deserted: the only disturbance coming from the traffic sliding down Roosevelt Road. Many of the gravestones sported photographs of the dead. Baresi had always found the practice creepy. When he was a kid, his mother used to take him to his grandfather's grave every Saturday. He'd always been rather frightened of his grandfather. He'd had a lazy eye that the tombstone photograph only emphasized.

'I've got to get the money back. And my credibility.'

'We'll get it back.'

'It was Matteo that brought him in?'

'Yeah.'

Baresi knew that the Boss was conflicted about Matteo – furious that one of his own had been gunned down, yet annoyed that he'd had to waste space in the family plot for such a 'stronzo'.

They stopped by a mawkish marble Madonna, and the Boss fixed Baresi with an icy stare.

'When you find him, get him to talk. Then stop him talking ever again.'

PART ONE

2006

CRIMINAL INVESTIGATION SQUAD – 2006

Erik Moberg, Chief Inspector
Henrik Nordlund, Inspector
Karl Westermark, Inspector
Anita Sundström, Inspector
Klara Wallen, Inspector

CHAPTER 1

'Did you see Liverpool on the TV last night?' Willi Hirdwall groaned as he threw his peaked cap down on the table and took his seat opposite Kasper Jensen. 'God, I wish The Blues played football like that.'

Måns Wallström laughed as Hirdwall slipped off his jacket and rubbed his hands together. It was bitterly cold outside and it was only the first of his rounds of this nightshift.

'Kasper doesn't give a stuff about Malmö. He's Danish.'

Jensen silently pushed a mug of steaming coffee across the table. Hirdwall nodded and cupped the mug, which sported the logo of Malmö FF, to thaw out his fingers. 'That's better,' he said as he sipped the strong black liquid.

Måns Wallström, a man with the leathery features of someone in his early sixties, glanced at the notice board in the guards' office and pointed towards the colourful holiday planner. 'I'm off next week, by the way. But the shipment goes out first thing Monday, so there'll be extra security lads in. Then you can all relax.'

'Going anywhere nice?' asked Hirdwall, swinging his legs onto the table and leaning back in his chair. He was over twenty-five years younger than Wallström. His nut-brown hair was slicked back in the style of an early Elvis Presley quiff. He was the joker in the group of security personnel at the Q Guard cash-handling facility on the edge of a dull, functional industrial estate on the outskirts of Malmö. Unlike Wallström and Jensen, Hirdwall was lean and wiry, but Wallström was sure that if push came to shove, Hirdwall could handle himself. However, that assumption hadn't yet been tested.

'Tenerife. The wife has set her sights on retiring there.'

'Oh, I heard you were taking early retirement.'

'Yeah. Offer too good to refuse, and what with all these cut-backs, I thought I might as well just go.'

'How will you cope with all that sunshine?' Hirdwall laughed. 'You'll miss all the wind and the rain and the snow.'

'I will, but Alice won't. And I've learned that for an easy life, it's best just to agree.' Wallström's attention reverted to the bank of monitors that, via a number of strategically situated cameras, kept a digital eye on various parts of the depot. Nearly every shadowy corner, alcove and doorway of the squat, drab, brick building was covered, as well as the spiked, metal perimeter fence and entrance gates.

Jensen pushed his chair back.

'I'm off to do my rounds,' he muttered as he got up to leave the comfortingly stuffy office.

Hirdwall watched his colleague plonk his cap on his head, do up his jacket and pick up his torch which, like everything else in the depot, was emblazoned with the company logo. When he was gone, Hirdwall pursed his lips.

'What's up with Kasper?'

On one of the screens, Wallström could see Jensen heading towards the main building from their office by the gate.

'Been like that for a few days.'

'He seems quite jumpy,' Hirdwall observed, his chair dangerously close to tipping over.

'Maybe something's up at home.'

'He's never been a bundle of laughs, but I've always put that down to his being Danish.'

'I'm sure it'll pass.'

'I've heard a rumour he's got money worries,' said Hirdwall as he languidly raised his legs off the table and righted his chair.

'Haven't we all?'

'Right enough,' Hirdwall agreed. 'But he won't solve them working for this lot. All that money in there,' he said, tilting his head towards the screens, 'and how much of it do we see? Bugger all.'

'Pension's good, though. I'll be picking mine up next year.'

Hirdwall raised his mug in a mock toast.

'Here's to Tenerife, then.'

The empty wine glass sat disconsolately on the table, asking to be refilled. Anita Sundström thought she'd better oblige.

'Same again?'

'Yes please,' replied a weary Klara Wallen.

Anita took their glasses to the bar and waited to be served. The Lilla Torg hostelry was already full of people kicking off their weekend straight after work. This evening, the place was particularly noisy, possibly because Christmas was only three weeks away. Festive decorations twirled and twinkled around the walls, and a large spruce, dripping with silver stars and golden baubles – and a few cheeky Nordic gnomes – sparkled in one corner, waiting to ambush unsuspecting passing drinkers.

As she waited, Anita's gaze rested on Wallen, who was delving in her handbag. She felt sorry for the woman; that's why she'd invited her out. It wasn't surprising that Wallen looked shell-shocked. Anita got the impression that she'd thought her transfer to the Skåne County Police headquarters in Malmö from the relative anonymity of Kristianstad would improve her career prospects. But after only her first week in the Criminal Investigation Squad under the less-than-benign leadership of Chief Inspector Erik Moberg, it seemed she was beginning to regret the decision. She might need more than this second drink. And it was Friday night after all; neither of them would be working over the weekend.

Anita unceremoniously plonked the glasses on the table,

and Wallen attacked her wine with gusto.

'Thanks,' she said, coming up for air.

'Don't worry. You'll get used to the team.'

'How do you put up with him?' By 'him', Anita assumed she was referring to Chief Inspector Moberg.

'I admit it's not easy. I've been with him a year now and I haven't been able to figure him out. He's like a bear with a sore head half the time.'

'He's been barking at me all week and he snapped at me for no reason today. And his size doesn't help: he's so overbearing,' Wallen added, grimacing.

'I know. Wouldn't surprise me if he has a heart attack one day.'

Anita was starting to regret her choice of wine. She shouldn't have ordered the cheaper stuff. But money was tight, as her ex-husband, Björn, was once again being slow with the maintenance payments for her sixteen-year-old son, Lasse. She looked at her new colleague and tried to sound encouraging: 'Moberg is difficult. But he's not a bad cop. He just doesn't know how to handle women despite the fact he's on his third wife. Maybe that's *why* he's on his third wife. He's highly combustible, which can be intimidating. And he hates incompetence, so any little slip...' Anita realized too late that she wasn't helping when Wallen retreated into her drink with a concerned expression. She quickly reeled in her negativity. 'But I must say I'm really glad to have you here. As the only woman on the team, it's been like fighting a war without any troops to back you up. That's the trouble: unless you look like a battleaxe, they don't take you seriously. Particularly someone like Karl Westermark.'

Wallen brightened at the young detective's name.

'He seems nice.'

'Don't be fooled. Anything in a skirt is a potential notch on his bedpost.' Wallen gave her a quizzical look. 'And, no, I'm not one of them, but it doesn't stop him trying. Last Christmas, his hand wandered where it shouldn't. The red mark on his face took a day to disappear.' She smirked at the memory. 'It bugs me sometimes; it's hard to do your job working closely with a guy you know is mentally undressing you all the time. So be warned.'

'He wouldn't hit on me, surely?'

'Don't bet on it. It'll happen.'

'But I've got a boyfriend! Rolf.'

Anita looked at her with sympathy. She was pleasant-enough looking in a mousy sort of way, but she didn't strike Anita as the most confident of people.

'Is Rolf from Kristianstad?'

'No. Ystad. But he's going to move to Malmö soon. I think he's worried the big city will corrupt me.' She gave a girlish giggle. 'He's been great, though. Just what I needed after my divorce.'

'Snap. Divorce, I mean. But I haven't managed to find a "just what I needed" yet.'

'Someone as attractive as you shouldn't find it hard.'

Anita was flattered, but she'd realized long ago that her looks could also be a curse, especially in the male-dominated polishus. The fact that she wore spectacles, kept her blonde hair tied back and didn't overdo the make-up didn't seem to put off the unwanted attention and stream of inappropriate comments from some of her colleagues.

'Harder than you think. It's amazing how often guys lose interest when it comes up in conversation that you're a cop – except the pervs who are turned on by uniforms!'

Wallen looked uncomfortable.

'I'm only joking. Well, sort of.'

Anita was clearly straying into an area that made Wallen uneasy, which made her wonder about Rolf's particular tastes. She swiftly changed the subject.

'Henrik Nordlund's lovely.'

'Haven't met him yet.'

'He's been at a conference in Gothenburg this week. Back tonight. Very experienced. I've known him for years. I worked my first murder case with him. I don't know if you remember that student who was killed at Knäbäckshusen? About ten years ago?'

'Yeah, I do actually.'

'Henrik led that investigation. Really frustrating. We knew who'd done it, but we were never able to find enough evidence to arrest the killer. He's still out there,' she said wistfully. 'Anyway, Henrik's a really genuine guy. He's the main reason I've been able to stick it out with Moberg. And he's the one person that Moberg defers to. He's a good, old-fashioned cop. You'll meet him on Monday.'

An awkward silence followed. Anita had run out of things to say: she'd used up most of her small-talk subjects during the week, and Wallen wasn't volunteering any more questions. This time, Wallen noticed that Anita's glass was empty again.

'Can I buy you one?'

Anita thought about it for a moment before declining. Making conversation with someone she didn't know that well for another half hour didn't appeal. She'd done her bit.

'No, sorry, must away. Lasse is going up to see his father tomorrow. Better make sure he's got everything ready.' It was a lie. It was true that Lasse was going to stay with Björn in Lund for a couple of nights, but he was far more organized than Anita could ever be. He would have packed already, and he'd probably have to wake her up in the morning, after giving himself breakfast, to say goodbye.

Anita rose from her seat, slipped into her thick, fur-lined coat and wrapped a bulky woollen scarf round her neck. It was freezing outside, though the snow was stubbornly refusing to fall.

As Wallen made to follow... 'Have a good weekend. See you Monday,' she called breezily.

It was just after one in the morning, and Willi Hirdwall was finishing his rounds. It was quiet except for his own footsteps and the sporadic hum of traffic coming from the E65 on nearby Ystadvägen. He'd walked the entire perimeter fence: there were no vehicles on the main drag into the estate and no sign of life on the small, rarely used track which bore off to the right just outside the gates. Now he was starting to feel the bitter, bone-numbing cold. The tarmac gleamed and glittered beneath his feet and he trod carefully so as not to slip. The beam from his powerful torch illuminated the building he was circling. It also picked out a couple of the security cameras. He flashed the light on and off twice at one of the cameras, which was his jokey signal to the watching Måns that he'd be back in a few minutes and that the coffee should be switched on. Facing the road that ran through the estate was a small sign sporting the discreet company logo – a red *Q* with the word *Guard* in black letters inside the Q's circle. With all that money sitting in the depot, the company didn't exactly want to over-advertise themselves. Willi knew that the stash of crisp krona notes was particularly large this week. With Christmas on the horizon, Skåne's ATMs would be under siege from shoppers and party goers. He knew there were euros and dollars in the depository, too. Many Swedes liked to get away over Christmas and New Year. He walked past a neat line of armoured security vans that would be wheeling out on Monday morning to restock the banks after the weekend.

Hirdwall tested the big armoured door that the vans would drive through to collect the cash from the loading bay. As always, it was firmly in place. It could only be electronically operated from the inside. A few paces beyond, he yanked at the handle of the door that was used by the employees who came in and out of the distribution and storage areas. This was also specifically constructed of reinforced steel, and a code was needed to gain access to the loading bay and the vault beyond. Satisfied that everywhere was secure, Willi headed back to the warm sanctuary of the security office.

It was around ten past two that Willi Hirdwall decided to slip off to the toilet for a quick cigarette. Officially, the guards weren't allowed to smoke, but none of the bosses ever inspected the bathroom at the back of the office. And the smell would have gone by the time the morning shift came on. He entered the small room, only just large enough for a toilet cubicle, a sink and a hand dryer. He opened the cubicle door, unbuckled his trousers, slid them down around his ankles and sat down. Comfortable, he fished out a half-empty packet of cigarettes. He flicked on his plastic lighter and torched the end of one of them. It glowed happily, and he drew on it contentedly. He'd been dreaming about this moment throughout his rounds. Now it was Kasper who was braving the temperatures that had plummeted as the night wore on. He yawned and stretched his legs. He closed his eyes momentarily. It was always around this time that he felt most tired when on nights. Still with his eyes closed, he took another drag.

As Willi Hirdwall enjoyed his cigarette, Måns Wallström was scanning the screens next door. Checking for any anomalies was automatic, and Måns's thoughts, though alert, also kept straying to that beach in Tenerife. Then, suddenly, something didn't seem quite right... where the hell was Kasper? He should have appeared by now. What was up with him? Willi was right – he *had* been on edge lately. It was as though his mind wasn't on the job. Måns hoped he would be more on the ball while he was off on holiday. He was about to call him on his walkie-talkie when the camera by the loading-bay door picked him up. Jensen was staring around, looking anxious. He checked his watch. He was now by the staff entrance to the distribution area. What the hell was he doing?

Wallström strode to the door and was outside the security office in a matter of seconds. He was instantly hit by the cold air, and it nearly took his breath away.

'Hey, Kasper! What are you doing?'

Jensen spun round guiltily. All of a sudden, Wallström heard the noise of an engine behind him. He swung round. Through the horizontal bars of the gate, he could make out a huge shape moving at speed along the road which led directly to the depot. As it came within range of the building's security lights, Måns could see what it was. An earth mover with a massive bucket on the front was heading straight towards him.

'Get out of the way!' Jensen shouted

The earth mover was clearly not going to stop. Wallström instinctively drew his gun and fired through the bars of the gate at the advancing machine. Two bullets pinged harmlessly off the giant bucket. Then, with a deafening reverberation of clanks and clangs, the gate crumpled and died before the relentless onslaught. The earth mover careered through the opening as Wallström tried desperately to get out of the way, but, in his panic, he lost his footing on the icy surface. As he fell to the ground, his gun spun out of his hand. The metallic battering ram kept going, and as Wallström was sucked under the massive rubber tyres, his piercing cry was lost in the thunderous noise of the pitiless machine.

CHAPTER 2

As Anita turned off Ystadvägen, an ambulance with flashing lights and wailing siren shot past her in the other direction. She wound her way onto the industrial estate of shadowy, anonymous, box-like buildings. She had to peer carefully through the windscreen, as her glasses were starting to fog up; the Volvo's excuse for a heater was only just beginning to work. It had taken her ten minutes to get her aging vehicle to start; it had an aversion to the cold. During her desperate attempts to coax the car into life, she'd even contemplated getting a taxi, but that wouldn't have gone down well and would have given Moberg and Westermark a hefty round of ammunition.

Ahead, she saw a uniformed officer directing her to the left-hand side of the road. She passed two abandoned police cars. Both had flat tyres. She stifled a yawn. The car clock showed 4.17. Her sleep had been rudely interrupted by a call from the polishus: Chief Inspector Moberg wanted her to attend a 'serious incident' on the E65 Industrial Estate, just beyond the Jägersro trotting track. No details were given. She'd lurched out of bed, quickly washed her face and hurriedly scribbled a note for Lasse, explaining that she'd been called out and that she probably wouldn't be back before he left. She deliberately didn't put anything about sending her love to Björn. Her relaxing Saturday had gone out of the window.

While most of the industrial units and warehouses she passed were modestly illuminated, the building at the far end of the road was a blaze of lights. And under the lights, there was a huge amount of activity. She parked the car next to a large metal piece of telecommunications street furniture, which was as near as she could get to the centre of it all. She spotted Karl Westermark talking to a couple of uniformed officers. He had that square-jawed Aryan look that Hitler would have approved of, and Anita suspected that his politics lay in that direction, if, that is, his mind ever wandered further than his next shag. When he saw her, he peeled away.

'Hope we didn't interrupt a night of unbridled nooky.'

'Piss off, Karl.'

They walked together through the twisted metal gate of the low, square, functional depot. It was clear that there had been some kind of break-in. Immediately in front of them was an incident tent. Beyond the tent loomed a massive yellow earth mover. The machine was nestled up against, almost caressing, a steel loading-bay door, several metres in width. The door was seriously indented and the left-hand corner was badly damaged. Part of the surrounding brickwork had also crumbled, leaving a small gap.

'What is this place?'

'Q Guard. It's a cash-handling facility.'

'Did they get what they wanted?'

'Oh, yes. Big haul. Don't bother trying to get money out of an ATM this week; there won't be any.'

A white-suited forensic technician emerged from the incident tent into the glare of the arc lights. Anita had expected to see old, cantankerous Petersson, but it was a strawberry-blonde woman instead. She grimaced ruefully at them.

'Better not go in there. The poor fellow was crushed under that thing,' she said, nodding in the direction of the brooding earth mover, whose shadow in the lights was double the size of the machine and resembled a menacing prehistoric creature. 'Not a pretty sight.'

'We'll let you scrape him up, then,' smirked Westermark,

who was clearly taken by the fresh-faced forensic technician. He reckoned she must be in her early thirties, like himself, and, as she headed off back to the tent, he was already having lurid thoughts about her prowess in bed.

'God, that's awful!' exclaimed Anita. 'Who was that in the ambulance?'

'One of the other security guards. Shot in the arm. He'll live.'

'Anybody else injured?'

'There's a third guard. Tied up by the gang. He's in the office with the freaked-out depot manager. Well shaken up.'

Before Anita could ask any more questions, from behind the enormous earth mover emerged the equally bulky Chief Inspector Moberg, with a timid Klara Wallen in his wake. Damn! Even Wallen had got here before her; that would give the new detective a few brownie points.

Moberg greeted her with 'Glad you could be bothered to turn up.' Biting her lip, Anita took his sarcasm on the chin – there was no point trying to explain about the car. He had that distorted anger in his voice that comes from being forced out of a warm bed at an unearthly hour on a glacial night.

'It must be clear what's happened, even to you,' Moberg said pointedly to Anita. 'It appears they smashed through the main gate some time after two. Made that hole in the wall, got into the building and the loading bay, then along to the vault door, which they blew to smithereens, and made off with the dosh. Don't know how much yet, but it's a lot. They were well away by the time we were called to the scene. Presumably, they came with some sort of van or truck. We've put out an alert, but my guess is, they'll have dumped the van, or whatever, and transferred the cash into something else by now.'

'That's if they're bright enough,' said Westermark.

'They're bright enough to get in and out of here,' came Moberg's surly reply as his cold breath billowed into the air.

'We're not dealing with the bloody *Jönsson Gang*.' They all knew the reference to the popular comedy heist films of the 1980s.

'Who raised the alarm?' Anita asked.

'Willi Hirdwall. He's the guy who was shot. Though I'm surprised he managed to make the call – he seemed pretty out of it. Think he bashed his head or something. The third one is talking to Henrik, though I'm not sure he'll get much sense out of him either. He's in a bit of a state. Not surprising when one of your colleagues has been flattened like a pancake. But the strange thing is, the building's alarm system should have been activated as soon as that thing hit that,' he said, gesturing to the earth mover and the battered door. 'It wasn't.' Moberg stamped his feet against the cold. 'Right. Sundström and Wallen, I want you to check out the security office. Hopefully, they've got CCTV, which might give us something to go on. Have a good look round. The alarm not going off needs checking. Karl, I want you to coordinate the search for the getaway van.' Anita noted, not for the first time, that it was surnames for women, first names for men. 'As far as I can see, they must have made off along that track just outside the gate. Seems to go round the back of the estate. They certainly made sure *we* couldn't get here in a hurry with those caltraps all over the main road.' Hence the punctured patrol cars.

They stood there.

'What are you fucking waiting for?'

Moberg stomped his way into the spacious, yet sparse, office of the depot manager. The manager was sitting behind a large desk strewn with trays, files and papers. In front of him was a computer and, with his eyes glued to the screen, he was talking rapidly on the phone, making grovelling excuses in English for what was, undoubtedly, a crippling business disaster. The robbery would seriously damage Q Guard's reputation with its banking and other customers. Months of PR crisis management and expensive schmoozing would be needed to restore even a smidgeon of faith.

In another part of the room, Henrik Nordlund was talking to Kasper Jensen, whose hulk was huddled uncomfortably on an ergonomic office chair. On seeing Moberg enter, Nordlund came over to report.

'I haven't got much out of him. He seems shattered. More mental than physical, as he hasn't anything in the way of injuries.'

'Shall I have a word?'

'No, no. Best not.' Nordlund understood his boss well enough to know he'd probably frighten the witness to death, and it was important to glean as much information as possible, as soon as possible. 'I'll get a preliminary statement out of him and then we can question him properly later.'

'OK. I'll have a word with the rabbit,' Moberg said, glancing over to the depot manager, who did look as though he'd been caught in the headlights.

The manager came off the phone. He was a middle-aged man of medium build, with thinning, unbrushed, reddish hair. He obviously hadn't had time to dress for the office and had thrown on his casual weekend clothes: a pair of jeans and a well-worn, blue jacket over a canary-yellow T-shirt.

'Chief Inspector Moberg.'

'Yes. I'm Artur Fält,' he said distractedly. 'This is just appalling. I've just come off the phone with the Head of Q Guard Europe.' He was almost frothing. 'Frankfurt,' he added unnecessarily.

'I can imagine he's not best pleased.'

'Precisely. He's getting onto America.' That sounded ominous. 'I don't understand how this could have happened.' His head kept moving like a nodding dog on the back shelf of a car, and his startled eyes were constantly scanning different parts of the room as though the answer lay somewhere within its featureless walls. Or maybe he was seeing this year's bonus going down the pan. Or his job.

'That's what we need to establish,' Moberg said curtly. He was in no mood to placate.

'Of course.'

'We were wondering why the alarm wasn't set off.'

'I have no idea. It's connected directly to the polishus. It's controlled from the security office at the gate.'

'On my brief inspection, the thieves certainly knew all about the site. It's been well planned, though they seem to have got lucky with the loading-bay door. The machine wasn't strong enough to smash it up entirely, but it made a hole.'

'It's the best on the market.'

'I'll need to get details of your staff.'

'You can't think—'

'We have to cover every possibility. The thieves seem to have known their way around.'

'My staff have all been thoroughly vetted,' Fält said unhappily.

'How many people work here?'

'We have forty-seven employees, including guards and cleaners. Some are part-time, of course, and many work shifts.'

'Doesn't seem that many for an outfit like this,' Moberg calculated.

'There have been a few cutbacks recently; new technology is being introduced... not as much need for human input.'

Moberg scowled: he had no time for 'new technology'. 'So, it was just the guards on the premises last night?'

'Yes. If it had been tomorrow night...'

'What do you mean?'

'Well, there would have been a lot more people about. We'd timetabled several shifts over the weekend to box up the money for Monday morning.'

'Do you know how much has been taken?'

Fält blanched. 'No, not yet. There was a lot of cash in there. Big week ahead for the banks, and some employers who pay early in December. As far as I can see, they haven't totally cleaned us out.'

'Probably took what would fit in their getaway vehicle.'

Moberg thought Fält was going to be sick.

'There's no possibility of recovering it any time soon?' the manager asked weakly.

'Fat chance. These guys are pros. You'll just have to claim on your insurance,' Moberg added unhelpfully. The chief inspector stood hovering over the distraught depot manager, deep in momentary thought.

'I just can't believe it,' Fält said, as though he were just awakening from a bad dream. 'Look, I've got more calls to make. Damage limitation.'

'I hope you're not forgetting that you've got a dead employee plastered all over your forecourt. And another one with a bullet in him.'

Fält was taken aback by Moberg's vehemence.

'Naturally, they're our top priority.'

Moberg turned away in disgust. He knew they weren't.

CHAPTER 3

The atmosphere in the meeting room was gloomy. This wasn't the weekend any of them had planned. Lack of sleep had made all except Henrik Nordlund irritable. Endless coffees since their return from the Q Guard depot hadn't done much to lift spirits. The only bright spot as far as Anita was concerned was that Karl Westermark was still out chasing down the getaway vehicle. Klara Wallen had put together a diagram of the cash-handling facility, and, together with photographs, had attached it to the board designated to the crime. A couple of other detectives, Falkengård and Gunnare, had been dragged in to boost the numbers. Anita knew them vaguely. Moberg came bursting into the room, coffee in hand. He put the cup down on the table with such force that the liquid splashed over the rim, leaving a black puddle.

'Right, let's not fanny around. Where are we?'

Nordlund stood up, went over to the board and launched into explaining the layout of the scene of the robbery. 'OK, this is Q Guard. Good diagram, by the way, Klara.' Wallen gave him a grateful smile. 'The right-hand third is the staff area: offices, kitchen, recreation room, toilets etc. This is completely separate from the left-hand section, which houses the vault and loading bay. There are three external entrances. One for the vans which use the loading bay, another for the staff who are responsible for the loading and the unloading. The third door is round the side and is purely for the use of the office staff. Both the outside security doors are constructed of a double layer of purpose-built reinforced steel, as is the internal door to the loading bay and the vault. The large loading-bay door is electronically controlled, the staff door and the internal door have keypads, and the vault door itself, which is made of steel-reinforced concrete, can only be opened with a two-piece key and a combination lock. The only windows in the building are in the office area. The place is surrounded by a metal fence and there's a main gate, with an adjacent pedestrian gate giving access to the road. The staff car park is outside the premises. Next to the gate is the security office for the guards. As far as we know, the earth mover smashed into the main gate around quarter past two this morning. The machine's a Komatsu WA-480-5 and is technically called a wheel loader. It weighs over twenty-five tons and does a top speed of nearly thirty-five kilometres an hour. No wonder it made mincemeat of the gate. Tragically, it ran over Måns Wallström in the process. We don't know what he was doing there; according to Jensen, his job was to monitor the security cameras. Maybe Hirdwall can throw more light on it.'

'Poor bugger,' Anita heard one of the officers behind her mutter under his breath.

'His Glock 17 was found, and forensics reckon it had been fired. We await details. It may take some time to get the full picture.' Moberg's impromptu groan indicated that he wasn't going to show much patience. Nordlund ignored the chief inspector and carried on. 'On arrival, the gang dealt with the two remaining guards. Kasper Jensen was on his rounds when he heard a crash, and he rushed to the front of the building, only to be confronted by an armed man in a balaclava. He could see the earth mover had smashed into the door. Anyway, he was shoved into the building through the gap, tied up and blindfolded. He says he has no idea what happened after that. The third guard, Willi Hirdwall, was in the security office by the main gate when he was shot. Despite loss of blood and concussion from a head wound, he managed to contact us as the gang were leaving. We haven't got the exact details of what happened there. Where are we with him?' he asked, turning to Wallen.

'The hospital is keeping him in for a while,' she faltered. 'His arm's OK, but they're a bit worried about the concussion.'

'Right. Let's hope we can question him later.'

'So all the guards are taken care of,' continued Nordlund. 'The gang – and we don't know how many there were of them – continue with the raid. Though the earth mover—'

'Let's just call it a bloody bulldozer,' Moberg interrupted.

Nordlund smiled. 'Though the *bulldozer* didn't actually manage to demolish the door, it buckled it enough to damage the wall and create a gap large enough for the gang to get into the loading bay and then through to the vault. The vault door can only be opened in the presence of the manager or, if he's away, the deputy manager. The gang didn't bother with such niceties – they blasted it open. So they arrived armed and with explosives. Then they bagged up the money – it was stored in bundles wrapped in airtight, waterproof plastic. Not all of it was taken – they left the lower denominations alone.'

'The raid was done and dusted in around twenty-five minutes as far as we can estimate,' butted in Moberg. 'The call through to here from Hirdwall came in at two forty-one just as they were leaving, but they'd allowed for a quick response, hence the caltraps all over the road. These guys knew exactly what they were doing.' Moberg let this information sink in before continuing. 'One of the main questions we've got to ask is why the alarm didn't go off when the loading-bay door was hit by the bulldozer.'

'Maybe it wasn't working,' ventured one of the officers behind Anita.

'Unlikely in an outfit like Q Guard,' Moberg huffed disparagingly. 'What we do know is the alarm not going off gave them more time before anyone appeared. The first patrol car got there seven minutes after the call from Hirdwall. The gate being knocked down would have been noisy, but no one was in the area at that time of the morning except the security guards on site: no other occupied buildings within earshot. And the bang from the explosion would have been somewhat muffled by the building anyway. They had a free hand. Presumably, we don't know how much they took?'

'Not yet,' confirmed Nordlund. 'The depot manager said it could be anything up to two hundred million kronor, and up to a million dollars and a further million euros in the mix.'

'Jesus!' Moberg whistled. 'What about CCTV? Surely that'll give us something.'

'I'm afraid not.' It was Anita's turn to contribute. Her mind went back to the early hours of the morning when she'd entered the security office. The warmth inside had been a blessed relief from the numbing night air. Her first impression was of unleashed vandalism. The security monitors had been completely pulverized by gunfire, and fragments of plastic and glass littered the floor. A forensic technician was already marking the positions of the spent cartridge cases. Amongst the debris, she could see blood stains near the door at the back of the office; there was also blood on the sharp edge of the metal frame. The technician pointed to a small hole in the wall where a bullet was buried – the one that had passed through the arm of the security guard. Judging by the trail of blood, the guard must have been between the door and the desk when he was shot and had fallen back against the doorframe and had then slumped to the floor. They would have to find out about his exact movements when they interviewed him. At least he was alive. Her mind went back to the CCTV. Though the screens had been destroyed, she'd come across enough similar systems to know that if the feed to the monitors was intact, they could recover the footage. Unfortunately, she hadn't got positive news to report.

'The box that feeds the monitors was dismantled. Someone knew the system and knew how to knock it out. Blowing out the monitors was for show.'

'Shit!' Moberg bellowed. 'Well let's get what footage we can from the other units and the roads leading into the estate. I know there won't be much, but we might pick them up coming in – especially that big fuck-off machine.'

Just then the chief inspector's mobile went off. 'Yes?' he bawled into it. He listened for a minute then said, 'OK, get forensics down there.' He flicked off his phone.

'That was Karl. They've found a burnt-out van outside Bara. Doubt forensics will find much, but we need to go through the motions.'

'It was a well-planned job,' opined Nordlund.

'You can say that again.'

'It took money to set up. You don't suddenly acquire a massive earth mover, sorry, *bulldozer*, that easily. And they needed professional know-how – that doesn't come cheap.'

'We need to look into who could mount such an operation.' Moberg glanced at his watch. 'Christ, I've got to see the commissioner.' He swung round to the diagram and sighed heavily. 'I've got fuck all to tell him.' He turned back, a scowl across his massive features. 'Henrik, can you sort out who does what? I may be upstairs for a while. His Majesty will be panicking about the press fall out.'

Moberg slammed the door on his way out. They knew he'd be in for a grilling. The imperturbable Nordlund watched him go before proceeding.

'We need to get a clearer picture of what went on. I've got a garbled statement from Kasper Jensen, but we'll need to talk to him again when he's in better shape. We also need to visit Willi Hirdwall to get his view – anything that might give us a lead. Unusual activity in the days leading up to the job…

anyone appearing suspicious… you know the sort of thing. I suggest you do that, Anita.' She knew that Nordlund trusted her in a way that Moberg clearly didn't. 'Take Klara.'

They discussed a few more details: CCTV footage in the surrounding areas, where the bulldozer and getaway vehicle had come from, background checks on the security guards and depot staff. And there was the glaring conundrum of the alarm.

'Anything else?' Nordlund asked, concluding the meeting.

'Just one thing,' said Anita.

After inspecting the security office, Anita and her colleagues had snooped around the damaged shutter and the loading bay and seen where the gang had blown the hole in the door to the vault. That had been the work of an explosives expert, and one of the things they needed to do was check out any known professionals in that particular field. But on leaving the scene of the crime, a nagging doubt had begun to nibble its way into her brain. And without Moberg around to flatten any suggestion she made, now was the time to voice it. If it had merit, Nordlund could pass it on; Moberg would give him a hearing.

'Everything about this robbery was meticulously planned: the bulldozer to smash the gate, the taking out of the guards, getting into the vault, escaping before anyone could get there, and the caltraps waiting for us when we arrived. And they somehow deactivated the alarm system and made sure there was no CCTV record of their visit. Nothing left to chance.'

'Your point?'

'What if the bulldozer hadn't made a hole? They couldn't be sure it would break through that door – as we saw, it's incredibly solid. They did make a gap of sorts, and I don't want to sound indelicate, but I don't think the chief inspector could get through it that easily.' Anita heard suppressed sniggers from the officers behind her. 'With time not on their side, the gang managed to take explosives in and carry a significant amount of money out of the building through that gap. It wouldn't have been that easy. What I'm saying is, it would have been quite a slow, tedious process. Unless they were all midgets, they'd have to bend down to carry the money through. But these guys appear to have got in and out pretty sharpish.'

'Luck,' suggested Gunnare.

Anita shook her head. 'An operation this well planned can't rely on luck. The loading-bay door was the one, big imponderable. Imagine all that planning, only to be thwarted if the door hadn't buckled and they couldn't break in. No. I think they must have been sure they would get in, whatever happened with the door and the bulldozer. Like the shooting up of the security monitors, crashing into that door was a case of misdirection.'

'How do you think they got in, then?' asked Nordlund.

'The only other way into that area is through the staff door – well, through the two doors. The one on the outside and the one between the loading bay and the vault,' Anita said, pointing at the board. 'Use that route, and they could take the explosives through unencumbered and remove the money unhindered.'

'But those doors need code numbers,' pointed out Wallen.

'That's right, Klara. And the codes are changed every twenty-four hours at midnight. They couldn't have known them in advance.'

Nordlund clicked his fingers loudly. 'I see what you're getting at, Anita. Using the doors would explain the speed of the operation and, as you say, the hole would divert attention.'

'Attention from what?' asked Falkengård.

Nordlund gave an appreciative nod in Anita's direction. 'That it was an inside job.'

'More specific than that,' said Anita gravely. 'One of the security guards on that shift must have been in on it.'

CHAPTER 4

The hospital was busy when Anita and Wallen entered just after four. It was the beginning of the 'flu' season and the people of Malmö were succumbing to ailments that they would happily struggle through during the all-too-brief summer months. They were shown up to the first floor, past a uniformed officer on the door, and into a single room. Willi Hirdwall was sitting on a chair next to his bed. So he wasn't at death's door; at least that should make things easier, thought Anita. His right arm was in a sling and there was a large plaster on the back of his head. His face was drawn and pasty beneath his flattened quiff: that of a man who had just had a life-or-death experience. The haunted eyes showed pain and confusion. He raised them as the two police officers entered the room.

'Hello,' said Anita. 'I'm Inspector Anita Sundström and this is Inspector Klara Wallen.'

Hirdwall just nodded.

'How are you feeling?'

'Bewildered.' He looked at his arm. 'And in pain. Never been shot before, so it's a new experience.' An attempt at a joke.

'Lucky the bullet passed through you.'

'Yeah. Didn't break the bone or damage any arteries.'

'Your doctor says you also have a head wound and possible mild concussion.'

'Yeah, I must have cracked it when I fell.'

'I know this has all just happened, but we do need to speak to you.'

Hirdwall shifted in his seat. He winced slightly as he moved his arm. 'I understand.' Before Anita could start: 'How is Kasper?' he said.

'He's badly shaken. But physically, he's OK.'

'Thank God for that. I just can't get over…' he gulped. 'Get over Måns. Christ, how could that happen? You know he was nearing retirement?'

'So we've been told.'

'His poor wife. She'll be distraught.'

Anita let that thought settle before proceeding.

'Basically, we need your version of events.'

'I'll do all I can to help. But, I'm sorry, things are still a bit hazy, at least what happened after I was shot.'

Anita eyed Hirdwall closely. Since her suggestion at the meeting that one of the security guards could be involved in the robbery, she'd been looking forward to assessing him. Could it be Hirdwall? The next few minutes would either bolster or allay her suspicions.

'Can you take me through the events of the early hours of this morning?'

He blew out his cheeks. 'I'll try. It's difficult to know where to begin. It was just like any other nightshift. Boring. Bit of banter with the boys. Regular rounds and then back to the office for a coffee to warm up. Well, me and Kasper did the rounds. Måns kept his eye on the monitors. His privilege… senior guy… most experienced…'

Hirdwall's voice trailed off at the mention of Wallström's name again. Anita gave him time to return to the gruesome reality of only fourteen hours ago.

'Kasper went out on his rounds about two. A bit after he'd gone, I went into the back for a crap and a ciggie. Sorry,' – realizing that he was addressing two women – 'I needed the toilet and took advantage of the quiet to have a cigarette. I was in the middle of my… business… when I heard a rumble close by and what I thought were a couple of shots, then this almighty crashing, thumping noise. I dropped my cigarette and got my pants up fast as I could. By the time I got into the office, there was this guy with a gun pointed straight at me. He had a balaclava on.'

'Did he say anything to you?'

'Told me to put my hands on my head.'

'What did he sound like? I mean his voice... accent? Local?'

Hirdwall scrunched up his face in concentration.

'Now you mention it: foreign. As in... I don't know. Spoke in Swedish, but I'm pretty sure he wasn't a Swede. Eastern European?'

Anita glanced at Wallen, who was taking notes. Was this their first piece of useful information?

'How did you end up getting shot?'

He shook his head.

'It was daft. Bloody stupid. When I went to the toilet, I left my gun on the desk. Gets in the way otherwise. The guy was glancing around the room, kinda looking for something, and I made a grab for the gun. He must have seen me and fired. Bam! I remember the pain and not much after that. I suppose I collapsed to the floor and must have hit my head against the doorframe on the way down. Well, that's where I was when I came to. Must have blacked out. I don't know how long I was down there; I just remember my arm hurting like crazy. My head, too. And blood and stuff. I think I just lay there.' He looked tortured and confused.

Anita didn't push it. 'Take your time. If there's anything at all you can tell me...'

After a while, he rallied. 'I think I remember coming round at some point, but it's all so hazy... there were sounds.'

'What sort of sounds?'

'Banging... smashing...'

'That might have been the CCTV being dismantled,' said

Wallen, looking up from her notebook.

'Makes sense,' said Hirdwall. 'And then I think someone else came in; there were voices. Then more noise – really loud... gunfire.'

'The monitors being blasted.'

'I remember just lying there, hoping they weren't going to kill me. I'm no coward, but I'm no hero either, not on my pay.'

'Can you recall seeing anything? What about the two guys? Was the one who took out the monitors the same one who shot you?'

'I'm sorry, it's all a blur.'

'What happened next?'

'I don't really know. I suppose I sensed at some point that they'd gone, and all I could think about was calling you. After that, I stumbled out of the office...' He physically shuddered, which made him gasp. Another shaft of pain. 'That's when I saw... Shit, it was horrendous! What was he doing out there? How did he end up under that fucking machine? I just can't get the image out of my head.'

He slumped into silence. Anita walked to the window and looked out. The lights were bright in the street outside, and the traffic was moving slowly along Carl Gustafs väg. The apartment blocks opposite were also well lit and reflected the spirit of the season, with nearly every window decorated with twinkling Swedish candoliers, each of the electric bulbs imitating the real candle flames that traditionally guided the faithful to church at Christmas. A time of hope – a time when criminals hoped to make a killing, she mused wryly. One group just had.

'Have you got all that, Klara?' she asked. Her colleague nodded. 'Now we get to the difficult bits.' Hirdwall's reaction to the next few questions would be telling.

'What difficult bits?' he asked quizzically.

'The bits we can't explain. First up: when the bulldozer hit the door, the alarm didn't go off.'

'You're right. That's struck me as odd, too; I've been thinking about it.'

'Can it be turned on and off from your office?'

'Yeah. Whoever's on duty turns it off when the place is opened for vans loading cash or bringing money in. But it was definitely on last night.' He bit his lower lip in thought. 'The guy in the office must have turned it off after he shot me. It can be done manually if you know what you're doing.'

'Well someone knew where it was and obviously knew how to do it. That would make sense. The gunman turned it off before the door was rammed.' Anita saw that Hirdwall was tiring. 'Are you OK to go on?'

'Sure.'

'Our biggest problem is how the gang got in and out so quickly. Did you see the hole that the bulldozer made?'

'Not really.'

'Well, it wasn't that big. We think that they must have got in and out another way.'

'There isn't another way.'

'The staff door?'

'That's always locked,' Hirdwall looked more animated. Then he paused. 'Did you find it unlocked?'

'No. It was locked. Doesn't mean they didn't use it.'

'It was certainly shut tight when I did my last walkabout around one.'

'Did Måns go out at all after you came back?'

'No. Anyhow, you must be wrong. You need a code to open that door, and another one for the internal door which leads to the loading bay and the vault. And the codes are changed every twenty-four hours at midnight. They couldn't have got to know that in... what, a couple of hours?' Anita stared at him. A slow realization of what she was implying crinkled his features.

'No, no, no, you're so wrong! You're talking about an inside job. No way! None of the lads would do that.'

'If the money was right?'

Hirdwall's mouth dropped open.

'You think it was one of us?'

'It's a line of enquiry.'

'You've got that wrong. Måns is... was straight as they come. He hadn't a bent bone in his body.'

'Kasper Jensen?'

'No. I can't believe he'd... OK, I didn't know him that well. He hasn't been with us that long.' He slipped into silence. Then, 'There *was* a whisper that he had money troubles. But who doesn't? He's got a family. And lately he has been a bit... distracted. Måns noticed it, too. We put it down to domestic tensions... I'm sure that's all it was.'

'Then if it wasn't Måns, and it isn't Kasper, there's only one left.'

Hirdwall looked aghast.

'You must be joking!'

CHAPTER 5

When Chief Inspector Moberg convened a meeting early on Monday morning, he was greeted by an array of tired faces. Their weekend had been wiped out and replaced with endless phone calls, revisiting the site of the robbery and hunting down and hassling people who were trying to escape work for a couple of days. The fear was that the money was long gone, especially if organized crime was behind the theft. That had become a growing suspicion, especially after Hirdwall's comment about his attacker possibly sounding eastern European. And soon, the aftermath of the crime from the public's point of view became all too apparent when many of southern Sweden's ATMs ran out of money. Anita had seen queues at machines as she'd driven home last night. The scramble for cash had been sparked by Sunday newspaper headlines screaming: *SWEDEN'S BIGGEST EVER CASH ROBBERY!* The amount the thieves had got away with varied wildly from eighty million to well over two hundred million kronor. The estimate that Q Guard had passed on to the police was around one hundred and thirty-five million kronor, and nearly a million in euros and about the same in dollars. It was certainly one of the biggest heists the country had ever seen, even at a time when cash depots, security vans and banks were being hit on a regular basis.

There was no preamble. 'Are we getting anywhere?' Moberg demanded before biting into his McDonald's Egg McMuffin. Anita suspected it wasn't his first of the day. Unlike the rest of his team, he'd been relieved to have an excuse not to be at home over the weekend. The alternative would have been Christmas shopping with his wife. They had no children of their own to buy for – thank God – but he had inherited a bunch of nephews and nieces, whom he couldn't stand and who tended to ruin his Christmas holidays. The situation at Q Guard had also got him out of a potentially excruciating Sunday lunch with his sister-in-law and her obnoxious undertaker husband. The only thing the two men had in common was dead bodies, and you can't spend a whole lunch talking about cadavers.

'We've got someone coming from forensics soon,' started Nordlund. 'Hopefully, we can get more information out of them. Weapons used, etcetera. Might give us further clues as to who's behind this.'

Moberg wiped his mouth with the back of his hand after the last of his breakfast had disappeared.

'We now think that the man who shot Willi Hirdwall switched off the alarm before they rammed the loading-bay door.'

'Makes sense. Where did the bulldozer come from?' A large photo of the offending machine took centre stage on the board.

'It was nicked from the stone quarry in Limhamn,' said Westermark. 'They just took it and drove it along the E6 round to the industrial estate. Bold as brass. I suspect someone at the quarry must have been bribed or threatened to allow them access. Anyway, we managed to pick it up on CCTV a couple of times along the route. On the last footage we were able to get hold of, it was followed by a white van.'

'The burnt-out van at Bara?'

'Probably,' said Nordlund, pointing at a photo of the vehicle. 'Ford Transit. Forensics are onto it, and we're following up van thefts in the last few weeks.'

'OK, they smash down the gate, crushing Wallström on

the way after he'd fired his gun, capture one guard and shoot another, turn off the alarm then bash a hole in the depot.' Moberg's summing up so far was succinct. 'And then you think, Henrik, that they didn't actually get in through the hole, but used the staff door?'

'It was Anita's thought.'

'More than just a pretty face,' Westermark said snidely. Anita couldn't even be bothered to glower.

'Are we taking this suggestion seriously?' asked Moberg as though anything that came from Sundström was unlikely to have much merit. 'The Dane… Jensen. He said he was taken through the gap.'

'He could have been lying,' Anita blurted out irritably. Her tone was to counteract Moberg's obvious scepticism.

'So, given that the three guards were the only people on the premises who would know about the new codes – did you say they were changed at midnight? – you're suggesting it's one of them on the inside.'

'It would also explain about them knowing where and how to switch off the alarm,' said Nordlund. 'I think Anita's onto something. For the operation to go smoothly, they must have been sure that everything would fall into place in advance. You couldn't set everything up and trust to luck. The only thing that did go wrong was Wallström. They couldn't have planned for that.'

'Looks like they were willing to kill, though. They did shoot Hirdwall.'

'But they only tied up Jensen,' Nordlund countered.

'They'd have probably tied them all up,' ventured Anita. 'Hirdwall was only shot because he tried to retrieve his gun.'

'That's true. And somehow, they must have been aware of all the shift patterns – who would be where at the crucial time. Again, possibly points to a security guard.'

'So,' Moberg continued, 'our villains load up the van; the

bagged-up bundles of notes are easy to carry. And before they leave, they fix the CCTV.'

'Yes,' Nordlund agreed. 'According to the manager, the parent company was about to install a new Samsung high-performance, megapixel camera system. As well as being sharper, they would be operated off site, and the gang wouldn't have been able to close them down.'

'Why bother to dismantle the CCTV at all?' asked Falkengård. 'They were all wearing balaclavas, so they would be almost impossible to identify.'

'They weren't worried about being identified,' Anita responded. 'They didn't want us to see that they were using the staff door. If we could see that, it would have been obvious that one of the security guards was in on it. It was to protect him.'

Just then, in breezed the fresh-faced forensic technician that Anita had seen emerging from the crime scene tent at the cash depot. She had a file under her arm. She was casually dressed in combat pants and had her hair scraped up into a bun. While the heads of the younger male detectives immediately turned to admire their new colleague, Moberg's face fell.

'Eva Thulin. Forensics,' she announced brightly.

'You again! Where's Petersson?' Moberg barked. He couldn't believe that he was going to have to deal with yet another woman. The force was going to the dogs.

Thulin was totally unperturbed. 'I thought you'd have heard. He's on sick leave. Stress.' She paused. 'I can see why,' she added with a sly grin which caught Anita's eye. Anita warmed to her immediately. 'Afraid you'll have to deal with one of his minions.'

'What have you got for us, then?' Moberg growled.

Thulin put the file down on the table. 'A helluva lot of weekend overtime went into that,' she said wryly. 'First, the details of Måns Wallström's death, and a gallery of gory photos to go with it. Want to see them?'

'No thank you. And I think we all know how he died. What else have you got?'

Anita admired the way that Thulin wasn't intimidated in the slightest by the formidable mountain that was Erik Moberg.

'Guns. Wallström fired two shots with his Glock 17 in the direction of the oncoming vehicle.'

Moberg huffed; they knew that already.

Thulin continued, 'I'm afraid I'm not familiar with the handguns that were used to shoot the security guard and demolish the CCTV monitors. They both used 9 mil ammunition, but we'll have to wait for the ballistics boys to give us more information.'

'Hirdwall mentioned his assailant sounding eastern European,' remarked Anita.

'Mmm. Could be something from Bulgaria or Romania,' opined Nordlund. 'Lots of different firearms floating about in that part of the world.'

'By the way,' said Thulin. 'Hirdwall was shot at close range.'

'He's told us that already,' Moberg said dismissively.

'Well, that confirms his story.'

'What about prints?'

'Sorry,' Thulin shrugged. 'Masses at the depot but none other than those of the employees, as far as we can establish at the moment. And nothing identifiable on the burnt-out van.'

'Anything else?'

'We're still looking into the explosives they used. We've got an expert coming down from Stockholm later today. He might give us some clues.'

'Basically, you haven't got much, have you?'

Anita couldn't believe how rude Moberg was being. The forensic technician flashed him a delightful smile.

'Sadly, we're not miracle workers. We're not paid enough.' She headed for the door. 'And I'll make sure I pass on your love to herr Petersson. I'm sure he misses you.'

After Thulin left, Moberg angrily paced up and down in front of the board while the others tried to suppress their smirks. Then he stopped.

'You can bet the money won't make an appearance for quite some time. The gang will lie low. Given the size of the haul and the slickness of the operation, organized crime's behind it: I can feel it in my water. If that's the case, we may never see the money again – it'll be laundered somewhere to pay for future operations. And if we do find the gang members, it'll be difficult to get them to talk – loyalty and fear will keep their mouths shut. Our only way in is to find out if one of the security guards really was in on it.' Turning to Anita, 'What was your impression of Hirdwall?'

'He seemed genuinely upset about Wallström's death. His account of what happened to him sounds plausible, if vague – he's still got concussion – and he *was* shot after all. And if he is telling the truth, he was either being very brave or very foolish, trying to grab his gun like that. He could be lying, I suppose, and there was some sort of mix up, resulting in him getting shot. But unlikely. And he did give us an indication that the man who shot him was from Eastern Europe.'

'We need to ask Jensen the same question,' suggested Nordlund.

'I think you and Sundström can do exactly that.'

CHAPTER 6

Nordlund was driving a pool car. Anita was relieved that Moberg had sent her off to Copenhagen to accompany the senior member of the team. Too often, she was partnered with Westermark. That was doubly dangerous: he drove like a maniac and his hands often strayed when he was changing gear. And Westermark would have treated the trip as a jolly and would want to spend time in Copenhagen that had nothing to do with the investigation. Sometimes, she thought Moberg deliberately paired them up just for the fun of it. She was quite sure they had titillating conversations about her behind her back.

They crossed the Öresund Bridge under leaden skies which still threatened snow, and made their way into Kastrup, once a small harbour community, now sucked into Copenhagen, and the site of Denmark's busy international airport. With a map on her knee, Anita directed Nordlund onto Kastrupvej, a long road that ran all the way to the Amager district. The newer houses and apartment blocks which had sprung up as the airport had developed gradually gave way to older, more traditional residences. On their right, they passed a church and several other buildings in the same style. Anita couldn't help but notice them; the complex was massive. The whitewashed walls of Filips Kirke, contrasting pleasingly with the clean, red-pantile roof, gleamed in the sullen winter light. The central tower with its familiar crow-stepped gables mimicked the architecture of Denmark's rural churches. Away from mercantile Christianshavn and the teaming city centre, this would have been a prosperous suburb at one time. They continued past a park and a large 1930s apartment block on their left, then, on Anita's command, Nordlund turned the car into a side street: Rumæniensgade. The building in front of them was similar to the one next to the park.

A woman's voice answered the intercom and let them in the main door. She didn't sound pleased that police officers were coming to her home. There was no lift, and they trudged up the narrow staircase to the third floor. There were two apartment doors on the landing, neither with a nameplate, so it was pot luck as to which was Kasper Jensen's. The woman who opened the left-hand door had long, dark, straggly hair and was in her twenties. Her drawn face was etched with worry and weariness. She was plainly pregnant. They could hear a youngster crying in the background.

She scowled at them. 'Do you really have to see Kasper?' The question almost came out as a whisper, as though she didn't want anybody else in the apartment to hear what she was saying. 'He's still so upset after that dreadful night. I don't know when he'll be able to go back to work.'

'Don't worry,' said Nordlund reassuringly in Danish. 'We only need to ask him a few more questions.'

It was only then that she reluctantly let them in. Judging by the number of doors leading off from the hall, it was a very small apartment for what was soon to become a family of four. She led them into the living room, which was modestly furnished. A wide bay window looked out over some allotments and trees on the other side of the road. The area would be pleasantly green come the summer. The unvarnished wooden floor had a couple of coir mats, grey with grime, which only added to the bleakness of the room. In the window recess was a Formica-topped table with three chairs, one with a baby seat attached. On the walls were a couple of dull reproduction paintings of Danish farmsteads, and a wedding photograph of a happy, carefree couple – a sharp contrast to the woman before them and the bulky shape slumped in front of the television that was Kasper Jensen. Wearing a black singlet top which showed off his muscles (he was built to be a security guard or a club bouncer), he was unkempt and unshaven, and it was obvious that he hadn't slept much recently.

'What are you doing here?' he said in some alarm. He'd spoken in Danish but they understood. Their presence in his home was obviously making him nervous.

'A few routine questions,' said Nordlund in an unthreatening tone. It was an approach that was much more likely to work than Westermark's trademark aggression. Nordlund took one of the dining chairs, placed it in front of the sofa and sat down. Anita perched on the other seat and took out a notebook, which she put on the table, ready to take down Jensen's answers.

'Do you mind if we speak in Swedish?'

Jensen didn't reply, his eyes drifting to the television.

'Can you turn that off, please?'

Reluctantly, Jensen pressed the remote and the screen went blank.

'How are you feeling?' Nordlund began.

'How do you think? It's been a bloody nightmare.'

'I understand,' Nordlund murmured empathetically. 'It's just we have to clarify a few things you said in your initial statement.'

'I was all upset when I made that. With what happened to Måns and all.'

'We thought that might be the case. Which is why we're here, not somewhere official. As I said, there are just one or two things we need to straighten out.'

'It's so horrible. I don't really want to go back there… to that night.'

'I sympathize, but we've got to catch these people. They

did kill one of your colleagues.'

Nordlund had neatly shamed him into cooperating.

'Now, when the bulldozer smashed through the gate, you say you were round the side of the building, out of sight.'

Jensen nodded.

'And when you came running to the front of the building, the bulldozer had already come through the gate. Why didn't you draw your gun at that point? You must have heard the shots that Wallström fired?'

Jensen cleared his throat. 'Didn't have a chance. One of them was waiting for me. He was armed.'

'And you couldn't identify your assailant?'

'They had balaclavas on. I already told you this the other night.' He was becoming tetchy.

'OK. So, when you were held up by the member of the gang, you were then taken inside the facility and tied up. Yes?'

Nordlund got a grudging 'yes' in return.

'And by that time, they'd driven the bulldozer into the door? I mean, by the time they were tying you up?'

'So?'

'And they took you through the gap that had been made?'

'Yeah.'

'It's just that we have a slight problem. The bulldozer did buckle and damage the door and part of the wall next to it, but it still blocked most of the entrance, and the hole it made wasn't that big. There wasn't a huge amount of room for the gang to carry out the money as quickly as they did. Their movements were hampered; they would have had to duck down. The whole procedure would have taken ages.'

'What can I say? I was shoved inside and tied up, gagged and blindfolded.'

'Through the hole in the door?'

'Yeah. Trussed up like a bloody chicken. It was like I was blind – but I did hear the explosion. Blasting the vault door.

Obviously couldn't see how they got the money out. I didn't even know Måns was dead until I was released.'

'Did you hear any of them talking? I'm thinking of particular accents. Scanian? Non-local? Foreign?'

'I heard one of them shouting. But it was impossible to tell.'

'The man who was armed... the one you ran into. Didn't he speak? Tell you to put your hands up or whatever?'

'Didn't have to. He was pointing a pistol at my face. He just indicated that I go inside.' As an afterthought: 'He took my gun.'

'Nothing was said while you were being tied up?'

'No. I've said that.'

Nordlund uncrossed his legs. A frown formed on his face.

'There's another puzzle which you might be able to shed some light on.'

Jensen flinched. 'I thought this was all straightforward. They burst in, took the money and took off.'

'We believe that the reason they could take the money out so quickly is that they didn't go through the hole at all. Battering the building was just a ruse to make us think that's how they entered. You see, we think they used the staff door.'

'But that's always locked.'

'We think someone opened it for them. Either that or the gang had the code.'

'Can't have. The codes only become available at midnight. I only found out the new ones when I started my rounds at one.'

'We still think that's how they got in and out. And if they did get in that way, the gang must have had help on the inside.'

Jensen suddenly looked scared. 'Don't look at me! I hadn't even got round to checking the door when everything kicked off.'

'Who did the rounds before you?'

'Willi.' Then more confidently: 'Check the CCTV.'

'We can't. The CCTV was dismantled. It's odd though, isn't it? because if Willi *had* unlocked the door, why shoot him?'

'Look, I don't know.'

'They seemed to have known there were three security guards on that night. I'm sure they didn't plan to run over Måns Wallström, but one of the gang went straight into the security office and took out Willi Hirdwall, and another was waiting for you when you came round the corner.'

Jensen just sat there silently.

'OK. Can you tell us how many intruders you saw before you were "trussed up like a bloody chicken"?'

'Three that I saw. The guy that had his pistol on me, someone was on the bulldozer thing and there was another one who helped the first guy tie me up and blindfold me.'

'And while you were being tied up and shoved away, you never heard any of them speak?' Jensen shook his head. 'Are you sure?'

'Look,' he said in exasperation, 'I've just told you. No!'

'Can't you just leave him alone?' They turned to the door and Jensen's wife was standing there with a grizzling toddler in her arms. 'He's been through enough.'

'You're right. That's enough for now.'

Jensen's relief was evident. His wife had come to the rescue.

Nordlund got to his feet. Anita finished writing and snapped her notebook shut. As they headed for the door, she spoke for the first time since their arrival.

'You haven't asked about Willi Hirdwall.'

'No, I…I haven't.' Jensen was flustered. 'How is he?'

'He's recovering. We're not sure if the gang thought they'd killed him. There was a lot of blood.'

'I didn't see.'

'You were the lucky one. Måns run over, Willi shot. You were only tied up.'

'What the hell does that mean?'

'Nothing. Just an observation. By the way, Måns's funeral is next week.'

'Right.' Jensen also stood, as though that would hasten their departure. 'I don't think I can take that. I'll send condolences,' he muttered.

Jensen's wife, still clutching the infant, showed them out. Nordlund gave the child a gentle smile and squeezed its little hand. It immediately quietened and stared at him with big blue eyes.

'It's going to be squashed in here when the next one comes.'

'We're going to move soon.' Her tone was conciliatory now that she knew they were leaving. 'Luckily, Kasper got a generous bonus from the company before all this, so we're looking around for somewhere bigger.'

Outside the apartment, Nordlund and Anita made their way towards the parked car.

'Keep on walking,' said Nordlund out of the side of his mouth. 'He's watching from the window. I want him to wonder what we're up to: why we're not driving away.' They were now just past their vehicle. 'I want him to sweat.'

They made their way along the main road and turned into the park they'd driven past. Except it wasn't a park. Behind a long hedge, among the leafless trees and thickets and wide lawned areas were sparsely dotted tombstones. Realization dawned: they had obviously wandered into the graveyard of the gleaming church. For a cemetery, it was decidedly under populated: there appeared to be no recent burials, so maybe the ground had been deconsecrated. Anita took out a pack of cigarettes and slipped one into her mouth. After lighting up, she took a long drag before blowing the smoke out slowly. She watched it whirl and mingle with the cold air.

'Isn't it about time you kicked that habit?' Nordlund observed. It could be her late father talking.

'I do, every month.'

They stood in front of a gravestone with a scrolled top and a Celtic cross. The memorial commemorated a number of Jensens who had died in the 1930s and 1950s.

'Family?' Anita queried after another lungful of smoke.

'Could be. Don't know if he comes from this area. We don't know enough about him.'

'He was certainly lying.'

'Oh yes.' Nordlund scrutinized the stone's inscriptions as though he was trying to conjure up images of the long-dead Jensen family.

'You think he's the man who opened up the staff doors?'

'If he didn't open them, he certainly gave the gang the codes. There's a glaring inconsistency in his story. If he was ambushed after hearing the gate being smashed in, as he claims, it was before the bulldozer made the hole because someone had to go into the security office to turn off the alarm...'

'When Hirdwall was shot – he didn't mention hearing that either.'

'...and the driver would be waiting for the go-ahead to ram the depot door. In that time gap, Jensen must have seen Wallström's body. He must also have seen the machine attacking the door because he says he wasn't tied and blindfolded until he was shoved inside.'

'And I don't buy him not getting his gun out. He must have heard Wallström's shots before the gate was demolished. Wouldn't it be natural for a guard to draw his weapon?' She puffed on her cigarette thoughtfully.

Nordlund was looking at one of the graves. 'I wouldn't mind ending up in a place like this.'

'I'll check out his bank account,' Anita said as she flicked some ash onto the grass.

'The bonus? Yes, that's highly unlikely. He's only been there six months. Companies aren't that generous.'

'It makes sense that it's payment up front. But is he actually part of the gang or just someone they've used?'

Nordlund moved away from the grave and onto the path. Anita dropped her cigarette, stubbed it out with her shoe and followed.

'If he *was* involved in the robbery, he doesn't seem too happy about it,' Nordlund mused. 'Not a man dreaming of riches ahead.'

'Wallström's death? That would be enough to freak anyone out, especially if it wasn't meant to happen.'

'Yes. It suddenly becomes blood money. Guilt. That's the key to cracking him.'

CHAPTER 7

Anita slumped down in a seat at the kitchen table. She'd already had a cigarette. Lasse didn't like the smell of smoke, so she had to go out and freeze on the open balcony. She knew there was a bottle of red wine that had been sitting in the cupboard for a fortnight, waiting to be opened. But first, she needed to make Lasse his evening meal. He was in his room doing his homework. She could never quite get over his dedication. When she was sixteen, she'd found too many distractions. Boys, to be more precise. Lasse didn't appear to have a girlfriend, or certainly no one he was willing to expose to his mother's scrutiny. He preferred to play football with his friends: that was his main preoccupation, which is why she'd bought season tickets for Malmö FF. It was a way of bonding with her son. Sometimes, work prevented her from going to matches, and one of his buddies would use her ticket. Björn hadn't shown the slightest interest, of course – his idea of sport was seducing his more attractive students. The marital split hadn't been amicable, and it had taken a long time before they'd agreed on her vacating their home in Lund. She'd stubbornly clung on to the house, even though, technically, it was a university property. Reluctantly, she'd eventually relented when Lasse was of an age to change schools. She knew she had been trying to piss Björn off and should have made the move sooner, as it was more practical living in Malmö once she was based at the polishus. The compromise they'd reached had enabled her to buy the *bostadsrätt* apartment in Roskildevägen, though the combination of mortgage and maintenance fee pushed her budget to the limit. And she was constantly battling to squeeze Björn for child support. Though he loved his dad, there was no way Lasse wanted to live with him full time, and Björn didn't want his son around to cramp his style, though he was quite happy to have him for the occasional weekend. It annoyed Anita that he didn't make more of an effort. Björn seemed to think that as long as he was charming, he could get away with anything, and people would excuse him his shortcomings. But Anita had learned the hard way not to forgive.

Oh, what the hell! She opened the bottle. She would have a drink before getting out the frozen meatballs. Sometimes, she felt guilty for relying so much on ready meals. She wasn't a natural cook, though she could rustle up some acceptable cuisine when she was in the mood. Often, she left it to Lasse, who was more than happy to whip up a mean omelette or an imaginative salad. In fact, he was becoming quite adventurous in the kitchen, and he was always tidying up after her. 'You're so messy, Mamma,' he would berate her good-humouredly. She sometimes marvelled that she'd raised such an organized, sensible child. Surely it wouldn't last: rebellion would begin and battles would ensue – inevitable with teenagers. But until then, she would enjoy the domestic serenity. She loved the apartment. It was a fresh start, a clean slate; the new home allowed her to escape the ghosts of Björn's infidelities. Of course, there had been some good, happy years when they were first married and Lasse was a child. That was before the silent serpent of deceit had crept into her life: undetected at first, and when it was discovered, the tears, recriminations, rage and broken promises had torn the marriage apart. Anita had tried to protect Lasse from the worst of it, and she'd picked her battlegrounds carefully, but it had been stressful and exhausting. Now, Roskildevägen was a place where they could both rebuild their lives. And they were succeeding. Well, it certainly felt that way with a refilled glass in her hand and the meatballs sizzling in the frying pan. She'd spice them up with a rich sauce spiked with sour cream and a bit of lingonberry jelly, just as Lasse liked it. She wasn't a complete slob.

After supper, Lasse had retreated to his room. He'd finished his homework and was rewarding himself with a game on the Xbox Björn had bought him on one of his guilt trips. Anita sat on the day bed in the living room with a cup of coffee, and put on a Santana album. Carlos Santana's soaring guitar rhythms always lifted her, and she let her mind drift. The first thing to kick a hole in her quietude was the thought of a blind date that she had foolishly committed to. Lasse had ribbed her when she'd tentatively started back on the dating scene. She'd dipped her toe in a few times with very mixed results. A couple had ended with sex, but nothing that led to a longer-term relationship; and another couple had been unmitigated disasters. She wasn't sure if she was really ready for any commitment. Her job was demanding enough, and she was always conscious of how Lasse may react to another man in her life. At first, she'd felt a slight sense of shame; she'd somehow still felt mentally committed to Björn. Ridiculous! Looking back, whenever Björn had been unfaithful, she'd had the strange idea that it was her fault – wasn't she a good enough wife?... wasn't she desirable enough?... wasn't she adventurous enough in bed? Her confidence and self-esteem had been knocked for six. So meeting these other men was awkward and nerve-racking. Her old school friend Sandra had fixed up this coming weekend's date. Sandra had reassured her that she was a beautiful, interesting and sexy woman. Damn it! She was! Of course, it didn't help that her work environment was male dominated, and that to many of her colleagues, women were just a bit of skirt: only good for one thing – or making the coffee. And unless you went along with the innuendo-laden banter, you'd be accused of not having a sense of humour and told to lighten up. She knew she was good at her job, but it was a constant struggle to prove it in such a misogynistic world. Of course, there were some genuinely nice men in the force. Henrik Nordlund was one, and she was grateful to have him as her mentor.

Anita had enjoyed going with Nordlund to Copenhagen yesterday; they had mutual respect and, for once, she felt she was doing real detective work without everything being clouded by the raging testosterone coursing through the corridors of the polishus. They were both in agreement that Kasper Jensen was involved in the robbery. To what extent, they weren't sure. They'd talked about Willi Hirdwall's possible participation, but it didn't stack up compared with Jensen's. Tomorrow, she would dig into both their backgrounds and their bank accounts. But whichever one of them it was, they were merely a means to an end. The real culprits were going to be more difficult to track down, especially if there was an organization behind them. The size of the seizure indicated that this wasn't the work of a few desperate individuals or low-level chancers. Anita thought back to the spate of robberies which had been plaguing the country recently. There had been a few big jobs in the last couple of years: a Securitas cash depot at Akalla in Stockholm had been raided in a similar way to the one on the E65 Estate – that had been done in the daytime, and the perpetrators had got away with twenty-six million kronor; in the same month, there'd been another cash-depot robbery in Hallunda, Stockholm; in November, two robbers had rammed a Securitas cash transport van and blown it up, taking five and a half million kronor; earlier this year, staff on a plane from London to Gothenburg had been threatened by men armed with automatic weapons, and the gang had got away with foreign currency worth eight million kronor; and only this summer, a secure cash-transport van had been waylaid at Arlanda Airport and the thieves had fled with nineteen million kronor. But all these were chicken feed compared with the Q Guard heist. To all appearances, it had been carried out by a small, slick team of focussed professionals who knew exactly what they were doing: in and out, no question of failure – quite unlike the Hallunda raid, where there were nearly twenty men involved and multiple vehicles used. This Malmö job must have taken months of planning, and it had gone without a hitch – except for the killing of Måns Wallström. That lifted it up a notch; murder was added to the charge sheet.

The twenty-nine-year-old Kasper Jensen had put a cash payment of fifty thousand Swedish kronor into his bank two weeks before the robbery. It wasn't a bonus from his Q Guard employers as his wife had suggested. It looked suspiciously like a down payment on services about to be rendered. Interestingly, it had wiped out his significant debt. There was nothing in his background to suggest that he was a potential criminal except for some minor juvenile scrapes. He'd only been with Q Guard for six months. Before that, he'd had various jobs, including work on building sites and as a nightclub bouncer, before becoming a security guard with a couple of companies in and around Copenhagen. He'd been unemployed for a few months before he was taken on by Q Guard, so life must have been financially difficult with a family to feed, hence the debt. The Q Guard job meant a daily commute over the Öresund Bridge, connecting Denmark and Sweden. Since the Bridge's opening six years before, more and more workers were moving in both directions.

Though the suspicions about Jensen were mounting, the Criminal Investigation Squad were also looking into Willi Hirdwall's background. He was thirty-six years old and his life had been fairly uneventful: he hadn't married as far as they could see and had been in steady employment. He'd been at Q Guard for three years. Before that, he'd worked as a guard on another industrial estate in Malmö after moving to the city five years ago. Previously, he'd done security work in Borås after leaving his native Kalmar, where he'd had a similar job at a large local factory. There was no unusual activity in his bank account. These were the facts. They didn't tell them anything about his family background, his love affairs, his political persuasions, his thoughts on life. For the human angle, they would have to delve elsewhere.

It was while Anita and Nordlund were ruminating about the two security guards that Westermark burst into the office.

'Coats on!' he said with undisguised relish.

They parked as well as they could in a street in Norra Sofielund. A long row of cars, including a police car which had got to the scene ahead of them, were almost bumper to bumper along the kerb, and Westermark had difficulty edging his vehicle into a gap; its backend remained jutting out into the road. It would be hard for motorists to pass, but Westermark couldn't care less what chaos it caused. 'It'll only get worse when forensics get here,' he said with shrug. A uniformed officer met them at the doors of a bland, three-storey, red-brick apartment building. Instead of taking them upstairs, he led them down some concrete steps to the long basement corridor that ran under the entire block. This was the part of the building which housed the residents' mesh storage cages. Behind their padlocked doors, most of the cages were filled with the junk and paraphernalia that wouldn't fit into the apartments above. When Anita, Nordlund and Westermark reached the ninth cage along, they saw the door was open. Inside, there was an eclectic mix of clutter: a couple of chairs, a broken table, several large boxes in a pile, a rather nice ornate mirror, an old bicycle propped up against the outside wall, and a battered mattress on the floor. Lying on the mattress was a raven-haired man in his thirties, casually dressed in an open-necked, red-and-white-checked shirt, blue jeans and new trainers. A simple silver crucifix nestled on his shirt front. He was on his back, his legs were splayed and his arms were either side of his head. For all the world, he could have been taking a quick nap, except his eyes were open – and there was a bullet hole in his forehead.

CHAPTER 8

They cleared out of the cage to allow the forensic technicians in. Westermark was delighted to see that it was Eva Thulin who had turned up. 'Haven't you lot given me enough to do already?' she quipped as she slipped into her protective clothing and went about her work.

'We need to find out from forensics a rough time of death,' said Nordlund. 'There was a shot, so someone must have heard something.'

'It might have been quite muted,' suggested Anita. 'There's so much stuff in these cages that the sound might have been muffled.'

'Who found him?'

'A woman called Anneli Forss,' said the uniformed officer who had brought them down to the basement. 'Came down here at around eleven this morning.'

'Can you speak to her, Anita?' asked Nordlund. 'Find out if she recognizes the deceased.'

Anita left with the officer to find Anneli Forss.

'Any ideas?' Westermark called playfully through the mesh.

Thulin turned to the smiling detective. 'Give me a chance!'

Westermark was sure he caught a hint of playful banter. This might be worth pursuing. He turned to Nordlund.

'It's all pretty neat. And no sign of a cartridge case. Could it be a professional hit?'

'Or made to look like one,' observed Nordlund.

*

Anita came out of Anneli Forss's kitchen with two mugs of coffee. The face of the woman sitting on the sofa was ashen. Anita had already established that she was twenty-five, worked shifts in the local ICA supermarket while doing a part-time course in event management, and had come from rural Finland two years ago. She placed a mug on the table in front of Forss and sat down opposite her.

'It must have been a shock.'

Forss nodded her head as she picked up her coffee and cradled the mug in both hands.

'Can you give me a time, as exact as you can remember?'

'Must have been just past eleven. I knew I had about an hour before my shift. I went down to get a suitcase. I'm meant to be flying home tomorrow.' Suddenly she appeared worried. 'Will I have to stay in Malmö? It's just that it's a pre-Christmas trip to see my family. I'm working over Christmas.'

'I'm sure if we can sort out everything now and get a statement, you'll be able to go.' Forss sank back into her seat in relief. 'So, just take me through what happened.'

Forss sipped her coffee first. 'As I said, I went down to the basement around eleven. My cage is the one next to that one… you know. I didn't see him at first. I got out the case and as I was locking up, I noticed this figure… lying on the mattress… on the floor. At first, I thought he was asleep. Then I saw his head – and then the blood. Around his head… on the back wall. I think I screamed. It's all a bit of a blur.' She put her mug down, as her hands were now shaking. 'Then I came back up here to phone the police. My mobile was here.'

'Thank you. I know it can't have been easy.' After a pause: 'Did you recognize the man?'

'Yes. I don't know his name, but he must live in the building, as I've passed him a few times at the front door. People don't talk to their neighbours much here.' That sounded typical.

'Is there anything you can tell me about him? Did you ever

see him with anyone? Did you see him at certain times of the day – or going out at night?'

'Not really. Oh, there was one time when I held the door open for him. He must have been out for a run as he had a tracksuit on and he was on his phone. He certainly wasn't talking in Swedish. Not sure what language it was.'

By the time Anita returned to the top of the basement stairs, the body was being carried out, followed by Eva Thulin.

'How did you get on?' Anita asked.

'OK. I don't think the deceased knew he was about to be shot. No defence wounds.'

'Which means he probably knew his killer?'

'Or the killer wasn't perceived as a threat. Which is more than I can say for that smarmy colleague of yours.'

'Westermark?'

'The young one. Trying to fix up a date while I'm examining a crime scene! No chance.' She held up her left hand with a thin gold wedding ring on it. 'Even this didn't put him off.'

'Nothing does.'

'I politely turned him down. I told him the cadaver had more chance than him.'

Anita was still laughing when she reached the basement. She was greeted by Nordlund. And a glum Westermark – he wasn't good at taking rejection.

'How did you get on?' Nordlund asked.

'Anneli Forss is sure our dead guy lived in the building, but she doesn't know his name. She did hear him on the phone one day – and he wasn't speaking in Swedish. She didn't recognize the language. I've had a look at the names of the residents by the main door. There are quite a few non-Swedes living here.'

'Bloody immigrants,' muttered Westermark. 'The place is crawling with them.'

They ignored him. 'Right, we'd better start knocking on a few doors.'

They started back along the corridor. As they followed Nordlund, Anita mischievously said to Westermark, 'That new forensic technician seems nice.'

'Huh! Lesbian.'

By the evening, they hadn't managed to establish the identity of the dead man; there was nothing to help them on his body. After a check with the residents' committee, they'd discovered the cage was attached to an apartment registered under the name of Magnus Svensson. They'd managed to talk to the immediate neighbour, who said that the man living there was subletting it from Svensson, who was working in Dubai. According to the neighbour, the man had been there for five months. Kept himself to himself. The only time they had actually spoken was when the neighbour had complained one night about blaring music that was keeping his baby awake. The man had grudgingly apologized, and it hadn't happened again. A search of the victim's apartment had yielded little – it didn't appear to be the home of someone who was intending to stay for long: very few clothes or personal possessions and no form of ID. And there was no sign of his mobile phone anywhere.

'So, how do you think it played out, Henrik?' Moberg was sat behind his desk, with empty sandwich packaging in front of him.

'Early forensics feedback indicates that there wasn't a struggle. Either the victim was taken by surprise or knew his attacker.'

'And when do they think the killing took place?'

'Initial assessment is that it was between one and three in the morning.'

'So, what was he doing down there at that time of night? And who would be down there with him? Someone who lives in the building?'

'Unlikely. We still have a few residents to speak to, but no one jumps out so far.'

'I presume any visitors have to buzz in?'

'Unless a resident has given them a spare key,' pointed out Nordlund. 'However the killer got in, it seems significant that the murder took place away from the man's apartment.'

'Too risky for a gunshot?'

'Partly. But they might have been down there for a specific reason. Something in the cage that he had and the killer wanted? I don't know.'

Moberg rose from his chair like a hippopotamus schlepping its way out of a waterhole.

'We need to wrap this up quickly. If we don't, the commissioner is threatening to take us off the E65 robbery and give it to Larsson's lot. And that's going to happen over my dead body!'

CHAPTER 9

Maybe Eva Thulin could dispel the air of frustration that had settled on the team by the next day. They had no real leads on the E65 Estate robbery. The press were asking questions about the heist, and no one at the polishus was supplying any answers. This just allowed the media to make up increasingly fantastical stories about the amount stolen (Q Guard were unwilling to admit publicly to the sum) and the exotic characters who could have carried out such a daring raid. Of course, just in case they were in danger of painting the gang as audacious Robin Hoods, they could balance their coverage by condemning with equal vehemence the fact that they had killed an innocent security guard in the process. And now the team had an unidentified corpse on their hands. It was little wonder that Moberg was making life very uncomfortable for everyone within bellowing range.

Thulin seemed unperturbed by the atmosphere of rumbling discontent in the room. She began to explain that she was there because she had something important to tell them about the shooting at Norra Sofielund. She confirmed that the victim was shot at close range – that was obvious given the confined space in the basement cage – and that she'd narrowed down the death to between two and three in the morning. Could it have been an execution? Moberg had asked. She couldn't say, but she did reiterate that there was no sign of a struggle or any defence wounds.

'For Christ's sake, tell us something we don't know!' Moberg thundered.

'OK.' Thulin pulled an enlarged photograph out of a folder and went over to one of the meeting-room boards, on which was pinned a solitary picture of the murdered man lying on the mattress. 'The right arm of the deceased,' she announced, attaching her photo. From just below the shoulder to just above the elbow, the skin was covered in an elaborate tattoo. Thulin was about to dispel their quizzical expressions.

'Quite a work of art, isn't it? You can see there's an arched crown at the top, and below that is a double-headed eagle with a shield on its breast. The shield is red with a white cross. These four things,' she said, pointing to the spaces between the arms of the cross, 'are called firesteels. A firesteel is a heraldic symbol, and this one, it is believed, originally stood for the Cyrillic letter S.'

'All very pretty,' said Moberg looking bored, 'but does it *mean* anything?'

'Indeed it does. The eagle and cross represent the national identity of the Serbian people across the centuries. This is a version of the coat of arms of Serbia.'

'A bloody Serbian. That's all we need!'

'More than that. There are numerous variations of these tattoos. One of the most common doesn't have the eagle, but has an extra crown on top and a surrounding embroidered mantle. What seems to link the wearers is that they are supporters of the Chetniks.'

'Chetniks?'

'A group of fighters who were formed in the Second World War at a place called Ravna Gora. Initially, they started up to resist the Nazis but nowadays are a rallying point for Serbian ultranationalists. They want an ethnically pure Serbia. Apparently, they haven't forgotten NATO's bombing of their country in 1999.'

'You seem to know a lot about this,' Westermark said sarcastically.

'It's all on the internet. Of course, you have to learn to read first.' Westermark looked daggers.

Next, Thulin produced a small evidence bag, which contained a crucifix. 'The deceased was wearing this round his neck. This type of crucifix is often worn by Serbian Orthodox Christians.'

'So, we've got a dead Serb nationalist on our hands,' groaned Moberg.

'Thought you'd better know,' Thulin said brightly. 'Hopefully, I'll have more for you on what weapon killed him at the beginning of next week. And any more scraps on the Q Guard job.' She left with a sweet smile.

'Right, at least we've got a nationality for our dead man. We need to find out about Serb expats in Malmö. See if any of them know who this guy is. He's bound to be a villain. This may be a tit-for-tat gangland killing.' The chief inspector now turned to the other wall of the meeting room: the one devoted to the robbery, where, in stark contrast to the two photos of the Norra Sofielund murder, there was much more material.

'We don't seem to be getting very far, do we? No sign of the money, no sign of the gang, a burnt-out van – and a fucking great piece of machinery.'

'By the way,' said Nordlund, 'the quarry didn't have anyone guarding it – or the bulldozer. Didn't occur to them that anyone would want to pinch something so big. The gang broke in, and somehow got hold of a key to start it.'

'Great. Come on, we've got to get some movement on this. The Danish guy… Jensen. You think he's in on it?'

'I think there's a good chance he's involved. Both Anita and I agree on that.'

Moberg took out his handkerchief and dabbed his mouth. 'Let's bring him in tomorrow. Rattle his cage and see what we can get out of him.'

'We'll need to get Danish cooperation,' said Nordlund. 'They won't take kindly to us arresting him without their knowledge.'

'I'll get the commissioner to clear it.' Moberg grimaced at the thought of his boss, whom he'd never got on with. 'I'll be glad when this new guy, Dahlbeck, takes over next year.'

At nine the next morning, Nordlund, Westermark and Anita were sitting in a car at the end of Rumæniensgade in Copenhagen. The snow that had fallen the night before was nearly all gone except for a few stubborn drifts along the kerb and in the cracks in the pavement. When another car drew up behind them, Nordlund got out. A middle-aged man stepped out of the other vehicle and greeted him with a friendly smile and handshake.

'Long time, no see, Henrik.'

'Nice to see you, Christian.'

A Danish uniformed policeman also emerged, and Anita and Westermark followed suit. Anita was reassured to see the officer looked strong and well built: more than a match for Kasper Jensen – they had no idea how quietly he would come.

Nordlund made quick introductions to Christian Tomasson. 'We go back a long way,' was all he offered about their obvious friendship and mutual respect.

They moved down the street and reached the front door of Jensen's apartment block. Tomasson turned to Nordlund. 'OK, Henrik, all yours. We'll stay put. We won't interfere unless it's necessary.'

'Fine.'

Nordlund pressed the buzzer next to Jensen's name.

After a pause, it was answered. 'Yes?' It was Jensen's voice.

'It's Inspector Nordlund again. We'd like another word.'

Silence at the other end. Then the door clicked. They went in.

Jensen was standing at the open entrance to his apartment. To Anita, he seemed even larger than the last time she'd seen him.

'Three of you?' Jensen queried suspiciously.

'We'd like you to come with us to Malmö. Answer a few more questions.'

'Haven't I answered enough already?' Jensen wore a frown of indecision.

'Stop pissing about,' butted in Westermark aggressively. As Westermark pushed forward and tried to grab him, Jensen's mind was made up. He swung a fist and caught Westermark on the chin, which rocked the detective back against the wooden banister. Jensen leapt back into his apartment and tried to slam the door. With his shoulder, Nordlund stopped the door from closing but in doing so, he was thrown off balance. Anita had quickly sized up the situation and was in the best position to rush into the apartment after the retreating Jensen. The Dane disappeared into the kitchen and the door thumped shut. She stood for a second, drew and raised her pistol and then, taking a deep breath, kicked the door open. The small galley kitchen was empty. A heavily breathing Westermark was just behind her.

'The fucking service entrance!' he shouted in her ear.

At the end of the kitchen, almost hidden by the cooker, was a door she hadn't noticed. It was slightly ajar. She rushed through it and came out onto a small landing with spiral backstairs winding their way down through every floor of the building. Shoved from behind by a fuming Westermark, she quickly started to descend, shouting for him to go the other way.

As she careered down the narrow stairs, she began to feel giddy, all the while expecting to meet a waiting Jensen round the next bend. She stumbled down the last couple of steps and burst out of the back door that opened into the little communal garden. There was Jensen standing stock still in the middle of a snow-speckled patch of grass. The reason for his immobility immediately became clear – just a few metres away stood Christian Tomasson, with a pistol pointing directly at him.

Tomasson gave her a knowing grin.

'Thought you might need a hand after all.'

CHAPTER 10

Kasper Jensen was twitchy. He was finding the atmosphere in the interview room oppressive. He couldn't get the image out of his head of Katrine coming round the corner of the street, with little Jon Dahl in his pushchair, just as he, in handcuffs, was being unceremoniously shoved into the Swedish cop car. She'd come running along the pavement, shouting hysterically at the police and then screaming through the window at him as the woman detective pulled her back. In floods of tears, she'd begged her to let her husband go. He'd done nothing wrong. But all to no avail. The female detective had got into the front of the car and the arrogant one – the one he'd punched earlier – had got in the back with him. As they drove off, he could see his distraught wife being restrained by the Danish cop who'd been waiting for him at the bottom of the back stairs. How on earth had he let things come to this? How could he have let Katrine and Jon Dahl down so badly when all he'd wanted was to give them a better life?

Opposite Jensen sat Henrik Nordlund and Karl Westermark. As he scrutinized the face of the younger of the two cops, Jensen knew he was in trouble; the guy looked as though he wouldn't stop short of violence. He could tell that he wouldn't be allowed to leave the room until he'd told them everything he knew. What Jensen didn't know was that he might have had an easier ride if Anita had won the battle with Moberg to be part of the interview team. She had, after all, come up with the idea of a security guard being involved in the break-in, and it was she who'd been there when Jensen was first interviewed in Copenhagen. But, as usual, Moberg had deferred to Westermark, and she and Wallen had been sent off to try and establish the identity of the basement murder victim.

For the benefit of the tape, Nordlund opened the interview with the time and the names of those in the room. What the tape didn't convey was the angry hostility that Westermark was exuding.

'We'd like to go over your statement again,' said Nordlund, his tone perfectly modulated.

'Why? There's nothing I can add to it.'

'Oh, I think there is!' Westermark came in aggressively. Nordlund gave him a sharp look and he retreated into simmering silence.

'OK. Maybe we'll talk about the bits in your statement which don't really add up. Firstly, we still think it's odd that you didn't draw your gun when you heard the shots and then the bulldozer crashing through the gate.'

'I didn't have time.'

'When you ran into the gang member who was waiting for you, there must have been a time lapse while one of the others went into the security office, shot your colleague and then turned off the alarm. At least a minute or so, I would think: plenty of time to see what had happened to Måns Wallström. But you said you didn't know about Måns until you were released.'

Jensen tensed at the mention of Wallström's name.

'I couldn't see him. He must have been under the machine.'

'If that was the case, the bulldozer hadn't yet hit the depot door. When we came on the scene, the machine was up against the door, and Måns's body was in full view from where you were standing. So, how, as you said in your statement, could you have been bundled through the hole it made if the hole hadn't yet been made?'

'Magic,' sneered Westermark.

'Moreover,' continued Nordlund, 'you must have seen someone emerge from the security office, give the driver the go-ahead and watch the attempt to smash through into the loading bay.'

Jensen didn't answer.

'Have you any idea why Wallström was out by the gate in the first place?'

Jensen shook his head.

'Can we have an answer for the tape?'

'No. I have no idea why he was there.'

'OK, let's get back to how the gang got into the building. As I told you before, we believe that the only sure way they had of gaining access was through the staff door. Relying on the bulldozer breaking through reinforced concrete and steel to make a hole large enough for their purposes was just too chancy. So the door it had to be. And we know they could only have learnt the codes from you or Måns or Willi.'

'Must have been one of them.'

'Cut the crap, you tosser! We know it was you.'

'Inspector!' Nordlund warned Westermark with a nod at the tape machine. He then waited a few seconds so that his colleague could settle down and the suspect imbibe his words of accusation.

'You can see why Inspector Westermark thinks it might be you, Kasper. You were the one who got off most lightly. Måns was mangled by the bulldozer; Willi was shot trying to retrieve his gun. But you...' He left the thought hanging. 'Awful what happened to Måns. Horrible way to die. You did see what happened, didn't you?'

Jensen flinched, though he still didn't speak.

'Let's think about why you would do it.'

'Money?' Westermark suggested helpfully. He was enjoying Jensen's obvious discomfort.

'That's a good reason,' agreed Nordlund. 'Let's think about your family, Kasper.'

'Keep them out of this!' Nordlund was pleased with the reaction. They were starting to get under the Dane's skin.

'We've been looking into your finances. I see you were out of work for a while. Not easy with a young child. And now you've another one on the way. An extra mouth to feed. Stuck in a small apartment.'

'I can manage.'

'Your wife told us about your company bonus.'

For the first time, Jensen's gaze dropped.

'Very generous of your new employers – and in cash. I know cash handling is their business, but don't they usually pay your wage directly into your bank? Strangely, when we made inquiries, Q Guard told us they hadn't paid any bonus. So that set us wondering: where did that cash you paid into the bank come from? Fifty thousand Swedish kronor.'

Jensen thought for a moment before raising his eyes to meet those of his inquisitors.

'Won it at the trotting. At Jägersro. It's just along from the depot.'

'Gambling man?'

'Yeah. That's why I told Katrine it was a bonus from the company because I didn't want her to know I had the occasional flutter.'

'So what race did you win on?'

'I can't remember now.'

'You're telling me that you won fifty thousand kronor and can't remember the winner? I would have thought you'd have at least cracked open a couple of Carlsbergs and celebrated the horse and driver.'

'It was over a number of races.'

'Now you remember,' mocked Westermark. 'You realize that we can check all this out at Jägersro?'

'It was through an unofficial bookie.'

'How convenient,' Westermark spat. 'Untraceable.'

Nordlund made a play of glancing though some notes. 'We've been talking to your colleague, Willi Hirdwall. The one who was shot, in case you've forgotten.'

'Course I haven't.'

'He said that you were "distracted" in the days running up to the robbery. What was on your mind? After all, you had a secure job at last, were expecting another child, and you'd had a windfall at the trotting. What did you have to worry about?'

'I don't think I was distracted,' he said, glancing down again.

'Måns noticed, too.' Again, at the mention of Wallström's name, Jensen became more twitchy. That was the button to press. 'The thing is, we're not just dealing with a major robbery here; when we catch those involved, they could well be charged with murder – Måns's murder.' Jensen's head jolted up. 'If we find, for example, that you've been involved, that could make life very difficult for you. You'd be locked up for years. First degree murder? Could be eighteen years. Imagine missing your children growing up.'

'Maybe your wife seeking solace elsewhere,' Westermark leered.

Jensen's fists tightened into ominous balls, and Nordlund jumped in quickly. 'Of course, if you were to help us, things might turn out differently. It's possible we can distance you from Måns's death. Cooperate, and I'm sure we can come to an arrangement with the prosecutor to secure a lighter sentence.' The older detective could see Jensen's mind working feverishly. 'I'll tell you what: while my colleague and I go out for a coffee, you can have a little think.'

Nordlund and Westermark stood up, their chairs scraping on the tiled floor. Westermark got to the door first and opened it. As they were about to head out, they heard Jensen mutter.

Nordlund turned. 'Did you say something?'

'I'll cooperate,' he mumbled.

Anita was still silently seething that she wasn't to be included in the Kasper Jensen interview when she and Wallen set off to pick up some lunch in Värnhem. They had been tasked with trying to find out about Serb connections in the city that might lead to identifying their corpse. Wallen, new to the area, was no help, and Anita wasn't much better placed. She knew there were a lot of people from the former Yugoslavia now living in the country. The first wave had been economic. Many came as part of a migrant work agreement in the 1960s to help Sweden cope with a severe labour and skills shortage. There had been a further influx later on as a result of the Balkan conflicts, when the old Yugoslavia disintegrated: not only Serbs but Croatians, Bosnians, and ethnic Serbs from Kosovo. It was recognized that some of the gangs that plagued modern-day Sweden had roots in these migrant communities. Anita and Klara both knew that approaching these people in order to get an ID on their body would be risky without back-up. After all, they may be talking to the very men who had put the corpse in the morgue in the first place. On the other hand, the killing might have nothing whatsoever to do with organized crime, and they would end up stirring up a hornets' nest for no reason. Faced with this conundrum, Anita had had a left-field idea. It resulted in a couple of phone calls.

'Who's this Luka character you're meeting later?'

'Luka Aleksić. He's a footballer.'

'A footballer?' Wallen laughed as they made their way along the pavement.

'Suddenly thought of him. Aleksić joined Malmö FF last season from OFK Beograd. Got him cheap but he had a great first season. Classy midfielder. Lasse thinks he's a genius. He's good but not that good.'

Wallen looked askance. 'How come you know so much about football?'

'I got into it through Lasse. Anyhow, I thought it likely he would've been adopted by the local Serbian community. He might know people to speak to who aren't on the wrong side of the law.'

'But doesn't the season end in October? Won't he have gone home?'

'He's been away, but he's back for a couple of weeks. So I'm meeting him outside the ground.' They came to the square and stopped for the traffic. 'And there's another reason he's worth talking to,' she said with a glint in her eye. 'He's drop-dead gorgeous.'

Jensen had a half-drunk cup of coffee in front of him. As he collected his thoughts, Nordlund sat passively opposite him while Westermark, a supercilious grin on his face, leant against the interview-room wall. He was feeling very pleased with himself. At last, the case was starting to crack, and it would reflect well on him that he was in on it when one of the perps confessed.

'I was short of money,' Jensen began tentatively. 'Before I got the job at Q Guard, I'd been out of work. It was hard with Katrine and Jon Dahl. We'd run up debts, but even with my new job, it was difficult to pay them off. The cost of the commute was crippling. And then Katrine got pregnant again.'

Nordlund noticed that Westermark was just about to jump in with an inappropriate quip. He shot him a glance and stopped it being articulated.

'With a new baby on the way, we knew we'd have to move to a bigger apartment. You've seen how small ours is. Then I was approached by a guy in a bar in Christianshavn. This guy just got chatting. Bought me a drink. We talked a bit. Turned out he worked in the security sector. Or so he said. Told him where I worked, and that was it. Ran into him again about a week later on the train back over to Copenhagen after work. Said he was doing bits of consultancy work in Denmark and Skåne. We went for another drink on the way home. But this chat suddenly got more heavy. He seemed to know I had financial troubles. He said he could make sure they went away. Better apartment, better environment for the kids to grow up in, cash in hand, treat the wife to a holiday. I was surprised he knew so much about me and I wondered what I'd revealed that first time in Christianshavn. Only later, it dawned on me that they'd done their research. I thought he meant he could use his security industry connections to get me a better job. When he told me what it was really about, I told him to fuck off.'

'Oh, yeah,' Westermark chided sarcastically.

Jensen glared at Westermark. 'I did!' he snarled.

'What changed your mind?' asked Nordlund quietly.

'I did go to Jägersro. All this guy's talk of making easy money. I thought if I had a bit of luck, I could get us out of the hole we were in. But I'm not a gambler. I blew money we didn't have; I just dug myself in deeper. I was such a fool.' Nordlund could tell that Jensen still couldn't reconcile himself to what he'd done. 'Then the guy came back. Knew all about my losses. I've no idea how. He said he'd give me fifty thousand kronor up front if I did as he asked, and then after the job, there'd be a heap more. He said the beauty of it was that I didn't have to do much and that no one would know I was involved. The way he painted the picture, it was win-win.'

'So, what exactly did he want you to do?'

Jensen's whole body was taut. He took a deep breath. 'He wanted me to switch off the alarm just before they arrived with the bulldozer. I told him that that would be virtually impossible, as Måns would be bound to spot me. But I did tell him where the alarm was and how to deactivate it. So all I had to do was get the new codes for the outside staff entrance and the interior door to the loading bay, let them in and make sure it was me who was doing the rounds and not Willi when it all happened. I had to time it so that I was at the staff door when they crashed through the gates. Then they would tie us all up and that would be that. I wasn't party to anything else.'

'You sure?' Westermark was sceptical. 'What about the layout of the place?'

Jensen took a deep breath. 'All he asked about was the corridor between the loading bay and the vault. No other stuff. But you've got to believe me, I never thought they'd hurt anyone.' Jensen looked distraught.

'But it all went wrong, didn't it, Kasper?' Nordlund said softly.

Composing himself, he took a long time to answer. 'I'd reached the staff door two minutes early. I was nervous as hell and panicked. Instead of waiting for the bulldozer to reach the gates, I started keying in the code, and Måns must have seen me on the monitors. He came running out and shouted at me just as the machine was heading for the gate. I yelled to him to get out of the way. Oh, shit!' Jensen's hulky frame started to shake like a rumbling volcano. 'I couldn't do anything! Måns... Måns whipped out his gun and fired.' He was really struggling now: tears were streaming down his face, and his voice faltered. 'He... tried... to get out of the way but he slipped on the icy surface.' His huge, bucket-like hands cupped his face, as though he was trying to blot out the scene of carnage. 'It wasn't meant to happen,' came a hoarse whisper from behind his thick fingers. 'If I hadn't lost my nerve, Måns would still be...'

Nordlund gave Jensen time to compose himself before asking him about Willi Hirdwall. Jensen confirmed that one of the men had gone into the security office and he'd heard a shot. For a moment, he thought that the gang had planned to kill all three of them, and it was with some relief that, after making sure both the staff doors were opened, he saw the bulldozer create the gap in the loading-bay door and adjoining wall. The machine operator carried on smashing into the building until the hole was just big enough to convince the police that it was indeed the means of entry. In the meantime, two of the gang had entered through the staff doors and had made their way along to the vault to set up the explosives. He'd heard the bang when the door was blown, and then the guy who'd gone into the security office took him into the loading bay and tied him up and blindfolded him. Before being gagged, Jensen told the man that Måns must have seen him on the CCTV. He was assured that before they left, they would put the surveillance equipment out of action. There would be no evidence of his involvement. He said the whole thing was a bit of a haze: he reckoned he was in shock after seeing what had happened to Måns.

'Other than the alarm and staff doors, are you sure you didn't give them any other information about the site: the layout... the loading bay, the vault... how many guards would be on duty?'

The Dane shook his head. 'No. Nothing like that. They seemed to know everything. Must have really cased the place beforehand. They just needed me for the door codes.'

'Have you received any money since?' Nordlund prompted.

'No. I wouldn't have taken it.'

This produced a disbelieving huff from Westermark.

'So, your "security consultant" hasn't been in touch since?'

'No. He said the money would come through after six months, when all the fuss had died down. Too dangerous, otherwise.'

'And you believed him?' guffawed Westermark.

'Was your contact one of the gang?' asked Nordlund

'Yes. He was wearing a balaclava like the others, but I recognized his voice. He was the guy who'd gone into the security office and then tied me up and told me that they'd sort the cameras. And he was the one giving orders.'

'As you'd seen him before, at least you'll be able to give us a description, right?' Jensen nodded reluctantly. 'That's a good start.'

'The guy was foreign. Well, Swedish but foreign.'

'Eastern European?'

'Yeah,' Jensen exclaimed in some surprise.

'That fits. Does he have a name?'

'Called himself Freddie. Probably not his real name. Medium height. Black hair. Ugly bastard.'

'That could describe a lot of people,' Westermark scoffed.

'Any distinguishing features?' Nordlund asked more helpfully.

'Not really.' He paused, deep in thought. 'Wait. One time, when he took his jacket off in the bar and he just had a T-shirt on, there was a big tattoo on his right arm. Well, I saw the bottom of it. Looked like the wings of birds, with claws and things. And a shield. Had a white cross on it.'

CHAPTER 11

Anita found herself next to a serried row of sweaty individuals who were cycling to nowhere. Not her idea of an early-evening activity. She could understand running round a park, which she had been doing since her move to Roskildevägen, because it was outdoors, and the scenery and the seasons were constantly changing. Here, the bikes were stranded, pinioned to the floor with no chance of escape, and their riders were slaves to imaginary distances covered. It reminded Anita of the Penrose Stairs... climbing, climbing, but never getting any higher.

She approached one of the staff at the gym: she had a Bran Fitness logo emblazoned across her chest. A young woman whose toned physique made Anita realize that it was about time she pounded the paths round Pildammsparken again. She hadn't had a chance this last week and she didn't want to go on this blind date tomorrow night clearly carrying excess weight. She asked if she could speak to the manager. The woman explained that he wasn't in, though he'd be around first thing in the morning.

It was her meeting with Luka Aleksić outside the undulating concrete lines of the Malmö Stadium's North Stand that had brought her here. The ground, which had been built for the 1958 World Cup, was starting to show its age, and there was talk of creating a brand new stadium next door. Only a ten-minute walk across Pildammsparken from her apartment, she had arrived a little early and had waited for Aleksić to emerge from a photo shoot that had been taking place inside, hence his return to the city during the Swedish off-season. Anita could see why the club had chosen him – he was the most photogenic member of the squad, and Malmö FF were making the most of him while they still had him. With his talent, he would soon be moving onto a bigger club in one of Europe's richer, more prestigious leagues – Sweden was a good jumping-off point for ambitious players from less glamorous footballing nations like Serbia.

When Aleksić came strolling out of the stadium in his smart, well-fitting suit, his long hair scraped back from his chiselled features into a ponytail, Anita found herself slipping into fan mode, and, initially, she had difficulty talking to this young, swarthy Adonis in an appropriately professional manner. She found herself mentally undressing him – or at least as far as his football strip – and inwardly rebuked herself. How often had she been disgusted by the men who did the same to her? Swallowing her hypocrisy, she steered her thoughts to Lasse and how excited he would be when she casually dropped it into the conversation that she had been chatting to his hero. Mamma would have a bit more kudos for a couple of days.

Aleksić was surprisingly shy and proved courteous. After a difficult start, they both soon established that English was the easiest way to communicate – his Swedish being very limited – and from then on, the interview went smoothly. Aleksić had made a number of Serbian friends during his time in the city, and he mentioned a couple of bars and a restaurant just off Östergatan where some of them met up. There was also a gym near Triangeln where a number of his compatriots worked. Some of the patrons were also from Serbia, and Aleksić himself went there quite often. Anita remembered that Anneli Forss had mentioned seeing the murdered man wearing a tracksuit. It would be her first port of call.

Even though it was a Saturday, Anita decided that she would return to the gym tomorrow morning. It would be easier to talk directly to the manager, as he would have a better knowledge of his staff and clients. As she walked out into the festive, brightly lit streets, she remembered, with a flush of embarrassment, ending her conversation with Aleksić by asking him for his autograph and descending into almost unintelligible babble trying to explain that it wasn't for her but for her son. She'd ripped out a page from her official notebook for him to sign: *To Lasse – Luka Aleksić*. She would surprise Lasse with her trophy over supper.

Wallen had volunteered to accompany Anita to the gym next morning. They agreed that Klara would ask around while Anita tackled the manager. The street outside was starting to fill up with Christmas shoppers, and a few flakes of snow drifted lazily among them. On entering the warm, rarefied atmosphere of the gym, Anita's glasses steamed up. She took them off to wipe them and as she did so, her gaze lighted upon a different set of riders on the phalanx of bikes. The people were new but their expressions of pain and exertion were disconcertingly the same.

Anita was shown into an office that didn't smell of perspiration. The unsmiling manager of Bran Fitness (Malmö) was called Boniek: a slender man with a shaven head and deep-set, dark eyes that accentuated his surliness. He was monosyllabic and unhelpful. Clearly, he wasn't intended to be the public face of the business. Anita spelt out why she was there and who she was trying to identify. She had a crime-scene photo of the dead man. Jensen had already identified him as his contact; now she just needed a name. She explained to the manager that she didn't want to show it to his members of staff as it was an upsetting image; she reckoned Boniek could take it.

'Yes.'

'Yes, you understand, or yes, you know this man?'

'Milan Subotić.' A name at last!

'Was he a customer or staff member?'

'Staff.'

'How long had he worked here?'

'Five months.'

'Where had he been before he joined Bran Fitness?'

'Stockholm.'

'Was he here at work on Tuesday? He was killed that night.'

'No. Sometimes he didn't show.'

'He wasn't reliable?'

'So-so.'

'If he was "so-so", why did you employ him?'

'He was recommended.'

'By whom?'

'Can't remember.' He was being annoyingly evasive.

'Was he working over the weekend?'

'I don't think so.' He glanced at a chart on a board. 'But he was here on Monday. Gave in his notice.'

'His notice?'

'Yes. Was going to leave at the end of next week.'

'Did he give a reason for leaving?'

'No.'

'Or indicate where he was going next?'

'No.'

'So when he failed to turn up after Tuesday, you weren't bothered.'

'No.'

Boniek wasn't exactly helping to paint a picture of his ex-employee.

'Did he seem worried about anything recently?'

'No.'

'Do you know what he did in his free time?'

'No. Some of the staff might know.'

As Anita left the office, she couldn't remember the last interview that had notched up so many 'nos'. At least she had come away with a name. Maybe the staff would prove more enlightening.

Half an hour later, Anita and Wallen were tucked in the warmth of a café, with steaming cups of coffee. Anita was also desperate for a cigarette but managed to suppress the urge.

'Well, other than the name, the manager was a fat lot of use. Either he didn't know anything about his employee or he was making sure I didn't find out too much.'

'At least you got the name, and some of the staff were more forthcoming,' Wallen reflected. 'I got the impression from a couple of them that the boss was afraid of Subotić. That's why he let him get away with things. Subotić didn't do much and often didn't bother turning up for his shifts. It sounded as though they all gave him a pretty wide berth. One said he wasn't the sort of guy you messed with.'

'Well, someone messed with *him*.'

When Anita entered The Bishops Arms in the Savoy Hotel, she wasn't exactly dressed to kill. Her pale-purple dress was short (but not too revealing) and she'd made the effort to put on some light eye make-up (but she'd gone easy on the lipstick). She wanted to come across as casually natural so that she was in a position to advance or retreat depending on how the evening was going. Initially, it was just for a drink and not a full-blown date, though the understanding was that if they struck up a rapport, a meal might be in the offing. Anita had made the conditions very clear to Sandra. She'd also set up an escape call. After an hour, Lasse was to ring, and if things weren't going well, she could make her excuses and leave for a family/work emergency (delete as applicable).

She hadn't had much time to change and come back into the centre of town. After discovering the name of their murder victim, Anita and Wallen had returned to the polishus and done some background checks on Milan Subotić. They established that he wasn't known to the local police, but when they widened their search, his name came up with an arrest in Stockholm for intimidating the owner of a beauty salon, though the charge was dropped and the case never went to trial. He'd come across to Sweden from Serbia in 1996 and was now a Swedish citizen. When Anita left to get ready for her 'not-a-date', Wallen said she'd just see if she could find out anything about him before he'd left Serbia. That puppyish keenness would soon wear off, Anita thought cynically. She'd told Wallen not to work too late. They would report their findings to Moberg and Nordlund first thing on Monday.

All that she had gleaned about Colin Culshaw from Sandra was that he was a doctor and had worked at the same hospital in Simrishamn where she was a nurse. He was English: over in Sweden on a six-month exchange programme. He was single and in this late thirties. Sandra had been pretty vague about his personal and professional curriculum vitae other than that he was spending his last three months in the urology department of Skåne University Hospital in Malmö. Obviously, he didn't know anyone locally, so Sandra thought it might be a nice idea if he linked up with someone who had spent some time in the UK; Anita fitted the bill.

The man who stood up at a table near the bar and smiled at her was a lot smaller than she was expecting. It wasn't often she looked down on a date. He had short, curly hair that was already greying at the temples, and his beady eyes came out on stalks when he saw Anita approaching, as though he couldn't believe his luck. He was somewhat overdressed for a relaxed drink: in a shirt and tie which wrestled with each other, and a suit that had the faint hint of a shine. Anita had braced herself for a shy man who had difficulty making friends, and she'd been worried that she would have to lead the conversation. That wasn't to be a problem.

'Hello, I'm Colin Culshaw. And you must be the fabulous

Anita,' he said, holding out a stubby hand. His mouth flapped like a windsock when he spoke.

'I'm certainly Anita, but I've never been called "fabulous" before.'

'Oh, Sandra's description was spot on.'

Anita slipped off her coat and put it over the back of her chair, making sure that her mobile phone was within easy reach. She made a mental note to have a serious word with her friend.

After fetching drinks from the now-crowded bar, Colin plonked himself down and shifted his seat a bit too close to hers.

'My friends call me CC. Cos I'm quick off the mark… like a motorbike. Vroom, vroom!' he chortled.

'Erm… I'll just call you Colin.'

'Fair dos,' he said, raising his glass. 'Bottoms up!' He took a huge swig of his beer, followed by a big breath as he returned the glass to the table. 'So, Anita, I hear you're a policewoman.'

'Yes. And I hear you're a doctor.' That proved to be a mistake, as for the next fifteen minutes, he talked about himself and the talents he'd brought to the urology department of the Royal Surrey County Hospital in Guildford.

'I always say I'm the chief piss-taker at work,' he said, rocking with mirth despite the fact that he must have used the same line a thousand times. When he saw Anita's lack of reaction: 'Piss-taker as in taking urine samples? And I also take the mickey out of people, you see.'

'I do understand the joke.'

Relentlessly, he continued in a similar vein, and when he started to go into excruciating detail about certain prostate procedures, which included a couple of off-colour finger-up-the-bum jokes, Anita realized that she shouldn't have instructed Lasse to wait as long as an hour before calling. Not only was Colin's conversation wearing, but his stories, full of his own self-importance and dull in the extreme, were all accompanied by a look – an intense gaze underneath a Roger-Moore-arched eyebrow – which said in no uncertain terms that this is the most interesting thing you'll hear all week, so pay attention! To break his verbal stranglehold on the dialogue, Anita jumped up the moment her gin and tonic was finished to buy another.

'Same again?' She knew the drill from her time in London.

'That's good of you. Swedes don't seem to understand the concept of rounds. Get 'em in then, sweetheart,' he encouraged jovially.

Ordering the drinks didn't take as long as Anita had hoped and as she wove her way back to the table, she felt like a hostage who'd escaped and was inexplicably handing herself back into captivity. Soon, Colin was telling her about his life in Guildford, which seemed to consist of going to quizzes at his local pub (which he always won), hobnobbing with senior members of the hospital staff (he kept dropping names of people she couldn't possibly know), and playing golf on his days off (though he seemed to have difficulty finding playing partners – Anita knew she didn't have to be a detective to solve that mystery).

Then salvation came when her mobile sprang into life.

'Sorry about this,' she said too hastily as she retrieved the phone from her coat pocket with the speed of a gunslinger. It wasn't Lasse. It was work.

'Anita here.'

'Hope I'm not disturbing you, Anita.' It was Wallen. 'Just thought you'd like to know that I've managed to get a contact name in Belgrade. We can follow it up on Monday when he's back in the office.'

'Excellent. Are you still at work?'

'I'm just leaving now. Meeting up with Rolf. I'll see you Monday morning.'

'Oh, no. I'd better come in.'

'Pardon?'

'I'll come back to headquarters now.'

'Really?' Anita could hear the surprise in Wallen's voice.

'Yes.'

'You want me to stay?'

'No, no. You have your meeting. That's important. Good luck with that.'

'OK,' Wallen said in slow puzzlement.

Anita snapped her phone shut before she caused Wallen any further confusion.

'Work?' Culshaw said with an understanding sigh.

''Fraid so.' She hoped her downcast expression was believable.

'God, I know that only too well, Anita. At the Royal Surrey my bloody pager is always going off. "CC, I'm so sorry but we desperately need you." It's constant.'

Anita gulped down the last of her gin and tonic then slipped her coat on in a trice.

'I'm so sorry about this.'

'Will you have to change back into uniform? I bet you look rather fetching in police togs,' he leered.

'I'm plain clothes.'

'Ah,' he said rather sadly.

'Anyway, it was nice to meet you and hear all about… you.'

'Can we do this again?' he said hopefully. 'I feel we've really hit it off.'

'Might be difficult. We've got a tricky murder on our hands. Very little free time.'

'Do you want my number?'

'Sorry, I really must dash.'

The last thing she heard was 'Don't worry, I'll get your number from Sandra.'

Outside, Anita took a deep breath. Pre-Christmas revellers were streaming across Mälarbron from the Central Station into the town. The bars and restaurants would be overflowing. Despite being surrounded by all this joviality, she was harbouring some dark thoughts: she'd never let Sandra set her up on a blind date ever again; she would never go out with a Brit; and if Sandra gave CC her number, she would commit murder.

CHAPTER 12

Moberg called a lunchtime meeting, though it was obvious he'd already eaten, judging by the sandwich wrappings stuffed into the bin. Outside, fat snowflakes were speckling the view from the window. The park beyond was now blanketed in a thickening layer of virgin white, and directly below, the traffic on Drottninggatan was moving gingerly. Eva Thulin was the last to arrive and as she took off her parka, flecks of wet snow sprayed the floor.

The atmosphere was a strange mix of excitement and frustration. Nordlund and Westermark had left the interview room on Friday in elation. Kasper Jensen's confession had supplied the first piece of the jigsaw. Now they had a first-hand account of the events that had taken place at the Q Guard site, and they knew how many men were involved in the robbery and most of their movements. Anita's theory about the use of the staff door had been correct. They also had a possible link to the man in the cage – if Jensen's Freddie and Milan Subotić were one and the same person. However, it was frustrating that having potentially identified another member of the gang, that vital lead was lying on a slab in the morgue. And what made it doubly vexing was that Subotić was the only one that Jensen had come into contact with – there was no way of identifying the other three. However, thanks to Anita, they at least had a name to go on. The chief inspector had grudgingly given her some mumbled credit and had told her and Klara Wallen to find out as much as possible about Milan Subotić and his movements on the day before he died.

When they had gathered, Moberg wanted action. What Anita and Klara had discovered about Subotić extended beyond his arrest in Stockholm three years earlier. He was a forty-seven-year-old Bosnian Serb born in Bijeljina, which had a minority Serb population. At some stage, he'd ended up in Belgrade and had racked up a criminal record in what had been the last days of Yugoslavia – he'd spent time in prison for aggravated burglary and putting two policemen in hospital. He'd been released when war broke out and had joined a Bosnian Serb paramilitary group: probably the Chetniks, as indicated by his tattoo. He may well have been involved in the Srebrenica massacre; certainly, he would have played his part in the general ethnic cleansing. Why he left Serbia after the conflicts is unknown, but he arrived in Sweden in early 1996, shortly after the Dayton Agreement ended the Bosnian War. Since then, apart from his arrest, he seems to have kept his nose clean, at least according to official records. In terms of his presence in Malmö, he had been in the city for five months, living in the apartment in Norra Sofielund, and had worked at Bran Fitness for the same length of time.

'Why do we let these fucking people in?' swore Westermark.

Nordlund gave him a sour look. 'Life in the Balkans can't have been easy back then. A lot of them were escaping genuine horrors.'

'What we don't know is if any of the other members of the gang are Serbians,' Moberg said as he viewed the photo of the dead Subotić.

'According to Jensen,' Nordlund again, 'Subotić was definitely at the scene of the crime – he recognized his voice and the build of the man. And he was the one in charge, giving the orders.'

'He also says that Subotić was the one who went into the security office and shot Hirdwall,' added Westermark. 'That fits in with what Hirdwall told Anita about his attacker having an eastern European accent.'

'Interestingly,' mused Nordlund, 'in Jensen's new statement, he says that Subotić spoke in Swedish to the man who tied him up, so we can speculate that not all the gang were eastern European.'

'It begs the question why Subotić was murdered,' said Moberg. 'Was it connected to the robbery? A falling out of thieves? Or is it pure coincidence, and he was killed for an entirely different reason?'

'They are connected.' They all turned to Eva Thulin. Anita noticed that Westermark had made sure he wasn't sitting anywhere near the forensic technician. She stood up and went to the board, to which she attached a photo of a crushed blob of metal. 'This is the bullet that went through Willi Hirdwall's arm. Our experts believe that it came from a Zastava pistol. Semi-automatic. Possibly a CZ99. The other bullets used to shoot up the monitors came from another pistol of the same model.'

'Where's this Zasty thing from?' asked Westermark.

'Serbia,' said Moberg.

'That's right,' Thulin confirmed. 'Zastava is a leading manufacturer of firearms and artillery. Has been since the middle of the nineteenth century. These pistols were used by the Yugoslav military and police before the Balkan troubles. After that, everyone was using them in Bosnia, Croatia, Serbia, and later in Kosovo... you name it.'

'Fits in with Subotić's background,' remarked Anita.

'Christ, I hope we're not dealing with the *Juggemaffian*,' Moberg groaned, referring to the Yugo Mafia, which had grown out of the mass immigration of Yugoslavian guest workers to Sweden in the 1970s.

'Not necessarily,' said Nordlund. 'Guns from the Balkans are everywhere after the conflicts there. However, one thing we can be sure of is that this wasn't just an ad hoc group with a good idea. Two much planning went into this.'

'Can I finish?' interrupted Thulin. This produced silence. 'As I said, there *is* a connection. The bullet that killed Subotić was from the same Zastava pistol that was used to shoot Hirdwall.'

This statement had an electric effect on the group.

'Yes! That's the concrete evidence we needed!' Moberg exclaimed triumphantly.

A satisfied Thulin then turned her attention to the robbery and gave the team a summary of what the explosives expert from Stockholm had had to say: 'He reckoned the gang used C-4. It's easy to use as it has a texture similar to modelling clay and can be moulded into any desired shape. It's also safer to handle than Semtex, which would enable them to get in and out more quickly. For people who have the right connections – and this lot clearly had – C-4 wouldn't be difficult to source.'

Moberg had the grace to thank Thulin as she left the meeting.

'OK. Now we know that Subotić was probably the leader, and the gang, by Jensen's calculation, consisted of four men. The robbery goes according to plan – except for crushing Wallström, of course – and they get away with the money. Where is it now? And why has Subotić been killed? What was he doing down in his cage at two in the morning? What more do we know about him?' He fired the questions at the team as fast as tennis balls from a launcher.

'His movements are unknown on the Tuesday,' Anita began. 'He didn't turn up for work. He often didn't, but his boss never reprimanded him.'

'Some of the staff thought the boss was afraid of him.' Anita was pleased that Wallen was speaking up.

'Subotić had given in his notice on Monday,' continued Anita. 'The boss – he's called Boniek—'

'Sounds foreign.'

'Yes, Karl, he's foreign. Polish. He said he didn't know whether Subotić was returning to Stockholm or getting another job locally. Now it seems the reality is that Subotić wasn't going to hang around after the robbery, but didn't want to draw attention to the fact. I've done some checking, and there may be a reason why Boniek treated Subotić with kid gloves – the establishment is owned by a Branislav Bilić. Hence "Bran Fitness". He's another Serb. I've been onto Stockholm to see if they have anything on this Bilić. They're sending stuff through. He's definitely on their radar, so there is a potential tie-in.'

'Well, follow that up. Find out what Subotić was doing in Stockholm; who he was mixing with. Don't let them bugger about. Actually, Karl, you can take over and liaise with them.'

The next day, Westermark was called to Moberg's office and went armed with the information that had come down from Stockholm. He'd enjoyed Anita's fury at having to hand over her Stockholm contact. Nordlund was already in conference with the chief inspector.

'Branislav Bilić is well known to our capital colleagues.' Westermark didn't need to consult his notes. 'He's another Serb; came over to Sweden in the late seventies as a young man. Has Swedish citizenship. His "business interests" are wide ranging: prostitution, drugs, cigarette smuggling… general extortion… along with legitimate companies like gyms and restaurants, though he may use these as fronts to peddle his other services. He's been around a long time and has worked his way to the top of his profession, if that's what you can call organized crime. He's always managed to keep out of the reach of the law. Good lawyers help. And intimidation: witnesses suddenly get amnesia, or don't turn up in court. Some are never seen again.'

'So, his tentacles have spread as far as Skåne?'

'A gym in Malmö and another in Trelleborg.'

'Perfect cover for setting up a local heist.'

'Exactly. And that's where our dead friend, Subotić, comes in. He's known to the Stockholm police. He's what is described as a "close associate" of Branislav Bilić. Disappeared from the capital some months back. My contact was interested to hear Subotić had turned up in Malmö.'

Moberg twisted in his chair and his desk shook.

'Any theories about why he might have been killed?'

'He thought it might be an inter-gang thing – unless he'd upset Bilić.'

'If Bilić *is* behind the robbery, it would be strange for him to get rid of Subotić so soon afterwards,' said Nordlund.

'Maybe Subotić was going freelance and Bilić didn't like it. Or he tried to take too much of the cash for himself,' pointed out Westermark, who could always be relied upon to approach matters from an angle of self-interest. 'Or he simply crossed Bilić in some way. Sounds as though the guy doesn't take prisoners.'

Moberg grunted. 'We're getting ahead of ourselves. This Bilić character may be the man behind the robbery, but without Subotić, it's going to be difficult to prove his involvement and a direct connection. We have to find the other members of the gang – and getting the money back wouldn't go amiss either.'

'If organized crime *is* behind this, the others in the gang might be out of the country by now, and the money salted away.'

'Ever the optimist, Henrik,' said Moberg sarcastically. 'Look, we've got to keep digging.' He stood up and stretched his huge frame, and the room visibly shrank. 'We can start by having another word with the other guard... Hirdwall. Anything that may have been missed. I'll send Sundström.'

'She can flash that lovely arse at him,' Westermark said salaciously.

While Moberg's face wrinkled into a knowing grin, Nordlund was clearly embarrassed at the comment.

'Not appropriate, Karl,' he admonished. 'Anyway, Anita can inform Hirdwall that he's no longer a suspect.'

CHAPTER 13

'I can't believe it!'

Anita had seen people register shock before, but Willi Hirdwall's was nearly off the Richter scale. His face was so creased in disbelief that Anita had to tell him twice that Kasper Jensen had been the man on the inside.

After a silence, while it was sinking in, the inevitable 'Why?'

Anita was sitting in Hirdwall's modest semi-detached home in Oxie, just south-west of Malmö. As she was making them a pot of coffee in the kitchen – Hirdwall's arm was still in a sling – he'd explained that Oxie was an ideal place to live: next to the E65, and a quick and easy commute to the industrial estate. The kitchen looked out onto a straggly bit of lawn, beyond which was a small wire fence and a broad, thickly wooded area of mature trees that ran along the backs of all the houses on that side of the street. The trees would help, Anita guessed, to muffle the sounds of the traffic on the busy dual carriageway. The two-bedroomed, rented house was plainly furnished, and there was a lack of personal items – most noticeably, no family photographs. The digging they had done on Hirdwall before Jensen took centre stage showed no sign of a wife, and little on family background other than that he'd been fostered and brought up in Kalmar. Hirdwall had noticed her looking around.

'Trying to weigh me up?'

'Not really,' Anita said guiltily, as she had been caught

doing exactly that.

'Don't worry. You're police. You're always sizing up situations, locations, people.' He smiled. 'Not much different to a security guard. We do the same. Is that person acting suspiciously? Or being too curious? Does that van parked opposite the gates really belong to someone going about their lawful business?' He shook his head. 'I'm sure you've done a background check on me. You'd be mad not to. I'm afraid you won't have found much. Parents dead. No siblings. Foster homes. A broken heart once. Mine, not hers. A Kalmar kid who hasn't done much with his life. But I like it here in Malmö. And I like my job. Until the other night, I thought I was good at it. God… I had no idea what was coming!'

'There was no reason why you should,' Anita said reassuringly. Then she'd dropped the bombshell about Jensen's involvement.

'The *why* seems to be money. Young child, another on the way. He was in debt. Tried to gamble his way out of trouble. Tellingly, the gang seem to have homed in on him. They knew he was a soft target. No one approached you?'

'No.' Hirdwall was still shaking his head. 'I'd have reported any approach. And I doubt Måns was a target either. Couldn't have a straighter, more honest guy.'

'It was remorse over Måns's death that did for Jensen. That wasn't in the picture that the gang's contact had painted.'

'I can understand. Kasper looked up to Måns. I must admit both Måns and I noticed something odd about him in the days running up to the robbery. He certainly seemed to have something on his mind, but we had no idea what he was getting himself into. I suppose we were pretty stupid – or naïve.'

'Not at all. Jobs like yours – and mine, I suppose – depend on trust among colleagues.'

Hirdwall picked up his coffee cup with ease. He grinned at Anita.

'Luckily, I'm left-handed, else I'd really be in the shit.' He sipped slowly. 'Not bad. I should get you round to make my coffee more often.' He put the cup down. 'So, who approached Kasper?'

'A man called Milan Subotić. Well, we're pretty sure it's him.'

'Have you arrested him? I haven't seen anything in the papers.'

'He's dead. Shot last week.'

'Christ! This guy... foreign?'

'Serbian. Bosnian Serb to be exact.'

'Was he the—'

'Man who shot you? We believe so. You were spot on with the eastern European accent.'

'Got something right, then,' he grimaced.

'Anyway, the upshot is that you're off the hook. No longer a person of interest.'

'That's a relief. Though in a way, I wish it hadn't been Kasper; I thought he was OK.' Hirdwall paused and looked pensive. 'Did he turn off the alarm?'

'No. Though he did tell them how to do it. His job was to open the outside staff door and the door leading to the loading bay.' Anita didn't give him any further information; that was all he needed to know.

'Hence your questions about the codes.'

'Exactly.'

Hirdwall drained his cup and stood up.

'I think I need something stronger.' He disappeared into the kitchen and returned with a whisky bottle tucked under his left arm and a glass in his hand. He placed the glass on the table and then manoeuvred the bottle down beside it. 'Do you want to join me?'

'No... thank you. Still on duty.'

Hirdwall one-handedly twisted off the cap and poured

himself a large measure.

'Still hurts like buggery.' He took a swig and licked his lips. 'That's better.'

Anita watched him enjoy his drink. 'I realize it's painful for you to revisit that night, but is there anything else you can remember? How's the head, by the way?'

'Much better, thanks. They kept me in the hospital for a couple of days, and I still have to be careful, but I *am* starting to remember a few more things. In fact, I was about to call you. Only this morning, something came back to me. I've been going over it in my head ever since just to convince myself it really happened. And now I'm sure it did.'

Anita's ears pricked up. This could be important.

'If you remember, I told you I was lying on the floor pretending to be dead, and I heard voices.'

'Yeah. We know there were four members of the gang. The one who shot you and sorted out the alarm was, we believe, Subotić. We have no further leads on the other three.'

'Well, I must have opened my eyes, because I remember seeing the guy who was taking out the CCTV.' Hirdwall swallowed another mouthful of whisky, which resulted in a cough. 'It took a bit of time. Probably only a couple of minutes, though it seemed like an age. The office was bloody hot; Måns liked it like that. Anyway, this guy was behind the monitors, obviously concentrating, and his balaclava must have been dead sticky in the heat and there'd be sweat getting in his eyes. So he pulled it off his face.'

'The balaclava? He pulled it up? Are you sure?'

'Yeah. He stood up and pulled it up. I'm sure.'

'Did you get a look at him?' Anita said expectantly.

Hirdwall sat impassively deep in thought. Then his eyes met Anita's.

'Yes.'

CHAPTER 14

'That's him.'

His voice wasn't emphatic. Measured.

'Are you sure?' Anita asked.

'Yes. One thing you learn as a security guard is to recognize faces: pick out distinctive features. I may have been fugged up that night, but looking at this photo, it's definitely him,' Hirdwall said.

'Do you know him?' she asked, turning to Nordlund, who'd been hovering in the background as she'd taken Willi Hirdwall through an extensive list of the usual suspects. The face they were staring at was that of a man approaching his fifties. It was grizzled and care-worn and looked older than its years. The bulbous nose, jowly neck and puffed cheeks indicated a lack of fitness and a fondness for alcohol. Anita could see that it was perfectly possible that the man could have been affected by the heat in the security office on the night of the robbery and had critically pulled up his mask.

'Oh yes. I remember him falling through a window trying to get out of a jeweller's he was burgling,' Nordlund said with the satisfaction of recalling a vital piece of information. '1992 if I'm not mistaken,' he added, as though embellishing an already correct answer to a quiz.

'So this guy is known to the police?'

'Yes, Willi. Bengt Rickardsson has been a frequent visitor here and a guest in the county's prisons.'

This was a result. Anita had been cautiously excited when Hirdwall had made his revelation the day before. She had been tempted to rush him straight to headquarters, but she could see that he was having conflicting thoughts about what he'd seen. Witnessing a crime was a traumatic experience, and the memory often played tricks. And, after all, Hirdwall *had* had concussion. How reliable a witness was he? Cases had fallen apart as a result of false recollections. So she'd decided to give him time. She would call back the next morning, and if he was still sure, she'd bring him in then. She'd try the rogues' gallery first, and if they had no luck there, they could at least put together a computerized photofit. But that morning, Hirdwall's mind was clear – he'd definitely seen the man's face.

And now they had a name. And a lengthy criminal record attached. And they knew where Rickardsson lived.

'He was a good choice for dismantling the CCTV. He's done that sort of thing on numerous occasions.' It was as though Nordlund was talking about an old friend. 'But Bengt's gone in too deep this time.'

They would have to go to Moberg with the information and see how he wanted to play the situation. Anita thanked Hirdwall for his help and arranged for a police car to take him home.

'This could make all the difference,' she told him gratefully as he was about to get into the patrol car.

'It's for Måns.'

Moberg was ebullient. 'Where does Rickardsson live, Henrik?'

'Down by the Bridge. Bunkeflostrand.'

'Shall we go and pick him up, Boss?' Westermark was keen to get on with it. 'We've got him fingered. Haul him in and if he doesn't want to play ball, I'm sure he can be persuaded.'

'No, not yet.'

Anita was surprised that Moberg didn't go with

Westermark's gung-ho suggestion. It would be typical of his style of policing.

'Let's keep him under observation. Maybe he'll lead us to the others. Better still, to the money. If nothing happens, then we'll bring him in.'

It was no surprise that Anita was given the first shift. Tedious work that wasn't helped by the fact that she had to share the car with Westermark. Bunkeflostrand was a featureless suburb of Malmö situated just south of the Öresund Bridge. They sat near the mouth of a drab row of flat-roofed, single-storey dwellings in a grid of similar streets. It was impossible to park near the house itself, as the road was too narrow and they would draw attention to themselves, so they were parked on the main drag into the estate. It was easy enough to blend in, as there were quite a few stationary cars: the lying snow discouraging residents from driving anywhere. The house was in view, and if Rickardsson did emerge, he would have to walk past their vehicle. As it turned out, he didn't show throughout their entire watch.

Between the awkward silences and unrelenting boredom, the conversation flitted between general moans about the polishus, the difficulty of a detective's lot and grouses about life in modern-day Sweden. Anita had done her best to avoid talking about the immigrant community – a hot-button issue with Westermark – but the subject raised its head when the murder of Milan Subotić came up. To nip his inevitable racist rants in the bud, she steered the conversation around to something that she'd been thinking about while they were on their third coffee.

'The pistol.'

'Which one?'

'The one that was used to shoot Willi Hirdwall in the security office.'

'And again to shoot Subotić in the basement. What about it?'

'Well, given that Subotić had used it in the robbery, we can suppose it was his pistol. So, why was he shot with his own weapon?'

Westermark caught his reflection in the rear-view mirror and smiled at himself before answering. 'The guy took him by surprise. Grabbed it.'

'But there wasn't a struggle. Yet somehow, his killer got hold of his gun and used it on him. And he must have known him – why else would he be down in the cage with him at that time of the morning?'

'So Subotić obviously didn't see him as a threat.'

'Another member of the gang? Or one of Bilić's other associates?'

'Could be…' Westermark was distracted. A man in a large, blue ski jacket and dark-green, woolly hat walked past them up the road. They watched him carefully. Westermark picked up his camera and followed the man's progress through the lens. 'Look, he's calling on Rickardsson.' He put the camera down. 'I'll try and snap him when he comes out.'

The man didn't surface for nearly two hours, by which time the light was starting to go. His appearance interrupted Westermark's story about a date he'd had at the weekend. 'She's got a great arse. Not as good as yours, of course. You know, yours has been voted the best butt in headquarters.'

'Ha ha. Honestly, Karl, you're pathetic. Haven't you got better things to do?'

Before he could reply, a light appeared in the doorway. Out stepped the man in the green hat, then he turned to shake hands with Rickardsson. Westermark had grabbed the camera and banged off a series of photos before stopping and slipping down in his seat as the man got closer. When he'd crunched his way past, Westermark sat up and flicked through the shots. 'Not much fucking use. Too dark – and that bloody hat!'

*

Westermark was right; the photos proved to be of little use in trying to identify the visitor. However, the next day, Wallen and Gunnare had more luck. The weather was finer and the snow was melting when what appeared to be the same man again visited the house. This time, he came out with Bengt Rickardsson, and they walked into the centre of Bunkeflostrand. They entered the local ICA supermarket, and Wallen followed them in. Gunnare waited in the car park and snapped some photos when they came out, bags in hand. Then the two men crossed to an eatery and spent an hour there. This time, it was Gunnare's turn to go inside. Again, when they emerged, Wallen got some shots. The pair then returned to Rickardsson's home, and an hour later, his companion left.

This time, the photos produced a name. It was Moberg who recognized the possessor of cropped, blond hair, a slightly wonky nose and rubbery lips.

'Alm. Sven-Olof Alm. Picked him up more than once. Thick as a plank but strong as an ox. Often been used as muscle. *And* he's Rickardsson's brother-in-law. Could well be another of our gang of four.'

Though Westermark was itching to bring in Rickardsson and Alm, Moberg was playing it cautiously. The surveillance would continue. If Alm *wasn't* involved, they still had to identify the other two robbers. After all, it was possible that one of them had killed Subotić. And even if that wasn't the case, with their leader dead, they might start to panic and make mistakes. With Subotić's name having been kept out of the press so far, they might not know what had happened to him. They might just think he'd done a bunk with the money.

It wasn't until the Saturday – another weekend out of the window for the team – that there seemed to be some more movement. Anita was with Wallen when Sven-Olof Alm arrived in a car and picked Rickardsson up. The two officers tailed them into the city centre, where they parked close to Möllevångs torget. Then they followed the two suspects to a café in the square, where they met up with a man who had already commandeered a corner table. The man was of stocky build and had what looked like, at a distance, a pockmarked face – Anita's view from her table near the counter was somewhat obscured. The table was also in the noisiest part of the room, so there was no way either she or Wallen were going to be able to overhear anything that was said. What she *could* see through the throng was that the man Rickardsson and Alm were meeting didn't look happy: in fact his entire demeanour was in sharp contrast to the festive buzz coming from the other customers. The three men were in earnest conversation, each leaning into the table, the intensity of which was only interrupted by a young waiter taking their order.

'Maybe they've got wind of Subotić,' Wallen speculated.

'Or can't find him,' said Anita.

As their coffees arrived, Anita's mobile bleeped. She took it out and saw she had an SMS; she didn't recognize the number. After another squint at their quarry in the corner, she flipped open the message: *I'd love to hook up for another drink. I really feel we connected. Let me know when it suits. Most of my evenings are free. Colin (Culshaw) – CCx*

'Oh, for God's sake! She gave him my number!' she muttered under her breath.

'What's up?'

'Oh, nothing. A minor irritation.'

Before putting her phone away, she asked, 'Klara, have you got a mobile on you?'

'Yes.' Wallen got it out of her bag.

'That looks fancy.'

'It's a Sony Ericsson. It's got everything,' she announced proudly. 'Rolf bought it for me when I started the new job.'

It put Anita's basic phone to shame, but it was just what was needed.

'Is the camera good?'

'Rolf says it's the best.'

'Right. Give it to me.'

Wallen reluctantly handed it over.

'What do I push to take a photo?'

Wallen showed her.

'OK. Smile!' The photo caught Wallen's puzzled expression, though only half her face was visible.

Anita handed back the phone. Wallen brought up the shot and grimaced.

'I'm not showing Rolf that.'

'It's not for him. It's for Moberg.'

Wallen looked more closely. 'Oh, I see. The other man.'

'It's not brilliant, but it might be enough to identify him. Look, when they leave, whatever they do or wherever they go, I want you to stick to the new guy. And if you get a chance to take any more pictures, do so. But be careful. We don't want to alert him.'

'You think he might be the fourth gang member?'

'Could be. If nothing else, we can eliminate him from the enquiry.'

Anita was about to order another coffee – she could see there was a couple hovering at the door waiting for a table to become vacant (they couldn't just sit there not drinking) – when the three men in the corner all stood up at once.

'Off you go, Klara. I'll pay for this. Ring me when you've got a chance.'

Wallen got to the door just before Rickardsson and the pockfaced man reached it. Alm had gone to the counter to pay. Anita stood up and waited for her turn to settle up. She noticed that Alm's wallet was bulging with bank notes. It seemed a lot for someone who, when not in trouble with the law, was just an occasional worker on building sites. Maybe he got paid in cash.

Alm extracted a few of the notes and handed them to the girl behind the till.

'Keep the change,' he grunted.

'Thanks,' said the girl in amazement. A healthy tip.

Alm ambled out.

The girl smiled at Anita as she was putting the money away.

'Before you do that, can I have a look?'

'I beg your pardon.'

Anita pulled out her warrant card.

'Police.'

The girl was shocked.

'Have I done something—'

'It's not you. I just need to take a look at the notes that man gave you.'

The girl handed over the three hundred-kronor notes as though they'd just caught fire. Anita felt them crackle between her fingers. Notes this crisp might have come straight from an ATM, but there had been a distinct shortage of available cash since the Q Guard robbery – and Alm's wallet had been bulging. She took a plastic evidence bag from her pocket and slipped the notes in.

'What about the—' the girl started to protest.

'Don't worry. I'll pay you back plus what I owe for our coffees.'

When she left the café, Anita's pocket was a lot lighter. There was also no sign of Rickardsson, Alm or their friend – or Klara Wallen.

CHAPTER 15

It was difficult to tell whether the male members of the team – except for Henrik Nordlund – were pleased or resentful that the two women had come up trumps as far as the Q Guard robbery gang was concerned. Their diligence and quick thinking had produced results.

After leaving the café in Möllevångs torget, Anita had headed back to the polishus with the bank notes that Alm had produced; she wanted to get them into the system as quickly as possible and have the serial numbers checked against those taken in the robbery. Then Wallen had called and asked her to meet her outside Malmö stadshus.

It was dark by the time they met up, and the area was busy with Christmas shoppers heading for home. Wallen explained that Rickardsson, Alm and the third man had walked out of the square. The mystery man had still been agitated, and Wallen, at a furtive distance behind him, had caught him saying 'We've got to bloody find him!' Anita speculated that 'him' might be Subotić; Moberg had been right to think that the other gang members might start to panic if they lost contact with their leader. The threesome had then split up when they reached Alm's car, and Wallen had followed the third man to an apartment block off the top end of Amiralsgatan, surreptitiously taking a couple more photos on the way. Minutes after her quarry had entered the building, she'd seen a light go on on the second floor. The block was a short walk from the City Hall, and when the two detectives arrived, they got into the building as someone else was coming out, and identified the apartment where the light had appeared. The name on the door was Peter Ljungberg.

Next day, they'd checked out both the apartment and Wallen's photos. The former had been sublet to someone called Dejan Kolarov – the agreement was for two months and was due to run out the following Tuesday – and from the latter, it was possible to identify the tenant. Yet another Bosnian Serb, Kolarov was known to the Stockholm police, and he had a reputation for handling explosives – a skill that had been picked up during the Balkan conflicts. Armed with his photograph, Anita and Klara had gone back to Bran Fitness, and one of the staff had recognized him as a visitor to the gym on a handful of occasions. Furthermore, Milan Subotić had organized his training régime, though that hadn't involved a huge amount of effort on Kolarov's part. They had spent most of their time chatting.

So they now had a link between Subotić and Kolarov. And Kolarov was connected to Rickardsson and Alm. Was this the foursome that had successfully cleared out millions from the Q Guard cash-handling facility?

They had their answer once the bank notes had been checked against those stolen from the depot – they were a match. The investigation team couldn't believe that Alm had been stupid enough to use money from the raid so soon. Did his fellow gang members know what he'd done? 'Told you he was a moron,' Moberg said gleefully.

'What now, Boss?' asked Westermark. His hardly contained excitement was reflected throughout the squad.

'Right. We need to move quickly before Kolarov leaves town. We'll bring all three in first thing in the morning. I'll sort out the prosecutor. Coordinated arrests. Don't want any one of them getting wind of the others being picked up.'

*

Anita and Nordlund were assigned to bring in Bengt Rickardsson. They were accompanied by two uniformed officers in case he resisted. At six o'clock the following morning, they crunched their way in the dark along the narrow pavement to Rickardsson's door. Nordlund rang the bell, which tinkled in the background. A light flicked on. It was a middle-aged woman in a pink dressing gown who answered. As soon as she saw the uniforms, a resigned expression crossed her face.

'What time do you call this? You want to speak to Bengt?'

'Yes please, Lena,' said Nordlund quietly. They had met before.

She turned her head and shouted 'Bengt!' then looked back at Nordlund wearily. 'What's he done?'

'I'm afraid it's more serious this time.'

Rickardsson arrived at the door in boxer shorts and a T-shirt, neither of which did anything to rein in his overhanging stomach. He rubbed his eyes to wipe away the sleep.

'Bloody Henrik Nordlund. Thought I'd seen the last of you.'

'I'm afraid not, Bengt. We need you to accompany us to headquarters.'

'What I have done now?'

'The Q Guard robbery.'

He burst out laughing. 'Bugger off. Too big for the likes of me. Got the wrong man. I was here that night, all night. Just ask Lena.'

Lena crossed her arms over her ample bosom. 'That's right. All night.'

'Well, we can talk about that in more detail at headquarters.'

Rickardsson sighed.

'Can I change?'

'I'd prefer it if you did.' Nordlund beckoned to one of the uniformed officers to keep an eye on him. 'And while you're doing that, we'll carry out a search. And before you ask, I've got a warrant.'

When they left half an hour later, Rickardsson called back to his wife, 'I won't be long, love.'

Even though they'd failed to find anything incriminating, Anita had her doubts that Lena would be seeing her husband any time soon.

All three arrests had gone according to plan. Dejan Kolarov hadn't answered his door, and the uniforms, on Westermark's instructions, had battered it down. But a sullen Kolarov hadn't resisted, and he'd been taken away. Nothing was found in his apartment to tie him in to the robbery, not even a burner phone; he'd obviously been too smart to be caught with any incriminating evidence. Sven-Olof Alm and his wife had objected loudly to being woken so early and fru Alm had shouted abuse at the officers as they searched her home. But it was here that they struck gold – a batch of bank notes from the raid worth nearly five thousand kronor. Now all three suspects were sitting in separate interview rooms.

Rickardsson yawned. He was wearing a blue tracksuit, his hair was a mess and he had about three days' stubble. Nordlund and Anita sat opposite him.

'OK, Bengt,' Nordlund started. 'Let's begin with the night of Friday-to-Saturday – the early hours of the second of December. Where were you?'

'Fast asleep, like any decent citizen would be at that time. At home. Just like my wife said.'

'All night?'

'All night.'

'So, you deny being part of a gang of four men who rammed their way into the Q Guard cash-handling facility on the E65 Industrial Estate?'

'Read about it. Big, big job. Too big for me. You should know that. You've seen my record.'

'We're all familiar with your record, Bengt. We also know your talent for dismantling CCTV cameras.' Nordlund consulted a thick file. 'We know you've done it a number of times: Helsingborg in 2001, Halmstad in 1995, and, famously, here in Malmö in '92 when you fell through that jeweller's window trying to escape. And they're just the capers where you were caught.'

'Look, I've gone straight since Helsingborg. Did my time. Promised Lena I'd keep my nose clean. I help Sven-Olof out with the odd building job these days. Bit of electrics… that sort of thing. Why would I risk that?'

'For a hundred and thirty-five million kronor,' Anita suggested. 'And that's not counting the dollars and euros.'

Rickardsson raised a slightly shocked eyebrow. 'That much?'

'Didn't you realize how much you'd taken?' she replied wryly. 'Didn't they tell you? Of course, you were only a small cog in a much bigger machine.'

'Don't know what you're talking about, darling.'

Anita didn't rise to the bait.

Nordlund jumped back in. 'Your brother-in-law, Sven-Olof. Do you know what he was doing that night?'

'No idea.'

'We're asking him right now.'

'You won't get anything out of him.'

'We already have.' This took Rickardsson unawares and he shifted in his seat. 'He's not the brightest bulb.' Rickardsson remained silent.

'You and Sven-Olof,' said Anita, 'went to a café in Möllevången on Saturday.'

'What of it?'

'You met a third man – Dejan Kolarov.' Anita could see that she had hit home. He wasn't expecting that.

'It's not a crime to have a coffee with someone.'

'How do you know him?'

'Met him in a bar one night. Got on. Decided on a *fika*.'

'Well, we find your *fika* friend rather interesting. He's connected to Milan Subotić.'

'Never heard of him.'

'Milan Subotić led the raid on the facility.'

'You've lost me.'

'It's more a case of you losing Subotić. Someone put a bullet in his brain.'

Rickardsson managed to remain impassive, though Anita spotted a brief flicker of doubt in his eyes.

'Anyway, let's get back to your *fika*. When you left the café, Sven-Olof paid for your coffees.'

'He's generous like that.'

'Maybe. But here's a strange thing. He paid with money stolen from Q Guard.'

Rickardsson bit his lip. It didn't take a psychic to know that he was secretly cursing his idiotic brother-in-law.

'Odd, don't you think?'

'I'm not saying any more without a lawyer.'

'That's your right,' said Nordlund. But it won't do you any good. You see, we know you were part of the gang that night.'

'Bollocks.' The protest was only half-hearted.

'We've got a witness.'

Dejan Kolarov had stopped talking to Westermark and Gunnare altogether. At first, he'd only spoken in Serbian, pretending he didn't speak Swedish. When Westermark had given this short shrift, he'd reverted to monosyllabic answers in Swedish, or no answer at all. He denied any involvement in the robbery. He wouldn't explain what he'd been doing in Malmö over the last two months. Then, to get a reaction, Westermark had brought up Kolarov's past criminal record. Since moving to Sweden in the early 1990s, he'd done time for a Stockholm bank raid involving explosives, and he was suspected of involvement in other robberies. What Anita had thought in the café were pockmarks on his face was, in fact, damage caused by a mistimed explosion during a job in pre-war Sarajevo. That particular robbery had been politically motivated: to raise funds for a Bosnian Serb militia group.

Westermark's usual aggressive interrogation techniques did little to unsettle the uncooperative Kolarov. Threats were batted away with indifference. The only time he appeared slightly fazed was when Westermark dropped into the conversation that Milan Subotić had been found murdered, and was it he, Kolarov, who had pulled the trigger? From Kolarov's reaction, Westermark judged that he hadn't been aware of the Subotić killing; now the remark overheard by Wallen – *We've got to bloody find him!* – made sense. After an hour, Westermark stormed out of the room and slammed the door. He didn't like to fail.

Moberg was having more luck with Sven-Olof Alm. It helped that he had more ammunition. First, he tried to pin Alm down to where he was on the night of the robbery. Alm, like Rickardsson, used the 'I was at home all night: ask my wife' line and, initially, wouldn't shift from his story until Moberg produced the cash they had found in his house. With Kasper Jensen's input, the team had worked out that it was Subotić who'd gone into the security office, shot Hirdwall and turned off the alarm; Kolarov had blown the vault door; and Rickardsson had dismantled the CCTV. They speculated that it was Alm who'd driven the stolen bulldozer, as he was used to working with machines on building sites.

'That was from a job. Cash in hand.'

'What job?'

'Oh... erm... down at Höllviken. An extension.'

'When was that?'

'Last week.'

'Address?'

'Not sure off hand.'

'And who paid this cash in hand?'

'I don't really want to say.' He made a clicking sound with his tongue. 'Nothing went through the books. Don't want to get anyone into trouble.'

'You're the one in fucking trouble!' Moberg suddenly yelled as he thumped the table. Alm jumped. He might have been tough, but he was no match for a raging, menacing Moberg. 'I'm not putting up with any more of this crap, Alm! The only way you could have got hold of these notes is from the Q Guard site on the night of the robbery.'

'I'm telling you the truth, Chief Inspector,' a crushed Alm said hoarsely.

Moberg suddenly changed tack, adopting the tone of a patient parent talking to a recalcitrant child. 'I don't think you've any idea what you've got yourself involved in. This is in a different league, Sven-Olof. It's not a case of you throwing your weight around and the occasional bit of GBH... the odd bungled burglary... nicking cars. We're talking big time here. This job was massive. Too massive for a dumbo like you to start splashing the cash. I bet the others didn't know what you were up to, did they? And whoever's behind this... Mister Big... isn't going to be happy. There'll be consequences, Sven-Olof, for you... your wife...your kids. Your stupidity has put them in danger.'

'You leave my family out of this.'

'But your biggest mistake was killing the security guard. That's murder!'

Alm visibly shrank. 'I didn't!' he whimpered.

'You were driving that bulldozer.'

'I wasn't,' he croaked.

'You drove the bulldozer from the stone quarry in

Limhamn. We've got you on CCTV.'

'But I was wearing...'

Moberg almost laughed. 'Wearing a balaclava. Yes, you were. So were the others: Milan Subotić, Dejan Kolarov, and your brother-in-law. But we still know who you all are. And now we've got all of you tucked up in our nice, cosy little police station. All except Subotić, of course – someone put a bullet in his head.' He could see Alm was stunned by the news. 'Told you you were mixing with a rough crowd.'

Alm now looked resigned, accepting his fate. 'Bengt had nothing to do with it,' he mumbled.

'Speak up!' snapped Moberg.

'Bengt had nothing to do with it. Subotić, yes. But I don't know that other guy you mentioned.'

'Oh sure; it was just you and Subotić,' Moberg guffawed scornfully. He put his face near Alm's. 'We know you were driving that bulldozer, Sven-Olof – the same bulldozer that flattened Måns Wallström. I'm sure it wasn't meant to happen that way. But it did happen, and you are going to take the fall.'

'Oh God,' Alm moaned.

Moberg let him stew for a couple of minutes before turning to Wallen.

'Of course, Sven-Olof could make things a bit easier on himself.'

'Could he?' asked Wallen, joining in the chief inspector's little game without knowing what on earth he was going to say.

'Oh yes. Maybe we could drop the charge from first degree murder to second degree, or even to manslaughter. Now that would change things quite considerably. Instead of looking at... what... eighteen years?... it'd be more like five or six.'

'Would that include time for the robbery?' Wallen asked.

'Oh, there'd be extra for that, of course. But at least he wouldn't come out an old bugger with nothing left to live for. It would come at a price, though.' Moberg was speaking as though Alm wasn't in the room. 'We'd need details of the robbery... who was involved... who was behind it.'

'And the money?' suggested Wallen.

'Good point, Inspector Wallen. Where the cash is stashed.' He then swivelled slowly to face Alm.

'Well, Sven-Olof, what's it going to be?'

CHAPTER 16

Malmö cast a gloomy aspect, with further snow clouds gathering and the wind off the Sound biting into those scurrying through the streets. This was the time when the *fika* came into its own: good to escape the rawness outside, sit round a table with twinkling tea lights, and let vigorously strong coffee and indulgent pastries fortify the inner soul.

It wasn't exactly a *fika* occasion in the Criminal Investigation Squad's meeting room, but there were buns and cakes a-plenty as the team compared notes on their various interrogations.

Westermark admitted he'd drawn a frustrating blank: Kolarov wasn't admitting to anything. But he did get the impression that the Serb hadn't known that Subotić had been murdered. He also reckoned that Kolarov was one of the same Serbian brotherhood as Subotić, as 'He has the same bloody tattoo!' When it was Nordlund's turn, he reported that he and Anita hadn't had much luck with Bengt Rickardsson either. Rickardsson had clammed up and demanded a lawyer when they mentioned there was a witness, but they were sure that he didn't know of Subotić's death, or that his brother-in-law had been spending cash from the robbery. 'He's an old pro,' summed up Nordlund. 'He won't be easy to crack because he knows there's more at stake with a dead guard in the mix. We'll need to get Willi Hirdwall on that witness stand.'

'Agreed,' said Moberg after demolishing another cinnamon bun. 'You didn't mention who the witness was?'

'No. I thought it best to keep Hirdwall out of it until we need him. So, as far as Rickardsson is concerned, it could have been someone who'd seen them at any stage of the operation, from the quarry to the getaway.'

'Good. I want to keep it that way. Until we know who exactly we're dealing with, we'll need to keep Hirdwall out of sight. He's vital. Alm isn't going to shop Bengt Rickardsson for obvious reasons. Or Kolarov – that's more to do with fear, I suspect. But I think I managed to put the frighteners on him, and he now realizes what he's got himself mixed up in. Once he knew he was in the frame for Wallström's murder, he got more cooperative, admitting he was there. I suppose he couldn't really do otherwise, as we've got his prints on the money from the café.'

'What a cretin!' Westermark interjected.

'Yeah, the silly bastard couldn't resist filching some of the cash. The stuff found in his house is with forensics. You can bet your bottom dollar, Alm's prints'll be all over it – but I suspect nobody else's. I haven't got out of him yet where they stashed the money, but a bit more pressure, and I think he'll spill all. I dangled the carrot of a reduced sentence. Making promises I don't know if I can keep; I suppose I'd better have a word with the prosecutor and see what we can do. I think Alm was almost relieved that Subotić is dead so he can blame everything on him. Subotić was definitely running the operation, but Alm thought the Serb was reporting to someone else.'

'Makes sense,' said Nordlund. 'Someone with the resources to back such a scheme.'

'Yes, that's what we have to concentrate on next. Alm was only promised six million. If that was the arrangement – each member getting a similar hand-out for doing the job – then the boss man walks away with well over a hundred. Plus the dollars and euros. Subotić and co. were set up as a specific team for the job. And a job this big smacks of organized crime.'

'Are we talking about this Bilić character?' asked Westermark.

'It fits. We know Subotić was an associate. We need to talk to Stockholm again to establish whether Kolarov is part of the same set-up. There's a good chance, as they all seem to be Serbs.'

'I'll check it out.'

'If we can prosecute the whole gang, then we've got a chance of reeling in the big fish. If Bilić *is* behind this, he must already be getting nervous that we've pulled his team in. After all, one of them might talk.'

'But you said that according to Alm, they took orders from Subotić,' Wallen pointed out. 'They might not know who the top man is.'

Moberg conceded the point. 'I'm sure an idiot like Alm was kept in the dark. But the other two might know.'

'Maybe that's why Subotić was killed,' opined Anita. 'Then there's no connection with Bilić.'

'Ah,' said Nordlund, 'but that presupposes that Bilić has got hold of the money already. We don't know when it was going to be divided up, and if the other three were worried that they couldn't get hold of Subotić, that probably hasn't happened yet. The money might still be out there.'

'Right!' Moberg said decisively. 'First thing tomorrow, I'll have another crack at Alm. A night sweating in a cell may make him even more talkative. We'll have a go at the others, too. At the moment, we've got fuck all on Kolarov and we won't be able to keep him in more than a couple of days without good reason. In the meantime, Sundström, I want you to have another word with Willi Hirdwall. Break it to him that we'll need him to testify against Rickardsson when the time comes. And see if he can remember anything else. We've got to nail these bastards!'

*

Anita sat in her kitchen feeling mortified. She'd just got cross with Lasse, who'd now shut himself in his bedroom with Grand Theft Auto. It had been unfair to take out her frustrations on her son. She'd been annoyed about Moberg's decision to send her off to see Willi Hirdwall. Other than to tell him he would be needed to testify when Bengt Rickardsson was brought to trial, there seemed little point in trying to squeeze any more information out of the poor guy; he'd been through enough. She had to admit that Hirdwall's role as prime witness would be vital as long as Rickardsson denied being at the scene of the crime and Alm still refused to rat on him. After all, they had no other evidence. But what had really bugged her was her exclusion from the process of exacting a confession from Rickardsson (Falkengård had been assigned that duty) and her summary dismissal to execute what she thought was a job any uniform could do. She felt she deserved to be in the thick of it, as she had played an important part in getting the investigation this far.

On arriving back at home, she'd had another SMS message from Colin Culshaw. This had prompted her to ring her friend Sandra and have a go at her for lining CC up in the first place. That had been peevish on her part and would cost her a placatory drink at some stage.

'I don't know what he's like socially, but he seemed nice enough around the hospital. Besides, he thanked me and said you'd got on like a house on fire,' Sandra had said defensively.

'I'd rather set *my* house on fire than put up with him again!'

Having miffed her friend, she set about cobbling together an evening meal for Lasse, who'd arrived home from football training and announced that he and his mates had gone for a takeaway pizza afterwards and he wasn't hungry.

She drove off next morning after apologizing to Lasse over breakfast. He had the grace to admit that he should have warned her he was eating out. He said he was trying to save her the effort of making a meal after a hard day at the polishus, which just made her feel worse. It was a bright morning, which lifted her spirits somewhat. There were still thick patches of snow along the sides of the road, but they were starting to melt in the weak sunlight.

Her thoughts wandered to Christmas. She would have to make her obligatory visit to Kristianstad to see her mother, who lived with her aunt. Anita's trips had always been short, as she and her mother had never got on, and, as a peace offering, she'd often left Lasse there for a couple of extra days when he was younger. Margita Ullman was not an easy woman. She had always been at odds with her lot in life and had taken out her bitterness on Anita. Anita was never quite sure what expectations she had failed to live up to. Maybe her closeness to her late father hadn't helped after her parents' divorce. Be that as it may, she still felt a responsibility for her mother and always tried to fulfil her filial duty, however irksome.

Gingerly parking her car in the slush, she could see Hirdwall waiting at the window – she had phoned him from the office the night before. He was no longer wearing his sling, and he gave her a wave, a cigarette clamped between his fingers.

He had prepared a thermos of coffee. 'I can do more for myself now.' He sounded proud of the achievement. The coffee was accompanied by a tin of *Pepparkakor* ginger biscuits.

'How are you feeling?' Anita began tentatively. It was important to keep Hirdwall onside. Besides, she found that she genuinely cared how he was.

'I'm getting better. Physically, anyway. Still wake up in the night in a panic sometimes.'

'You know, I can arrange for you to talk to someone. What you've been through… it might help.'

'Thanks. But Q Guard have already organized a couple of sessions for me. I must admit, I always thought these trick cyclists were a bit of a con, but I think, now, I've changed my mind.'

'Can you get away somewhere, perhaps? I know you've got no family as such… friends? A change of scene might help as well.'

'No… no family to speak of; Kalmar's in the past. Not many friends, either. Not round here, anyway. I suppose I'm a bit of a loner. Haven't a clue who my neighbours are, except the grumpy guy next door who complained I'd left my car in his parking space. I didn't know it was his,' he chortled; the incident seemed to have amused him. 'I suppose I got on with Måns the best.' He went quiet as he held a biscuit in mid air. 'I went to his funeral last week,' he said softly.

'I would have gone but I was on surveillance that day.'

'Something to do with the case?'

'Yes. The man you identified.'

'Did you find out anything?'

'We've brought him in. And the other two.'

'That's great news.'

'Partly,' Anita said guardedly. 'One of them is talking. Not the one you identified – Bengt Rickardsson. The squealer is his brother-in-law. And the third one's a Serb called Dejan Kolarov.'

'Wasn't the one who died a Serb?'

'Yes. The only problem is, we haven't really got anything concrete on the two keeping shtum.'

'What about my ID of Rickardsson?'

'That information was invaluable. But in order to make the charge stick, we need you to go that little bit further.'

'How?'

'Would you be willing to testify to seeing Rickardsson on the night of the robbery?'

Hirdwall winced. 'You mean put my head above the parapet?'

'Yes. For Måns.'

'Do the police do courses in emotional blackmail?' He gave a rueful grin. 'Of course I will.' It suddenly dawned on Anita what she was asking of him. If they were really dealing with Bilić, he had a reputation for getting witnesses to change their minds. They'd have to keep an eye on Hirdwall.

'Look, I know it's unlikely, but has anything else occurred to you since we last spoke about that night, or the lead up to it? Anything that might help us? Some daft little detail... I don't know. We don't want any of these people walking free because we haven't got enough evidence.'

Hirdwall stood up and wandered over to the window. Droplets of melting snow were pattering to the ground from the roof of the house opposite.

'I've replayed the events of that night again and again until my head aches.'

He turned back towards Anita and shrugged.

'Nothing?'

'I wish I could tell you more but, I'm sorry, I can't.' She could sense his exasperation.

'Willi, you've done enough already. Just identifying Rickardsson has given us a major breakthrough.' She hoped that would be some consolation for him.

She gulped down the last of her coffee. 'I'd better go. Oh, I tell you what. I've got photos of all four of the gang. You might as well see who you were up against. Don't know, might jog a memory.'

Hirdwall came and sat next to her as she took out the images.

'This is Bengt Rickardsson – you know him, of course.'

'Oh yes.'

'This one is his brother-in-law – Sven-Olof Alm.'

'The one doing the talking?'

Anita nodded.

Hirdwall shook his head. The face clearly meant nothing to him.

'This is Milan Subotić. He was the leader.'

'The prick who shot me?'

'Yeah. Sadly, we can't bring *him* to justice.'

'He got what he deserved.'

Finally, she produced Dejan Kolarov's photo. This also produced a shake of the head. Then, slowly, Hirdwall's brow creased into a frown. 'Sorry, give me that.' He took Kolarov's photo and screwed up his eyes. He stared at it as though mesmerized. Then he looked again at Subotić, then back again to Kolarov. 'Wait… wait, wait, wait…'

CHAPTER 17

Willi Hirdwall held the two photographs, one in each hand.

'It's them!'

'What do you mean?'

Slowly, he laid the photographs of Subotić and Kolarov down side by side on the coffee table.

'I've seen them before. Together.'

'Where?' Anita demanded, her voice urgent.

'Outside the depot.'

'When?'

'About a couple of weeks before the robbery.' Hirdwall's eyes sparkled. 'I'm good at faces.'

'I remember you saying.'

'The reason they didn't register at first is because they were out of context: mug shots like this,' he said, waving a hand over the photos. 'But now I remember – Telenor.'

'What's Telenor got to do with it?' Anita was thrown; what was he talking about?

'There's a big metal box near the car park. It's to do with broadband.'

'Yeah. I parked next to it on the night of the robbery.'

'Måns and I had just finished our shift. Then we'd had a meeting before leaving, to fix up the latest rota, so we didn't get away until about nine that morning. We were driving out – Måns's car was in front of me. Just next to the box, there was a white van – no company livery on it. The front of the box was open, and two guys in Telenor overalls were fiddling with something inside it. Måns stopped his car and slid down his window to have a word with them. He was always paranoid about people hanging around anywhere near the site. Didn't trust anybody. I must admit, I was a bit hacked off because I just wanted to get home and get some kip, but I was stuck behind him. He was chatting to them through his window – I couldn't hear what they said because my window was up, but I could see their faces clearly.' He tapped Subotić's photo. 'It was this one he was talking to. This guy' – pointing at Kolarov – 'just stood there. Kol...'

'Kolarov.'

'Kolarov. Whatever was said, it ended in a joke because these two were laughing, and they waved at Måns as he drove off. I forgot about the incident until I saw these. Måns never mentioned it, and I forgot to ask.' He paused. 'That's it.'

'And you're sure it was these two?'

'Dead certain.'

Anita slowly gathered up the photos.

'You'd swear to it?'

Hirdwall nodded.

'They must have been reconnoitring. Do you think you can you work out the exact day you saw them?'

'I can ring the office and check when the rota was sorted.'

'That would be great.'

Anita burst into Nordlund's office.

'We've got a connection between Q Guard and Kolarov.'

She quickly retold Hirdwall's story. She'd waited at his house until he'd rung his office and confirmed that it was on the morning of Friday, November 17th – fifteen days before the robbery – that he'd seen the supposed Telenor van.

'I've confirmed that Telenor didn't send anyone to that location at that time. And, of course, they haven't got employees called Subotić or Kolarov. It's clear what they were doing.'

'Well done, Anita. Can you pass that onto Karl? It'll give him something to use against Kolarov.'

'How did you get on with Rickardsson?'

'Blank. He stonewalled us. It gets monotonous when someone says "no comment" in the same voice for over an hour. His lawyer was dozing off. We're going to have to rely on your friend Hirdwall. Do you think he's up for it?'

'Yeah, I think he is.'

Westermark had Gunnare for company. He hadn't been able to shake or intimidate Dejan Kolarov. He hadn't resorted to the 'no comment' ploy, but most of his replies were either monosyllabic or sarcastic. Westermark took a much-needed break, in which he'd smacked the water cooler in annoyance when his plastic cup failed to appear. After Anita had had a word with him, he returned to the interview room with renewed vigour. He was on his own, as Gunnare had disappeared somewhere. He deliberately didn't switch on the recorder.

'Where were you around nine o'clock on the morning of Friday, November the seventeenth?'

'In bed. I work nights.' Kolarov's speech was thickly accented.

'We know that – that's when you blow up safes and vaults. We know exactly where you were that morning.'

'So why you ask?' he shrugged.

'You were outside the Q Guard site pretending to be a Telenor engineer. You and your dead mate, Milan. Casing the joint.'

'What "casing joint"?'

'You know fucking well!' Westermark shouted. 'Looking around – working out how you were going to rob the place.'

'Crap.'

'We've got a witness. He saw you there.'

'I was not near that morning; you make things up,

policeman.' He injected a shot of venom into his voice.

When Westermark didn't get the reaction he was expecting, he lost his temper.

'Take that smirk off your fucking face! This guy also saw you in the security office on the night of the robbery. You came and shot up the monitors. He's going to send you down.'

Kolarov looked steadily at Westermark and smiled. Westermark realized he'd gone too far. Anita had warned him they were keeping Hirdwall under wraps until Moberg was ready to produce him. And he knew there was no way Hirdwall could identify Kolarov from the night itself.

'You say security guard can identify me?'

Westermark could see Kolarov working out who that must be. He tried to backtrack. 'I didn't say it was a security guard.'

Too late. Kolarov's smile broadened. 'I speak to lawyer now.'

It was Moberg who emerged from his interview room the most triumphant. 'I know where the money is! Alm is so shit scared that he's going down for murder that he blurted it out. Come on. Let's go!'

Two cars left headquarters in a hurry. Nordlund drove the first with Moberg sitting next to him and Anita and Westermark in the back. Behind them came a patrol car with three uniformed officers. Once out of the city and past the E65 industrial estate, they headed along the main road in the direction of Svedala. Anita felt claustrophobic, as Moberg's massive frame was blocking out the light in front of her, and Westermark was using their proximity to rub his knee against hers.

'Sven-Olof was singing away once he thought I'd do a deal with him,' Moberg said loudly above the noise of the engine. His exhilaration was palpable. 'He admitted that they drove the getaway van to near Bara. Transferred the money into another van and took it to a farmhouse. That's where we're going. Once the cash was unloaded, Subotić drove them back into town. It was while he was in the back of the van that Alm swiped his notes.'

'Is he still not giving anything away about the other two?' asked Westermark, giving himself an excuse to lean across Anita to speak to the chief inspector.

'No. Can't see us getting anywhere with that. And he still maintains that Subotić gave the orders and they had no idea who he was dealing with. So the buck conveniently stops at Subotić.'

Once past Svedala, they reached the roundabout that led to Sturup Airport. Moberg gave the instruction to turn off.

'To the airport?' Nordlund asked in surprise.

'No. There's a turning to the left just up here.'

The cars veered onto a snow-covered, wooded side road and soon had to slow down, as the tarmac was rutted and uneven. At one point, the wheels of Nordlund's car began to spin as they strained to grip the slushy surface; even the winter tyres couldn't cope. There were no tracks ahead, so no vehicles had been up this way for at least a couple of days. The birches and pines became denser, and the light struggled to infiltrate them as they drove further into the wood. Without warning, they suddenly came across a clearing, on the edge of which stood an old, dilapidated farmhouse. The peeling wooden walls and grimy windows gave the place a melancholic, desolate air. Beyond it, they could see the frozen fringes of a small lake, devoid of any signs of life. Overhead, the silence was split by the growling throb of an aircraft flying low over the trees as it came in to land.

The team parked in front of the house – no sign of life there either. But it was a different building that Moberg was interested in. Forcing his frame out of the car, he trudged through the snow, heading straight for the ugly, squat construction next door – a corrugated-iron garage with double doors held by a rusty padlock. This, too, had seen better days, and no one could accuse it of being secure, but then who would think of looking for millions of kronor in such a ramshackle place? Moberg unceremoniously kicked the doors open, the lock proving no match for his size 46 boot. They were immediately hit by an oily smell, though there was no vehicle inside. Moberg flicked a switch by the door, and a strip light buzzed and eventually flickered on. The garage was empty except for an area at the end where there were a few tools and old oilcans on a long wooden workbench. In the centre of the concrete floor were some stained planks of wood covering a basic inspection pit.

They all gathered behind the chief inspector, holding their collective breath.

'Down there, there should be over a hundred million kronor. Who would like to do the honours?'

Westermark immediately volunteered, and quickly, with the help of one of the uniformed officers, started pulling back the planks. They came away easily: evidence that they had been recently replaced. After shoving the fifth piece of wood to one side, Westermark jumped into the pit.

'Give me a torch.'

The officer handed one down.

Westermark switched it on and let the strong beam drift around the space and penetrate the darkest corners.

The silence was almost physical. Then it was broken by Westermark's cry:

'Boss! It's all fucking gone!'

CHAPTER 18

Chief Inspector Moberg tucked into a chocolate bar. He watched as Karl Westermark picked up a newspaper at the magazine stall. Their early-morning flight from Malmö's Sturup Airport hadn't yet been called. Other sleepy-eyed passengers were sprawled on chairs or were milling around, waiting for the Stockholm plane that would carry them home for the festive season or to the swish stores of the capital for some last-minute shopping. The two policemen had an entirely different itinerary. The irony of taking a flight from so close to where the money from the Q Guard robbery had been stored wasn't lost on the chief inspector, but it was that very circumstance that had led them to Sturup's departure lounge on this twenty-third day of December. Surely the proximity of the airport was no coincidence.

Initially, Moberg and the team had reacted badly to the farmhouse's empty garage. Hopes so quickly raised had been instantly dashed. Where had the money gone? Moberg had charged into Sven-Olof Alm's holding cell and yelled at him: 'Are you fucking playing me for a fool?' But it soon became transparent that Alm was equally baffled, then as the news hit home, his puzzlement turned to anger. Had Subotić and whoever he was working for planned to do the dirty on them all along? That bastard, Kolarov, must have had something to do with it, too. (Excellent, thought Moberg gleefully, now Kolarov's definitely in the frame.) But despite his ravings and recriminations, Alm still wasn't willing to sell his brother-in-law down the river.

The team had established that the farmhouse in the woods had been bought eight months previously by a Stockholm-based property company that was traced back to the Branislav Bilić empire. Follow-up flight checks over the last seven months had shown that Bilić had made three day-return trips to Sturup during that time, the last of which was eight days before the robbery, on the 24th of November. On none of the occasions had he visited his Bran Fitness centre in Malmö, or the one in Trelleborg. Subotić had made two similar trips to Stockholm and back within that time frame. It was all pointing in one direction – to Branislav Bilić. He was behind the heist. He had to be! He had the money and the wherewithal to mount such an operation, and it was becoming abundantly clear that he had scooped up the whole lot without having to pay for the services of the gang he'd employed. And the icing on the cake, as far as Bilić was concerned, was that Subotić was dead and the other three were in custody.

The farmhouse hadn't yielded any prints from Bilić – he would have made sure of that – but the gang hadn't been so careful when hiding the money in the early hours of the 2nd of December. In the garage, forensics had found two sets of prints down in the inspection pit – Alm's and Kolarov's. They knew that those two must have helped hide the cash on the night of the robbery: Alm had admitted as much. Rikardssson and Subotić must have been there, too. But which of them had removed the stash? The most likely candidate was Subotić, either on his own behalf or Bilić's. Whichever it was, he ended up dead.

What Moberg couldn't fathom was why Bilić would need to get rid of Subotić: the leader of the gang and possibly the brains behind the whole operation. It had been Subotić who'd recruited Kasper Jensen; maybe he'd done the same with the rest of the gang – all specialists in their own way. Had Subotić wanted more than Bilić was willing to share? A fatal falling out? Or had Bilić planned to rid himself of the gang all along? The others – with the possible exception of Dejan Kolarov – didn't seem to know of the Subotić-Bilić connection. With Subotić's death, there was no direct link to the Serbian boss. Putting the three gang members away behind bars only solved part of the problem as far as Moberg was concerned. There was no proof of Bilić's involvement, and Moberg was convinced he was literally getting away with murder – and with a hundred and thirty-five million kronor plus extras. Faced with this dilemma, the chief inspector saw the only way forward was to shake things up. He and Westermark would pay Branislav Bilić a visit.

The train from Arlanda airport into Stockholm was on time, and Moberg and Westermark wandered down from the central station towards Gamla Stan, the old part of the town. The snow was thicker up here and lay charmingly on the white rooftops of the churches and quaint, tightly-packed medieval buildings: perfectly in keeping with the season. The sky was clear and bright, and the water surrounding the Gamla Stan peninsula shimmered in the sunlight. The atmosphere was festive, but the jollity was lost on Moberg: he hated Stockholm, and Stockholmers in particular – too rich, too frivolous and too up their own arses – and he didn't think much of Christmas, either.

They went down a narrow street squashed between high buildings, and stopped outside the Belgrade Kitchen restaurant. The restaurant was closed at that time in the morning, and Moberg wrapped a mighty fist against the glass door. He knew from colleagues in the capital that this was the best place to find Bilić. The gang boss was a man of habit: he rose at five each morning and had his lunch early. He came to the Belgrade Kitchen at eleven to eat before it opened to the public at twelve.

It was now ten past eleven.

A man of medium height walked casually towards the door through the neat rows of tables. He was smartly dressed in a crisp white shirt and dark suit. His thick black hair was slicked back, accentuating his granite cheekbones and large dark eyes. What attracted immediate attention was the livid scar that cleft the right-hand side of his face from temple to mouth. Was it a sneer or a suppressed smile that greeted them as he languidly opened the door?

'Yes?'

'We'd like to speak to Branislav Bilić,' Moberg growled. Beside him, Westermark was striking his toughest pose.

'He's busy.'

'I'm sure he's not too busy to speak to the police.' Moberg and Westermark produced their warrant cards in unison as though they had practised the routine.

The man seemed totally unimpressed. Still blocking their path into the establishment, he didn't move a muscle.

'As I say, he's busy. He's having his lunch, and he doesn't like being disturbed while he's eating. Ruins his digestion. Maybe you can talk to me, and if what you have to say is important, I'll pass on the message.'

'What's your name?' Moberg demanded.

'Dragan Mitrović. Not that it's any of your business.'

'Look... Dragan...' – Moberg injected venom into the name – 'we've flown all the way up from Malmö at some bloody ungodly hour this morning, so I'm not going to piss about on your doorstep. I want to talk to the organ grinder, not the fucking monkey.'

With that, he barged his way past Mitrović, who had been taken off guard by Moberg's unexpectedly sudden movement. Westermark followed in the chief inspector's slipstream. Moberg strode between the tables, laid out in Christmas colours, towards the end of the room, where there was a festively decorated bar. Seated at the table nearest the bar sat a slim man in his fifties, whose sartorial taste resembled that of an ordinary 1960s businessman. Smartly dressed in jacket and tie, he had neatly cut grey hair and was clean shaven. He was not handsome: his nose was slightly too large, his eyes too sunken and his mouth too thin. He looked innocuous enough, but Moberg could envisage him in army fatigues, transformed into a brutal soldier who would stop at nothing to ethnically cleanse what he regarded as his spiritual homeland. Moberg knew that Bilić had been brought up in Sweden but had returned to the Balkans during the conflicts to serve in one of the militias. It was no surprise that he surrounded himself with those he had fought alongside.

As they burst in, Westermark noticed the barman reaching down behind the counter. A hidden gun; Westermark was ready. But there was no need to panic – yet. Bilić said something sharp in Serbian, and the barman withdrew his hand. As the chief inspector towered over the table, Bilić carried on eating as though nothing had happened. Mitrović stood menacingly behind the policemen. Westermark suspected that he, too, was armed.

Bilić stopped masticating. 'I'm afraid the restaurant doesn't open until twelve.'

'We're not here to eat,' boomed Moberg, brandishing his warrant card. 'But don't let me stop you finishing your burger.'

'This is not a burger,' Bilić said with disgust. '*Pljeskavica*,' he corrected. 'It's a spiced meat patty made of pork, beef and lamb. It's excellent with chopped raw onion and tomato slices' – he indicated the fare with a chunk of bread. 'And this is *pogacha* bread. It's a popular combination with our clientele; I highly recommend it.'

Moberg realized that he was failing to intimidate Bilić, so he hauled up a chair and sat down. He still dwarfed the Serbian.

'I've come about the robbery at the Q Guard cash depot in Malmö.'

'Read about that. Quite a haul.'

'We're wondering where you've put it. The money that is.'

Bilić tugged a piece of bread apart. 'I have no idea what you're talking about.'

'We think you have. Your men were involved.'

'How do you work that out?' The bread disappeared into his mouth.

'The man who ran the operation was Milan Subotić. He was what you'd call an associate of yours.'

Bilić arched an eyebrow then paused, allowing himself time to chew and swallow his bread. 'It is true that Milan did the occasional job for me. He is a cousin of Dragan here. But he certainly wasn't in my employ.'

Moberg swivelled round in his chair to face Mitrović. 'You know someone shot him? Right here,' he said, tapping the centre of his own forehead.

If the ploy was to wind Mitrović up, it didn't work. He simply glared malevolently at Moberg without saying a word. The chief inspector judged that his cousin's death was old news, and returned to Bilić.

'Another of your fellow countrymen is currently enjoying our hospitality. We believe that Dejan Kolarov, a man of explosive talents, is also one of your associates.'

'You are mistaken. I have heard the name. Never met the man.' Bilić returned to his food.

'We found it, you know. The farmhouse near Sturup Airport. And we know you flew down there on a number of occasions, one of which was eight days before the robbery.'

Another mouthful then another pause for mastication. Moberg's patience was running out.

Bilić looked up from his plate. 'I have business interests down in the south.'

'But you didn't go anywhere near your gyms.'

'I didn't go to the gyms. I was meeting up with some associates.' A thin smile played on his lips. 'Legitimate ones, in case you're wondering.'

'Look, Bilić, let's not beat about the bush. You planned the robbery – or paid to set it up. Two of your men were directly involved. You made regular trips to keep an eye on the operation and after it was done, the cash was stored at the farmhouse. Now the money's gone. You moved it. The problem is that your team killed one of the security guards, so they're all going down for that. And then, for some reason, you got rid of Subotić. Was Dragan's cousin getting too greedy? Or was he a weak link? You see, these deaths were big mistakes. They left trails; it's all unravelling. And it all leads back to you.'

Bilić had had enough to eat and he pushed his plate away.

'As I see it, Chief Inspector, all you've got is speculation: no real evidence. And as for the men you claim carried out this crime "going down", as you put it, all you seem to have in your favour is the rather nebulous testimony of a security guard. Just his word.'

Moberg was stunned. Where the hell had that come from? No one was meant to know about Hirdwall; he was being kept under wraps until the time was right. Unless Bilić was referring to Jensen. But no... something about the Serb's demeanour made him think it wasn't Jensen he was talking about. Shit! He had to retreat and regroup.

The chief inspector rose from his chair and clipped the edge of Bilić's table. His plate fell off and broke as it landed, and the remains of the meal were strewn across the floor.

'This is just the beginning. We'll be back!'

Bilić was totally unfazed. '*God jul!*' he said pleasantly.

Moberg stormed towards the door, Westermark scuttling after him.

'Hey!' Bilić called after him.

Moberg swung round angrily.

'Where shall I send the bill for the broken plate?'

Moberg was fuming. 'How the hell did he know?' he furiously addressed the sky as though appealing to the gods. Westermark's mind was racing. His thoughts went back to his disastrous interview with Kolarov and his stupid *faux pas*. What if his boss found out? Moberg got out his phone. 'Sundström's got pally with Hirdwall. I'll send her round to check on him tonight. We might have to move him.'

CHAPTER 19

Anita had spent Friday night and most of Saturday in Kristianstad for the pre-Christmas get-together with her mother and her aunt. Lasse had come, too, in his role of helpful nephew, dutiful grandson and general peacekeeper. Anita, as usual, had been counting the hours before it was time to leave. She always found her visits depressing: the two women were like a tragic Greek chorus, forever chanting about the woes of the world and their unfulfilled lives. And, of course, Anita couldn't do anything right. Admittedly, she didn't help her cause. One stick she gave them to beat her with was her smoking. She had taken some snus with her to tide her over, but there were a couple of occasions when her mother so riled her that she had to disappear into the garden for an illicit cigarette. She felt like a naughty teenager. And that was exactly how her mother still treated her. Only twenty-four hours, but it dragged oh so slowly. She couldn't stop thinking about her Christmas at home with all the usual cheesy songs on the radio – Adolphson & Falk's *More Christmas*, Tommy Körberg's version of *O Holy Night* or Chris Rea *Driving Home for Christmas*. Oh, how she wished she was! She and Lasse would watch rubbish on the television, and together prepare the dinner – the *julbord* of ham, meatballs and herring. Bliss! Then came the call from Moberg in Stockholm, asking her to swing by Oxie and check up on Willi Hirdwall on her way home. Even then, they didn't get away until nearly eight, as her mother was fussing over Lasse in a way that she had never done over her.

'Just make sure he's all right,' Moberg had instructed. 'And for God's sake, don't mention that Bilić knows that a security guard is our witness. If he digs around, he'll come up with Hirdwall's name. We don't want him getting scared and pulling out.'

'How does Bilić even know we've got a witness?' Anita had worried that this might come out before they were ready. Given who they were up against, she was under no illusions as to the possible danger Hirdwall might be facing.

'Wish I knew. At least if Bilić does find out who he is, because he lives in a rental, it won't be easy for him to track him down. That'll buy us some time. When I get back, I'll look into organizing a safe house. Of course, nothing will happen until bloody Christmas is out of the way.'

It had been snowing nearly all the way back from Kristianstad, and obviously here, too. Anita turned off the E65 and drove through the tree-lined outskirts of Oxie. It was almost the perfect Christmas-card scene – it just needed a few *tomtar*, the mischievous gnomes of folklore, frolicking in the foreground. Now the snow had stopped, and a bright waxing crescent moon hung in the sky. She parked outside Hirdwall's house, the third one along from the end of the street. There was a light coming through the blinds from what she knew to be the living room.

'Are you OK staying here?' she asked Lasse. 'I won't be long.'

'I'm fine,' he replied, popping his headphones back on.

She walked up to the door. All was quiet except for the faint hum of traffic from the E65 beyond the trees behind the houses. She rang the doorbell. Hirdwall answered and greeted her with a smirk.

'More questions? It's Christmas tomorrow. Don't you ever stop working?'

'Don't worry. This is a brief social call. Making sure you're all right.'

He asked her in and she followed him into the living room. The electric fire was on, the television was playing quietly, and the smell of long-smoked cigarettes pervaded the room. Hirdwall's only concession to the festive season was the obligatory candolier in the window and a miniature plastic Christmas tree in the middle of the dining table. There was a can of beer and an open packet of crisps on a stool next to an armchair.

'Want a drink?'

'No thanks. My son's in the car outside, so I'll be quick.'

He slumped down into the armchair.

'As you can see, I'm planning a quiet Christmas. I've never really been into all that stuff. With no family to speak of, I don't have to make an effort. Suits me fine.'

Anita perched on the edge of the sofa.

'Lucky you,' she said with feeling, mentally spooling through the last twenty-four hours. 'We're keeping it low-key, too. Just me and Lasse.'

'I've promised myself a sunshine Christmas one of these days. I had thought about Thailand, but the tsunami rather put me off.'

'Yeah, that was just awful. I couldn't believe the number of Swedes who died.'

'Mm. Perhaps Spain would be safer. Or Morocco might be nice.'

'It's good to dream. How's your arm?'

'It's on the mend.'

'Look, I just wanted to make sure you're OK.'

'You worried I won't testify?' This was accompanied by a knowing grin.

'Not at all,' she said hastily. 'It's just you've been through a traumatic experience.'

'Sure. I'll be fine. Q Guard have arranged those counselling sessions I told you about. And don't worry; I'll be there in court if you need me when the time comes.'

Hirdwall showed her to the front door.

'Remember, if you need to talk about anything, just give me a ring.' She handed over a card with her number. '*God jul!*'

The door closed behind her and Anita walked down the short path to the road. She slid back into the car and turned the ignition key. The car struggled into life.

'Everything's fine.'

Lasse took off his headphones and nodded.

She drove carefully along the road in the opposite direction from the way she had come. She hadn't gone far when she noticed a van parked on the part of the street adjoining a stretch of open waste ground. She could see there was no one in it.

'How long's that been there?' she asked Lasse.

'Dunno. A few minutes? A couple of guys got out and headed off towards the trees back there.'

Anita slammed on the brakes, and Lasse lurched forward and groaned as his seat belt bit tightly.

'They went round the back?'

'That's what I said.'

Anita slammed the gear stick into reverse and shot back, weaving her way along the road as fast as she could, in a fountain of flying snow.

'Whoa, what are you doing?'

The car screamed to a halt in front of Hirdwall's home. Anita quickly reached across to the glove compartment in front of Lasse and pulled out her pistol.

'Shit, Mamma, what's that doing there?'

'I keep it there in case I'm tempted to shoot your *mormor*. Look, stay here and keep your head down.'

'What do—'

'Just do it!' Anita snarled.

Instead of following her impulse to burst into Hirdwall's house, Anita slipped down the side of the building. She didn't know the area, but she remembered the view from Hirdwall's kitchen window, and imagined it would be easy enough for the men in the van to go into the wood abutting the main road and come out at the back of any house on this side of the street. Her fingers were cold and steady as they gripped the butt of her pistol. In contrast, her heart was pumping wildly.

Keeping low, she sneaked along the side of the house through to Hirdwall's rear garden. The light from his back windows, together with the moon, was enough to illuminate the snow-covered lawn. Then her heart missed a beat. There were footprints – two sets – making tracks from the fence towards the house. Gingerly, she crept towards the back door, keeping well under cover. As she drew nearer, she could see that the door was open, and through it, she could hear raised voices, though she couldn't distinguish what was being said. Now she was faced with a dilemma. Should she rush in? If the men were armed, she would expose herself and might endanger Hirdwall. Or should she wait for them to come out? At least then she'd have the element of surprise. But what if they were about to kill him? Wait, and it might be too late.

The decision was taken out of her hands when Hirdwall was suddenly pushed through the door. He was immediately followed by a tall man in a winter jacket and a woollen hat pulled down over his ears. Anita caught the glint of the handgun he was pressing into Hirdwall's back. Then the second man appeared. She couldn't see whether he was armed or not. The three of them crunched their way towards the shadow of the trees. Then Anita made a decision. She ran forward and fired a warning shot into the air. The men spun round.

'Don't move!' she shouted.

The man with the gun fired instinctively, without aiming, and the bullet smashed harmlessly into the brickwork of the house. Anita threw herself to the ground and again fired off an aerial shot so as not to accidently hit Hirdwall. Another return bullet spat into the snow close to her shoulder. She ducked, and rolled over in the snow twice before she was in a position to fire again. In front of her, she could see Hirdwall on his knees, and the two men already disappearing into the blackness of the wood. Shaken, she took a few moments to compose herself, then she got to her feet.

'Are you OK, Willi?'

Hirdwall was cradling his injured arm.

'Yeah,' he said through gritted teeth.

She helped him up. 'Get back into the house.'

Once she was sure he could walk, she ran back down the side of the house onto the street. The van was driving off. Unsteadily, she made her way along the icy pavement in the hope of glimpsing the number plate, but it was too late: the van was too far away, and moments later, it was gone.

She stopped to get her breath back. The adrenaline rush she'd experienced back in the garden was subsiding as quickly as it had kicked in. That was a close shave. She got her phone out and called the polishus, but she knew there was little hope of finding a patrol car close enough to spot and catch up with an anonymous white van heading out of Oxie on the E65. On her return, Lasse was standing by the car. He looked petrified.

'Mamma! Mamma, are you...' He couldn't finish. He fell into her arms and she clasped him to her. Her eyes began to water and as she held her son tightly, she realized how close that second bullet had been.

'I'm OK, darling. Come on inside with me. The police are on their way.'

They went into the house and found a dazed and frightened Hirdwall standing in the middle of the living room. He was shaking.

'They're gone.' She tried to sound reassuring.

'How did they know where I live?'

That was a question that Anita would dearly have liked to know the answer to.

'I don't know,' was all she could offer.

'They were going to kill me, weren't they?' he gasped.

'Look, you can't stay here. You'd better come to our place for Christmas.'

CHAPTER 20

In early April, Malmö was emerging from hibernation. The days were lengthening, the parks were burgeoning with new life, and the city was tingling with fresh hope as it shed the constraints of winter.

The feel-good factor was also rife among Chief Inspector Moberg's Criminal Investigation Squad, who were optimistic that their efforts over the past few months would be rewarded: the trial of the three remaining gang members of the Q Guard robbery was due to start in two weeks' time (Kasper Jensen was being dealt with separately). All the evidence had been assembled for Prosecutor Egleholm: all three suspects could be placed at the scene; Sven-Olof Alm had identified Dejan Kolarov as one of the gang; and Alm had also confirmed that Milan Subotić had been the leader of the operation, though not necessarily the brains behind it, and Kasper Jensen's testimony had backed this up. The only frustration was that Alm stubbornly refused to finger his brother-in-law, Bengt Rickardsson. However, they had Willi Hirdwall waiting in the wings to clear that hurdle.

Though the team were confident that those responsible for the robbery and Wallström's death would be put away, their enthusiasm was tempered by the fact that they were no closer to discovering who had killed Subotić (this had led to the delay in the trial, as the police were convinced the two crimes were linked) and that there was no sign of the stolen millions. Both these issues were now assumed to be down to Branislav Bilić.

Why he had had Subotić murdered was a question that still needed answering, but the disappearance of the money was easier to fathom – it had been neatly moved from its hiding place in the farm garage shortly after the robbery. Moberg speculated that Bilić had planned to do the gang out of their share all along, and that might possibly explain why he had eliminated the main man.

Furthermore, they were sure that Bilić was behind the attempt to kill Willi Hirdwall in Oxie that snowy night before Christmas. How Bilić had so quickly discovered who he was and where he lived had baffled the team. How he even knew that they had a security guard as a witness was particularly troubling. An unofficial internal investigation hadn't thrown any light on the matter. Moberg hadn't noticed Westermark's uncharacteristically lukewarm involvement in the inquiry – though Anita had. She was sure Westermark had had something to do with it. But what she was unsure of was whether the two men who turned up in Hirdwall's garden were trying to abduct him or kill him. Probably both. The most likely scenario was that they were going to abduct him first in order to find out what he knew, and then dispose of him later. Of course, Anita's unexpected appearance had spooked them; if they'd been caught, the police might have been able to establish a direct link to Bilić. It was a lack of any demonstrable connection which was obstructing the team's efforts to hook the big fish.

Willi Hirdwall had naturally been shocked by events. While Moberg organized a safe house down in Skanör, Hirdwall had spent the few days over Christmas at Anita's apartment. It had been a strange experience for them both, tinged with worry that Bilić's men would return. Lasse had been unhappy with the idea at first, but when Hirdwall had proved to be an unobtrusive guest, he thawed and actually took to the older man; he even let Hirdwall play on his Xbox with him. Anita also had to admit that she rather enjoyed Hirdwall's company

– having a man around who didn't try and make a pass at her was a pleasant change. Hirdwall willingly helped round the house when needed and kept out of their way when he thought that she and Lasse wanted time to themselves. He was the perfect house guest. When he was eventually picked up by an unmarked police car and taken to Skanör just before New Year, the apartment felt rather empty.

Hirdwall was the first to admit that what he had experienced had traumatized him. Someone was trying to make sure he didn't make it to court, and he was now having doubts about the wisdom of testifying. He'd been assured that if all went well, his testimony wouldn't play a major part in the trial – Alm was the man who would seal the gang's fate. During the months of Hirdwall's comfortable incarceration, Anita had seen him regularly. Moberg felt that as she had established such a good relationship with him over Christmas, she should be the one to provide the support and reassurance he needed to make sure he didn't backtrack.

'I think we've got everything we need,' said Prosecutor Egleholm. 'You've done a good job, Erik.'

Egleholm was a dapper man with a high forehead – a sign of intelligence, Moberg had been led to believe. His mannerisms were very precise, reflecting the meticulous way in which he gathered evidence. He was ever cautious – maybe because he was only a few years off retirement – and sometimes Moberg had been exasperated by his exaggerated thoroughness, which often stymied the chief inspector's bullish impatience to see cases rapidly concluded and brought to court. But it had to be said that Egleholm's methods had resulted in a high percentage of successful prosecutions, as he took the time to factor out failure.

'I'm still not happy about Bilić,' Moberg grunted.

'We might not get him this time, Erik. But it'll lead to cracks in his organization.'

Moberg couldn't see that happening. To him, Bilić was in a win-win situation: he was sitting on a stolen fortune, and with the gang safely banged up, there would be no repercussions.

Egleholm was reading his mind. 'I think we've at least got him rattled. Otherwise, why would he try and have Hirdwall killed? He's worried that things will come out in court. The key is Kolarov. One of Bilić's own. Once he gets it into his head that Bilić was behind the money being moved, he'll realize that either Bilić didn't trust him and the rest of the gang, or that he never intended to pay them in the first place.'

'Well, I hope the prosecution makes that crystal clear.'

'Oh, we will,' Egleholm said with a thin smile.

Göran Gyllensten made his way down the corridor. He was still getting used to the smells of incarceration: men cooped up in their cells most of the day. It was only his second year in the prison service and he was still learning how to cope with the divers criminals in the Malmö Detention Centre, which was conveniently situated behind the polishus. Gyllensten had joined the service with an optimistic outlook and a fervent belief in the power of rehabilitation. It wasn't a view shared by some of his older, more pessimistic colleagues, whose trust had been broken too many times. Gyllensten, however, refused to be discouraged by their intransigence and cynicism, and he turned a deaf ear to their complaints – the inmates were pampered, the governor was too soft, the cells were turning into 'bloody IKEA showrooms', etcetera, etcetera. But he wasn't so wet behind the ears that he thought the men he was dealing with were saints underneath their tough exteriors. Or that a compassionate prison service could automatically mend someone who'd been dealt one of life's poor hands. He was learning to recognize the hopeless cases, but many of his charges were fundamentally decent people who, through circumstance or need beyond their control, had been led astray. Sven-Olof Alm seemed to be one such case. Gyllensten had had a number of discussions with him over the last three months. Here was a man who'd had his head turned by the promise of unimaginable wealth. He'd got in with the wrong crowd. Gyllensten knew his background: he was being charged with robbery and manslaughter. Despite causing the death of a security guard, he was being charged with the lesser crime because he'd provided the police with inside information on the Q Guard heist. It was a national story, still making the front pages after four months. And now the trial was imminent, Gyllensten and his colleagues were on high alert, aware that by cooperating with the authorities, Alm had made himself a target. The criminal fraternity didn't like a grass.

Gyllensten had nearly reached the end of the corridor. Alm's cell was the last in the row. He was taking him a mobile phone. With the trial only a fortnight away, Alm was allowed to speak to his lawyer once a day at a specific time. It was nearly six – the hour arranged for the call. As Gyllensten reached the cell, he stopped. There was something wrong. The door was slightly ajar: it should have been locked. Had someone messed up? He knew that Alm had been allowed a session in the gym an hour earlier. Tentatively, he pushed the door open further. Alm was lying curled up on his bed, his face to the wall. An odd time to sleep. Maybe the gym session had exhausted him.

'Sven-Olof! Wake up! Time for your call.'

No response.

Gyllensten stepped over to the bed.

'Sven-Olof!'

He shook the prone figure. Then he noticed the pool of blood on the bedding. He grabbed Alm's shoulder and half-turned him over. More blood – everywhere. The body was cold, and the face that stared up at him was a mask of fear.

*

Within an hour of finding Sven-Olof Alm dead in his cell, the ructions were reverberating around the polishus. Moberg had stormed out of the bar where he was having an early-evening drink with an old police buddy, spouting a flood of imaginative invective that would ensure a future ban from the premises. Prosecutor Egleholm, usually a picture of mannered calmness, was in a panic. Both had been hauled up to the commissioner's office. The rest of the team broke off whatever after-work activity they were involved in and were back at their desks awaiting Moberg's return from the top floor. In Anita's case, she'd just crashed in front of the television with a cup of Earl Grey tea. It was after eight when they were called into the meeting room.

'How could it have happened?' Westermark opened with the obvious question.

'They've no idea. There'll be a full investigation, and no doubt heads will roll. They'd better,' Moberg added bitterly. 'You can be sure of one thing: Bilić is behind this. Two weeks before the trial and our star witness is knocked off in one of our own cells. For fuck's sake! My bet is a bent warder was bribed to leave the door unlocked and a couple of the other inmates went in and did the business.' He was so furious that spittle was forming on his lips.

'Where does that leave the trial?' asked Nordlund.

'In tatters. Well, almost. The commissioner has put pressure on Egleholm to proceed. We'd look stupid not to.'

'We've only got two of the gang left. Have we enough on them?' Nordlund's question was in all their minds.

'We've still got Willi Hirdwall.'

'This is really going to expose him,' said Anita.

'That's the way it's got to be. He can identify Bengt Rickardsson. That should be enough to put *him* away. Kolarov's the problem.' He looked pensive, and for the benefit of himself as well as the team, he proceeded to summarize the situation:

'Hirdwall placed Kolarov outside the depot masquerading as a Telenor engineer. Kolarov was with Subotić, who we know led the robbery, a fact which will be corroborated by Kasper Jensen. That ties him in. We've got his fingerprints at the Sturup farm, but that's meaningless because we can't prove the money was ever there. And we don't have proof that he was actually part of the raid unless we can get Rickardsson to cooperate. And after his brother-in-law's murder, he's hardly going to do that. It's a question of how much the court will accept the confession of a dead man.'

The fury seemed to have left Moberg; dejection had set in.

'Will Hirdwall deliver once he knows what's happened to Alm?' It was another pertinent question from Nordlund. 'They tried to kill him, too, remember.'

'We've nothing else. He's *got* to testify. Sundström,' Moberg said with a glum stare, 'it's up to you to make sure he does.'

CHAPTER 21

The wind tousled Willi Hirdwall's hair. He'd grown it during his months in the safe house. He was revelling in the freedom of a walk along the edge of the sea. Anita accompanied him, her own hair tied back, though the odd annoying strand escaped and forced its way across her eyes. Above, grey clouds scudded across a threatening sky. The swift change in the weather reflected Anita's pessimistic mood. In the distance was the hazy outline of the Öresund Bridge: a pencil sketch on the horizon. Behind them were rows of gaily coloured beach huts, which would soon be opening their doors to desperate sun-seekers. The sand beneath their feet was strewn with pungent seaweed.

'It must be serious if you've dragged me out here, Anita, though I'm grateful to get out. Blow away the cobwebs.'

'It is, Willi,' she said without looking at him. She'd taken the last drag of her fortifying cigarette and thrown away the butt.

'Well, spit it out.'

This brought her to a halt.

'Right. Erm... there's no other way to say this: Sven-Olof Alm was found dead in his cell last night.'

She couldn't register his immediate reaction, as he was staring out to sea.

'Suicide?'

'No. Stabbed to death.'

An urgent internal investigation had been immediately launched, but Anita knew it would be some time before all the circumstances surrounding Alm's death would be known.

Hirdwall reflected for a while. 'You reckon this Serbian gangster was behind it?'

'It's the logical conclusion.'

'So, they succeeded with him, but not with me.' He paused and faced Anita. 'Yet.'

'They'll not get *you*. You're safe with us.'

'But for how long? Wasn't Alm meant to be safe?'

He began to move again, and no words were exchanged while they progressed along the beach. A flock of gulls circled noisily overhead.

'Your evidence is more important than ever. You can place Rickardsson at the scene. And you saw Kolarov and Subotić carrying out surveillance at the site.' 'Will that be enough? I mean for Kolarov? Have you got more on him?'

Clearly, Hirdwall was aware of the possible ramifications. There was no point in lying.

'Not much. But we've still got Alm's testimony.'

He gave her a withering glance. 'So, you want me to stand up in court and do my best to send down the two guys who aren't dead yet, knowing that someone has already tried to kill me.'

Anita nodded. 'I guess so.'

He stopped and stared out to sea. The silence was almost palpable.

'For Måns,' she said in a small voice.

Turning to face her: 'Don't give me that guilt shit; that's cheap. I expect better of you, Anita.'

'Sorry.' She felt dreadful. She shouldn't have mentioned Wallström. 'Look, I know we're asking a lot. But if you don't appear, no one will be brought to justice.'

Hirdwall scuffed a lump of seaweed with his shoe.

'I want to do this, I really do. But I'm shit scared. What's going to happen to me when all the fuss has died down and

Kolarov comes waltzing out of prison after his five minutes away? These people are bloody terrifying. I'll be yesterday's news. You lot can't keep me bottled up forever. I'll be out there somewhere,' – he waved his hand in the air – 'a sitting duck. What sort of life is that? Constantly looking over my shoulder. I don't know if I can...' His voice drifted off.

'I know, but there *is* a solution, Willi. I've discussed it with my boss and the prosecutor.'

Before heading down to Skanör to meet with Hirdwall, Anita had been closeted with Moberg and Prosecutor Egleholm. She'd propounded this exact scenario. It would take a huge amount of courage for Hirdwall to testify, given the background to the case and the subsequent deaths. She insisted that she had to be in a position to offer him an incentive; she knew that the thought of living under protection for years wouldn't appeal to the Hirdwall she'd befriended over the last few months. Moberg had been keen on the idea Anita had put forward – Egleholm less so.

'Yeah? What?' He was sceptical.

'It would mean leaving Sweden. Starting again somewhere else.'

She let it sink in.

'We can arrange witness protection. New name, new passport, new life.'

'Is this the cost of doing the right thing?' Hirdwall bent down and picked up a shell.

'Look, Willi. No one would blame you if you walked away from all this right now. But we have to face the facts. I can't guarantee that if you don't testify, Branislav Bilić won't still seek you out. He doesn't like loose ends. He knows you were there, and you can't unsee what you saw. And if you do walk away, we won't be able to protect you at all.'

He examined the shell. 'It's pretty, isn't it? I wonder what happened to its owner – eaten by some marine Bilić, I presume.'

He let out a huge sigh. 'So it looks like I'm stuck between a rock and a hard place.'

'I suppose you are.'

'Well, I haven't much to keep me here, have I? Maybe a new life is what I need.' He chucked the shell into the sea.

The train rattled over the Öresund Bridge. In the distance, the Turning Torso, the highest building in the Nordic countries and a potent symbol of modern Sweden, seemed to do a dance as Anita viewed it at speed through the bridge's trelliswork of girders. Next to her sat Willi Hirdwall, also staring out of the window, and as the Torso got smaller and smaller and further and further away, she wondered what he was thinking. Not that he was Willi Hirdwall anymore. According to the new passport she'd handed over to him an hour before, he was Mikael Mosten. In four hours, he would be taking off from Copenhagen and flying to New York. After much discussion, he'd decided that he wanted to go to America. It was the land of opportunity – the American dream that hundreds of thousands of Swedes over the last hundred and fifty years had hoped would become a reality. He planned to go to Minneapolis, as it was full of people of Swedish descent: 'I think I might feel at home there.'

At least Sweden was bidding him a glorious farewell in the May sunshine. Hirdwall had fulfilled his end of the bargain at the trial and had helped to ensure it wasn't a total disaster. He'd been a very credible witness, and his testimony had played a vital part in convicting Bengt Rickardsson. The case against Dejan Kolarov hadn't exactly collapsed. He was going to serve time, but not nearly enough as far as the team were concerned. Hirdwall had testified, under intense questioning from the defence, that Kolarov, in the company of Milan Subotić, was the man Måns Wallström had talked to at the Telenor box. It sparked the most dramatic moment of the trial: Kolarov had shouted at Hirdwall that he was lying, and he threatened to cut out his tongue when he got out. It was this incident that had finally persuaded Prosecutor Egleholm that witness protection was needed.

The Skåne County Police hadn't come out of the whole experience with much credit. They had only brought two of the gang – three if you counted Kasper Jensen – to justice, and one wouldn't be in captivity for long. Along the way, they'd lost their key witness while he was supposedly safe in detention (the culprits still hadn't been identified), failed to solve the murder of the gang leader, and still hadn't found the missing millions. And they hadn't been able to lay a finger on the organized crime boss whom they believed was behind the whole operation. It didn't seem that justice had been achieved for Måns Wallström.

Anita and Hirdwall alighted at Kastrup train station among the jostling holidaymakers heading for the world's hotspots. Hirdwall blended in, and Anita was confident he would continue to do so in his new life. On the platform, officials were waiting to usher them up to the airport concourse and into the departure lounge, bypassing normal security. Everything had been prearranged. They were given a small room with a view of the tarmac lined with waiting planes. Anita had been told to stay with Hirdwall until he was escorted onto his flight. Food had been organized, and they shared a half bottle of red wine.

Hirdwall raised a glass. 'A toast. To Anita Sundström, who saved my life... and gave me a new one.'

'Just doing my job.' It sounded inappropriately trite, but she was flattered by the recognition.

'I'm going to miss you, Anita. You've kept me going all these months. It's been hard.'

'I'll miss you, too, Willi.' She meant it. They'd got to know each other well. They had talked about music, battled over politics, found common ground with Malmö FF, and even shared the odd confidence: his lost love, her divorce. And latterly, they'd discussed the hopes and dreams he had for the future.

He drained his glass.

'Don't take this the wrong way,' he said with a guffaw. 'But I hope I'll never see you again. If I do, something will have gone very wrong.'

Anita laughed, too. She raised her glass.

'Here's to never seeing you again!'

PART TWO
PRESENT DAY

CRIMINAL INVESTIGATION SQUAD – PRESENT DAY

Anita Sundström, Chief Inspector
Klara Wallen, Inspector
Dan Olovsson, Inspector
Khalid Hakim Mirza, Inspector
Pontus Brodd, Inspector
Bea Erlandsson, Inspector
Liv Fogelström, Technical Assistant
(currently on maternity leave)

CHAPTER 22

'Cabin crew, prepare for landing.' Twenty minutes earlier, the pilot had announced they would soon be approaching Arlanda Airport, and the weather locally was clear and a pleasant twenty-three degrees. The captain's voice was friendly and confident: just the kind of voice the passengers had needed when the aircraft was bumping and juddering its way through the turbulence over the Atlantic.

Salvatore Baresi downed the last of his Valpolicella. He wriggled in his seat. His arse was sore and he was desperate to stretch his legs. It was only his second transatlantic excursion – the first had been when, as a teenager, he'd visited Italy with his mother to see her family in Tavernelle, a small village up country from La Spezia. As a kid from Chicago, it was like landing on Mars and being sucked in by aliens. He'd hated the whole experience, except for his friendship with a local girl who'd caught his eye. But the relationship had never got any further than a couple of chaste afternoons in an ice cream parlour in the local town: her brothers had made sure of that. He would much rather have vacationed with his father's relations near Naples, but his parents had divorced by then. Now, in his forties, he looked back on that trip with a certain degree of nostalgia; he was still raw from his mother's passing two years ago. Since then, the Gentiles had been his family. They nurtured, protected. Owned.

The attractive blonde SAS stewardess came round with a bin bag to collect the last-minute rubbish. If she was typical of Scandinavian womanhood, he would enjoy Sweden. He'd done his research: it seemed to be a civilized country with neat, tidy towns, expansive countryside and lots of water. He liked water. On his rare days off in Chicago, he was always drawn to the beaches along the shoreline of Lake Michigan. He closed his eyes, and his mind wandered to lazy swims, girls playing volleyball on the sand and the tantalizing smells wafting from the seafood restaurants. Suddenly, he was jolted back to reality: this trip was business, not pleasure. His orders from Giuseppe Gentile were unequivocal – find Micky Mosten, retrieve the money he'd stolen, and then, slowly and painfully, kill the bastard. Gentile had had his pride hurt and his reputation dented. The Columbians had lost their heroin in the FBI raid and they blamed the family for the loss, which Gentile had felt duty bound to pay for even though he hadn't taken possession of the merchandise. And in the confusion caused by the arrival of the Feds, Mosten had absconded with the five million dollars that he and Matteo Nesta had been entrusted with to pay for the drugs. Then Micky had compounded his betrayal by shooting Matteo! Baresi couldn't get his head round why he'd done that. True, the boy was an imbecile; perhaps he'd been trying to stop the Swede. Whatever... Matteo was Giuseppe's son-in-law; he was family. You don't rub out one of Gentile's own and get away with it. And what had upset his boss even more was how the Feds had known about the exchange in the first place. Had someone leaked the location? Or had they been under surveillance from the start? Now their relationship with the Columbians, if not shattered, was decidedly strained, which made any future deals difficult, even dangerous.

For six months, they had searched high and low for Micky Mosten. Baresi began to think about why he'd trusted him in the first place. Easy: he'd been plausible, affable and had made people laugh. They'd enjoyed some great nights out, especially down in Vegas. And Gentile had taken a shine to him, too – and that didn't happen often. Micky always did a good job – he became an efficient bagman – and he was loyal and honest: every dollar of protection money was always accounted for. And he'd been trusted enough to do the first exchange with the Columbians. Giuseppe had had little faith in Matteo – he was a willing donkey but with fewer brains, and Micky had been sent along to keep an eye on him. On that occasion, everything had gone without a hitch. So what had gone wrong the second time? And why had Mosten done the dirty on them all, and in such a stupendous fashion? After the disastrous raid, the Boss had demanded action. It had been galling to see the Feds boasting about the haul – exaggerating the street value to make it sound even more impressive than it was. Also galling that there was a warrant out for Micky's arrest for Matteo's murder. It was a matter of honour that Gentile should even that particular score, yet now it was a race to see who got to him first. Every known Swede in Chicago and Minneapolis (where Micky had moved from) had been shaken down for information, and they'd discovered that shortly after the bust, he'd flown to New York and then on to Berlin. He hadn't had time to change his name or get a new passport, so that bit had been easy. Then the trail had gone cold. But you need a long spoon when supping with the devil, and Micky's luck wasn't about to hold with Giuseppe Gentile on his case. Two days ago, a contact in the Chicago police department on the Gentile payroll had given them a vital lead: the FBI had been tipped off by Interpol that someone resembling Mosten had been caught on CCTV at Copenhagen Central Station. They'd also discovered from an American-Swedish friend of Mosten's in Minneapolis that he'd originally come from a place called Kalmar. So that's where Baresi was heading.

The plane's engines throttled back and the descent began.

Three days later.

The man beamed contentedly as he savoured the last mouthful of his espresso, then he placed the small cup back on its saucer. The sun was shining with a dazzling brightness. He turned his face to its warmth and pushed the over-priced designer sunglasses he'd bought in the town further onto his nose. Alicante was living up to its Roman description of the City of Light. The Cafe de la Playa next to the wide Explanada de Espãna was a great place to people watch. The sun was not at its height at this time of the morning, so many folk were enjoying a cool amble in the shade of the palms which flanked either side of the marble concourse. The Explanada, with its red, ivory and black mosaic tiles, mimicking the movement of the waves of the nearby Mediterranean, is perhaps the most famous maritime promenade in Spain and attracts locals and tourists alike. Most people, sensibly, would retreat indoors when it grew uncomfortably hot – though a number of British holidaymakers could always be found on the beach under the distant ramparts of the Castillo de Santa Bárbara. Through the trees and the elegant street lamps bobbed the masts of the yachts gently swaying in the marina. Maybe he would buy a boat. After all, he was born by the sea.

He checked the time with his new Rolex watch. A quick stroll and then he'd still have time to make his appointment. He would return this evening for a meal and a bottle of Rioja (many of the local wines were too sweet for his taste). Someone had introduced him to Rioja many years ago and now that he'd developed a taste for it, a regular bottle was becoming a staple ingredient of his new life.

He picked up his smart Barbour black leather briefcase. Appearance was important and he was pleased with his. He wore a crisp white shirt with his lightweight camel Brioni suit. He'd heard the Italians made the best suits. OK, perhaps he was a little overdressed for the middle of an Iberian summer (his only concession to the climate was to dispense with a tie), but now that he could afford it, where was the harm? It had been a long and winding road to the white beaches and blue skies of the Costa Blanca, but now he was where he could settle. He already had a nice apartment close to the kind of bars, restaurants and shops he liked to frequent: authentic Spanish, not teeming with tourists. He might even start indulging in more cultural pursuits. Improve himself. And soon, after his appointment today and one last trip away, he'd have the wherewithal to buy that secluded *finca* up in the hills. A country retreat where he could keep a low profile. The best of both worlds. No looking over his shoulder. No carrying out other people's orders. No ties. After he'd made that final trip.

He wandered over to the edge of the Explanada de Espãna. He paused to watch a luxurious craft ease its way from its mooring and head out of the marina. Two attractive women in summer dresses were already clinking wine glasses, and he could hear the tinkle of their laughter carry over the water. The sound matched his mood. It was going to be another good day.

He glanced at his watch again, smiling at its opulence and his extravagance. Time to head off to the bank. He started to walk briskly up the Rambla Méndez Núñez, the bustling artery which linked the port to the city. Either side of the three-lane road was an eclectic mix of traditional and modern buildings rising from a wide tree-lined pavement, a large area of which was devoted to al fresco dining. As he walked, he recollected, with some embarrassment, his first visit to the bank. On that occasion, he'd hit a serious problem. It had taken all his strength of mind to hide the crushing wave of disappointment that had engulfed him after the initial shock caused by the clerk's explanation of his predicament, and it had taken some verbal agility on his part not to arouse suspicion. Afterwards, he'd got blind drunk and had shed a few tears of frustration. But after sobering up the next day, he realized that all was not lost and that he would return.

So here he was again, outside the white-stuccoed building with grilles on the windows. He hesitated for a moment, gave his briefcase a playful slap and headed through the tall, pilastered portico. Once inside, he skipped confidently up the cool stone steps.

CHAPTER 23

Anita was up to her eyes in administrative chores. Performance reviews, duty rosters, reports and forms, time sheets, case evaluations... the list was endless: all to be gathered, collated and tested against quality control parameters. What the hell was she doing with all this shit? she wondered for the umpteenth time as she clicked *send* on her computer and another piece of useless information sped off to some faceless bean counters hidden away in another part of the polishus. Then there were the budgetary considerations. Commissioner Theo Falk was forever apologizing for them, but he was having to run a tight ship and had to keep on top of departmental spending. Among the many contentious issues, overtime was arguably the most problematic. The late Erik Moberg had never cared about such nuisances. It was only in the latter stages of the chief inspector's reign that Anita had appreciated the battles he'd been willing to fight on the team's behalf. She was only six months into the job, and already the sheer volume of administration was starting to pall. She looked back on her time with Moberg with nostalgia and felt a growing respect for the man she'd spent many years at odds with. At least towards the end of his life, they'd reached a mutual understanding. Which is more than could be said for Anita's nemesis, Alice Zetterberg. She'd been Moberg's successor (and Anita's immediate predecessor) and had gone out of her way to make her life as difficult as possible, so much so that Anita had resigned from the force. Now Zetterberg had gone, pushed out by the new commissioner, who had been a contemporary of both Anita's and Zetterberg's at the Police Academy in Stockholm. Commissioner Falk had been responsible for bringing Anita back into the fold as chief inspector, a move which had generally been met with approval. Zetterberg, meanwhile, after a series of blunders and the big-time messing up of the Liberty Conference case, had been banished to Östersund in Jämtland County – far enough north that she couldn't do too much damage. It had thwarted her dreams of a cushy government job in Stockholm, for which she blamed Anita. Yet another thing for which she would never forgive her. When she discovered that she was being replaced by her *bête noire*, she was described as being 'incandescent' by someone high up in the polishus.

Anita felt she had a good team. Though she didn't get involved in all the day-to-day duties, she had confidence in those under her, with the possible exception of Pontus Brodd. Brodd was a bit of a passenger: a lightweight who contributed little to the squad. He was quite happy to be carried and didn't seem to notice the resentment this caused. Furthermore, he was forever trying to suck up to the *boss* (as he called Anita, much to her annoyance). She was careful as to the assignments she gave him. Usually, she partnered him with Dan Olovsson, whom she regarded as the ultimate safe pair of hands. Anita relied a lot on Olovsson's calm experience, a quality that had been missing from the team since the tragic death of Henrik Nordlund. Olovsson was also proving to be something of a mentor to the affable, elfin Bea Erlandsson. Bea had never been a shrinking violet, but now she was visibly blossoming, the shadow of Zetterberg and the constant digs about her sexuality having been removed.

And then there was Hakim. Though she would have baulked at the idea of being accused of favouritism, Anita couldn't hide her delight at being back in harness with Hakim Mirza. Not only was he a fine detective, he was a good friend, and the brother of her son Lasse's partner, Jazmin. Anita and Hakim had been through a lot together, and their relationship had been cemented by mutual empathy as well as adversity. They had a chemistry which had even survived the aftermath of Liv Fogelström's shooting. Hakim's girlfriend had been permanently confined to a wheelchair after that, but now they were married and had a baby son. Typically, Liv hadn't allowed her disability to interfere with her career – as Anita's technical wizard, she was a vital cog in her wheel. (So vital that Anita selfishly begrudged her being away on maternity leave.)

Strangely, despite her unquestionable competence, most of Anita's problems now revolved around Klara Wallen. The two women had known each other since Wallen had first joined the Criminal Investigation Squad back in November 2006 and they were thrown straight into the infamous Q Guard robbery case. At the time, Anita had done her best to help Wallen integrate into a team dominated by the intimidating Erik Moberg and the obnoxious Karl Westermark. Over the subsequent years, Anita and Klara had had an on-and-off relationship, often swayed by Wallen's then boyfriend, Rolf, whom Anita thought to be over-possessive and controlling. Rolf thought Anita was interfering and a bad influence on Klara, and had discouraged their friendship. Now Rolf was yesterday's news, and Anita had hoped that with her return to the team, she and Klara would be able to reconnect. But it was not to be. Wallen had been aloof from the moment Anita had walked into the squad room, and had pointedly snubbed the suggestion that they revive their old habit of going out for an after-work drink. Wallen had a large axe to grind: when Anita had resigned from the force, because of her years of service, she had seen herself as the senior detective within the group, and after Zetterberg had been moved on, she thought her promotion was in the offing. Then, to be pipped at the post by Anita waltzing back as chief inspector and be subjugated to her when for years they'd been on equal footing was maddening and humiliating. Moreover, she saw it as favouritism – a suspicion which wasn't without foundation. A number of people within the polishus had noted that Falk seemed to be carrying a torch for Anita, though she seemed totally oblivious to the fact. As far as Anita was concerned, they had just been friends at the Police Academy and he was a useful ally in her job. She may have become more tolerant and less impulsive as she'd grown older, but her emotional antennae were often found to be defective. It had never occurred to her that her own elevation was seen by Klara Wallen as a snub. It was only when Hakim had had a quiet word, she realized that Klara would need careful handling.

At the moment, Wallen was playing a leading role in clearing up the stabbing of a teenager outside his school. The culprit – another student – had been arrested that morning and was being interviewed. This would be some good news, Anita thought with relief, to report to Commissioner Falk at their late-afternoon meeting. Then, when the necessary paperwork was completed, she would go home and take a long shower and then talk to Kevin.

Kevin Ash was her long-distance lover. A British detective based in Cumbria, after years of begging and cajoling and trying to circumvent the problem with all kinds of impractical ideas (he had even asked her to marry him!), Kevin had eventually accepted that they would never be able to live together, as neither really wanted to uproot from their respective countries. It was a price he was willing to pay to keep the relationship going. On the plus side, he had to admit that it added to its freshness and vitality, and, ironically, the trust he had in Anita a thousand miles away was far greater than the trust he'd had in his ex-wife (the marriage had foundered because of her infidelities). On her part, Anita had been more than happy with the arrangement, yet now that she was in an increasingly stressful job, she missed Kevin's strong moral support. They spoke regularly on Messenger, and she valued his advice. He understood the pressures, and she could talk through her problems and worries in a way she could no longer do with her colleagues. Theo Falk had indicated that his door was always open, but confiding in her boss wasn't the same, and Kevin had become her safety valve, which he was quite happy to be.

August Skoog waddled like a duck into the sauna. He was trying to keep the weight off his painful left heel. He was beginning to think the plantar fasciitis was never going to go away. Inside, the heat was rising, and his naked wife, Gudrun, was already building up a sweat as she sat on the towel on the wooden bench. Her eyes were closed. August took in the body that he knew so well. They'd been married for fifty-two years but, with a painful stab to his heart, he knew that they were unlikely to see their next anniversary. That had been the consultant's rather blunt prognosis on their visit to Skåne University Hospital in Malmö three months earlier. Apparently, treatment was useless at this stage, as the cancer hadn't been detected until far too late. If only August had been firmer and more insistent. Gudrun hadn't been well for a while, but he couldn't persuade her to see a doctor. She always put other people first and pooh-poohed her own problems. She was far more worried about his own heart condition and said it was important that he got that sorted out first.

August whipped off the white towel wrapped around his waist and laid it carefully on the wooden bench next to his wife. He eased himself down with a now familiar groan. His blotched belly hung over his upper thighs. He knew he'd put on too much weight recently as the damn foot had made him inactive. And he was drinking more than he should. Worrying about Gudrun was the root cause of that. How was he going to face life without her? He gently squeezed her damp hand and she gave a little murmur of acceptance. He gazed at her.

To him, she still retained hints of the youthful beauty that had once captivated him. The shapely body of the woman he had fallen in love with had filled out over the years but then, quite suddenly, with the rapidity of a fallen leaf drying in the sun, the flesh had wizened and withered as the cancer bit deep.

He fought back the tears. He was trying to be strong for her just as she had always been a rock for him, but he was struggling with the realities of the situation, and in the sanctuary of his workshop, he'd often found himself seated at his bench crying over the horror and injustice of it all. The workshop had been a happy retreat since they'd retired and moved to Löderup nearly twenty years ago. August had a talent for creating little wooden artefacts – bowls, paper knives, candle holders… that sort of thing – that had been sold at a local craft shop. It hadn't been for the money – just something to do. And he'd used his carpentry skills to improve the house: from new windows and wooden doors to creating the sauna which Gudrun loved so much. That was where they relaxed and let the aches and pains of advancing age dissipate with the steam.

Gudrun opened her eyes. 'What was that?'

'What do you mean?'

'That sound.'

'I didn't hear anything, my love. Probably a stray cat.'

Gudrun sank back and closed her eyes again. August felt a slight pressure on his hand. She was trying to squeeze it with what little strength she had left. 'August. I think I can hear something.'

He opened his eyes and wiped away the sweat. He kissed her lightly on the head.

'I'll go and check.'

CHAPTER 24

Hakim was scrolling through photos of his son's naming ceremony. Held in his garden on Sunday afternoon, it had gone well. The sun had shone, and friends and family had enjoyed the occasion. Lasse and a friend of Liv's had been invited to be non-religious godparents, and they'd made good but not-too-serious speeches evincing their commitment to their pastoral roles in little Linus's life. The baby – diplomatically named Linus Uday (after Liv's late dad and Hakim's own father) – had slept much of the time. Uday had previously expressed his horror that the baby wasn't going to be brought up as a Muslim, but Anita had pointed out that he wasn't going to be brought up as a Christian either. Hakim and Liv were adamant that Linus could make up his own mind when he was older. However, Uday was only partially placated and Anita could see that, as far as he was concerned, that was not the end of the matter.

Anita relished Hakim's pride in his new family. The responsibility suited him, as did his new clean-shaven look. He was still gangly, though his movements were less awkward than they had been in his early days at the polishus. He seemed happy in his own skin: relaxed, confident and self-assured. An altogether more contented Hakim. Anita was also pleased that he and his sister Jazmin, Lasse's girlfriend, had buried their many hatchets, thanks to the phlegmatic natures of their respective partners. Jazmin and Lasse were still not married – another bone of contention with Uday – but Anita's daughter-out-law

(Jazmin liked that) was wilful and independent and was unlikely to be drawn by the protestations of her father. Of course, both father and daughter were careful to keep the cart on the wheels for little Leyla's sake. Anita's granddaughter, now six, had type 1 diabetes and needed constant monitoring.

'It was a lovely day,' Anita remarked as Hakim showed her yet another batch of photos. Lovely but tiring; Anita had been exhausted by the time she got home. As well as playing a conciliatory role with Uday, she had also played a unicorn, a pet-shop owner, a ferocious lion, a spy and an alien with her granddaughter. Leyla was definitely going to end up on the stage!

Anita was quite relieved when Hakim put his phone away. There was only so much appreciative nodding one could do.

'Did you see that thing last week about the old couple in Löderup?' he said as he headed towards the door. 'That's your old part of the world.'

'Well, it's not far from Simrishamn. Some of the kids at my school came from there,' recalled Anita.

'Really sad. Sounds like a suicide pact. Apparently, the wife had terminal cancer.'

Anita couldn't really conceive of a love that was so strong that two people would want to end their lives together. She'd be horrified if Kevin sacrificed himself for her, however ill she might be. She'd certainly not do it for him.

Five minutes after Hakim had left her office, the phone rang. It was Commissioner Falk. Could she come up and see him? So what was this all about? She'd already reported on the school stabbing, and Wallen and Olovsson were working closely with the prosecutor on the case.

Theo Falk greeted Anita with a beaming smile. He always did. He liked any excuse to call her up to his office or pop into hers. He'd always had a soft spot for her – well, more than a soft spot if truth were told. On his appointment as commissioner to Malmö, he'd sought her out in a professional capacity, but also for personal reasons. His disappointment was real when he discovered she had a partner – albeit in another country – and it was immediately apparent that she had no romantic interest in him and just regarded him as a friend. However, the knowledge hadn't deterred him from inveigling her back into the force despite some opposition from a couple of the most senior ranking members in the polishus (most notably Prosecutor Blom). But Falk had got his way. He hadn't exactly broken any rules – more like reinterpreted them. Ironically, the Liberty Conference affair, which had been so disastrous for Alice Zetterberg, had been a triumph for Anita, and that had won the day.

'Anita, come in and take a seat.'

'I hope this is important, Commissioner. I'm very busy; all those reports don't write themselves.'

He ignored the dig – and he wished she wouldn't call him 'Commissioner', but she had stuck rigidly to the formalities from the moment she was appointed. He tapped a pile of newspapers on his ridiculously large desk.

'Did you read about the couple who committed suicide in Löderup last Friday?'

'Funnily enough, Hakim remarked on that just before you rang.'

'August and Gudrun Skoog. Both in their eighties. Found by a nurse who was visiting – Gudrun had terminal oesophageal cancer. She only had a short time to live, possibly a matter of weeks. By all accounts, they were devoted to each other. They moved to just outside Löderup when they retired twenty-odd years ago. He shot her dead in their sauna before turning the gun on himself. The feeling is that he couldn't face living without her and didn't want her to suffer any more.'

'Suicides are sad and often unnecessary, but maybe not in

this case. But I don't see how this has got anything to do with me.'

'The case is being handled by Ystad, and in normal circumstances, they would see it through. The problem is that the pathologist's report came through this morning, and there may be more to it. The thing is, they'd been in the sauna overnight before they were discovered and all that heat had affected the skin. Some had peeled off – apparently a bit like a snake shedding a layer. There were also internal burns. All to be expected in the circumstances. But then the pathologist found something else. There was evidence of trauma which he could not explain.'

'Any note?'

'No note. By the sound of it, we may be looking at suspicious circumstances. Why anyone would want to kill an old couple like that is unfathomable. But I want your team to take over the case.'

'What about Ystad?'

'They requested it, actually. They don't feel they have the resources for such an investigation if it turns out to be murder.'

'Don't tell me – cutbacks?'

'Well, it…' He gave up. It was pointless trying to explain the enormous pressure he and other commissioners were under to cut costs. 'Anyway, I want you to go over there and liaise with an Inspector Joel Grahn.'

'I'll send a couple of the team.'

'No, I want *you* to go. If this does turn out to be murder, we might have some lunatic out there. Then there'll be mass panic – nothing worse than old folk being murdered in the safety of their own homes to get everybody twitchy. I want this solved quickly, one way or another, and you're just the person to do it.'

CHAPTER 25

Inspector Joel Grahn was waiting for them when they drew up outside the Skoogs' house. It was a brisk ten-minute walk from the village of Löderup, which is half way between Ystad and Simrishamn. Like many villages in Skåne, Löderup is primarily linear – a long main street, with houses and shorter side roads feeding off it. It has a shop, a school, a garage and a building supplier, and an attractive step-gabled, whitewashed church. The village is well situated – just a short drive from one of the coast's many attractive beaches, though that has not yet been reflected in the property prices, which are just that bit cheaper than those by the sea. Anita had always liked the place and could see herself living somewhere like it one day.

The Skoogs' home was accessed by a dirt track off the main road to the north of the village. It was a quiet spot, with trees surrounding two sides of the building. The house itself looked interesting. Solidly constructed of 1930s red brick, the size was deceptive: it was built on a rise and was higher at the back than the front. What turned out to be the living room had a large bay window, next to which was a pleasant porch leading to the main entrance. Above the porch, a pretty balcony surrounded by a white picket fence announced itself as the main feature of the property. Climbing roses and splashes of hollyhocks completed the picture. On the right of the house was a car port with an old Volvo estate inside, and to the left was the obligatory flagpole; today the blue-and-yellow national flag hung limply on its halyard as though in mourning.

Anita, Hakim and Bea Erlandsson were greeted by Grahn: a young cop with puppy-dog eyes that shone with the enthusiasm of the unjaded. He was probably a few kilos overweight, which had the disconcerting effect of making him look cuddly: not really the right image for confronting hardened criminals but perfect for reassuring old ladies that their missing cats were sure to be found.

After brief introductions, Grahn took them inside the house. The front door opened directly into the living room with the bay window. The room also included a dining area, the table poignantly set for a meal which the Skoogs never got to eat. Odd, thought Anita, why set the table if they were about to kill themselves? Grahn took them into the hallway, through a door opposite the kitchen and down some steep wooden steps which led into the cellar. This basement area was huge, and despite being partly built into the embankment, it was light and airy, as it had some windows looking out onto the back garden and a glazed outside door at the far end. One section had been converted into a workshop. This contained every woodworking tool imaginable: planes and sanders, chisels and saws, all neatly hung on hooks or stored on shelves. In one corner was a pile of off-cuts and in another was an industrial-sized lathe. Along the main wall was a well-worn workbench, complete with vice and clamps, next to which was a beautiful oak door, lying on its side. It was not quite finished; the polish was waiting to be applied. Under the window, on three long shelves, were samples of the craftsman's work – some completed and some in progress. Affixed on the wall opposite the workbench was a metal cabinet. Its length indicated a store for hunting rifles.

They continued their tour.

'August Skoog was a carpenter. Ran a successful business before he retired here.'

'Where was that?'

'Kalmar.'

'He was good. He built this,' Grahn said, opening another door. Anita had been in quite a few saunas in her time, but this was the smartest domestic one she'd ever seen. It was immaculately finished off in light spruce and had been well maintained. Spoiling the clean lines, however, were spatters of dried blood, now five days old, on the back wall and benches. Anita wished they'd been able to view the crime scene straightaway.

'It was a horrible sight,' Grahn said with a shiver. 'I went outside to be sick,' he admitted candidly. 'My first...'

'We've all been through that,' Anita said reassuringly.

'Their skin was sort of peeling and kind of hanging off. They'd probably been boiling for around fifteen hours. We found Gudrun Skoog lying slumped on the floor. It's thought she was actually sitting when she was shot in the head, side on. August was lying near the door, here.' He indicated the spot. 'He'd also shot himself in the head – or so we believed – and had dropped the pistol on the floor. It only had his prints on it.'

'So, initially, a suicide pact was the obvious conclusion,' commented Hakim.

'But strange that a devoted husband would have left his wife in such a position even if he was about to kill himself,' Anita observed. 'No dignity in it.'

'Did August own the pistol?' Hakim asked.

'Yes. He had two pistols and a couple of hunting rifles. There's a gun cabinet in the workshop. The key was still in the lock.'

'Why would he need four guns?' Hakim could never get his head around the number of firearms people had in Sweden.

'It's well short of the sixteen that people are allowed,' commented Erlandsson with disapproval. She agreed with Hakim and had made it clear on numerous occasions what she thought of Swedish gun laws. Gun owners generally used their weapons for hunting and in shooting clubs, and the laws were notoriously strict, but Erlandsson thought they should be tighter still.

'He had the correct permits for all of them,' countered Grahn. 'Apparently, he took up hunting when he first retired and had been a member of a shooting club back in Kalmar, hence the pistols. That's another reason why we thought it was a straightforward murder-suicide pact. What appeared to confirm it was the fact that Gudrun had terminal cancer and had only weeks left to live. The one in the throat.'

'Oesophageal cancer,' Anita volunteered. 'My mother died of that.'

'I'm sorry.'

Anita shrugged.

'Anyway, according to the locals, August was distraught and didn't know if he could face up to life without her. Drinking a lot, apparently, though there was no alcohol found in his blood.'

'And then the pathology report…' prompted Anita.

'Yeah… yeah, that seemed to change the whole picture. They might have been physically abused. August had been beaten about the head and his nose was broken, but this didn't show up immediately as he'd blown his brains out.' Grahn turned pale as he remembered the scene. 'And Gudrun's left cheekbone was fractured.'

Anita let her gaze drift around the small room, trying to imagine the Skoogs enjoying their sauna. What had they done to deserve such a horrific end?

'What areas did forensics cover?'

'Just down here. There didn't seem any point looking anywhere else at the time. It all seemed straightforward.'

'If it *had* been suicide, why would they have done it in here?' Erlandsson wondered. 'And naked?'

'Contained? More clinical? Less messy than another part

of the house?' opined Grahn. 'Their robes are hanging up just outside.'

'So they must have been in here when the possible intruder or intruders arrived.'

'The table was set for a meal,' mused Anita. 'What is the estimated time of death?'

'Roughly between six and seven, early evening.'

'And I believe there was no note.'

'None that we found.'

'Right. Hakim, let's get forensics down here again. They need to go over the property, top to bottom. See if you can get Eva Thulin. She'll be thorough.'

'Do you think this is some sicko?' asked Grahn.

'Possibly. We may have a psychopath on our hands' – Anita took out some latex gloves – 'but if our victims *were* beaten, it could be something personal. Or whoever was in here was trying to get some information from them: after something valuable. Let's see if we can establish if anything is missing. Money, jewellery and so forth.'

Anita let Hakim and Erlandsson go round the two upper floors while she concentrated on the basement. Down there, besides the sauna and the workshop, there was a large utility and drying area with a washing machine. Laundry was still hanging up ready to be ironed. She then, accompanied by Grahn, opened the outside door and went into the garden.

'No signs of a break in?'

'No. This door and the front door were both unlocked. I suppose at that time of day, they would be.'

'The intruders may have come into the house this way.'

'Makes sense,' Grahn agreed.

'Has it rained much in the last five days since the killings?'

'Yeah, some heavy downpours over the weekend.'

Anita clicked her tongue in annoyance. 'That would have washed away any footprints – and tyre tracks.'

In contrast to the tidiness of the house, the garden was shambolic. The grass was long, the flower beds were in urgent need of weeding and the raised vegetable patch had been sadly neglected: the salads had bolted and the brassicas had been eaten by caterpillars. Anita suspected that Gudrun had been the one with green fingers and it had all got too much for her. The garden was large, with a number of fruit trees, and at the bottom end, it merged into open ground, scrub and pockets of woodland.

'What do we know about the couple?' asked Anita as Grahn stuffed a snus bag in his mouth.

'August was eighty-seven and Gudrun eighty-four. Came here in 2004. August was brought up along the road in Borrby. He'd always wanted to return to the area when it was time to retire. And, apparently, Gudrun was happy to do so, as the summers in southern Skåne were better for her arthritis. From what I can gather, they were well liked and joined in community activities. No one seems to have a bad word to say about them.'

'Any children?'

'No. Not their own.'

'What do you mean?'

'They fostered a lot of kids when they were in Kalmar.' For some reason, the remark rang a vague bell with Anita, which she wasn't able to connect to any particular thought. 'That seems to have been Gudrun's life's work.'

'Any next of kin?'

'The only one we can trace is an elderly cousin of August's in Borrby. She's been informed.'

'Well, you can be our local eyes and ears.' Grahn seemed pleased that he was still going to be involved in the investigation. 'The first thing you can do is talk to the cousin.' Anita realized that the case was starting to get her adrenaline pumping after what seemed like weeks trapped behind her desk.

'Anita!' Hakim called from an upstairs window. 'I think you should take a look at this.'

Anita, followed by Grahn, made her way to the upper floor and into a small bedroom that overlooked the garden. Hakim was there with Bea Erlandsson. The room contained a single bed; a bedside table, on which there was a lamp with a floral patterned shade; a chest of drawers; and a narrow built-in wardrobe. Judging by the immaculate finish, the furniture was surely August's work.

'What am I looking at?'

'Well, firstly, this bed has been slept in. The Skoogs' bedroom is along the corridor.'

'Maybe August snored. Couples do sleep in separate rooms occasionally.' Whisky set Kevin off snoring and more than once, he'd been banished to Lasse's old room.

'Possibly, but what about this?' Hakim opened the top drawer of the bedside table and extracted a half-empty packet of cigarettes. Marlboro.

'Did the Skoogs smoke?'

'I haven't found any evidence elsewhere in the house,' said Erlandsson.

'Perhaps August was a secret smoker.'

'The health warning is in French,' Hakim pointed out. 'And I haven't finished yet. Here's the most interesting bit.' With the flourish of a practised magician, he opened the wardrobe. The only item in there was a man's blue suit.

'What size was August?' Hakim asked Grahn.

'Quite small. Stocky. Overweight.'

'Well this obviously wasn't his. This would fit a taller, thinner man. And it's an Emporio Armani, according to the label,' said Hakim, feeling the cloth. 'It's certainly a cut above the clothes hanging up in the main bedroom.'

'Yeah, pretty expensive,' agreed Grahn admiringly. 'Over twelve thousand kronor at a guess. Always fancied one myself.'

'Not on your salary,' said Anita dryly. 'Try the pockets, Hakim.'

'Ah,' said Hakim after a few expectant moments, 'what have we here?' He produced from one of the suit jacket's side pockets two small pieces of paper. He scrutinized the first. 'A receipt for two packets of Marlboro from a *bureau de tabac* at the Gare du Nord in Paris, dated Saturday, the second of July. I doubt if August would go all the way to France to get his cigarettes.'

Anita grinned. 'OK, we have French cigarettes and a suit for a tall man. So, who might this belong to' – she took the suit out of the wardrobe and laid it on the bed – 'and why is it here?'

'A guest? Someone staying in the house? That would also explain the cigarettes.'

'But why would anyone leave such an expensive item hanging in the wardrobe?'

'Because they intended to come back and fetch it?' Hakim speculated.

'Or because they had to leave quickly,' suggested Erlandsson.

'Whoever owned it was here shortly before the killings. Look at this.' Hakim gave Anita the other piece of paper he'd taken out of the pocket. 'Another receipt. A meal at the Harbour Hotel in Ystad – the fifth of July. The Skoogs were murdered three days later.'

'So our suited man was in Paris on the second, in Ystad on the fifth, and the Skoogs were killed on the eighth. Right. This room gets special attention from forensics. And tomorrow, we'll come back and go door-to-door round the village to find out as much about the Skoogs as possible, and any recent visitors they had. The first thing we've got to establish... who owns this suit.'

CHAPTER 26

Anita went back to Löderup the following afternoon. The sun-kissed vista which was Österlen was looking at its most beguiling and beautiful – the greens and the yellows of the orchards and the cornfields, as intense as those in a Van Gogh painting, were inflamed by the empyrean brightness. The neat, well-kept villages and high-towered, substantial churches reflected the wealth created by this cornucopia. A land of peace and prosperity: a veritable Garden of Eden. In sharp contrast to the grizzly discovery in the Skoogs' basement.

Hakim, Erlandsson and Brodd had been sent off early to do the door-to-door enquiries. It was a necessary, yet grindingly tedious, job that as a chief inspector, Anita could now avoid. A perk of her promotion, and it wasn't the only one, the most significant being a much-needed pay rise. During her year of self-imposed exile from the force, her meagre savings had soon been depleted, as her work at the tourist information centre had hardly covered her basic weekly costs. Now she would no longer have to clothes shop at Lindex or the second-hand chains. What bliss! As she passed a sign to Tomelilla, she promised to indulge herself with a trip to Eckerlunds. She mused that the unpretentious town was an unlikely setting for such a fashionable store.

She made her way to the Skoogs' house, where the squad were to meet up and report what they'd found out. Eva Thulin and her forensic team had been and gone. They gathered in the garden. Bea Erlandsson had raided the local shop for snacks and drinks and they sat round a beautifully constructed, wooden garden table they'd found in a shed. Another of August's pieces, they reckoned. Anita put down her bottle of sparkling water.

'Right, Joel, how did you get on with Gudrun's cousin?'

The young detective's moon-shaped face beamed at being addressed by his first name by a senior officer.

'Britha Skoog is in her early nineties, but she's all there upstairs,' he said, tapping his forehead, 'though she did go off at a few tangents. First thing I learned was that August wasn't a smoker. He used to visit her regularly after returning to Österlen, though he hadn't come round much in recent months. That backs up what the locals have said – the Skoogs seem to have retreated from village life. Understandable, I suppose. August had been depressed about Gudrun. And the last time Britha saw him was about a month ago – she couldn't remember the exact date – and she thought he was drunk. She wasn't totally surprised when she heard he'd committed suicide.'

'Could it still be suicide?' Hakim wondered aloud. 'The circumstances seem right. Depressed husband putting his beloved, dying wife out of her misery – then putting himself out of his own.'

Anita frowned. 'I'm not so sure. What about the table being set? And what about that unfinished door?'

Grahn had an answer for that. 'There's a door missing upstairs. It looks as if August was replacing all the doors – some of the upstairs ones are new and match the one in the workshop.'

'Which emphasizes my point. Why would he kill himself in the middle of what was obviously an important project for him? It just doesn't make sense. And what about the physical injuries? We have to take those into account.'

'Maybe Gudrun hadn't known what he was going to do and lashed out... I don't know... perhaps he slapped her to calm her down.' Hakim didn't sound convinced by his own argument.

'I doubt she would have had the strength to resist him, let alone attack him,' said Anita, 'and a slap wouldn't have fractured her cheekbone. No, I think we've got to look at these deaths as suspicious.' She took another sip of her water: there was no breeze to temper the sun's relentlessness. Turning again to Grahn, 'Did you find out from Britha whether the Skoogs had any regular visitors?'

'She met a couple of friends from Kalmar who holidayed here once or twice. She thinks they might have been former neighbours. She remembered the name – Beijer – because she has a friend of the same name. And she thought that one or two of their many foster children had visited over the years. There was one who'd since got married and came and showed off his kids. She remembered Gudrun was particularly proud, as he'd been a handful as a child; many of them had been. And there was someone who came across from Malmö a few times in their early days in Löderup. She couldn't remember any of the names, but we may have one lead. When August made his last visit, he was sitting in her kitchen, rambling about all sorts of things – he was drunk, remember. She was baking and wasn't really listening. But she does recall asking him if he'd left Gudrun on her own, and he said Klas was keeping an eye on her.'

'Klas? Klas who?'

'No idea. He went off at a tangent and she didn't get any more out of him.'

'OK, let's see if we can track any of these people down. There must be social services records for the foster children. What about the villagers? Anything from them?'

'Universally liked as far as I can gather,' said Hakim with a shrug. 'Genuine shock at what's happened.'

'Before Gudrun got ill, they joined in village life,' added

Erlandsson. 'She clearly loved kids and liked to help down at the local school; she worked with some of the slower ones on their reading. August got involved in community projects and did little joinery jobs for people, as well as selling his wooden artefacts at a craft shop near Borrby.'

'Had they upset anyone locally?'

'Not that we can tell,' answered Hakim.

'Anything unusual recently?'

'I had a long chat with a man at the garage.' Anita was glad that Brodd had managed to make himself useful. 'He said he'd seen a Danish car pass through the village a few times shortly before the couple died.'

'Registration?'

'No.' Brodd opened his notebook. 'A red VW Golf. At least ten, eleven years old. Had a noticeable dent in the driver's-side door. Mechanics notice those sort of things.'

'Dates?'

'Not specific. But it was during the week of the killings. And he'd also seen it a few weeks before, sometime in June. He was surprised that the owner hadn't got round to fixing the bodywork.'

'Could have been a holidaymaker,' said Grahn. 'Österlen is a big tourist area, especially at this time of year. Lots of Danes have holiday homes around here.'

'True. Still, we need to follow it up. Pontus?' Anita gave Brodd a look as he closed his notebook with a groan. 'Hakim, when do we expect to hear back from forensics?'

'Eva said in a couple of days.'

'So all we've got so far is an unknown man missing a smart suit. He may have nothing to do with any of this, but we need to be in a position to discount him. Anything else?'

'This is a long shot,' said Erlandsson quietly. 'Last night, I was going through the national records of recent similar situations where supposedly devoted couples ended up killing themselves: murder-suicides. One somewhere near Gothenburg, and the other outside Västervik. Both in quiet, rural locations like this one. One of the detectives in Gothenburg had doubts about the killings there, which made him look around to see if there were any other instances. Wife killed by husband, husband kills himself, just like we possibly have here. In neither of the cases – Gothenburg or Västervik – did the husband have a history of violence...'

'Do we know if August had?' Anita queried.

'Not that we know of,' answered Grahn. 'Nothing in official records. But I'll ask around. His cousin might know.'

'...then this detective looked further afield. Apparently, in the north-west of England, a senior coroner's officer, making a freedom of information request across Britain, discovered thirty-nine cases between 2000 and 2019 of older couples found together in similar circumstances. Five particular cases are being reviewed.'

'So, what are you saying? You're not seriously suggesting this is the work of a serial killer?' scoffed Brodd through a mouthful of crisps.

'I suppose we can't discount the possibility,' Anita said guardedly. Despite the preponderance of serial killers in much of Scandinavian crime fiction, she knew the real figures didn't bear this out. 'Have a word with whoever up in Gothenburg, Bea, but I don't want it to be too much of a distraction at the moment.'

It was time to wrap things up. Anita needed to get back to Malmö for yet another pointless meeting. 'OK. While we wait to hear back from Eva Thulin, I want that Danish car found. Is there a connection to our mystery man? How did he get here? And someone visit the Harbour Hotel in Ystad and see if we can match a customer to that suit. And we need more on the Skoogs' life in Kalmar in case there's any link to their past. I want the usual things checked out – phones, bank accounts, etcetera. And Hakim, have a word with the pathologist who did the post mortem and see if he can provide us with any more information.'

Anita scanned their surroundings. A beautiful, tranquil place that had witnessed two brutal deaths. But who was responsible?

CHAPTER 27

The following Sunday afternoon, Anita was sitting in McDonalds with her granddaughter. She knew Lasse and Jazmin probably wouldn't approve, but Leyla had begged her grandmother, and Anita had given in.

The day had been a special outing. Anita was happy to indulge the little girl, as she hadn't had as much time for the family since taking over as chief inspector, and she was feeling guilty about neglecting them. It wasn't the most relaxing way of spending a precious Sunday off, but she wouldn't have swapped it for the world. They'd already been to the cinema complex on Storgatan to watch *Sonic the Hedgehog 2*. Leyla had loved it so much, she'd stood excitedly throughout virtually the whole film, so caught up in the action was she (fortunately, they'd been on the back row). And between them, they'd munched through an enormous tub of popcorn. What the hell! – the child didn't get many treats. As long as she fed the correct information into Leyla's Personal Diabetes Manager, the insulin pod would do the rest. Anita still marvelled at the technology, but she knew she had to get it right – a mistake could have dire consequences.

She watched Leyla tucking into her nuggets and chips (more insulin – naughty *farmor*!) and listened happily to her chatter. The child took after her mother in that respect – her father wasn't the most talkative of people. Anita was proud of both parents in the way they'd adapted and learned to cope with Leyla's type 1. It had been a steep learning curve, but now working out the carbs, keeping an eye on her blood glucose, changing her insulin pod and all the other things they had to remember concerning her condition were all pretty much second nature. Of course, there still remained that niggling element of worry at the back of their minds – that would probably never go away – but they had learned to live with it. After Leyla had finished her meal, she began to play with the free game that had come with it. While she was distracted, Anita turned her phone back on and found that there were two messages – one from Lasse to say he was back home and she could bring Leyla back any time. The second was from Theo Falk. Could she call into his office at eight o'clock tomorrow morning? There was no reason given, but it was probably to get an update on the Skoog business. She had to admit that the case had got her investigative juices flowing once more, and the challenge of unravelling the mystery and bringing the killers to justice gave her a buzz. She found that it was homicides that were the sharpest test of her mental acuity, and she needed that kind of stimulus to keep her energized. Even during her year out of the force when she got involved in Magda Forsell's private investigation, dangerous though it turned out to be, she'd never felt more alive. And she was good at her job: even working in an independent capacity, she'd cracked the case and saved a man's life into the bargain. That had been gratefully acknowledged by Theo Falk and had led to her reinstatement. She owed Falk a lot and she would do her best to repay his faith in her.

'Come on Leyla, time to head for home.'

'Oh, *farmor*, can't I have some ice cream?' Leyla said in a deliberate little-girl voice, her big brown eyes gazing pleadingly up at Anita.

Farmor tried to frown. Ice cream really wasn't good for her granddaughter and Anita would have to tweak her insulin yet again. But, ever the sucker for Leyla's charms, she caved in. 'OK. Just a small one.'

*

Theo Falk, dressed immaculately in a dark suit, was sitting behind his desk. A pot of coffee and two cups and saucers were at the ready. Anita wasn't used to such sophistication in the polishus. The meeting must be important, especially this early on a Monday morning. His neatly cropped hair was now shot with grey (the pressures of his elevated position, no doubt) and his waistline was expanding (too many high-profile lunches and not enough exercise in between), yet he was still the amiable cadet she'd met at the Police Academy. At the time, everyone had agreed that he was too nice to make it, but he was obviously made of sterner stuff than they'd thought. What hadn't changed was the permanently startled gaze which had earned him the unflattering sobriquet of 'The Goldfish'. Whenever they met, Anita found it difficult to erase the mean moniker from her mind.

'Morning, Anita,' he said with a broad smile. 'Please, take a seat. Coffee?'

She'd already had two that morning, but this coffee would be far superior to her own at home, so she smiled and thanked him.

Falk brought his chair round from behind his desk so that they sat opposite each other. Anita started to fret – posh coffee and a face-to-face chat. What had she done? Since becoming a chief inspector, she'd been conscious of feeling more vulnerable. She could take criticism – she'd got used to that under Erik Moberg and, particularly, Alice Zetterberg. But now every decision she made could be questioned not only by her superiors but by those under her as well. She sometimes wondered if she was in way over her head. And it sometimes kept her awake at night. What was it called? Imposter syndrome?

'How's the Löderup case going? Do you think it's murder?'

At least he'd got straight down to business.

'It's pointing in that direction. The pathologist believes

that violence was inflicted on both the victims, and he agreed with me that the bruising found on August Skoog's body couldn't have been inflicted by Gudrun, as she would have been too physically weak owing to her cancer. As for August, according to his cousin, he had no history of violence. In fact, he sounded a bit of a pussycat; Gudrun was the strong-willed one. Which means there must have been a third party in the sauna that night – or more than one. We're now thinking that whoever was in there knocked them about first before setting up their deaths to look like suicide. August's own gun was used, helping with the deception, and it all seemed to fit with the circumstances: wife weeks away from dying and husband unable to contemplate going on without her. And maybe the perp thought the heat of the sauna would obscure the injuries. And if it *was* murder, it begs the question: why beat them up before killing them?'

'A psychopath? Or perhaps a revenge attack?'

'Doubt the former, but there might be something in the latter. The team and I reckon that maybe the killer was after something.'

'Something hidden in the house?'

'As far as we can tell, there's nothing obvious missing, but, of course, we don't know what we're looking for. Gudrun's purse was intact; her bank cards hadn't been touched. Nor had August's, and he still had a couple of five-hundred-krona notes in his wallet. The bedroom was pristine – no sign of a search or Gudrun's jewellery being disturbed or anything like that. But the killer was after something: something tangible that was hidden in the house perhaps – or information.'

Falk sipped his coffee delicately.

'What we did find of interest was in a spare bedroom. Someone had clearly been staying there: we found a half-empty packet of cigarettes in a drawer, and an Armani suit – not August's – was hanging in the wardrobe. In one of the pockets was a receipt for the cigarettes from a *bureau de tabac* at the Gare du Nord in Paris. There's an outside chance that this mystery man is someone called Klas – August's cousin heard him mention a Klas who was looking after Gudrun the day he visited her. We also know that three days before the murders, this same man had lunch at the Harbour Hotel in Ystad. Anyway, Hakim talked to the waiter who was on that day. The guy was definitely there; the waiter clocked the suit. But the rest of the man's description was a bit on the vague side: in his forties or fifties, short blond hair. It wasn't helped by the man wearing dark glasses.'

'During lunch?' Falk sounded appalled.

'He was eating in the beer garden. Hot day. But another thing the waiter remembered was that the guy paid in cash.'

'Unusual.'

'Anyway, we're pretty sure that whoever left the suit was the man who dined at the Harbour. Maybe forensics will help identify him.'

'Only if he's got a record. Is that likely?'

'We live in hope. What we do know is that he spoke Swedish. Also, there was a Danish car seen in Löderup the week of the killings – an aging VW Golf. Not unusual in itself, but it had been seen there the previous month, too. Distinguishable because it had a distinctive dent in the driver's door. Pontus Brodd is trying to track it down but has had no success so far.'

Falk raised an eyebrow. If redundancies had to be made, Brodd was near the top of the list.

Anita missed the significance of the look. 'We need to see if there's any connection between the man in the suit and the Danish car, though that doesn't seem very probable. If you can afford to wear an Armani suit, you're unlikely to drive around in a bashed-up Golf.'

'OK. Anything else?'

'Well... it's hardly worth bringing up but...' Anita briefly filled Falk in on Erlandsson's theory.

The commissioner's face was a picture of horror. 'Jesus! The last thing we need is a serial killer roaming around bumping off senior citizens. Do you give this any credence?'

'Not really, but we have to look into every eventuality.' In Anita's new position, she couldn't afford to dismiss the idea out of hand; she had to be seen to cover all the bases so there was no possibility of official comeback. The top brass were masters of hindsight.

Anita finished her coffee. Why couldn't she get her own to taste this good? 'We're still waiting on forensics. I'll let you know if they've come up with anything.'

She eased herself off the chair.

'No, wait, Anita. This case isn't the only reason I asked you to come this morning. There's something else.'

Alarm bells started ringing in Anita's head.

'I need your help. Your cooperation, actually.'

'Cooperation?'

'Yes. Help yourself to more coffee.' Anita was tempted, but her bladder said no. 'We've been contacted... well, *I*'ve been contacted by the FBI.'

'The FBI, as in the Federal Bureau of Investigation?'

Falk nodded. 'The very same. It's to do with a murder case in Chicago which happened during a drugs bust organized by the Bureau.'

'Chicago's a long way from Malmö.'

'Indeed. However, the FBI think that the person responsible for this murder may be here in southern Sweden. He was spotted on CCTV in Copenhagen Central Station in June. So we have an Agent Paige McBride flying over tomorrow. We've agreed to give her all the help we can to trace the suspect.'

'Fine. But what has this got to do with me?'

'I want you to liaise with Agent McBride.'

'Why?'

'Because your English is faultless.' That was a bit lame; there were a number of other senior officers whose English was perfectly adequate for such a task.

'Look, Commissioner, I don't really have time to babysit this FBI woman. The Löderup case is taking up most of our waking hours. On top of which, we're going to be short-staffed soon. Dan Olovsson's already taking his long summer vacation now that the school stabbing has gone to the prosecutor, and others are also due holiday, me included. Add to that Liv Fogelström on maternity leave, and Hakim's paternity leave coming up...' She drew a breath. 'Well, you can see where we stand.'

Falk flashed her an indulgent smile.

'I know all that, but I thought you'd be particularly interested in this.'

'Why?'

'Because of the man the FBI are trying to track down.'

'Do I know him?'

'It's a Mikael Mosten, known as Micky.'

She stared blankly at the commissioner.

'You might remember him better as Willi Hirdwall.'

CHAPTER 28

'I just can't believe it!'

Anita was conscious of bending Kevin's ear yet again but she knew it would be a sympathetic one. Being a detective himself, he knew the score, and in recent months, she'd found herself relying more and more on his wisdom and advice. She was fully aware that she'd taken him for granted and used him mercilessly in the past, but now that she was in a more stressful and demanding role, she was beginning to wake up to the fact that she missed him more than she had previously cared to admit. He brought fun into her life with his daft humour, and even some of his annoying habits could actually be quite endearing. She wasn't sure that they could ever cohabit – at close quarters she might lose her appeal, as she wasn't the easiest person to live with. But absence makes the heart grow fonder and all that; to Anita, there seemed to be some truth in the old adage. She was beginning to think that she would like to spend more time with him. Not remotely practical, of course.

'What, that this guy... Willi... could have killed someone?' He shook his head to show he understood. He was in the living room of his rented home near Penrith with a half-drunk glass of beer by his side. She had interrupted him as he had settled down to watch the Test Match cricket highlights on the television. What devotion – she was oblivious to the ultimate sacrifice he was making!

Willi Hirdwall had been playing on her mind all day,

even though that morning, there'd been a breakthrough in the Löderup investigation. Eva Thulin had FaceTimed Anita to give her a heads up on the forensics report. She now had confirmation that the old couple *had* been beaten – Eva and her team had found blood spatters that were unrelated to the injuries inflicted by the gunshots and were consistent with a physical assault.

'Anything on the "visitor"?' Anita had asked.

'Sorry, not much. He'd definitely been in other parts of the house, including the basement area, but I'm afraid we don't have a match for you. It doesn't mean he hasn't got a criminal past, of course: it's just that the records may have been expunged by now.'

Anita was well aware of the law. Criminal records are deleted any time between three and twenty years after the offence, depending upon its severity.

'Now I'm in charge, I expect more helpful results, fru Thulin!'

'If you turn into Alice Zetterberg, you won't see me for dust, Chief Inspector Sundström!' she said with a grin. 'You can do your own forensics!'

So nothing much there from Thulin. But then there'd been a loud, excited knock on Anita's door, heralding the news she was hoping for.

'We think we might have got a name for the mystery man!' Hakim exclaimed.

'Great!'

'He's possibly a Klas Karlin.'

'Ah, the "Klas" mentioned by the cousin. How did you find him?'

'I got on to social services in Kalmar. The Skoogs fostered a child called Klas Karlin from 1985 to 1987. He'd be around thirteen when he went to live with them. That would make him around fifty now. That would fit with the age of the guy in the Harbour Hotel.'

'And if he'd kept in touch over the years, he'd know about Gudrun's illness, hence the visit.' Erlandsson had followed Hakim into the office.

'So, *if* the mystery man is the foster child,' Anita speculated, 'we have someone from the old couple's past staying with them during the week they were killed. I wonder why he left his suit – did he intend to return?'

'As I said before,' put in Erlandsson, 'he may have left in a hurry. Perhaps he had a row with the Skoogs, or something had gone wrong when he was living with them as a kid and he'd been planning revenge for some reason. If he'd spent some time in the house, he'd probably know where the guns were kept. He ends up killing them and has to get out as fast as he can.'

'That's a possibility,' Anita said cautiously. 'Of course, Klas the foster kid may have nothing to do with any of it. Before we jump to conclusions, we need to find him to establish whether he *was* the man staying at Löderup, or if there's another Klas floating about.'

'I've never told you about the Q Guard cash-depot robbery, have I?' Anita asked Kevin as he'd been about to pick up his glass of beer. He put it down again, as he knew he had to pay attention.

'No.'

She went on to fill him in on all the gory details of how the police had screwed up.

'We've all made mistakes.' Kevin's reassurance didn't ameliorate the bitter memories of that investigation. They were best forgotten, but now Willi Hirdwall – or Micky Mosten – was about to reopen old wounds.

'I spent many hours with Willi. I liked him. Christ, I trusted him. He never struck me as someone who could kill anybody. I think there's been some mix-up. Or did I just get it wrong?'

Again, the maggots of self-doubt that had been plaguing her since her promotion were working on her brain.

'You're a good judge of character, Anita. You've proved it over and over. You only have to look at me!' he grinned.

She allowed herself a smile, but she still had misgivings.

'I love you, Kevin.'

Kevin was startled.

'Where did that come from?'

'I don't know. I miss you.'

'Me, too. I mean I miss you, not me.'

Anita laughed. 'Thanks for listening.'

'Any time.'

'This Agent McBride is flying in tomorrow night. I've got to meet her at the Clarion at Kastrup for breakfast. You know I'm never at my best first thing in the morning.'

'Just think, it'll be on expenses, so you can stuff yourself.'

'You always see the positive side of things. Actually, if you remember, I've eaten there before, and the breakfasts *are* amazing. Look, I'll let you get back to whatever you were watching.'

'It's finished now,' he said a little sadly.

'Sorry.'

'Don't apologize. I love you and I'm always here for you.'

'I know.'

Anita took an early train across the Öresund Bridge and got off at the airport station. The Clarion Hotel was up an escalator and just before the Metro stop for trains into Copenhagen. It was a tall building of no great architectural merit on the outside, but internally, it was another matter. Through its doors, it provided travellers with the best in modern comfort and service. A palatial reception area of elegant yet simple Danish design opened into a high atrium piercing the centre of the accommodation floors. Off the reception was a plush, spacious dining area and bar. Last year, Anita had treated herself to a night there before an early morning flight to Manchester on her way to visit Kevin. It was a luxury she could ill afford, but it had been worth it. She'd been given a well-appointed room with great views over the Sound and the city, but the thing she remembered best was the stunning self-service breakfast spread. So, despite having to get out of bed earlier than she would have liked and making the monumental effort to look half decent, she was anticipating, with relish, her early-morning meal.

A statuesque woman with short-cropped, flaxen hair was waiting impatiently. She had a long face with a square jaw and wide mouth, and bright, piercing blue eyes. Anita couldn't decide whether she was attractive or not, but there was no disguising the fact that she was worth a second look and would attract admirers at the polishus. Anita knew from her profile, which had been sent from Chicago, that she was forty-three years old.

'Hi, I'm Anita Sundström,' Anita said, holding out a hand and smiling a welcome.

For a moment, she thought the woman wasn't going to return the gesture.

'Agent Paige McBride, Federal Bureau of Investigation,' she said rather formally as though someone like Anita wouldn't know what 'FBI' stood for. The handshake was perfunctory.

'Nice to meet you. Look, maybe we should have breakfast first.'

McBride almost sighed. 'Coffee will do me fine.'

Anita's heart sank: she could see her breakfast disappearing out of the window. No, stuff it; the woman would just have to wait.

After picking a table for two next to a group of four Swedish businessmen who appeared to be hung over, Anita went through to the serving area, which was groaning with everything from the ultra-healthy to the artery-clogging. Anita had her eye on the latter (she loved bacon and scrambled eggs: it reminded her of her time living in Britain) but decided she'd better go for more wholesome fare. For some reason, she found herself worrying about how McBride would judge her.

Once seated, Anita tucked into her bowl of museli and plate of crispbread, cheese and cold meats. The American glowered at her; there was no small talk. 'No sign of Micky Mosten?' McBride hadn't even touched her coffee.

'No one of that name has entered Sweden as far as we can tell. Not by plane or ferry. And there are regular border checks our side of the Öresund Bridge, but that doesn't mean he can't have slipped through.'

Again, the suppressed sigh. It gave Anita the distinct impression that McBride thought she was dealing with a bunch of hicks.

'Change of name?'

'The name Willi Hirdwall hasn't come up either.'

McBride did at last deign to have a sip of her drink.

'We understand that Micky was under witness protection. Can you tell me about that? We got his original name but we couldn't find out much else.'

'Willi Hirdwall wasn't a criminal. He was a security guard at a Q Guard cash facility in Malmö that was hit. In fact, he took a bullet. He became a key witness because he could identify one of the gang. It put his life in danger because the raid had been carried out by a Serbian criminal organization based out of Stockholm. We put three behind bars. Unfortunately, though we knew it was a guy called Branislav Bilić who was financing the robbery, we never could find enough evidence to pin it on him, and we never retrieved the money. Bilić is now presumed dead, having disappeared after an internal coup. His successor is an old acquaintance of mine. At the moment, he's sitting in a cell' – she waved her hand vaguely in the direction of the Bridge – 'just across the water.' She still broke out in a cold sweat whenever she remembered meeting Dragan Mitrović for the first time. Armed with several charmingly expressed threats, he'd been waiting for her in her apartment one evening. 'Anyway, Bilić attempted to have Willi – Micky Mosten to you – killed to shut him up before the trial. I was there when they tried. After the trial, because we couldn't bring Bilić in, it was too dangerous for Willi to stay on in Sweden. We handed him a new identity and a new life in America.'

'Well, for a non-criminal, he must have changed his spots.'

'Doesn't sound like the Willi that I got to know.'

'I don't know about the Willi that you got to know,' McBride said scathingly, 'but this is the guy who acted as a bagman to a would-be godfather and ended up blowing away the would-be godfather's son-in-law.'

Anita just couldn't reconcile what she'd read in the file that had been sent over from Chicago with the man who'd spent Christmas with her all those years ago.

'Bagman?'

McBride looked at her as though she'd said something monumentally stupid.

'Someone who collects or distributes illicit money for gangs or organized crime.'

'Ah. I was seconded to the Metropolitan Police in London for a short time. A bagman over there is an assistant to a detective.'

'Whatever. Your buddy Micky got in with some serious players in Chicago. Giuseppe Gentile…' McBride realized that the Swedish businessmen on the next table had ceased talking and were listening to their conversation. She stopped and gave them a stare that would have melted a glacier, and had them scurrying from the dining room. Anita was impressed. 'Gentile is old school and there is nothing gentle about him. How Micky got mixed up with him, I have no idea. I think he befriended Matteo Nesta.'

'Who's he?'

'Who *was* he? Gentile's son-in-law – the sap that Micky put a bullet into.' This didn't square at all with Anita's view of Willi Hirdwall. But, despite Kevin's reassurances, she'd been wrong about a number of people before.

'How did it happen? We haven't really got the details other than that you're after him and you think he might have come back to Sweden.'

'Oh, we believe there's a high probability that he's hiding out here. He's skilled at blending in with his own folk. Lived in Andersonville. It's a part of Chicago that's full of Swedish stock. Got the word from the community that he was likely to head to Scandinavia. It fitted in with him being spotted at Copenhagen Central Station on June fifteen. We got that from Interpol.'

It was on the train back over the Öresund Bridge that McBride filled Anita in on the events that had led the American officer to fly across the Atlantic to hunt down her quarry. And that was exactly how she viewed her assignment.

'As I said before, Micky… OK, let's call him Willi from now on as you'll end up getting confused…'

Anita bridled at her patronizing tone.

'…Willi was a bagman for Giuseppe Gentile. Gentile was into the usual rackets – prostitution, cigarette smuggling, extortion and dabbling in narcotics – as well as a number of legit businesses so that he could keep a veneer of commercial respectability and wash some money while he was at it. Willi used to waltz along with some heavies and collect the "debts", pick up the pimps' earnings, deal with pushers and hand over the cash for smaller drugs supplies or be on hand to shove a bribe in the direction of corrupt politicians – and cops. Anything like that and Willi was your smooth-talking, go-to guy. We knew about Gentile's activities and Willi's role but we were waiting for something big to come along before pouncing.'

The train was now thundering over the Bridge and for a moment, McBride's attention was caught by the outline of the Turning Torso in the distance.

'We got an anonymous tip-off that there was to be a big drugs exchange,' she continued. 'Columbian cocaine. Turns out it'd come in stashed in auto body parts. Street value, several million dollars. Gentile was going to lay out big bucks by his standards. He tended to deal in narcotics small-time, so the size of this particular shipment wasn't really his normal thing: he'd always been careful and made sure he didn't muscle in on other territories and upset the status quo. Our best guess is it was Matteo's brainchild. The douchebag getting ideas above his station, if you know what I mean. Anyways, the meet took place at an old factory unit, and we were waiting. We had a big team there, but maybe someone or something spooked Willi cos he split the moment we swooped. Matteo got away, too. Except *he* didn't get very far – I found him with two bullets in his back. We cleaned up on the merchandise so the narcs were happy, and we mopped up a whole bunch of nasty people, but no sign of Willi – or Gentile's money. Without the cash, we couldn't trace it back to Gentile and put him behind bars.'

'So, you reckon Willi shot Matteo?'

'Who else? It wasn't any of our guys. The bullets didn't come from any police weapons. They came from the gun we found where Willi must have dropped it while carrying away five million smackers. His prints were on it. Open and shut. That's why my mission is to track him down, arrest him and oversee his extradition back to the States, where he'll face justice.'

Anita was finding it hard to fathom. How had Willi Hirdwall changed so much?

'No wonder you're looking for him.'

McBride slid her a mirthless grin. 'I doubt we're the only ones: Gentile wants his money and reputation back.'

CHAPTER 29

At ten o'clock that morning, Anita assembled the team so that they could meet Agent McBride – and she meet them. Anita had quickly briefed them about the Q Guard robbery and Willi Hirdwall's role within it. She wasn't entirely sure how the arrangement with McBride would work. Would it be a joint effort, or would the American do her own thing, asking for help only when it was needed? Anita hoped for the latter. She hadn't warmed to the FBI agent, and it soon became clear that her fellow detectives didn't take to her either (with the possible exception of a starstruck Brodd, who seemed to think Scarlett Johansson had joined the team). After the initial introductions, McBride, in slow English, took them through the events of the Chicago narcotics raid and the subsequent murder of Matteo Nesta. She imparted the information like a school teacher trying to explain a complicated subject to a group of not-very-bright children.

'We know that Micky Mosten was known to you as Willi Hirdwall and was given witness protection to start a new life in the US. He started his new existence in Minneapolis, where he had a number of jobs, before moving to Chicago. There, he fell in with Giuseppe Gentile's organization. He became a bagman – that is someone who collects or distributes illicit money for gangs or organized crime.' McBride gave Anita a condescending smile. 'Nothing to do with assistants to British detectives.'

McBride produced a blown-up photograph of a man in a

crowd. He was wearing a newsboy cap and glasses.

'Micky Mosten. AKA Willi Hirdwall.'

'Are you sure it's him?' Anita was doubtful.

'He was on an Interpol watchlist. Identified through facial recognition software. It took them a while to work through the system. It's definitely him.'

Anita had to acquiesce. He would have aged in the last fifteen years – he'd be in his fifties now.

'This was captured at Copenhagen Central Station on June fifteen. This is our first link to him since he took a flight from New York to Berlin using his Mikael Mosten passport. That was January seven. Then a total blank. Not a sighting for months until this one. Where was he between Berlin and Copenhagen? And where has he been over the last month? He can't have flown anywhere unless he managed to get a new passport, which is, of course, possible – he can sure afford one on the money he took off with. Anyway, we believe that he was heading for Sweden – his native country after all – easier for him to blend in, and he's got the money to lose himself. Big country, small population. Probably why so many 'Nam draft-dodgers and deserters ended up here. Of course, he'll know we'll be after him and he'll keep a low profile wherever he is.'

'What's he like?' asked Hakim, who wasn't around at the time of the Q Guard robbery.

'Despite what your chief inspector might believe, Micky… Willi is a dangerous man. He got himself mixed up with organized crime, which is why the FBI are acquainted with him. He's a liar and a thief and a drug dealer and, as we now know, a murderer. Make no mistake, he's ruthless: he had to be as a bagman for a mobster. He's also affable, charming and sociable – qualities which helped him worm his way into the Gentile clan.'

'The way you're describing him, it sounds like you know

him personally,' remarked Anita, who was pissed off with McBride's condescending attitude.

'Never met him, but he was under surveillance for a number of weeks before the bust. We monitored his activities along with those of other members of the Gentile organization. And over the last six months, I've had plenty of time to study him further. 'Course, we've also done a psychological profile on him, so we know how his mind works. That's why we think he's here, blending into a familiar background, just like he did in the Swedish communities in Minneapolis and Chicago.'

'But the Gentiles are Italian,' Wallen said pointedly.

'Sure, but that was work. His home life was in predominately Swedish neighbourhoods. That's where he felt safe.'

'But he had to leave Sweden because he wasn't safe: his life was in danger. So why would he come back?' Anita remonstrated.

'Times change. The threats to his life may have gone, and people won't know him now. When was it he left Sweden?'

'2007.'

'Fifteen years,' she said emphatically, as though that proved her argument. 'I'm sure he's back.' Her glare said that the matter wasn't up for debate. 'And I'm here to find him. I'll call on your local knowledge if and when it's needed. Any questions?'

'The FBI have a very good reputation for achieving success,' said Erlandsson. 'I was just wondering how such a well-planned operation as your drugs bust could let two people slip so easily through the net.'

Anita could see McBride bridle – nice one, Bea!

'It shouldn't have happened, but even the best-laid plans don't always work in the moment. You might find that out if you ever get the chance to deal with the higher echelons of crime.'

An awkward silence followed.

'Pontus, would you take Agent McBride up to the commissioner's office?' Anita chose Brodd, as he seemed to be the only member of the team not to be riled by the agent's abrasive approach. Turning to McBride, 'Commissioner Falk would like to meet you and discuss how we can help your investigation.'

'I'd like a private office to work in,' McBride said. It came out more like a demand than a request.

'You can use Dan Olovsson's. He's on holiday at the moment.'

'Ah, the famous Swedish holidays. How long is this guy away for?'

'Nearly four weeks.'

'Jesus.'

'Hopefully, you'll get your man before Dan gets back,' said Anita.

Brodd escorted McBride to the door.

'Who the hell does this patronizing bitch think she is?' Wallen muttered in Swedish as McBride was leaving.

'Pardon?' said McBride sharply.

'I'm just saying what an interesting case it is,' Wallen replied sweetly.

It was later that afternoon when Theo Falk rang down.

'How's Agent McBride settling in?'

'She's closeted in Dan Olovsson's office. Busy making phone calls as far as we can see. She's also asked for the Q Guard robbery files for some reason. I don't know what she hopes to learn from those.'

'Good. Keep her happy.'

'Not at the expense of my team. They're already collecting money for her leaving card.'

'Oh, I can understand that.' She'd obviously got on the wrong side of Falk, too. 'But, Anita, as well as giving her our full co-operation, I also want you to keep an eye on her. I don't want her getting all trigger-happy and causing mayhem when she finds Hirdwall. This is not America.'

'Yet.'

'Look, can someone take her to her hotel tonight?'

'Where's she staying?'

'The Clarion at Malmö Live.'

'The FBI don't stint on accommodation.'

'They've got better budgets,' he said ruefully. 'Anyhow, get her there safely. And, Anita, please don't make waves.'

Just as she was putting the phone down, Brodd rushed into her office.

'Ah, the very man I wanted to see. Pontus, can you take our American guest to the Clarion when she finishes work?'

'Yes, yes,' he said distractedly. 'But, listen, I've found the car!'

'The red Golf?'

'Yeah. The only problem is that it doesn't fit our timelines, so it may be irrelevant to the investigation. It was crossing the Bridge on Friday, the eighth at 17.04.'

'So it was leaving the country before the murders.'

'No. It was coming the other way – into Sweden. The trouble is, the information I got from the garage in Löderup put the car passing through the village a few times earlier in the week. But I can't find any sign of it going back over to Copenhagen before its return on that Friday.'

'Are we talking about two different cars?'

'No. The one on the Bridge had a large dent on the driver's-side door. It's very noticeable: you can even see it on the CCTV. Two cars of the same age and colour are unlikely to have the same damage. Besides, once I got the registration, I rang the garage and it prompted the guy's memory. He reckoned it was the same one he saw that week and in June.'

'It's odd. But we don't have a sighting of the car in the Löderup area on the day of the murder, so it's unlikely to be connected. A dead end, I think. Never mind. Still, good work, Pontus.'

'Thanks, Boss. Oh, by the way, I'll add the name of the owner to the file. It's a Kasper Jensen.'

CHAPTER 30

For the second time that week, Anita was stunned. She was still astonished when follow-up enquiries the next day revealed that it was the same Kasper Jensen who had been the security guard involved in the Q Guard robbery back in December, 2006. Now forty-five, single (so his marriage hadn't survived prison), living in the same area of Copenhagen and working as a shelf stacker in a supermarket, it was extraordinary that his name should come up in their investigation just when his fellow security guard, Willi Hirdwall, was being hunted for murder.

She called Klara Wallen into her office.

'Kasper Jensen. Another blast from the past!' Wallen, too, was incredulous.

'An inglorious past.'

'And at the same time our loveable American friend is after Willi Hirdwall.'

'Yes. A bizarre coincidence or what? I honestly can't see any possible connection to the Skoogs or Löderup, but we have to eliminate Jensen from our enquiries. Could you check him out? Pontus has his address. We know he was in Sweden on the day of the murders. In fact, he was crossing the Bridge about an hour before the Skoogs were killed.'

'That would give him just enough time to get to Löderup and do the deed.'

'I know. That's why he might need an alibi.'

Wallen pulled a face. 'He's not going to take kindly to

seeing us again after what happened last time.'

'Take Pontus with you as back up. *You* know Jensen, and *he* found the car.'

'OK.'

'I bet that now she's got a high-profile murder on her hands, I'll be sidelined.' Klara Wallen was behind the wheel of the car as she and Pontus Brodd made their way over the Öresund Bridge.

'She's sending us to check out this Kasper Jensen, isn't she?'

'Exactly. Because he's unlikely to be involved. "We have to eliminate him from our enquiries,"' she said in a mock-Anita voice.

Klara Wallen had grown closer to Pontus Brodd in recent months. She was still resentful of Anita's promotion and she couldn't moan to Hakim, Erlandsson or Liv Fogelström, as they were clearly in the Sundström camp. Dan Olovsson was diplomatically silent on the subject. At least she could bend Brodd's ear.

'Queen bloody bee. All lovey-dovey with the commissioner. And now she'll be prancing around with that American cow.'

'I don't know. She's all right. Quite hot, actually. McBride, I mean.'

'Really?' Wallen said in some disbelief.

'Yeah. I took her to her hotel last night. She asked me in for a quick drink. Quizzed me about Anita and the rest of us.'

'Why?'

'Don't know. She just seemed interested. I talked the team up.'

'Talked yourself up, more like. I think she made it plain what she thinks of us at that meeting yesterday. The sooner she catches Hirdwall, the sooner she'll be gone.'

'You know this Hirdwall character?'

'Yeah. The Q Guard robbery was my very first case after my transfer to Malmö. In my first week, actually.'

'I gather Anita doesn't think Hirdwall is the killer type.'

'That's one thing I can agree with her on. He didn't strike me as the sort of person McBride was describing. He was just in the wrong place at the wrong time. The poor guy was frightened for his life. According to McBride, he seems to have had a total change of character. Unless we all got him wrong.'

They pulled off the dual carriageway and entered the urban outskirts of Copenhagen.

'What was Kasper Jensen like?'

'Family man who got himself into debt, which made him easy for the gang to manipulate. Well, that's what his defence counsel argued at his trial. He thought the money would transform his life. It did, but not in the way he'd imagined. He cracked under questioning easily enough because he was so shocked by the death of his colleague that night. Guilt got to him.'

'Criminal with a conscience?'

'Yeah. But don't expect a warm welcome when we see him.'

They were now progressing up Kastrupvej. Bredegrund was a street immediately off the main road. It encircled a five-storey block of red-brick, balconied apartments. At one end, it overlooked Jensen's old home. Wallen drove round the building. Propped up against the wall close to the entrances were numerous bicycles. Across the way, the residents' cars were parked on a strip of rough ground. And there was a red VW Golf. They parked close to it, and Brodd got out and inspected the car. He checked the number plate and ran his hand across the telltale dent.

'This is definitely it. Jensen's car.'

'He should be at home, then.'

When Wallen pressed the buzzer next to Jensen's name,

there was no answer. She tried again.

'He's obviously not in,' said Brodd. 'Shall we wait?'

Wallen didn't answer as she pressed the next buzzer along. A deep male voice eventually answered. 'Yes?'

'Hello. This is Inspector Klara Wallen of the Skåne County Police. We're trying to locate your next door neighbour, Kasper Jensen.'

'Kasper's not here at the moment.'

'Do you know where he is?'

'Enjoying the sun.'

'Where?'

'Majorca.'

'Majorca?'

'Him and his girlfriend. Last minute thing.' The man chortled. 'Typical Kasper. Soon as he gets money, he spends it!'

'Do you know how long he'll be away?'

'A fortnight. I'm looking after the Crown Princess while he's away.'

'The Crown Princess?'

'His cat.'

Wallen tried to sound patient. 'So when is he due back?'

'Flew out at the weekend. You do the maths.'

'Right. I want you to phone me as soon as he returns.'

'Really?'

'Yes, really. I want you to call the Skåne County Police in Malmö. And ask for Inspector—

'Klara Wallen. I remember.'

'You'll do that?'

'All right, then.'

'Thank you.'

Wallen turned to Brodd. 'Well, that was a waste of time.'

CHAPTER 31

'Well?' Anita enquired.

Hakim smiled. 'Found something out, Boss.'

'Don't you dare call me that!'

'Sorry. Just winding you up.'

'This had better be good. Klara and Pontus haven't been able to find Kasper Jensen. He's on holiday in Majorca.'

'So, we can't rule him out yet?'

'No,' she said as she pushed her chair away from the desk. 'Apparently, the holiday was last minute. Suddenly, he has some spending money, according to his neighbour. Sounds like history repeating itself.'

'What history?'

'Oh, nothing. Look, are we sure that no money was taken from the Skoog place?'

'As sure as we can be. But I've come across something very weird. I've been checking out the couple's bank account. They banked with Nordea in Ystad. The day before he died, August deposited four thousand euros.'

'You mean the krona equivalent of four thousand euros.'

'No. I literally mean four thousand euros.'

'That *is* strange. Where would he have got that from? Have they been abroad recently?'

'Not that we're aware of. The bank thought it was slightly odd but didn't question it, as August was a long-time customer. Besides, he liked to deal in cash. People often paid him in cash for the wooden objects he sold.'

This was a conundrum.

'Could he have made something large enough or valuable enough for someone to pay him the equivalent of...' – she made a quick mental calculation – 'over forty thousand kronor? And is it significant that he goes to the bank the day before his death? Was it the four thousand euros that the perp was after?'

'It's not a life-changing sum,' said Hakim. 'I don't think you'd commit a brutal double killing and carefully stage a suicide for forty thousand kronor. The more I think about it, the more it strikes me that whoever did it had a much greater motive and knew exactly what they were doing.'

'As in a professional hit?'

'Not exactly. But someone who knew about guns and could cover their tracks.'

'Which makes me think that it's a revenge killing. Either the perpetrator's own revenge or on behalf of someone else.' Anita was thoughtful for a few seconds. 'Maybe there's more to the Skoogs than we know.'

'Possibly. But there's nothing obvious. We're still looking into August's business interests, and the other thing is the fostering. According to the little that social services would reveal, Klas Karlin was a bit wild as a kid. "Difficult" was the word they used. Got into trouble. They didn't say exactly what kind and they've no record after he left the fostering system. And if there was anything involving the police, it wouldn't be on record now as it was over twenty years ago and the official slate would have been wiped clean. And we haven't found anything since. Anyway, that's why the Skoogs took him in. Gudrun Skoog in particular was able to handle kids with behavioural problems. They never fazed her, and she gave them the sort of love and security that was missing from their lives. His time with the Skoogs seems to have been one of the calmest periods of Karlin's young life.'

Anita blew out a breath. 'Gudrun sounds like a saint. Not

the sort of person someone would want to take revenge on. Maybe August was the problem.'

'Firm but fair seems to be the assessment of him. At least that's how he was at home with the foster children. I've no idea about his business but I'll keep digging.'

'Any sign of Klas Karlin?'

'No. We're trying to trace him, but no joy yet. We can't find anything official. Car ownership, tax etcetera. Which may point to him living abroad since his Kalmar days.'

Hakim made his way to the door.

'Oh, Hakim, how is Bea getting on with her serial-killer angle?'

'I know she's been talking to Gothenburg and she's been trying to get hold of the relevant detectives in Västervik.'

'I hope she draws a blank,' Anita said with feeling.

The next day, late afternoon on the Friday, the team had a catch up on the Löderup case. There was nothing they could do about Jensen's red Golf. The general feeling was that it was a distraction – he *had* had time to commit the murder and he appeared to have been in the Löderup area immediately before the killings because of the sighting of his car on the Bridge, but they couldn't establish any link with the Skoogs. Jensen's photo had been sent through to Joel Grahn to see if anyone in the village had seen him, but Grahn had come up with a blank, which made the team think that Jensen must have been travelling to and from somewhere in the vicinity, not visiting anyone in the actual village. Maybe it was his girlfriend.

Next, Bea Erlandsson dismissed the serial-killer theory, much to Anita's relief.

'The methods employed in the two cases of supposed murder-suicides differ too much. Like ours, in the Gothenburg case, the physical violence was totally out of character. The husband beat his wife using a rolling pin and then throttled himself with a metal coat hanger. Not easy to do. It was the discovery of trauma in our case that made me think there might be a connection. At Västervik, a gun was used – husband shot his wife before turning it on himself. No signs of violence prior to the shootings – just acceptance. Our killings had a bit of both, but I can't see any pattern.'

'Thanks, Bea. That's another avenue closed. What about herr Suit?'

'We can't locate Klas Karlin,' said Hakim with annoyance. 'The fact that he seems to have disappeared might mean that he does have something to do with it. He knew the Skoogs – he'd been fostered by them in Kalmar. There might have been something in their shared history that finally pushed him over the edge.'

'A long time to wait. But carry on, Hakim. How do you envisage the scenario,' Anita asked, 'bearing in mind that the Skoogs must have welcomed herr Suit into their home? After all, he slept there and left an expensive item of clothing in the house.'

'True. He turns up at their door; we don't know if they were expecting him or not. They might have invited him to stay for old times' sake.'

'Maybe he heard that Gudrun was dying?' suggested Wallen.

'Possibly. Or was there another reason? Perhaps he had his own agenda. He wants something they have – or something they know. A contentious issue... led to an argument... led to physical violence. Whatever it was, it all gets out of hand. He's stayed in the house before, so he'd probably know about the gun cabinet. It's in the workshop next to the sauna. Easy enough for him to get a gun and threaten them. Perhaps he got the information he wanted then had to kill them to keep them quiet. OK, it's only speculation.' Hakim shrugged. 'What we also don't know is how he actually got to the Skoogs' house, or to Ystad for his lunch at the Harbour Hotel. There's an hourly bus from Ystad to Simrishamn that passes through the village, and we're talking to drivers to see if they recognize the description of the man at the Harbour – or at least his suit. If it was by car, we haven't identified any vehicle yet, and the heavy rain would have washed away any tyre tracks in the dirt outside the house.'

'Then there's the four thousand euros,' Anita remarked.

'Exactly. Can't explain that.'

'Well, whoever owns the suit, Karlin is the only name we've got to go on at the moment.' Anita could feel the frustration in the room. 'We do believe that whoever is behind this knew about guns and was either experienced or clever enough to set it up to look like suicide. If our mystery man turns out to be Karlin, what sort of motive would he have? Let's stick with the revenge theory for a moment – something hidden in the past. I think it might be an idea if you went to Kalmar next week. We've got to find this guy.'

'Well, it doesn't look like he lives in Sweden,' said Hakim. 'He doesn't pay tax or own a car here. He could live in France, of course – remember the cigarettes.'

'Wherever he is, the boy must have done good,' observed Brodd. 'That suit.'

'Could Kasper Jensen be Klas Karlin?' asked Erlandsson.

'No,' said Wallen. 'We did a background search on Jensen back in 2006. Besides, their ages don't match.'

'We'll give Kalmar a try and if no luck there, we'll have to spread the net wider. Perhaps get on to the *Préfecture de Police* in Paris,' said Anita. 'OK, anything else?'

'The Skoogs' phone records,' chirped up Erlandsson. 'I've been through their home phone, and also a Doro mobile that was on the couple's bedside table. Nothing unusual. As you'd expect, lots of calls to and from the doctor's surgery and the hospital. A number of local calls, including several from

August's cousin Britha Skoog. There were a couple of recent ones from Kalmar. These were from the Beijers.'

'The neighbours?'

'That's right.'

'So nothing from herr Suit?'

'Doesn't look like it.'

'So he could have just turned up out of the blue. He might not have known about Gudrun's illness at all.' Everybody went quiet. 'OK, let's call it a day. We'll gather first thing on Monday. Who's on over the weekend?'

'I am,' said Erlandsson.

'All right, Bea. If any information about Karlin comes in, get straight on to me.'

'Will do.'

'Right. Have a good weekend, everyone.'

An hour later, Anita gathered up her things. She hadn't any specific plans for the weekend – she'd probably spend some time with Leyla, and there was her usual Sunday morning chat with Kevin. She felt tense and on edge and she knew she wouldn't be able to unwind. The case had stalled almost from the outset. If only they'd been called in right at the beginning, they might have had a better chance. All they were doing was playing catch-up. As she walked down the corridor, she noticed Agent McBride still working in Dan Olovsson's office. She thought she'd better pop in and ask if she was making any progress. Falk's words about keeping an eye on her came to mind. Anita knew that since her arrival, McBride had hardly left the office except for spending a few hours away the previous afternoon. Brodd was Anita's unwitting informant – he saw himself as the agent's unofficial chaperone.

Anita knocked on the door and entered.

'Just making sure everything's OK.'

'All's fine.'

'Do you require any help from us at the moment?'

'Nope.'

Anita hovered awkwardly. Then she blurted out: 'Do you want to go for a drink?' It was an invitation she immediately regretted the second it left her mouth.

'No. I've still got work to do.' Thank heavens for that!

'Right, I'll leave you to it.'

'Oh, just one thing. Your Willi Hirdwall.' The *your* sounded accusatory.

'What about him?'

'I've been going over the Q Guard robbery file. It was a big job, certainly for here.'

Of course, they always do things bigger and better in America, thought Anita snidely. 'Yes. About thirteen million dollars in *your* money. And there were real dollars in the mix.'

'Was any of the money recovered?'

'No.'

'Isn't that strange that nothing's ever turned up?'

'Not where organized crime is concerned. I'm sure Branislav Bilić recycled it somewhere.'

'Possibly. Is Bilić's organization still active?'

'Probably. As I told you when we first met, Bilić was deposed and disappeared a few years ago, and his number two, Dragan Mitrović, took over. It's believed he was responsible for his boss's vanishing act.'

'Yeah, I remember. And this Mitrović is now banged up.'

'Yes, here in Malmö. But I'm sure that doesn't stop him running his operations.'

'I've heard the Swedish prison system is soft.'

Anita had to agree, but she wasn't going to let another slight past.

'Are you telling me that your gang bosses don't still control their empires from their prison cells?'

McBride ignored the question. 'Don't you think it's odd that Willi Hirdwall was involved in an organized crime robbery in Sweden, and then in the States, with the new life that *you* gave him, he hooks up with a similar outfit?'

This was a ridiculous comparison. 'Hirdwall was only involved with the Serbian gangsters over here as an innocent bystander.'

'Are you sure?'

'He was shot, for God's sake! And Bilić tried to have him killed to shut him up. Look, I don't know what happened in America to make him do the things you say he's done, but here, he was just a man trying to do his job.'

'I can't believe he had no criminal record of any kind. He was fostered, yet no juvenile misdemeanours.'

'Firstly, criminal records have a time limitation on them in Sweden. If Hirdwall had one, it would have been expunged by now—'

'You've got to be kidding!' McBride's incredulity at the Swedish judicial system was increasing by the minute.

'And secondly, are you trying to say all foster children do bad things?'

Again, McBride ignored Anita's question. 'I've been through the file in detail. It doesn't sit right. Why was Milan Subotić bumped off, for example? There seems to be a lot of incompetence, or maybe complacency. And how could you lose Sven-Olof Alm?'

'Subotić was one of Bilić's men – anything could have gone wrong there. And do you never have murders in *your* jails?' said Anita aggressively. She wasn't going to be lectured to by this damn outsider. 'Why are you fixating on something that happened sixteen years ago? Shouldn't you be concentrating on the present and finding the killer you let escape instead of raking up an old investigation that has no bearing whatsoever on the here and now?'

With that, Anita turned, wrenched the door open and, just in time, stopped herself from slamming it behind her.

CHAPTER 32

That bloody woman! She had not only got under Anita's skin, she'd also got her thinking. She'd spent the last fifteen years trying to forget about the Q Guard fiasco; her only consolation had been that she'd helped an innocent man start a new life. Now McBride was sowing seeds of doubt. How could Mr Nice Guy Willi Hirdwall have turned into some kind of gangland hoodlum? It just didn't seem possible. But of course, Anita had no idea about his life in America and what could have caused him to change so dramatically. The conundrum plagued her all night. She tossed and turned and pummelled her pillow; eventually, she put the light on and went into the living room to read. But little registered – Willi's face kept staring out at her from the pages. She went back to bed and turned the digital clock to the wall so she couldn't keep tabs on how long she'd been awake. After what seemed like hours of wriggling and squirming and waging war on the duvet, she dropped into an uneasy unconsciousness.

Anita awoke feeling tired. At some stage during the night, she'd decided to speak to her journalistic contact (the only one she trusted) Martin Glimhall, the leading crime reporter on the *Skånska Nyheter*. She knew Glimhall well. He'd helped her out on numerous occasions, most memorably when she was tracing the background to the *Estonia* ferry disaster; they'd also worked closely together at the time of the murderous intrigues surrounding the Liberty Conference last year. She knew he'd written a book about the Q Guard robbery – *Caught off Guard* – which had come out a few years after the event. She'd allowed him to interview her about the crime, but she couldn't bring herself to read the finished account; that would have been far too painful. After a much-needed cup of strong coffee, she phoned him and they arranged to meet for an early-Saturday-evening drink at The Pickwick. Glimhall was always more loquacious with alcohol in him.

Anita hadn't seen Glimhall in a while – she'd been busy getting her feet under the table in her new role as chief inspector and he'd been sensitive to the shift in their relationship. The evening was warm and they sat at one of the bench tables outside the pub. Other customers had had the same idea, and they were surrounded by happy people enjoying their weekend.

'So, how's the new job?' Glimhall asked after his first long draft of beer. He looked smarter than she'd ever seen him before, with a well-ironed shirt and a new blue linen jacket. Perhaps the influence of his latest girlfriend. He'd shaved, too, and his thinning, blond/grey hair had been neatly coiffured. He still had the jowly features, of course, which gave him a rather baleful look, and there was no disguising his tall frame, which was hunched over the table, but the new image suited him.

'It's all right.'

'Only *all right*?' There was a mischievous sparkle in his eye. 'Must be better without Zetterberg, surely.'

'Of course it is. But there's too much admin and not enough investigating.'

'That's the trouble with authority. That's why I could never stomach being an editor. I like to be out there, sniffing around. So, what can I do for you, Anita? Can I smell a story?'

Anita retreated into her glass before answering.

'Not at the moment.' Their conclusions on the Skoog murders had not been made public, and it was still believed by the press to be a suicide pact. 'It's not something that's happening now. Your book about the Q Guard robbery...'

He gave her a broad smile. 'So you read it?'

'Of course I bloody didn't! I'm not going to read about myself ballsing up a major investigation.'

'It wasn't just you.'

'I played my part, though, didn't I? You were pretty hard on us from what I hear.'

'With good reason. But I was kind to you, Anita. You were a mere sprat – you'd only been with Moberg a year. He was the big fish who got it in the neck – and the force as a whole.'

'We probably deserved it.'

'So, what's your interest now? It's ancient history.'

'It was.'

'Oh yeah?' She'd stimulated his journalistic antennae.

'Something has emerged.'

'New evidence?' He was now so intrigued that he stopped drinking.

'Not exactly. What conclusion did you come to about the robbery?'

'In what way?'

'Do you think the way it panned out in court made sense?'

Glimhall picked up his glass but didn't lift it to his mouth.

'Pretty much. I highlighted the obvious failings, and there were some unanswered questions – some of the pieces just didn't sit well.'

'Like?'

'Milan Subotić's killing. Who was behind that?'

'Branislav Bilić.'

'Was it? I put forward various theories, but none was incontrovertible. But at the end of the day, I couldn't escape the fact that the bullet that killed him was from the Zastava pistol he'd used in the robbery, which brought it back to the Serbs. I did try and approach Bilić, but I didn't get an audience. I spoke to Dragan Mitrović, though. One pretty scary guy.'

'Yeah, we've met a few times.'

'Well, you can imagine he didn't give anything away. I knew he was Subotić's cousin and I got the impression he was upset by the killing. Maybe it *was* Bilić behind it, and that might have ultimately triggered Mitrović's coup.'

'Then Bilić just disappeared.'

'Yes. Not even a body to explain that one away. Then there was all that money. I can't believe none of it ever turned up, except for the few kronor pinched by Sven-Olof Alm, of course.'

'Yes. His stupidity gave us the in.'

'You spotted that, you see. I gave you credit for that one.'

'Too kind.'

'I can imagine them salting the money away, but it should have emerged eventually, even in dribs and drabs. I mean, you can't use our kronor anywhere except here in Sweden.'

'Could have been changed into other currencies.'

'Even so, with that amount, some would eventually find its way back here. Foreign banks – even Serbian ones – wouldn't want a hundred and thirty-five million kronor blocking up their vaults.'

Glimhall drained the last of his beer and stood up. 'Another?'

'Just a half.'

'Oh, Anita, you disappoint me.'

'OK. All right then.'

'When I get back, you can tell me what's started all this. I'm sure you're not here merely for the pleasure of my company.'

While he was gone, Anita thought hard. She had to decide how much information to impart. Glimhall was a good sounding board and they had had mutually beneficial relationships before.

'Off the record?' Glimhall was doing a balancing act any circus would have been proud of: Anita's drink, a whisky for himself and an accompanying beer chaser, and a couple of packets of peanuts were deftly deposited on the table as he slid onto the bench opposite her. His new woman obviously hadn't curbed his alcohol intake. He gave her a knowing grin.

'Definitely off the record, Martin. In time, it might produce a juicy story. Unfortunately.'

'Why unfortunately?'

'Well… the name Willi Hirdwall cropped up recently.'

'The security guard who was shot.'

'That's the one.'

'In what way has he "cropped up"? I could never find out what happened to him. The police were very tight-lipped, you included. Tried to trace him but no joy.'

'I can't really say. It's just that's he's been involved in something. Abroad.'

'Something illegal?'

'Yes. It's just that I spent a lot of time with him before the main trial, and he really didn't come across as… oh, I don't know, that type. I've met a lot of criminals in my time and he never—'

'Are you asking me if I think he might actually have been involved in the robbery?'

'I suppose I am.'

'It did cross my mind. But I didn't give it any credence. He *was* shot after all, and Kasper Jensen was found to be the inside man.'

'Glad to hear you dismissed it.'

'You'd have known that if you'd been arsed to read my book,' he said with a chuckle before downing his whisky in one. 'Of course, if it's still playing on your mind, there is one person you can ask.'

'Who?'

'Your friend Dragan Mitrović. There's a man who knows where the bodies are buried – literally. And he was there when the robbery was planned. You might have more luck than I did, especially as he's behind bars. Use your feminine charms.'

'I'm a bit long in the tooth for that.' She half smiled. She'd visited Mitrović in prison once before; if she turned up again, he'd think she was stalking him! But it was worth a try.

'This had better be good, Reza. I should be spending Sunday with my family.' Hakim had only agreed to meet his old school friend because Reza sometimes came up with useful information. After leaving school, their lives had taken very divergent paths – Hakim's into the law, Reza's into the outer fringes of it. Hakim still didn't really know how he made a living beyond the confines of his second-hand store, where nothing ever seemed to be sold to non-existent customers. The same junk was sitting comfortably in the same places every time he visited. Yet Reza was always smartly turned out, and his cars, changed almost more regularly than little Linus's nappies, were always flashy and expensive. Hakim had learned not to ask too many questions. It suited them both.

'Tell me about that lovely family of yours. How is Liv?'

'She's good, thanks.'

'I do envy you. It's hard work living up to my cool-dude, bachelor image. Sometimes, I think it would be nice to go home to a good woman and snuggle up in front of the television with a camomile tea.'

'Is that how you see my life?'

'Of course! And you've got a kid now. I must come and meet it sometime.'

'It's a *he*. Linus.'

'Good Iraqi name. Your dad must love that!'

'Very funny. His second name is Uday. Keeps Dad quiet.'

Hakim gazed round the shop at the now-familiar paraphernalia cluttering the place: racks of musty clothes, dodgy electrical equipment, aging furniture which wasn't stylish enough to pass off as retro, cracked ceramics, unloved LPs, poorly painted pictures in battered frames, and a plethora of unidentified objects lying around ('unidentified lying objects' – Hakim smiled at his own pun). No wonder the shop was always empty. There was no way it could compete with the efficient second-hand chains, but he supposed that was the point. Reza didn't want the inconvenience of customers. This was a front for whatever activities he really made his money from. And as his name had never surfaced in any police enquiries, Hakim had long ago stopped speculating about his friend's sources of income.

'Coffee?' Reza offered. Hakim declined – he'd sampled Reza's coffee before.

'Look, Reza, as I said, this is my day off. Why am I here?'

'What's wrong with wanting to see my old friend Hakim, who just happens to be in the police? And if during a casual chat with that old friend, I just happen to pass on a bit of street gossip, what's the harm in that?'

'OK, what's this gossip?'

'Well, this is only hearsay, mind you, but according to the grapevine, someone was trying – and I believe successfully managed – to acquire an illegal shooter.'

'What kind of shooter? Rifle? Handgun?'

'Handgun.'

'Is that so uncommon?' Hakim knew all about the availability of guns in Sweden. August Skoog's collection was a case in point.

'Not in itself, but the person who was trying to acquire one was an American.'

'An American?'

'The word is that he works for a criminal organization over there. Don't ask me what. Put it this way: no one was going to stand in this guy's way, not with his connections.'

'Wonder what he's doing over here?' Hakim didn't like the sound of this. 'What type of handgun?'

'Don't know. That's not my thing.' Hakim knew Reza only went so far.

'And when did this "successful transaction" take place?'

'A week or so ago. I'd have told you sooner but I've only just heard.'

After catching up with more mundane news, a thoughtful Hakim left the shop. An armed American gangster loose in Malmö was not good. Who was he intending to shoot?

CHAPTER 33

'Willi Hirdwall?'

Anita had grabbed hold of Hakim first thing on Monday morning. He'd passed on Reza's tip-off as soon as he'd left his shop, and Anita hadn't liked the sound of it at all. Her brain had gone into overdrive and she'd come to the conclusion that if he was from a criminal organization, the American might well have Hirdwall in his sights.

'Agent McBride told me that the Italians would be after Hirdwall. If this guy *has* been sent over by Gentile, I wonder how he knew that Hirdwall was here.'

'McBride knew. The mobsters have connections as well as the FBI: even connections in the FBI, I would imagine. And he was seen in Copenhagen, so he's been somewhere in this neck of the woods. If they can't find him in the States, Sweden is an obvious possibility,' replied Hakim.

'I don't know. Would you come back to a place you might be recognized if you'd pinched all that drug money? I would lie low somewhere else.'

'I suppose it's easier for a Swede to hide among millions of other Swedes.'

Anita picked up the coffee she'd brought in with her. She took a sip. She pulled a face – it was lukewarm.

'But why come back here? I mean specifically Skåne. Wouldn't you just lose yourself in the wilds? Heavens above, if there's one place on earth you can get lost, it's Sweden. And then there's Bilić's lot to consider. I know the chief is out of the picture, but there are still some Indians who've got a score to settle. We'd better check what's happened to Bengt Rickardsson and Dejan Kolarov. Kolarov didn't do much time, but Rickardsson did. Probably out by now.'

'I'll get Bea onto that.'

'Thanks. Now, where are we with Klas Karlin? Nothing came in over the weekend.'

'We're in contact with the Paris police to see if he can be tracked down there.'

'Good.'

'I'm going back to Nordea to see if I can find out more about August Skoog's banking habits. There's something distinctly odd about the euro payment – and the timing.'

'You think he might have been involved in something fishy?'

'Maybe. We still don't know enough about his joinery business. Maybe some of that wasn't above board. My trip to Kalmar might throw something up. Your revenge angle.'

'Possibly,' Anita said cautiously. 'Though if someone hated August enough to kill him and his wife, would they wait nearly twenty years to do it?'

'But you still want me to go?'

'Yes. We'll talk about that later today. In the meantime, I'm going to visit an old acquaintance.'

Before Anita left the polishus, she popped into McBride's office. The American agent was glued to her laptop and didn't raise her head when Anita entered.

'Thought I'd better let you know.'

This was enough for McBride to tear her gaze from the screen.

'We've had a tip-off about an American here in Malmö after a handgun. Apparently, he found somebody to supply one.'

'What kind?'

'The source didn't know. It's just that there's a chance that it's someone after Willi Hirdwall. They wouldn't risk travelling through an airport with a gun. Someone sent by Gentile? Just a thought. '

'Description of the American?'

'Haven't got one.'

Again, that exasperated, I'm-dealing-with-a-load-of-hayseeds look.

'It might be to do with something entirely different, of course, but I thought I'd better mention it.'

'OK. You've mentioned it.' McBride returned to her laptop.

Anita found herself swearing colourfully as she left the building. Fortunately, it wasn't verbalized.

It took a while to negotiate the sequence of locked doors. Each was opened then slammed behind her. Anita had always hated visiting people in prison: she found the feeling of claustrophobia associated with the idea of incarceration overwhelming. And visiting this particular prison always brought back unhappy memories. But she had to admit that the inmates these days enjoyed freedoms that their forebears would only have experienced in their fantasies. This policy of rehabilitation and the relaxation of restrictive measures within the prison system had its critics, but Dragan Mitrović wasn't one of them. It had allowed him to retain tight control over his criminal empire. Eventually, Anita was ushered into a light, airy room, the bars on the window the only indication of its employment. A table and four functional but comfortable chairs were positioned in the middle of the space. She took a seat and was greeted by a lopsided smile from Mitrović as he entered the room. She nodded to the prison guard that it was all right to leave them.

'We can't go on meeting like this: people will talk.'

Mitrović didn't exude quite the same confidence he'd shown during her last visit, when she'd come to ask him about people-trafficking across the Baltic from Estonia. He was thinner – more gaunt – and his eyes were not quite as bright. His facial scar, its prominence now contested by other deepening furrows, was less sinister. But the raven-black hair was still dyed to within an inch of its life, and, as always, he was neatly turned out: the creases in his trousers as sharp as the knives he was famed for using. But there was no denying that age was catching up with him.

'I hope they've been treating you well over the last three years.'

Anita had the disconcerting impression that their paths had only crossed recently: his charisma was pervasive.

'Is it that long ago?' He shook his head. 'I hear that you are now a boss yourself.'

'Only in a small way. My gang is not as big as yours.' The comment amused Mitrović.

'Well, Anita, what can I do for you this time? Are you plundering my past again?'

'In a way. I'd like you to cast your mind back to the time before you took over your...' she struggled for the right word.

'Business,' Mitrović supplied helpfully.

'OK. Business. Your managing director then was Branislav Bilić.'

'Sadly missed.'

'And sadly never found.'

'A mystery to all of us.'

'He was behind the Q Guard robbery down here in Malmö: Christmas 2006.'

His black-olive eyes bored into her.

'That was never proved.'

'True.'

'I remember two policemen barging into the Belgrade

Kitchen while Branislav was having his lunch. Their behaviour was rude and their accusations unfounded.'

'Yes, I missed that particular jaunt.'

'I gather neither gentleman is with us anymore.'

'No.' She wasn't willing to elaborate. 'Perhaps we could indulge in a hypothetical situation?'

'I don't mind playing games. I've nothing else in my diary for today.'

'A gangland boss... say, based in Stockholm for argument's sake... decides to rob a cash-handling facility in... Malmö, for example. He needs a team. He puts together four specialists under the supervision of a trusted lieutenant from his home country. Along the way, this lieutenant recruits one of the facility's security guards to act as an inside man. But the robbery doesn't go entirely to plan and a second security guard is killed and another is shot. Shortly afterwards, the trusted lieutenant is found murdered in the basement of his apartment block. And the money, which has been stashed at a secluded farm, disappears. And, here's the thing: there is no trace of it over the next sixteen years. Naturally, the police assume that the gangland boss successfully salted it away and disposed of the said lieutenant. Yet they are still perplexed that none of the stolen cash has ever surfaced, and they continue to wonder why the trusted lieutenant was killed. Especially as the dead man was the cousin of the gangland boss's own right-hand man.'

Mitrović said nothing for a while, and Anita found herself shifting uneasily in her seat.

'Why now?'

'Something has come to light.'

He shook his head. 'I doubt if some*thing* has come to light. But perhaps some*one*?'

Anita tried to remain poker faced. 'I can't say.'

The glint in his eye worried her.

'You want to know if your hypothetical gangland boss really was behind the killing?'

'Yes. We assumed that the trusted lieutenant had either got too greedy or the boss was distancing himself from the robbery. And given that the lieutenant was the cousin of the right-hand man might explain why the boss disappeared without a trace.'

'That's a lot of assumptions' – Mitrović pointed a finger at Anita – 'but I can tell you one thing. Milan wasn't killed on the orders of Branislav Bilić. You didn't get it right then, and I doubt you'll get it right now.'

'And the cash?'

Mitrović gave an expansive shrug.

Dragan Mitrović was returned to his cell. The door was shut but not locked. He waited for the guard's footsteps to fade before he took out a mobile phone concealed under the washbasin. He took off the plastic wrapping, switched it on then keyed in a number. It was soon answered.

'Do you know where Dejan Kolarov is these days?'

He listened to the reply.

'Tell him to get back to Sweden. He's got some unfinished business to attend to. I think Willi Hirdwall may be back.'

CHAPTER 34

As soon as Anita returned from the prison, she was told that Commissioner Falk wanted to speak to her. Ten minutes later, she was in his office. Falk got straight down to business.

'Do you know how Agent McBride is getting on?'

'Haven't a clue.

Falk was clearly disappointed.

'Has she made any progress in finding Willi Hirdwall?'

'She just sits in her office most of the time. We haven't been able to trace him through the usual channels and up until now, I haven't given much credence to McBride's theory that he's here in Sweden.'

'Up until now?'

'Well, perhaps now I'm not so sure.' She then went on to mention Reza's tip-off and her notion that there might be a connection to Hirdwall. 'Of course, I may well be totally wrong about that.'

'Have you told McBride?'

'Yes. She didn't sound too impressed. I don't think we're living up to the FBI's expectations, or maybe they started at a low base.'

'Rubbish. I'm sure we can teach them a thing or two.' – Anita doubted that –'She's off to Kalmar tomorrow morning.'

'She didn't tell me that.'

'Part of our agreement to cooperate with her was that she had to keep me informed of her movements, especially if they took her out of the Skåne County area. I've had to inform

Kalmar's police chief that she's going there.'

'Did she say why?'

'Willi Hirdwall came from there.'

Of course, Anita remembered that.

'She wants to find out more about his background. Something about results from psychological profiling. Going back to his roots. Americans seem obsessed with roots.'

'Well, she can go with Hakim. I'm sending him to find out more about the Skoogs and track down one of their foster kids.'

'Good. But not Hakim. I want you to go. You can keep a weather eye on Agent McBride while you're there.'

'Oh, come on! I've got enough on my plate at the moment.'

'Just up your street, I would have thought.' There was a twinkle in his eye. 'Surely, you're not going to pass up the chance to get out there and do some real detective work? Aren't you always complaining that you're chained to your desk? Well, here's an opportunity to get back to your first love.'

'Real detective work doesn't include babysitting a seriously unpleasant FBI agent.'

'You don't have to babysit her. Just make sure she's not straying beyond her remit. I don't want her to go all Dirty Harry.'

'I think you're showing your age there.'

'Besides,' Falk said with a smile, 'I suspect you have more in common than you realize.'

There was an answer to that, but Anita bit her tongue.

'That's settled then. Make sure you stay at the same hotel as she does.'

'It'll be pricey.'

'I'll make the budget stretch.'

Hakim was relieved that he didn't have to go to Kalmar – and even more so when he discovered that he would have been accompanying Agent McBride. Anita could tell the team sympathized with her plight – even Klara Wallen felt sorry for her, especially when Anita diplomatically put her in charge of the Skoog investigation while she was away. The two of them analyzed and summarized the team's progress so far: not an encouraging exercise. Klas Karlin still hadn't been found, and they hadn't heard back from the French police, or the Danish police, who'd been alerted in case he materialized on the other side of the Sound. No other leads had emerged, and Anita told Wallen that she'd agreed with the commissioner that if nothing came to light while she was away, she'd hold a press conference on her return from Kalmar and announce that the apparent suicide was actually murder – that might bring something, or someone, out of the woodwork. They were still without a real suspect and any sort of motive. Maybe her trip and some background research on the Skoogs would instigate the breakthrough they so desperately needed. She'd made contact with the Beijers, August and Gudrun's old neighbours, and she'd fixed up to call on them the next afternoon.

After the meeting broke up, Erlandsson caught her.

'Hakim asked me to check on the whereabouts of the last two of the Q Guard robbery gang.'

'Any luck?'

'Bengt Rickardsson got out four years ago and has spent most of his time in and out of hospital. Heart problems.'

'He was always overweight. And Dejan Kolarov?' She still remembered his dramatic threat to Willi Hirdwall in court.

'Served two years and then left the country after being paroled. Presumed to have gone back to Serbia or Bosnia and Herzegovina.'

'So neither of them is likely to be a threat to Hirdwall. Thanks, Bea.'

'You know, when I was with the Cold Case Group, we looked into the Milan Subotić killing. It was after Alice

Zetterberg arrested the wrong person for the Knäbäckshusen murder and she held that embarrassing press conference in front of the commissioner and prosecutor.'

Anita gave Erlandsson a wry grin, remembering that she had unmasked the real killer, and Zetterberg's publicity coup had been very publicly punctured.

'She was determined to find cases that you'd been involved in and hadn't been solved.'

'Why doesn't that surprise me?'

'Anyway, we soon gave up on the Subotić case as there were no obvious new clues. We concurred with the original conclusion – Bilić removing him for whatever reason.'

'I bet Alice didn't take that well.'

Anita rushed along the platform of Malmö Central Station, the wheels of her old cabin bag screeching behind her. She was cutting it fine. Her alarm hadn't gone off for some reason, and she was immediately on the back foot. She'd frantically got her bag together, having, of course, neglected to pack it the night before as any sensible person – certainly Lasse – would have done, and after a lightning shower and half a cup of scalding coffee, she'd run out of her apartment in a panic.

McBride was waiting impatiently and made great play of consulting her watch as a sweating Anita approached. Breathless, she didn't have time to apologize, as McBride leapt up the steps onto the train and walked straight down the aisle to their pre-booked seats. Anita hauled her case onto the rack above their heads: McBride's was already neatly in place. As Anita sank into her seat, the train began to slip out of the station.

'Timekeeping not your thing?' McBride observed acidly.

'At least I made it' was her only retort.

They were out of the city limits before Anita felt composed enough to ask McBride how her investigation was going.

'I'm still putting out feelers.'

'And you really think he's here?'

She gave Anita a sour look. 'I wouldn't be here otherwise.'

Anita gave up. She got the distinct impression that McBride didn't want her along. It was going to be a long three hours. She turned her attention to the countryside outside the window. Either side of the track were vast swathes of ripe cornfields, some already succumbing to the attentions of mighty combine harvesters stirring up great billows of dust. With its wide open skies, this was the Skåne – the breadbasket of Sweden – that Anita loved. They'd already passed through Lund and soon they would be in Hässleholm, where the serious forests began, and the train would be funnelled into a never-ending expanse of pine and birch, only broken up by the occasional stretch of water and small town.

McBride spent most of the time engaged with her laptop, and for the first half of the journey, they hardly exchanged a word. After Växjö, Anita went to answer a call of nature, though it was more to give herself a break from her companion than to relieve her bladder. On her way back to her seat, she paused to take in the fleeting scenery: the landscape had changed from trees and small lakes to even more trees and bigger lakes.

Settling herself down once more, Anita began to drift off to sleep. She was jolted awake by her phone going off. She banged her head on the window as she frantically retrieved the jingling handset.

'Hi Klara. Anything to report?'

'Yes. Something really weird. Hakim's just called in. He's been back to the Ystad Nordea bank to check on the four thousand euros that August Skoog paid in the day before he died. And you're not going to believe this.' Wallen paused for effect.

'Well?' Anita prompted tetchily.

'The euros, though still legal tender, were first issue.'

Anita wished Wallen would come to the point. 'So?'

'The bank checked them out. They come from the Q Guard robbery.'

CHAPTER 35

Anita was wide awake for the rest of the journey. Even McBride had taken note that the call had had an immediate impact on the chief inspector, though she refrained from asking why. And Anita had no intention of telling her for the moment. It had nothing to do with the hunt for Willi Hirdwall.

The implications of Wallen's revelation swirled around in Anita's head. How was it possible that some of the Q Guard money had turned up after sixteen years? And why now? And why only such a small amount? And why was it in the Skoogs' bank account? Could they have had something to do with the robbery? It seemed inconceivable. They had moved to Löderup a couple of years before the heist, so they were around when it took place. Could August have had a connection with the gang? And if he had, why hadn't the money been used before? The Skoogs lived in a nice house – and they were clearly comfortably off – but there was nothing to indicate that they were particularly rich. Hakim had found out that they had nearly half a million kronor in savings. Not a vast amount. Anita would have expected more from someone who had sold a business, even allowing for the fact that they'd been retired for nearly twenty years, but Hakim had discovered that they'd made generous charity donations over the years, particularly to causes involving children, so that would account for their modest reserves.

So was there any significance in the timing of the deposit and the murders? As Hakim had pointed out, it was unlikely that the killer or killers would have gone to such lengths to stage a suicide if they were only after the four thousand euros. Unless the motive was the very fact that the Skoogs had allowed the stolen money to surface at all. But then that brought Anita's reasoning back to the gang: Rickardsson, with his poor health – and Kolarov. As far as they knew, *he* wasn't in the country. That might need checking. But even if he was, how on earth would he know about the Skoogs' bank deposit? Or for that matter, how would anybody know? Her mind drifted back to Mitrović's reaction to her question about the money. What had his shrug meant? That he knew where the money had gone? Or that he had no idea?

Then a fresh thought pushed the others into the background. Kasper Jensen! Was this the connection to the Skoogs that they had failed to find before? Jensen's car had been seen in Löderup in June and again in the days before the old couple were killed. And he *was* in Sweden when the murders took place. They knew he had time to get across to Löderup. He could have got to the house without driving through the village if he'd approached from the north along Örumsvägen. There were only a few houses along that route down from National Road 9. They would have to check any possible sightings of the red Golf on that road on that evening. But it still seemed a stretch for Jensen to be in league with August Skoog. Jensen had been out of prison for over ten years, so the timing was in itself bizarre even if they were linked. And if Jensen did know where the money was, why hadn't he extracted it earlier? This was a man who had lost his wife and children and worked stacking shelves in a supermarket. Hardly someone who could get his hands on a fortune – and that presupposed that Bilić hadn't salted away the money after the robbery. Anita's head was throbbing by the time the train reached its destination.

The weather was now hot and sticky despite the force of the wind coming off the Öland Sound. They headed into Kalmar's 'new' (though it dated back to the mid-1600s) fortified town on Kvarnholmen. This island area was built after the original town had suffered greatly during the endless wars with the Danes, whose lands stretched as far as Kalmar's borders, and is now linked to the rest of the city by several bridges. The rectilinear streets with their quaint cobbles were not designed for Anita's and McBride's wheeled cabin bags, which clacked and jumped their way to the hotel. This infuriated the American: 'Haven't they heard of tarmac?' Eventually, they reached Stortorget, the island's heart. This elegant square, with its array of impressive 17th-century buildings, is dominated by the magnificent cathedral, which wouldn't look out of place in France or Italy. The basic building is cruciform with a tower in each angle but, as with other fine examples of High Baroque architecture throughout Europe, the addition of pilasters and pediments, domes and finials transformed it into a thing of opulence and splendour. As the two women crossed the square, the cathedral's orange stuccoed walls glowed in the late-morning sun. Opposite the cathedral was the less ornate but still imposing town hall, and close to this was their hotel. This, too, had a rich history, but Anita was too tired to take it in – the journey and the heat of the day had sapped her energy, and she was grateful that she didn't have to share a room with McBride: memories of sharing with Alice Zetterberg on their trip to Malta during the Knäbäckshusen cold case investigation were still fresh in her mind.

After she'd dumped her bag and freshened up, Anita made a call to Joel Grahn. She asked him to make enquiries at all the properties on Örumsvägen to see if anyone had seen the red VW Golf on the evening of the Skoogs' murders. Afterwards, she went off for a coffee and sandwich before taking a taxi to the Beijers' home. McBride didn't say where she was going, but Anita had the feeling she would be heading for the police headquarters; she was clearly determined to find out if Willi

Hirdwall had any kind of criminal past, despite what Anita had told her about the time limit on records. Anita had suggested she try social services. She thought McBride was on a wild goose chase, but if she wanted to waste her time and the FBI's money, good luck to her.

The taxi made its way out of the centre and on to Stensövägen before turning off into a peaceful street of neat detached properties and well-tended gardens. The Beijers' smart white house peeked out above a neatly clipped hedge. Under the red-pantile roof nestled an upper storey with a balcony, upon which was a cosy arrangement of two seats and a small table. Next door was a house of similar design. This had belonged to the Skoogs.

Anita was greeted warmly by Oskar and Ann Beijer as they ushered her into their living room. The room was immaculately tidy: not a crumb on the floor or a cushion out of place. The wide picture window overlooked the front garden. The furniture was from the 1980s, a period when style won over comfort. Anita judged the Beijers were in their seventies. Oskar was tall and thin. His short, grey hair, goatee beard and spectacles gave him the serious, studious air of the teacher he had once been. Ann, shorter and plumper, had unruly curls and an infectious smile. Both appeared fit, and the reason soon became apparent when two West Highland terriers burst into the room and yapped round Ann's feet. When one of them attempted to lick Anita's ankle, Ann fussed them out of the room in the doggy-child language adopted by many cynophiles.

'Sorry about that,' apologized Oskar. 'Please sit.'

Coffee had already been prepared and was accompanied by biscuits and a plate of freshly-baked vanilla hearts: shortbread pastries dusted with icing.

As Oskar poured out the coffees he said, 'It's absolutely dreadful what has happened to August and Gudrun. We just can't believe it. Suicide is such a drastic step. I know Gudrun was seriously ill and August was at his wit's end, but all the same...' His voice trailed off.

'So, so sad,' chimed in Ann. 'We can't get over it.'

'I know it's tragic,' Anita added sympathetically, 'but I'm afraid I have to tell you it's more serious than we first thought. This is not official yet – I must impress upon you that this must remain confidential for the time being – but we are treating the Skoogs' deaths as suspicious.'

'Oh no,' squeaked Ann, clutching her face in shock.

'I told you,' Oskar said to his wife with the air of someone who'd been proved right. Probably always thinks he's right, thought Anita as she weighed up her hosts. 'I just couldn't believe that August would do such a terrible thing. He wouldn't have had it in him.'

'That's why I'm here: I need to know more about the Skoogs and their life before they moved to Löderup. So far, we've found no local suspects or motive for their deaths. So now we're working on the possibility that the motive may be rooted in their past.'

'They were ideal neighbours,' Ann ventured. 'Gudrun was the kindest person you could possibly meet. Nothing was too much trouble. And she had the patience of a saint.'

'She had to have with some of those foster children,' put in Oskar with a knowing raise of an eyebrow.

'What about August? I was wondering about his business. Did he run into any trouble?'

'I don't think so,' said Oskar. 'He was very skilled. He made his own dining table and chairs: that's how good he was.'

'That's right,' Ann confirmed. 'And all the doors upstairs.'

'He built up his business from nothing,' said Oskar, taking back control. 'We moved here forty years ago. Twentieth of June, 1982, to be exact.' His pedantry suited Anita. People like Oskar were reliably accurate. 'They were already here and August was on his own except for an apprentice. By the time he sold the business and they moved to Löderup, he employed about ten people.'

As far as Anita was concerned, the business angle was unlikely to be fruitful. And even if there had been some serious bad feeling somewhere, the time lapse mitigated against an aggrieved employee or customer catching up with August and killing him now.

'I'll tell you what I really came to see you about. It was one of the boys that Gudrun took in. According to August's cousin, someone called Klas visited them before the Skoogs died. We've found out from social services that one of their foster children was called Klas Karlin. This may or may not be the Klas who turned up at Löderup. Do you remember him?'

'Yes,' said Ann.

'Difficult child.' This was said with some feeling by Oskar. 'I taught him. He was a handful. I don't know how Gudrun coped with him, and one or two of the others.'

'She was so good with them. She really cared about them. And both she and August made sure they didn't cause trouble for the neighbours.'

'Huh. They took it to school instead. Klas was always getting into trouble. And then he went from bad to worse.'

'To be fair, that was after he left Gudrun's care,' Ann said defensively. 'He always had a nice smile and we'd have the occasional chat. He liked my vanilla hearts. Oh, please do take one, Chief Inspector.'

'It's Anita, and thanks.' The pastries looked tempting. She swallowed her first mouthful before asking, 'What do you mean by bad to worse?'

'Petty crime to start with. Stealing cars. Joy riding. Then stealing to order.' Oskar was warming to his theme.

'I know Gudrun was very upset,' said Ann.

'As I was saying,' – Oskar was clearly annoyed at his wife's interruption – 'that was just the beginning. The car thefts brought him to the attention of the police. It started while he was still at school. Then he really moved up a gear. No pun intended,' he said seriously. 'He got in with a pair of armed thugs and started raiding supermarkets. Stealing the takings. They went too far at one place in the centre of town. They beat up the manager, who wasn't being cooperative. It was touch and go whether he would make it. Fortunately, he did. All three of them were caught. Though Klas hadn't played a part in the assault, he was regarded as the ringleader of the group. He was sent to prison – for a couple of years, I believe.'

'When was this?' Anita asked.

He stroked his goatee thoughtfully. 'He must have come out around the mid nineties.'

'That explains why we couldn't find a record for him.'

'I know Gudrun did see him again,' said Ann. 'Down in Löderup.'

'August's cousin mentioned someone who'd been troublesome in their youth but had moved on and had a family. He visited the Skoogs and showed off his children. Could that have been Klas?'

'No, I think that sounds like Josef. Gudrun was so pleased with the way *he*'d turned out.'

'But you say Gudrun did see Klas again?'

'Yes. When they first moved to Löderup. She said he'd turned into an upright citizen. Another credit to her.'

'I doubt that,' Oskar scoffed.

'Don't be so hard on him, dear.'

That fitted in with what Britha Skoog had told Joel Grahn. Someone had come across from Malmö in the early days of the Skoogs' retirement.

Oskar continued to revile the Klas Karlin he remembered. 'You didn't have to teach him! That was what was so galling – he was intelligent. If he'd channelled his energies into something more worthwhile instead of getting into trouble, he could have made something of himself.'

'He did try,' insisted Ann. 'And don't you remember, after he came out of prison, his foster brother helped him?'

'Yes, I do remember now. You're right.'

Anita wasn't sure where the conversation was going. So Klas Karlin had a criminal record, but seemed to have got his life back on track. He'd visited Löderup after the Skoogs had first moved to Skåne. So if Karlin was the same Klas who'd stayed with Gudrun the day August visited his cousin Britha, why had he recently reappeared so suddenly? Ruminating on this, she was only half listening to the Beijers when she was forced out her reverie by the mention of a name.

'Sorry, Oskar, who did you say Klas moved in with?'

'Willi.'

'Willi who?'

'Willi Hirdwall.'

CHAPTER 36

'Are you all right, dear?' Ann Beijer asked in concern.

'No, it's OK. Just the name. It means something.'

Anita's mind raced over the known facts. Willi Hirdwall had been fostered in Kalmar. He himself had told her that, she remembered. Of course, they hadn't delved any more deeply into his past during the Q Guard robbery investigation because it seemed neither apposite nor necessary – they had quickly identified Kasper Jensen as the inside man. If they had probed further, the connection to the Skoogs would have emerged sixteen years ago, though it would have had no bearing on the case then – and it wasn't exactly relevant now. It was just an odd coincidence that Willi Hirdwall knew Klas Karlin.

'Did you teach Willi Hirdwall, too?'

Oskar had now taken off his glasses and was polishing them with a handkerchief.

'Yes, I did as a matter of fact. He was a year, no, two years ahead of Klas. Now *he* was a lovely boy.' He popped his glasses back on.

'Lovely boy,' Ann cooed in agreement.

'He might not have been the brightest bulb in the box, but he was a hard worker and honest. Respectful, too. You don't see much of that around these days.'

Again, this backed up Anita's initial opinion of Hirdwall: the antithesis of the picture painted by McBride.

'And look at the way he took Klas under his wing,' Ann said approvingly.

'He did that.' Oskar turned to Anita. 'They'd become close when they were living with August and Gudrun. And Willi was there for Klas when he came out of prison. Everybody supported him – Gudrun even got August to give him the odd job to do while he was still on probation.'

Anita finished her coffee even though it had gone cold. She was done here. She'd got the background she wanted on Klas Karlin. She stood up.

'I don't suppose you have any idea where Klas Karlin might be now?'

'I'm afraid not,' Oskar said decisively.

'Don't worry. It's just we're having a bit of trouble tracing him.'

'Goodness, you don't think…'

'No. We just need to eliminate him from our enquiries.'

Anita shook their hands. 'That vanilla heart was delicious.' Ann giggled in delight.

Oskar escorted her to the front door.

Before she left: 'Actually, herr Beijer, I knew Willi Hirdwall many years ago. He helped us out on a big robbery case in Malmö.'

Oskar looked askance. 'Are you sure?'

Anita frowned. Why was he doubting her? 'Of course I am. He was very brave. Put himself on the line.'

'When was this?'

'2006, into 2007.'

Oskar shook his head vigorously. 'I'm afraid you're mistaken.'

Anita was trying not to lose her temper. 'I don't think so.'

'I'm sorry, Chief Inspector, that's quite impossible. Willi Hirdwall died in 1998.'

*

Anita was back in the Beijers' living room in her uncomfortable chair. Ann, her face creased in perplexity, was in the process of clearing the cups away. Oskar stood by the fireplace with the smug expression of someone who'd been proved right yet again.

'Let me get this straight. The man you knew as Willi Hirdwall is dead?'

'Correct,' said Oskar.

'Did your Willi Hirdwall work as a security guard?'

'I believe he did.'

'So, what happened to him?'

'He drowned. He'd got into sailing. He and a friend were out somewhere off Öland. The weather turned quickly and they must have been caught. I think they both lacked experience. Anyway, the boat overturned. They found the wreck a couple of days later, washed onto the island. Neither body was recovered.'

'And this definitely happened in 1998?'

'Gudrun and August were so upset,' said Ann. 'I think Willi had been a particular favourite.'

Anita was trying to mentally navigate her way through the confusion that this information had caused.

'So your Willi Hirdwall can't have been our Willi Hirdwall,' Oskar stated baldly.

'Quite,' Anita replied distractedly.

Ann suddenly put down the tray that she had been about to take out and turned to Anita. 'It's odd you asking about Willi.'

'What's odd?' Oskar said sharply.

'Well, a little while ago, a couple of weeks perhaps, a man came to the door. He was asking about him, too.'

'You never told me,' Oskar said accusingly.

'It was when you were away on that golfing trip to the west coast. By the time you came back, I'd forgotten about it.'

Anita, now in full charge of her faculties, jumped in. 'Who was this man?'

'Charming. American. Large man. Made me think of a boxer. Very friendly.'

'Did he have a name?'

'He didn't give one, and I'm afraid I didn't ask.'

'What exactly did he want to know?' Anita demanded.

'Well, my English is a bit limited but from what I could gather, he was over from America and was tracing his ancestors: trying to find relatives. He had some Hirdwalls in his family tree. He knew that Willi had been fostered but thought he might be related to Willi's grandfather. I don't know how on earth they work these things out. The internet I suppose. I must admit, he seemed a bit swarthy for someone with a Swedish background, but I'm sure there's been lots of intermarriage over there. Such a hotch-potch.'

'Did you tell him Willi was dead?'

'Yes, I did. He was disappointed, though I got the impression he wasn't totally surprised.'

'Did you tell him anything else?'

'Well, he knew that the Skoogs had fostered Willi. Must have been to social services. He'd tried next door first, of course, but the people there now didn't know anything, so they sent him round here. He said he'd love to meet the Skoogs if they were still alive. He was really interested in finding out more about Willi's life.'

'You gave him the Skoogs' address?'

'Yes,' she said cautiously. 'Did I do something wrong?'

'No, no. Don't worry. Now think carefully, Ann. When exactly did he come to your house?'

'Oh, oh dear me,' she twittered anxiously.

'Calm down,' Oskar commanded. 'Think! It was when I was away. I left here at ten in the morning on Wednesday, the sixth, and came back the Saturday evening: that was the ninth.

I was back home by seven. It was obviously sometime in that time period.'

'That's right,' Ann said brightly, as though she'd been let off the hook for some misdemeanour. 'It was the morning after you left.'

'That's the seventh,' said Anita. 'Are you quite sure?'

'Yes. Yes, I am.'

That was the day before the Skoogs were killed.

CHAPTER 37

Oskar Beijer had given Anita a lift back to the hotel. She had calls to make and she wanted to find McBride. The FBI agent wasn't around, and Anita realized that she didn't even have the woman's phone number. That summed up their lack of communication. In her hotel room, she rang headquarters to speak to Wallen. She wasn't in, so she spoke to Hakim. She explained the revelations that had come to light that afternoon.

'So your Willi Hirdwall *isn't* Willi Hirdwall.' She could hear his incredulity. 'So, who is he?'

'Obviously someone who assumed his identity. Hirdwall had no next of kin, so it would have been easy. Whoever it was knew he was dead and knew enough about him to steal his identity.'

'Klas Karlin?'

'He fits the bill. They knew each other; they were friends and only a couple of years apart in age. But there's something that doesn't quite sit right. Obviously, Karlin knew the Skoogs and had visited them years ago – and had returned recently. But if Karlin *is* Hirdwall, why did he bother to come back and see them in the first place? Why not just lie low in Paris or wherever he's been hiding since his escape from America? According to McBride, he had five million dollars with him.'

'Maybe he heard that Gudrun was dying.'

'Possibly. But what a dangerous thing to do. He must know people are after him, and, of course, he could have been recognized by someone from his past life.'

'The Skoogs knew him. Could Karlin have killed them?'

'I don't know. I can't think why he would.'

'They might have blown his new identity.'

'I doubt that. I get the feeling they were very protective of the kids they took in, even after they'd left. Anyway, we might have someone else in the frame. This American who called on Ann Beijer. Supposedly tracing his family tree. She gave him the Skoogs' address the day before they died. If he's one of Gentile's men...'

'Might be the same guy that Reza mentioned: the one looking for the handgun.'

'Exactly. Though the timing's not right. The guy got the gun *after* the murders. And we know that one of August's own guns was used for those. Anyway, I've got Ann Beijer's description of the man. We may need to find him. The question is: if he did make contact with the Skoogs, did he get there before or after they were killed?'

'How about Agent McBride? She might know something about him.'

'Yeah, I need to find her. And I need to compare notes on Willi Hirdwall. The man I knew lied about who he really was, so what else did he lie about?'

Anita lay down on her bed. She had a headache coming on and she felt physically drained after her revealing talk with Ann and Oskar Beijer. She dozed for a while and woke with a start. She must get up and track down McBride. She went into the bathroom and rinsed her face. As she raised her head, the image in the mirror stared mournfully back at her. She studied it closely. She was starting to age: a few more wrinkles, more grey hairs. But what the hell! She straightened up and gave herself a shake. She wasn't bad for her fifty-three years – Kevin didn't think so, anyway. She headed back into the bedroom. Through the window, she could see the square – and there, crossing it, heading towards the hotel, was Paige McBride. Anita quickly grabbed her bag and headed down to the lobby to catch her.

McBride had beaten her to it and was nowhere to be seen. Anita asked the receptionist if he had seen the American lady. He indicated the entrance to the bar. Anita glanced at her watch. It was half past five. Maybe a drink was a good idea. A glass or two might loosen the tension between them and get them on a more amicable footing.

McBride was perched on a bar stool in the pub that was attached to the hotel. Incongruously, the pub had a Scottish theme: the profusion of tartan was a giveaway, as were the walls, replete with everything from ancient golf clubs to a portrait of Bonny Prince Charlie. The FBI agent was sitting by herself in front of the long, polished wooden counter, behind which were several shelves groaning with bottles of whisky. McBride was about to order.

'Let me buy that,' said Anita.

McBride eyed her suspiciously. 'OK.' She twisted round to the barman. 'Make it a Talisker. Forget the ice.'

Anita took the stool next to her. They were the only customers.

'I'll have a red wine,' said Anita. 'The nearest to hand,' she added before the barman could ask what type she wanted.

McBride picked up her glass and raised it as though she was about to make a toast. 'The only thing I got out of a bad marriage to an American Scot was a taste for Talisker.' She downed half of it in one gulp.

'Bad day?' asked Anita.

'I've had better. I went to the police, who were worse than useless. But I had better luck with social services. They had a Willi Hirdwall on their books. Turns out the foster parents were called Skoog. That's the same name as your murdered couple, isn't it?' Anita was surprised she knew about that. It was soon apparent how: 'Pontus Brodd told me all about your case.'

He would, thought Anita. 'Well, yes, they are the same people. I went to see the Skoogs' old neighbours this afternoon. It was quite revealing. I was actually making enquiries about someone else when Willi Hirdwall's name came up. *Your* Willi Hirdwall. Apparently, he died about twenty years ago.' McBride didn't react and took a large swig of her whisky. 'So Micky Mosten wasn't Willi Hirdwall. He just said he was.'

'I'm not surprised,' said McBride. 'He's a slippery son of a bitch.'

'It makes me wonder what lies he was telling us at the time of the robbery,'

'I told you there was a lot about that case that didn't add up.' McBride used the same snarky tone of voice as Alice Zetterberg. Anita thought she'd love to put the two of them in a room together and see which one could out-bitch the other.

'You may be right.'

'Has it ever occurred to you that Hirdwall might have had something to do with your robbery?'

'Not really. We looked into him, but we found the inside man very quickly, so we didn't pursue him any further.'

'And how did you find the inside man?'

Anita had to think back. 'We discovered that he was in trouble financially. He was an easy target for the gang. They offered him a way out of debt.'

'How did you find out about his debt?'

'Well… I can't remember.'

'It's in the file. It was Hirdwall first mentioned it.'

Anita had to admit that it was. 'Are you saying he played us all along?'

'It's just a thought.'

It was a thought that was starting to gnaw at her brain. She was still trying to process the possibility that Hirdwall and

Karlin were not only connected, but one and the same. But it wasn't a theory she was going to discuss with McBride until she knew more.

McBride plonked her empty glass down loudly on the bar and looked steadily at Anita. 'I think Willi Hirdwall is capable of anything.'

'For someone you've never actually met, he's really got to you.'

'I don't like failure. The bust was carefully planned and he got through the net. And whatever I think of the Gentile family, Hirdwall killed one of his own. You don't do that.'

Anita could never get her head round the warped morality of criminals.

'One thing I did pick up that might interest you. An American, claiming to be tracing ancestors, called at the Beijers – the neighbours of the Skoogs – asking about Willi.'

McBride was all attention.

'Ann Beijer told him that Willi was dead, but gave him the Skoogs' address. This was the day before the killings. Now, I have no idea if he followed that up, but it sounds mighty suspicious.'

'Description?'

'Large – or well-built – swarthy complexion with high cheekbones. Said he was like a boxer. And black hair. Very polite.'

McBride cocked her head towards the barman and nodded. He took her glass and topped it up with the minimum of fuss.

'Sounds as though it could be one of the Gentile mob.' She took the glass and gulped down the full shot. 'Could you take me to the Beijer house? I'd like to see if she can identify the man from my computer files. I need to know who I'm up against.'

*

It was nearing eight when Anita and McBride, sitting in the back of a taxi, were on their way back into central Kalmar. The Beijers had been surprised at Anita's swift return and were taken aback by a belligerent McBride. Eventually, after some placatory explanations on Anita's part, Ann identified one of the suspects that McBride showed her on her iPad.

'Gentile really does want revenge if he's sent Salvatore Baresi: he's a seriously nasty piece of work. He's been part of the Gentile set-up for years. Brutal and effective is how he's been described. An enforcer. He's only been put away once, and then he got out on appeal; two witnesses changed their statements. It's dangerous characters like Baresi that your precious Willi Hirdwall has been associating with.'

'I get the picture,' Anita said with tired resignation.

'You've fucking well got to pick up Baresi.'

'Easier said than done. As far we know, he's not done anything illegal. An implausible impersonation of an American Swede isn't an arrestable offence.'

'What about the gun in Malmö? You can pick him up for that, surely?'

'We'll put out a description.'

'I suggest you find him quick. Because if Baresi gets to Willi Hirdwall before I do, you'll not only have a dead man on your hands, you'll find yourself in the middle of a shitstorm.'

CHAPTER 38

Anita rose early and had a quick breakfast. There was no sign of McBride – the last time she'd seen her, she was making a beeline for the Scottish bar after their return from the Beijer home. She headed out of the hotel and stepped into the early-morning sunshine. Stortorget was almost deserted, as were the streets that radiated from it; there would be little activity until the shops opened at ten.

She made her way to the station, crossed the road opposite and strolled past the marina. She was enjoying the weather; the constant wind of yesterday had dropped. A couple of yachts were manoeuvring out of their berths on their way to the Öland Sound. She carried on past the train terminus and over the narrow strait of water which separated Kvarnholmen from the rest of the town until she was in Stadsparken. Now she was almost within touching distance of the magnificent Kalmar Castle. The huge moated medieval fortress, modernized in the 16th century in a style fit for a renaissance king, dominates the city and the Sound. Anita remembered seeing it once before, on a holiday with her mother and aunt. As they'd crossed the Öland Bridge (the longest in Sweden, her mother had told her), she'd been amazed at its splendour. Sadly, she reflected that she hadn't been able to visit it then and nor would she be able to visit it today. She sighed. Another time. Maybe she would bring Kevin. Kalmar was the sort of town he would love.

She walked through the leafy gardens, absorbing the atmosphere, and only pausing to say hello to a statue of

Gustav Vasa, one of Sweden's most famous monarchs. Then she doubled back and found a seat overlooking the castle. As she gazed up at the great bastion of strength, its sense of history and permanency almost overwhelmed her and she began to ruminate on her own insignificance and ephemerality. Then the noisy chatter of some children close by abruptly ended her brown study. She shook herself and dragged herself back to the matter in hand. Willi Hirdwall. What was that all about? Throughout her career, she had always relied on her gut feeling and subsequent judgement. She'd made mistakes, of course, but on the big calls, she'd usually got things right. So how could she have got Willi Hirdwall so wrong? He wasn't even Willi Hirdwall! Yet he'd been so convincing, so sincere. Over the months he'd been in the safe house, she'd built up a genuine connection with him. She'd presented him with the freedom and anonymity that she felt he deserved after having had such a traumatic experience. But now it was starting to look like she'd been conned. And she wasn't the only one: the senior figures on the investigation had also been taken in. But it couldn't be denied that it was *her* faith in Willi that had been a deciding factor in his rehabilitation. *She*'d been his advocate. How could she have judged his character so badly? Not a good trait in a cop. Christ, what a mess!

It was with a huge sense of relief that Anita got back to the polishus. A couple of days in the company of the FBI agent had stretched her patience and her nerves. McBride had an aggressive intensity that was wearying, and her small talk was non-existent. Anita still had no idea what the private person underneath all the arrogance and swagger was like, as the American never seemed to let her guard down. And she seemed obsessed with tracking down Willi Hirdwall – it was like an itch she couldn't scratch. So much so that Anita began to suspect she had some kind of psychological problem.

OK, the son-in-law of a Chicago mobster had been killed and someone had to be brought to book, but the guy had been part of a vicious criminal outfit, and, presumably, Chicago's streets were a tiny bit safer without him. Maybe McBride was some kind of control freak – the drugs operation hadn't gone totally as planned and it was getting to her. She couldn't be seen to fail; it was a sign of weakness. Anita had always regarded that as more of a male phenomenon.

She'd called Wallen and Hakim to her office so that they could catch up.

'Any further developments on the euros that August Skoog took to the bank?'

'Nope,' replied Hakim. 'Other than that they are definitely from the robbery. Bea and I have been back to the house in Löderup, and there is no sign of any more of the cash.'

'Where on earth could he have got hold of it?'

'He couldn't have been involved in the robbery?' queried Wallen. 'I mean, in a way that we don't know about?'

'The Skoogs *were* in Skåne then. And there *is* a connection: Willi Hirdwall was one of their foster kids. Except he drowned years before, so the Hirdwall we dealt with was someone else. He could be Klas Karlin, who was fostered by the Skoogs at the same time. We know from the Beijers that Karlin had a criminal past. Car theft initially, then supermarket robberies, where a manager was nearly killed. Spent a couple of years inside.'

'There's no record,' said Wallen.

'Over twenty years since his release. So, did Karlin assume Hirdwall's identity? And if so, why?'

'To make sure he could get a job,' opined Hakim. 'No criminal record to put off employers, especially in security.'

'He certainly wouldn't have got that job at Q Guard,' Wallen stated emphatically.

'Right, say, hypothetically, that Karlin assumes Hirdwall's identity after the boating accident. He inherits Hirdwall's life and his employment record. He comes to Malmö and gets a similar job before ending up at Q Guard.'

'That fits,' confirmed Wallen.

'He's faced with a life choice – either he goes straight or he doesn't. Our friend McBride was questioning whether Hirdwall was involved in the robbery. She pointed to the fact that it was he who nudged us in the direction of Kasper Jensen.'

'That's true,' said Wallen. 'I was with you at the hospital when he did.'

'Your memory's better than mine.'

'My first big case. Everything made an impression on me then.'

'So he might have done that deliberately… but I still can't work out how he was involved. If he was, why did they shoot him? And why did Bilić, who we know was behind the robbery, try to have him killed?'

'We believed at the time that Bilić was behind Subotić's murder because he was trying to neutralize the gang, or the connections that led back to him. And if Hirdwall was one of them, it would make sense to kill him, too.'

Wallen had a point.

'I understand that,' agreed Anita. 'But why was no attempt made on Jensen's life?'

'He didn't know anybody in the gang other than Subotić, and then Subotić was killed anyway.'

'They got to Sven-Olof Alm. I suppose he knew too much.' Anita was still trying to think the business through. 'And why have two guards on the inside?'

'To ensure that nothing went wrong on the night?' suggested Hakim.

'An extra mouth that might blab? I doubt it. And if they were trying to silence Hirdwall on the night of the robbery, why didn't they shoot Jensen too? Nothing makes sense.'

'Getting back to the money,' said Hakim, 'what if August

just found it somewhere?'

'It's a thought, Hakim. We've always assumed that Bilić moved it. What if he didn't? What if it's still out there, and August did just come across it?' There was a brief silence as they pondered this.

'I don't think that works, Anita,' said Wallen. 'If all that money is just sitting there and August did find it, why would he only take four thousand euros?'

'You're right,' said Hakim. 'I think I was being fanciful. It's not as if he had any more hidden in the house – we looked.'

'So someone must have given him the money.'

'Karlin?' proposed Wallen.

'That would fit in with his movements,' Anita agreed. 'We think he was around the same week August went to the bank. But even if Karlin was the Hirdwall of 2006 and he knew where the money had been hidden, how could he possibly know where it had been moved to? And why has it surfaced now?' Anita gave an exasperated grunt. 'If we can find out where August's money came from, we might be able to work out who killed him and Gudrun. The timing can't be a coincidence. We've got to find Karlin.'

'Still nothing from France,' said Hakim.

'The trouble is, despite what McBride believes, Hirdwall or Karlin or Mosten or whoever the hell he is may never come back to Sweden again.'

He got out of the shower and vigorously rubbed himself down. He wandered naked into the living room of the apartment. It was yet another gloriously sunny day –already thirty degrees – and he opened the door to the balcony. A slight breeze, warm and welcoming, played against his skin. This was the life! Spain had been a great idea. The seductive finger of Freedom was beckoning him. He just had one last trip to make. That would do it.

He wandered into his bedroom. The bed needed making and its dishevelment brought a smile to his face. The woman he'd met in the bar on Rambla Méndez Núñez had been responsible for the disarray. She was an English divorcée looking for a good time and, judging by her uninhibited enthusiasm, she'd found it. He hoped she'd still be on holiday when he came back; he would only be away for a few days.

He began to dress. A clean shirt and neatly pressed chinos. He wanted to look the part. Next to the bed was a half-filled cabin bag, and next to that was a shoulder bag. Plenty of room for what he needed. From the bedside table, he picked up his Rolex watch and admired it for a few seconds before slipping it on his wrist. Then he opened the top drawer and took out the plano glasses he used in public places where there might be CCTV, and his new passport. He gave the cover a cursory glance and smiled: *Den Europæiske Union*, *Danmark*. He flicked it open. There was the photograph of Robert Olsen staring back at him. He squinted at it. He was now used to the blond hair. He put the passport in the inside pocket of his jacket, which was hanging on the back of a chair. With luck, he wouldn't need it – that was the beauty of train travel through the EU – but he always took it just in case he was stopped.

He closed the case, zipped up the shoulder bag and took them into the living room. He had just enough time for a cigarette out on the balcony. He sat on the sun chair, shut his eyes and enjoyed the nicotine permeating his system. Traffic noise thrummed in the background and he felt his muscles relax in the heat. He reflected on the tortuous route that had brought him to this little piece of heaven. One more step and his journey would be complete. Then he would live life on his own terms, secure at last. He stubbed out his cigarette and stood up. He'd walk to the Alicante-Termino and soak up the atmosphere of the town – his town. Almost there.

CHAPTER 39

'Be nice to her.'

'Is that the best advice you can offer?' Anita groaned. Kevin wasn't being of much use. She wasn't in the best of moods. Commissioner Falk had wheeled her out for a press conference to announce that the deaths of the Skoogs were now being treated as suspicious, but any details that the press could latch onto were withheld. She loathed appearing in front of the media, as she always felt self-conscious and constantly worried that she'd give an answer that could be misconstrued, or twisted to create a more lurid headline.

'Look, the secret to dealing with the McBrides of this world is to let them talk about themselves. She sounds as though she's up her own arse, which means that she thinks she's the most interesting person in the room. Make her feel that she is, and she might open up.'

'I'm not sure I really want her to open up,' Anita said doubtfully.

'Take her away from the work setting. Might relax her. Show her some sights.'

'She didn't show the slightest interest in Kalmar, and that's a very attractive town.'

'Yeah, but she was there in a professional capacity.'

Anita was sitting on her bed, talking to her phone. Kevin, at the other end, was sitting on a garden chair on his small patio. It was ten in the evening in Sweden, nine in the UK. She could hear a lumbering tractor in the background. The daylight was going, but he was illuminated by the light above the back door. The weather was still and warm and he had a bottle of beer in his left hand.

'Anyway, it sounds as if you're really going to have to try and cooperate with her. How long's she going to be around?'

'Don't know. I did try and get rid of her. When I discovered that Klas Karlin and Willi Hirdwall might be one and the same person, I told her about the Paris connection and advised her to go there. Didn't work. She seems convinced he's either still here or, if he's left the country, he'll be back.'

'And you say this American gangster is on the loose?'

'Baresi's somewhere. We've put out his description to all the forces between us and Stockholm. I'm sending the team back to Löderup to ask the locals if they can identify him from his mug shot. And to warn them, if they do see him, under no circumstances to approach him. He sounds dangerous.'

'Gawd, how exciting! We don't get much in the way of Mafia activity round Penrith. Unless you the count the farmers: some of them are impenetrable. The most exotic it gets is the annual influx of Romanis for the Appleby Horse Fair.'

Anita smiled, fondly remembering her trips to Cumbria and how peaceful it all seemed. Then she forced herself back to the issue in hand. 'The thing is, Baresi may have killed the old couple. For what reason, I've no idea. Or it may have been Kasper Jensen. Then again, it could have been Klas Karlin. That's why I have to work with McBride. The man she's after may turn out to be the man I'm after.'

After ending her call to Kevin, Anita turned her attention to the papers strewn over the bed. They were from the pre-digitized files on the Q Guard robbery. She knew she shouldn't have taken them out of the polishus building, but getting a small slap on the wrist was the least of her worries. She was in the process of going over the statements made by Willi Hirdwall, desperately searching for clues to his duplicity that she missed at the time.

An hour later, she yawned for the umpteenth time and gave up. Even if Willi had been playing them – and, in hindsight, there were signs that that was possible – she still couldn't work out what his involvement might have been. She would sleep on it.

The train zipped across the Öresund Bridge under a cloudless blue sky. The sea was calm, with barely a ripple, and the iridescent blue water shimmered in the sunlight. A distant tanker was silently ploughing its way through the Sound from the north, while to the south, the sails of the serried ranks of wind turbines stationed off the coast, normally rotating in a frenzy, were merely idling. Anita wasn't sure what the day held in store. She'd taken Kevin's advice and had held out an olive branch to Paige McBride. Showing her the sights of Copenhagen might give them a chance to bond. Life was difficult enough without McBride making waves at the polishus. The Criminal Investigation Squad were getting sick of her; her obsession with Willi Hirdwall was driving them all crazy. So when McBride, to Anita's surprise, accepted her rather lukewarm invitation, it was with mixed feelings of relief and trepidation that she steeled herself for the outing.

They got off at Copenhagen Central Station and crossed the road to the Tivoli, the city's famous amusement park and pleasure gardens. It had been Copenhagen's premier attraction for a hundred and seventy-nine years, but McBride didn't fancy it. The mention of the National Museum was met with a shrug and a grimace. The prospect of the Christiansborg and Rosenborg Castles didn't so much as raise a flicker of interest. The only thing that seemed to get the American's juices flowing was seeing the statue of the *Little Mermaid*. When Anita warned her that it would be quite a walk, she agreed that a boat cruise round the harbour and canals, passing Hans

Christian Andersen's fictional creation on the way, sounded a good option. Anita threw in the promise of a bar afterwards, and the idea was sold. At Nyhavn, they managed to squeeze onto a boat already packed with tourists. As their craft slipped out of its berth and steered its way past a plethora of tall-masted sailing vessels and the beautiful, brightly coloured 17th-century maritime buildings which lined the harbour, even McBride looked interested. Anita smiled, stretched out her legs and absorbed the atmosphere. The happy chatter from the other tourists on the boat, and the buzz from the cafés, bars and restaurants along the quayside, already doing a bustling outdoor Sunday-morning trade, began to tranquilize her mind. Add the glorious weather and the open water to the mix, and it was no wonder that a sense of calmness and well-being overcame her. She hadn't felt so relaxed for a long time. And then she realized that McBride had got out her phone and was taking photos! Success!

Leaving Nyhavn and turning left, the boat entered Inderhavnen, the wide stretch of water which separates the Zealand part of the city from Christianshavn, and Amager Island beyond. The waterfront on either side had long ago exchanged traditional commercial premises for stunning architectural statements of a modern Denmark. The glass behemoths of the Royal Danish Playhouse, the Royal Danish Opera House and the Blox building all produced 'wows'. When they swung round and came close to the *Little Mermaid* sitting on her rock, McBride actually whooped, giving an unsuspecting Anita a fright. After that, the American visibly relaxed and continued to snap away while they chugged their way through the aquatic maze. The 'Not bad.' uttered by McBride when they got off at Ved Stranden made Anita's day. On their way back towards the Tivoli Gardens, they found seats outside the Axelborg Bodega. Opposite the bar was another architectural wonder: the Axel Towers. The five copper-coloured, cylindrical towers in question, all of different heights and fused together in a graceful flow by curved extensions, tastefully blend with the city's old architecture. Not usually a lover of modernism, Anita liked them: they had an elegance that was pleasing on the eye. McBride, more interested in a different kind of cylinder, suggested two ice-cool Tuborgs while they perused the menu. Anita recommended the platter with three traditional open sandwiches. The ingredients were unspecified and it was pot luck as to what the waitress would bring, but it sounded too adventurous for McBride – she chose Grandmother's egg cake with pan fried pork and chives. When their meals arrived, it was Anita who was the happier with her choice.

'Neat place.'

'The bar or the city?' Anita asked after swallowing a delicious mouthful of seafood sandwich.

'The city. I like big cities. Malmö's a bit…'

'Provincial?'

'Something like that.'

'It's a cosmopolitan city to us,' she said defensively. 'But compared to Chicago, well…'

'That's not where I come from. Born and raised in Minneapolis.' Anita's command of North American geography was a bit hazy, so she wasn't entirely sure where Minneapolis was. Somewhere in the middle?

'And it's a big city?'

'Not exactly. But with Saint Paul on the other side of the Mississippi, it's not exactly small.' Anita adjusted her thinking when the Mississippi was mentioned. In the south? She'd surreptitiously consult her phone when she got a chance. McBride drained her beer. 'Another?'

'Why not?' She might as well, as McBride seemed to be lightening up a bit. Anita caught a waitress's attention and ordered two more Tuborgs.

'Minneapolis is full of Swedes.'

'And Irish or Scots?'

McBride laughed. 'You mean McBride? Scots, actually. No, that's my married name. I was brought up a Lindsten.'

'I knew a Lindsten at school. Wilda Lindsten.'

'Yup. It's Swedish. Folks were both of Swedish extraction.'

'You've kept that quiet.'

The waitress produced two more cold, foaming glasses of beer. It was the perfect antidote to the heat of the day.

'So you swapped Swedish for Scottish?'

'For a while. When me and Jim split, it was too much of a hassle to change everything. I was known as "Mac" in the station anyway. Would have confused my colleagues if I'd gone back to Lindsten – some of them have shit for brains. Made my life easier.'

'So you're really an American Swede.'

'Sure am. And proud of it. My mom's grandparents came over from Sweden at the turn of the century – the last one of course. Apparently, they never learned to speak English. Their daughter married into the Swedish community – there were a hellava lot of Swedes in Minnesota by then. Still are. My own folks met at an event at the American-Swedish Institute in Minneapolis, which says everything. I didn't know Dad's parents, as they died when I was very young, but Mom's parents looked after me a lot when I was a teenager after my folks divorced. They used to speak Swedish in the house. Liked to keep the language and traditions alive even though neither of them ever saw the old country. And they used to get a Swedish-language newspaper at home – there used to be Swedish newspapers all over; I believe there were hundreds at one time. My grandparents used to get *Svenska Amerikanaren Tribunen*; my mom still reads *Nordstjernan* occasionally. I'm not great at speaking Swedish, but I understand enough.'

'Enough to understand what Klara Wallen said at that first meeting?'

'Oh yeah!' They both laughed. 'Thought it might be useful not to let on.'

'I'll drop that into the conversation the next time I see Klara.' Anita savoured a mouthful of cold pork from her second sandwich. 'Where did the name Paige come in?'

'There was a lot of family pressure to call me Ingrid or Greta, but Mom thought it would be better for me to have a more American name. The fact that it's Latin or Greek or suchlike didn't register with them. Pity. I think Greta would've suited me.'

'I know a lot of people emigrated from Sweden to the States. We were a poor country back in the day.'

'I remember learning that a third of the Swedish population left to escape famine and poverty. America must have seemed like heaven to them. Plenty of land to farm in places like Nebraska, Kansas and Illinois – and Minnesota, of course. There's even a place called Malmö Township in the state. And those who didn't make a go of it in the countryside headed for the cities like Minneapolis and Chicago. When I was growing up in Minneapolis, we still did all those weird Swedish things. Like lutfisk at Christmas. I hated that.'

'Me too!'

Silence followed as they concentrated on their food. Anita had got more out of McBride than she'd expected. She decided to keep it going.

'So how did you end up in the FBI?'

McBride gave a rueful pout.

'Joined the police in Minneapolis. That's where I met Jim McBride. Handsome as hell, but hell to live with. Or maybe I was. Other women couldn't keep their hands off him and he didn't do much to dissuade them.' It was a story that Anita could relate to. 'Boy, did we have some fights! Too much drink, too much pressure at work. Cops should never marry cops. Anyways, I was in homicide by then. A chance of a transfer to

Chicago came up and I grabbed it. Left Jim for a fresh start. Chance to blow away the stench of a toxic marriage in the Windy City. After I'd been there for a couple of years, I was approached by the local FBI. It was a no-brainer. And it's all been good until—'

Anita's phone interrupted McBride's flow. It was Klara Wallen. 'Sorry, I'd better take this.'

McBride went back to her beer.

'Hi Klara. What's up?' Anita listened intently. 'No, no. I'm already in Copenhagen. I'll go. What's the address?' Anita scribbled something on her beermat. 'OK, I've got that. I'll let you know how I get on.' She slipped her phone back into her pocket.

'Something come up?'

'Yes. Kasper Jensen, the security guard involved in the Q Guard robbery – he's back in town. As soon as we've finished here, I'm going to see him.'

'Can I come, too?'

Anita took a sip of her beer. It tasted good.

'All right.'

Twenty minutes later, they were on a driverless Metro train heading out towards Kastrup. Anita explained to the FBI agent about Jensen's car being seen in the Skoogs' village in the days before their murder, and that it had also been spotted on the Bridge, coming into Sweden in the late afternoon of the day of the murder. There was still no evidence that Jensen had been heading for Löderup that night, and Joel Grahn had had no luck in identifying the red Golf on the road north of the Skoogs' house around the time the killings took place. But there was no denying the car had been in the vicinity at those crucial times, and a few weeks earlier in June. Jensen had some explaining to do but if his account was plausible, at least that would be one less suspect. Leaving just Klas Karlin and Salvatore Baresi in the mix – unless there was another possibility they hadn't factored in.

They alighted at Lergravsparken Metro station and walked through the park from which the stop took its name. They strolled through the Sunday afternoon activity: families picnicking on the grass, dogs sniffing in the undergrowth, kids playing on the swings, joggers pounding the footpaths, and couples enjoying a leisurely promenade. They made their way to the top of Kastrupvej and along to the apartment building that Jensen now occupied. The last time Anita had been in the area was to arrest him. It had been a bleak midwinter then. Summer now made it look and feel totally different. The allotments occupying the tract of land between where Jensen had then lived and now resided were bursting with colour, both decorative and edible: a profusion of flowers, fruit trees, herbs and vegetables soaking up the sun's energy while their owners fired up their barbecues and cracked open their Carlsbergs.

Kasper Jensen greeted them with a 'What the fuck do you want?' before grudgingly letting them into his apartment. He was much changed from the muscle-bound security guard of fifteen years ago. The once-firm contours had run to fat and his gut was bursting out of his T-shirt. His face was red and bloated: the visible effect of too much alcohol. But despite his personal appearance, Jensen's apartment was neat enough – and he'd clearly found himself a girlfriend to take on holiday. She wasn't in evidence.

He reluctantly took them into the living room.

'Shit, I remember you now,' he said to Anita. 'You haven't aged well.' The nasty remark hurt her more than it should have, and she had to restrain herself from saying 'Ditto'.

'Have a nice holiday?' she asked pleasantly in Swedish as she took a seat. McBride remained standing. She would have to try and understand what was said as best she could.

'It's no business of yours whether it was nice or not,' he

replied in the same language.

'It's just I heard you'd come into some money.'

'Fuck! Are we going through this all again? You were asking the same shit the last time I saw you.'

'And you gave me the wrong answers. Look where that got you.'

'Yeah – losing my wife and kids,' he said furiously.

'It's OK,' she said, waving him back into his chair, which he'd half risen from in his anger. 'I'm only here to ask you some routine questions.'

'Look, lady, I've done nothing wrong. I stack shelves in a fucking supermarket. I keep my nose clean. I'm not going back inside.'

'As I said, it's OK,' Anita said reassuringly. 'I'm just here about your car.'

'My car?' He was totally nonplussed.

'Yes. The red VW Golf. That's yours, isn't it? The one with the dent on the driver's-side door?'

'Have I been caught speeding?' he said mockingly. 'That thing's not capable of breaking any speed limit.'

'We'd just like to know why you were passing through Löderup in the first week of July.'

'What?' he shouted. 'Where the fuck is Löderup?'

'It's in Skåne. Between Ystad and Simrishamn.'

'I don't know what you're talking about.'

'OK, let's be more specific. Friday, the eighth of July. Your car was seen crossing the Bridge, heading into Sweden. That would be about a week before you went on holiday.'

Jensen thought for a moment. 'Ellie. I was going to spend the night with Ellie.'

'Who's Ellie?'

'My girlfriend. She was the one I took on holiday.'

'Where does she live?'

'Staffanstorp. Other side of Malmö. She's Swedish.'

'We'll need her name and address.'

'Why?' he said aggressively.

'To ask her to confirm what time you arrived.'

'No. I don't want the fucking police hassling her. And why do I need an alibi? What have I supposedly done?'

'We're investigating the murder of an elderly couple outside Löderup.'

He recoiled in horror. 'You don't seriously think I've got anything to do with it? I don't even know where Löderup is.'

'We just want to eliminate you from our enquiries.'

'I've heard that one before,' he muttered sarcastically. 'Anyway, why on earth are you talking to me about it?'

'As I said, your car was seen in the area not long before the murders took place. And, secondly, some of the money from the Q Guard robbery has just turned up.'

This last remark immediately deflated his growing rage. 'What?' He appeared genuinely incredulous. 'Some of the money's turned up? Where?'

'I'm afraid I can't tell you that, but there is a connection to one of the victims.'

'Shit! After all this time,' he said reflectively. Suddenly, he seemed to be aware of the gravity of his situation. 'Look, I know nothing about this couple. I don't follow the news, especially in Sweden.'

'Right. So you'll have no objection to us talking to your girlfriend.'

'She's not here. Went home yesterday. Back at work tomorrow.'

'I'll get someone to speak to her.'

'Fine, fine. Ask her.'

'In the meantime, your car. How come it was in Löderup but you know nothing about it?'

Jensen looked away. 'I don't know.'

'You must know, Kasper. If you don't tell us, we'll draw the obvious conclusion: you were there and could in some way be involved with the murders.'

Anita could tell Jensen was struggling with an inner turmoil. She waited while he wrestled with himself. McBride watched intently. At last, he came to a decision.

'Look... erm... I let someone use it.'

'Who?'

'An old friend, that's all. He wouldn't harm anyone.'

'Has this old friend got a name?'

Jensen was surprisingly reticent. 'He doesn't live in Copenhagen. Just borrows the car when he's here on business. So he can't be of any interest to you.'

'Kasper, I need a name,' Anita insisted.

He took a deep breath, then, reluctantly, in a small voice he said, 'It's Willi.'

McBride, who had been trying to follow the conversation, stiffened.

'Willi?' said Anita slowly. 'Willi who?'

'Willi Hirdwall.'

'The man you worked with at Q Guard?'

Before he could answer, McBride burst out, 'Where is he?'

This startled Jensen. Anita held up her hand to stop McBride going any further.

'Willi Hirdwall borrowed your car at the beginning of July?'

'Yeah. But he didn't really want people to know. I don't know why. Just his way. But he did pay for it.'

'The money for your holiday?'

'Yeah.'

'So he gave you enough money for a holiday for two for the use of your crappy old car? Doesn't seem a fair exchange.'

'You don't understand. It wasn't an exchange. He said he was looking out for an old workmate. He knew I'd been in prison and my life had turned to crap. He felt sorry for me.' He sighed. 'I can't afford to be too proud to accept a bit of charity.'

Anita glanced at McBride.

'How did you meet him again?'

'He just turned up out of the blue sometime last month. Wanted to see how I was getting on. He was just the same, really. A good guy.'

'Did he tell you what he'd been up to since the robbery trial?'

'Yes. Said he'd gone to America. Set up a business and done well.' McBride was grinding her teeth in the background, desperate to get involved. 'But he'd had enough and was coming back to Europe.'

'Why borrow your car?'

'Said it would be fun. Remind him of his youth. I don't know... some such reason.'

'And you didn't think it was odd?'

'I didn't give a toss. He gave me a thousand euros the first time. And five thousand the time before this. Paid for the holiday. Said I deserved it as life had treated me badly.'

'It's guilt money,' said McBride in English.

'What does she mean? Who is she, anyway?'

'I mean,' McBride continued, 'that your *good guy* was the one who pointed the cops in your direction all those years ago.'

'That's rubbish!' Jensen's English was quite good enough to refute her claim.

'It's true,' Anita confirmed. 'We think that Willi was involved in the robbery somehow.'

Jensen shook his head wildly. 'No, no, no. Willi was shot. It was me who opened the fucking doors and helped—'

'Wait a minute,' Anita stopped him in his tracks. 'Wait a minute! You said he paid you a thousand euros the first time. And another five the time before *this*. What do you mean by "the time before this"?'

'I told you. That week you talked about.'

'So what's "this time"?'
Jensen was silent
'When?' yelled McBride, shoving her face close to his.
'This morning.'

CHAPTER 40

If he never came back to Sweden, it would be the bright churches sprinkled around the countryside that he would miss. Churches like those he had just passed in Ingelstorp and Valleberga, and the one in Löderup that was coming into view up ahead. He found the churches of Spain, with their cloying Catholicism, too claustrophobic. Formal religion had always been wasted on him, but he could still find solace in the plain simplicity of his home country's Lutheran places of worship. Without ostentation, they exuded a fundamental godliness which was pure and unexacting, unlike the richly adorned basilicas that demanded veneration and adulation. If there were a God, surely He must see through all that incense and flummery. And if there were a God, he hoped He would look kindly on Gudrun. She'd taken him to church a couple of times when he'd first moved in with her and August, but then he'd refused to go any more. He realized it had saddened her, but she hadn't tried to press it further. Yet now, he found himself praying that she would be spared any more pain and suffering. He hadn't known what to bring her this time. She could no longer eat the chocolates she used to love. And she wouldn't live long enough to appreciate or enjoy any kind of trinket. He'd bought a small Spanish crucifix, but he wasn't sure whether he'd actually present it to her. The flowers he'd picked up in Ystad might be better. August had been easy – a bottle of single malt.

Past the church, he turned left off Österlenvägen into the

now familiar Storgatan. On his right was the village school where he knew Gudrun had helped with the kids. The long main street was bathed in vivid sunlight as he drove beyond the garage and the village shop. He'd avoided going to places which he knew the Skoogs frequented in case any awkward questions were innocently asked. Just outside the village, he passed yet another church – Hörups – perched loftily on a rise on his right. Soon, he was turning off along the old farm track that led to the Skoogs' home. He didn't intend to stay more than two nights this time; he didn't want to hang around longer than was necessary for appearances' sake. Gudrun and August were always pleased to see him, and the old couple were so proud that he was now so successful in the world of commerce after such humble and troubled beginnings. Of course, he kept the exact nature of his business vague. The truth would crush them. He was already feeling guilty that he couldn't tell them that this would be his last ever trip. Maybe, when the dust settled, he could fly them down to Spain for a holiday. The sun would do them good. If Gudrun lasted long enough to make the journey. Though he knew her cancer was terminal, August had always been guarded about how long she had left.

He drove the car to the front of the house. He could see August's Volvo Estate. They must be home. He fetched the bottle of whisky and the bunch of flowers and took them to the front door. He pressed the bell and heard it tinkle inside. No one came. He rang again. Still no answer. He put down the bottle and tried the door – it was locked. Maybe they were round the back in the garden. He walked round the house, but still no sign. He tried the back door. That, too, was firmly shut. He couldn't understand it. The car was here yet the house was deserted. Had they gone for a walk? That was unlikely. Gudrun tired too easily.

Then it occurred to him that maybe something had

happened to Gudrun. There was no way he could find out; he didn't have August's mobile phone number. That had been deliberate. He'd avoided using phones of any kind in Sweden. The first time he'd visited them, he'd just turned up. They were delighted after not seeing him for so many years, and though he said he would book into a hotel, they'd insisted that he stay with them, and any other times he was on business in Skåne. The arrangement suited him; it meant he could keep a low profile. He'd put on his suit and go to his non-existent meetings during the day and come back for a meal with the couple at night. They had no suspicions of his true intent. All they could see was his affluence and his success. He did have one awkward moment when August had commented on the car. Why was he driving such a battered old vehicle? Surely he could hire a decent car or afford a taxi? But working on the premise that the best lies always have an element of truth, he'd managed to wriggle out of that one, explaining that he was doing a favour for a friend who'd fallen on hard times: instead of giving him charity, he'd paid for the hire of his car. And, of course, the Skoogs, in their naïvety, had believed him. He had to admit that he'd probably always sought their approval and now that he'd won it, it was all based on a lie, or a series of lies. It made him feel hollow. These were the only people who had showed him unconditional kindness and love, and he was deceiving them.

Worried though he was about what had happened to the old couple, he had to put sentiment aside. He took the bottle and flowers back to the car and took out his cabin bag. It would be easier to do this while no one was around. He went back round to the garden and headed for the trees.

Anita and McBride had returned to the polishus. On the way back from Copenhagen, Anita had called all the team members and ordered them into work. Wallen and Erlandsson had been dispatched to Staffanstorp to speak to Kasper Jensen's girlfriend to establish if his alibi could be corroborated, Brodd was told to check the CCTV footage from the Öresund Bridge to see what time Hirdwall had crossed into Sweden, and Hakim was given the job of putting out an all-points bulletin on Jensen's car. Anita then called Joel Grahn. He was hosting a barbecue at the time, though he was happy to abandon it to help. He would go round to the Skoogs' place and see if Willi Hirdwall turned up there. Anita advised him to take at least one uniformed officer with him just in case Hirdwall was uncooperative.

McBride had joined Anita in her office, now centre of operations.

'Told you he'd be back.'

'How could I have doubted you, Paige?' Anita admitted with a twinkle in her eye. Maybe she'd misjudged the FBI agent. And maybe she should pay more heed to psychological profiling. Despite spending all that time with Hirdwall, clearly McBride knew him better than she did, and *she* hadn't even met him. 'What I can't get my head round is why Hirdwall would turn up here at all. This appears to be the third time. If he's sitting on five million dollars, why risk coming back to Sweden? It can't be just to visit the Skoogs, though they're probably the nearest thing he had to family. And why borrow Jensen's car?'

'Everything he's done is to keep him under the radar,' said McBride. 'He hasn't flown in to either of the local airports – Copenhagen or Malmö – so he's probably using trains. He was spotted at Copenhagen Central, remember.'

'Yeah. No border checks if he's coming from France.'

'As to why he keeps coming back: I reckon it's your robbery. He's connected. I just know he is. You say the money has never surfaced up until now. Maybe he knows where it is.'

'Or maybe August Skoog found it somehow.'

'Possible. Perhaps that's why he was killed.'

That was something that hadn't occurred to Anita. Could the Serbs be involved? Dragan Mitrović had been unforthcoming on the subject of the money. Did he know where it was?

Her phone rang. It was Wallen calling in from Staffanstorp. Jensen's alibi checked out. He'd reached the girlfriend's house at around half-past five. This was confirmed by a neighbour, who moaned that that they had starting bonking shortly after his arrival. Thin walls. He couldn't have been at Löderup at the time the Skoogs died.

Shortly afterwards, Hakim came in.

'Pontus found no sign of the Golf crossing the Bridge anytime today.'

'What's he playing at?' said McBride in frustration. 'Is there another way? A route that's not as noticeable?'

'I suppose he could have crossed on the ferry,' said Hakim. 'Helsingør to Helsingborg. It's a long way round. It would add two to three hours to his trip. The Bridge only takes minutes.'

'But the ferry's not an obvious place to check. Paige is right. Everything he does is to keep out of sight. You and Pontus check all this morning's ferries.' As Hakim left the office, Anita turned to McBride. 'Where the hell is he?'

The traditional hotel room had had a boutique make-over and was more comfortable than he'd expected. He'd spend the night here, and tomorrow, he'd find out where the Skoogs were and say his goodbyes. He knew it might be the last time he saw Gudrun. That was a painful thought. He'd counted out some more money to give to August. It wouldn't buy Gudrun's life back, but it might help in some way. He owed them so much. And, even though they'd remained in ignorance of the fact, they'd helped him in another way over the last sixteen years. Out of his window, over the road, he could see two large ferries in dock. The daily sailings to Poland. The thought struck him that that might be an even safer way to leave Sweden this last time. It would avoid him travelling through Copenhagen, where there was always the danger that he might be spotted. And it would be a more interesting route back to Spain. He could take his time; he had now bought himself that precious commodity. Kasper's car? He'd call and tell him where to pick it up. It would scarcely be a hardship after all the money he'd given him.

He took the small kettle into the bathroom and filled it up, then pressed the button to start it off. He yanked at the tube of Nescafé – why were they always so difficult to open? – before letting the granules slide into the coffee cup. While the kettle boiled, he sat down in the armchair by the window. Yes, Poland was a good idea. He would ask about getting a ticket. Lazily reaching over to the table, he picked up the copy of *Skånska Nyheter* which he'd got from reception. He flicked it open and suddenly held the newspaper deadly still. He recognized the woman in the photograph on the second page. It was Anita Sundström. She was now a chief inspector and the image had been taken at a recent press conference. The article was by a journalist called Martin Glimhall. He began to read and as he read, his mouth dropped open and he could feel bile careering towards his throat. He thought he was going to be sick. Gudrun and August Skoog were dead! Not only that, but their deaths were being regarded as suspicious. He was oblivious to the kettle boiling in the background until it switched itself off. The newspaper was now shaking in his hands and he had to lay it down. He threw his head back and groaned. How could this possibly have happened? Who would want to kill such good people? They had spent their lives helping others. He screwed up the newspaper and threw it to the floor. Then, slowly, the implications of their deaths started to dawn on him. Had their murders something to do with what he'd been up to? No, it wasn't possible. How could anyone know of his connection to the Skoogs? Christ, the Serbs! Had *they* found out? But how? Oh my God! August knew when he was coming back. Had they tried to get him to talk? What if the old couple had been tortured? His brain reeled at such a horrific thought. But, if they had told the Serbs what they knew, surely a reception committee would have been waiting for him? Or maybe the Skoogs hadn't told them anything and had died as a consequence. The thought was almost too much to bear.

He forced himself out of the chair and went to the mini bar. He took out a miniature gin and drank it down in one gulp. He would have to put his revulsion to one side. He had to think practically. He'd done what he'd come to do, so he'd check out that ferry today. Now it was even more imperative to get out of Sweden as quickly as possible. He remembered Anita Sundström as a good officer. She was thorough. She'd have gone into the Skoogs' background. His name might have come up, and that of Willi Hirdwall. She knew him well from all those dull months in the safe house. That made her dangerous. He calmed himself and tried to think rationally. There was nothing to link him to August and Gudrun now; the police wouldn't even be aware that he was in Sweden. All he had to do was to keep his head and disappear as soon as he could.

His heart slowed and his breathing returned to normal. He'd have that coffee. As he poured the water into the cup and watched the granules liquify, a dreadful thought hit him like a hammer blow.

The suit! His fucking suit was hanging in a closet at the murder scene!

'Hirdwall's not here.'

Joel Grahn was calling in from just north of Löderup. He was standing in the Skoogs' garden. 'I've been here fifteen minutes. Everywhere is locked tight. No sign of anybody.'

Anita thought for a moment. Confirmation had just come

in that the red VW Golf had been on one of the Helsingør to Helsingborg ferries that shuffled across the Öresund Sound every half hour. The crossing took twenty minutes. He'd been on the 11:40, so he would have reached Helsingborg by twelve o'clock. The distance between Helsingborg and Löderup, according to Hakim's smart phone, was 141 kilometres. That was about two hours, so he'd have got there at around two. It was now four-thirty. That's if he'd been making for Löderup. Or he might have been going somewhere else first. Even if he'd turned up at the Skoogs' earlier, he would have found it deserted. And if he'd already heard that they were dead, would he have gone there at all? Anita couldn't make her mind up.

'Can you hang around for another half hour?'

'Sure.'

'Thanks.'

It was after ten o'clock in the evening before he went to the hotel car park and drove off out of Ystad. He'd waited until dark. He had to be careful. He'd already prepared his escape route and had purchased a one-way passenger ticket to Świnoujście in Poland for tomorrow's 13.30 sailing.

This time, he'd taken the precaution of avoiding driving through Löderup, and he'd approached from the north. He felt nervous and unsettled at the thought that he'd have to break into the Skoogs' home. It was ridiculous – they could hardly object, yet it was like betraying their trust. He turned off the main road and dimmed his lights. The night was clear and starlit, and it was a relief to disappear under the dark canopy of the trees which lined the drive. He brought the car to a standstill in front of the house and got out. All was quiet except for the incessant chirping of crickets. The evening air smelt sweet. The earthy scent reminded him of his last visit, when he'd sat out in the garden in the gathering dusk, sharing a few drinks with August. Gudrun had gone to bed early, and the old man had reminisced about their life together in Kalmar.

He went round to the back of the house and stood by the glazed door into the workshop, listening. An owl hooted in the wood. Then he held up the torch he'd purchased that afternoon and smashed the glass with the butt end. He jumped guiltily as the sound echoed into the night. He reproached himself for being stupid: there was no one around to hear. He leant in and flicked the latch and gingerly opened the door. Once inside, he switched on the torch and made his way through the workshop and up the wooden stairs leading to the ground floor. His footsteps sounded heavy and loud. He pushed open the door at the top of the stairs and flinched. The kitchen door stood open. Moonlight was flooding in through the window, giving the objects in the room an eerily animate appearance; he could almost sense the presence of the Skoogs. Do the dead ever really leave this earth? He shook his head. After all he'd been through, he shouldn't be crapping himself at a few shadows.

Following the beam of light from his torch, he continued his progress through the house to the spare bedroom on the top floor. He wondered if he'd left anything else besides the suit. He couldn't remember. He entered the room and went straight to the wardrobe. His heart pounding, he yanked open the door and flashed his light inside. The suit was gone! The one thing that could prove he'd been in Sweden. Shit, shit, shit! His mind whirred. The police must have it! They'd have realized immediately that it didn't belong to August. What could they glean from it? Fingerprints? Where he'd bought it? They might be able to trace it back to Alicante! Anything in the pockets? Again, he couldn't remember. Jesus! They might even try and tie him in with the murder! He really had to get out of Sweden as quickly as possible. He made his way back to the stairs. What was that? A sound? He froze. Christ, this was getting to him. He must stay composed. He listened carefully. Nothing. He had to get out of there.

He flew down the stairs and was heading for the basement door when a sound from the kitchen made him stop. He swung round and there, to his horror, illuminated by the light from his torch, was the figure of a man.

'Hello, Micky.'

CHAPTER 41

'Long time, no see.' The voice could crack Brazil nuts.

He couldn't move. It was as though his feet had grown roots in the wooden flooring. A cold sweat of fear broke out all over his body. There, dwarfing the kitchen chair in which he was nonchalantly sitting, was a bear of a man wearing gloves. And in one of those gloved hands was a Makarov pistol. And the pistol was pointing straight at him. It was the last person he expected to see – or wanted to. How in the name of God had Salvatore Baresi tracked him down to a lonely house in the Swedish countryside? This was a nightmare! Baresi... with a lethal weapon! He just didn't know what to do. The man was vicious and violent. If he killed him cleanly, that wouldn't be so bad. But it's what he might do to him before he killed him that really terrified him: he'd seen Baresi in action before.

'Micky, Micky, Micky,' the big man said, shaking his head. He waved the pistol at him. 'Put the light on so I can see you properly.'

He still couldn't move. His wanted to vomit, but he knew he mustn't show how afraid he was. He must play for time; delay the inevitable and think of a way to escape. He forced his arm to move, and his finger flicked the switch. The light revealed a grin on Baresi's face as wide as Lake Michigan.

'You've put me to a heap of trouble, Micky. It's about time you showed your ugly mug; I've been hanging around this dump of a country of yours long enough.'

'How did you find me?'

'Not quite as clever as you think, are you Micky? Or as careful. You were spotted on CCTV in Copenhagen station last month.'

'Who by?'

'Interpol. They fed the intel back to the FBI. Which reached the Chicago cops – and Mr Gentile has sources there. Then all he had to do was put two and two together.'

How could he have been so stupid? Fucking technology! What chance did anybody have these days? Taking some deep breaths to keep calm, he did some mental calculations.

'So, if the FBI knows I'm here, they've probably sent someone after me, too.'

'Makes sense. And there were two cops hanging around here earlier – like they were expecting someone. Isn't it just dandy that so many people crave your company?'

How could this be happening? The whole world was after him. Baresi was right: he wasn't as clever as he thought.

'But why would the cops think I'd come here?'

'Yeah, why do you keep coming here?' Baresi said, playfully cradling the pistol on his lap. 'The old couple wouldn't tell me.'

'What do mean?' he said in alarm.

'They told me when you were coming back, but not why. After some persuasion, they told me that you were in business. You in business!' he scoffed. 'I knew they were lying.'

'You fucking bastard!'

'Take it easy, Micky. Don't make this more difficult for yourself.'

'Gudrun and August didn't know the *real* reason I was here; they just thought I wanted to see them. They couldn't have told you. There was no need to kill them.'

'I can say one thing for them: they were trying to protect you.'

'But why shoot them?'

'Hadn't much choice. I came in the back and this naked

guy appeared brandishing a piece. I didn't take kindly to being threatened. It sort of went downhill from there.'

'Gudrun was dying, for Christ's sake.'

'Then I was doing her a favour.'

He just wanted to punch the fucker in the face and hang the inevitable consequences. No, he must keep his self-control.

'Enough,' Baresi said, rising from the chair. 'Down to business, Micky. Except you're not Micky, are you? Before I came over here, we found out from our source that your name was Willi Hirdwall.' It was clear that Baresi expected him to say something. He didn't. 'Except it ain't Willi Hirdwall either. I found that out in Kalmar.'

'You've been to Kalmar?' he said incredulously.

'Skoogs' old neighbour. Nice lady. Ann.'

'Shit. You didn't harm her, did you?'

'I'm not an animal. We had a pleasant conversation. Found out that Willi had died nearly twenty-five years ago. And, once I showed your photo to your friends here, with a little persuasion, they recognized you as one Klas Karlin. Though I wouldn't be surprised if that wasn't your real name, either. So who the hell are you?'

'Klas Karlin.'

Baresi laughed. 'You're not exactly a Klas act. Not as far as Mr Gentile is concerned. You not only upset him, but a bunch of Columbian *spiks* who are having second thoughts about supplying us. So, before I put you out of Mr Gentile's misery, where is the money you stole?'

Anita wearily pushed open the door of her apartment. It had been a long day. The morning had been more enjoyable than she'd expected, and she felt she'd achieved some successful bonding with Paige McBride but then, with the bombshell delivered by Kasper Jensen, the day had rapidly deteriorated as it turned into an exhausting, tense manhunt for Willi Hirdwall.

She threw her bag on the day bed and kicked off her shoes. Coffee or wine? She was so tired, she couldn't decide. She switched on the television. A couple of talking heads were debating the work-life-balance question. Right on cue, her phone buzzed.

It was Hakim. 'I know you've probably just got home, but I thought you'd better know straightaway. I've just had a call from the guy I spoke to at the Harbour Hotel when I was finding out about the lunch receipt. He says the same man's back. Booked in this afternoon.'

'Klas Karlin?'

'No. A Robert Olsen.'

'Sounds Danish. Has your guy got it right? He didn't exactly give us a clear description last time.'

'Seems positive. And it *is* our man.'

'How can you be so sure?'

'He noticed an old red VW Golf in the hotel car park when he came in for his shift. He only clocked it because their usual guests drive "cooler cars". Didn't fit with Robert Olsen's "cool gear". I get the impression he's a snob.'

'Right.' Her tiredness had disappeared. 'I'm going over there.'

'Want me to come?'

'No. You get back to the family. I'll pick up Agent McBride. But one thing you can do: get on to Joel Grahn, even if you have to drag him out of bed. Tell him to meet me outside the hotel in an hour and to bring a couple of uniformed officers with him. I don't want to take any chances.'

Baresi followed Karlin down to the basement. Klas was frantically trying to work out where the mobster was going to shoot him. In the house? That might be dangerous, as the police might be back at any moment. And he certainly couldn't make it look like suicide again. Outside? But what about the noise? It was a still night and the sound would carry. In the trees? That would work. Make him dig his own grave. Then he realized that the most sensible solution from Baresi's point of view would be to make him drive somewhere – take him to a secluded spot where it would be easier to dispose of his body. One thing was certain – the Italian had had time to plan his execution.

At the bottom of the stairs, Baresi switched on the light and pushed the pistol into Karlin's back.

'Make for the sauna.'

Fitting, he supposed, that he should die in the same place as the only two people in the world who'd ever shown him any love. He was almost resigned to his fate, then the thought of what this monster had done to August and Gudrun suddenly enraged him and an unyielding obduracy took over – he was not going to let Baresi get away with it.

They entered the sauna and Baresi pushed him down onto the wooden bench.

'Now Micky, my old buddy. You still haven't answered my question.'

'Gentile's money's not here.'

'That's not helpful.'

'It's in a bank. A couple of banks, actually.'

'Very prudent, I'm sure. Well, let's go pay these banks a visit, shall we?'

'They're in another country.'

Baresi pointed the pistol at Karlin's head. 'In that case, there's no point in my hanging around here any longer. Mr Gentile sends his regards. Bye, Micky.'

'Wait, wait! I've got money. Way more than I took in Chicago.'

'No use to me if it's in another country.'

'No, no, you don't understand. It's here.'

'In Sweden?'

'No. Here!'

'Here? In this house?' Baresi said sceptically. 'Are you kidding me? 'I've been through this place and I didn't find a cent.'

'It's out there.'

'In the garden?'

'In the trees. There's an old, disused concrete septic tank. I remember August having it cleaned out when they first moved here. That's how I knew it was there.'

'All very fascinating, Micky, but I'm losing patience.' Baresi's hand tightened on the pistol.

'It's full of money. It's kronor, but it's at least eleven million dollars' worth.'

Baresi's eyes opened wide. 'Eleven million?'

'Yeah. That's more than double what I took from Gentile.'

'And where did this money come from?'

'A robbery. Back in 2006. A cash depot in Malmö.'

Baresi was silent, then he chuckled. 'So, that's it! That's why our police contact came up with another name for you. Witness protection?'

'Kinda.'

'But hang on a minute. If all that money is out there, why didn't you get it before?'

'I couldn't. At the time, I was under police protection and then I had to get away before others involved in the robbery got to me. That's how I ended up in America. Why do you think I keep coming back now? I take bits at a time. But there's still the equivalent of eleven million left. Think of that. You go back to Gentile with twice what I took. And he wouldn't miss a million if you skimmed a finder's fee off the top.' He could see Baresi's interest stirring. 'In exchange for just letting me slip away.'

'My orders are to recover the money and kill you,' Baresi said baldly.

'Say you got the money, but couldn't find me.'

'Remember there's the *chooch* lying in Mount Carmel. No one misses him except Antonella. But that's not the point. Family honour. The Boss took it personally because he doesn't like his beloved daughter getting upset.'

'Just *say* you killed me. I'll disappear. Completely. No one will know.' He could tell Baresi was wavering.

'Let's take a look.' Baresi reached down and yanked Karlin to his feet.

They made their way through the workshop and crunched over the broken glass from the back door. Baresi held the gun in one hand and the torch in the other. They walked across the moonlit garden and Karlin led him towards the trees. The grass was damp beneath their feet and the owl was still hooting somewhere up ahead. They entered the woodland and ploughed their way through the tangled bushes and arboreal detritus of a forest floor. After a few minutes, the torch picked out a pile of old and withered branches which appeared not to have grown naturally but to have been placed there by human hands.

'It's here,' said Karlin.

'Show me,' Baresi said impatiently.

Karlin bent down and started to clear away the debris. A rectangular slab of concrete was soon revealed. In the middle of the concrete was a large round metal cover.

'Lift it!' Baresi ordered, waving the pistol at the cover.

Karlin leant down, found the familiar iron ring and pulled. The first time he'd come back, the lid had stuck fast after lying untouched for nearly sixteen years. It had required all his strength and ingenuity to open it. This time, he raised it without too much effort. He slid the cover to one side to reveal a hole giving access to the tank beneath. The gap was big enough to take a man, even of Baresi's size. By the light of the torch, the mobster could see a large rectangular space, in the corner of which was a mound of something covered by a faded tarpaulin.

'That the money?'

'Yeah.'

'Eleven mill, you say?'

'That's right. It's all yours, Salvatore.'

Baresi waved his pistol. 'I want to see it. Get in.'

Karlin was reluctant. He knew that once down there, Baresi could shoot him and cover up the tank and he'd never be found. But he had no choice. He eased himself down. With his feet on the floor of the septic tank, the opening was just above his head. He bent down and pulled the tarpaulin off the mound. There, underneath, were five large, sealed plastic bags. With his back to Baresi, who was hovering above him, he fiddled with the first bag. The money was neatly wrapped within another layer of plastic, just as it had been prepared all those years ago for depositing in the Q Guard depot.

'I can't see what I'm doing. You'll have to shine the torch in more.'

He half turned, still shielding the bag.

'Point it down properly.'

Baresi shifted to the edge of the opening, bent over slightly and stretched out his hand holding the torch to direct the beam further into the tank.

'Bit more. Over here.'

As Baresi leant down a fraction further, Karlin grabbed his wrist and yanked it with all his strength. The Italian, off balance, crashed down onto the concrete above. As he fell, the pistol went off and the torch dropped into the tank. Karlin clung like a coconut crab onto Baresi's arm, waiting for some reaction from the big man. There was no movement. He could hear the owl again. Eventually, after what seemed like a lifetime, he let go and retrieved the torch. Baresi's body was blocking part of the gap above him. He had to somehow move it to get out. He tried to push it away, but couldn't get enough purchase. Then inspiration struck. He piled up the money bags and eased himself onto the top. This gave him just enough elevation to push his upper body through the gap. Then slowly and laboriously, he rolled Baresi's body far enough away from the entrance so he could hoist himself through. Sweating profusely and breathing heavily, he collapsed on the ground.

All was silent except for the flapping of the birds disturbed by the sudden report of the shot. Karlin wondered if Baresi was dead. He shone the torch on the big man, and its beam picked out a large gash where his head had smashed onto the concrete. But he was still breathing.

What should he do? He reached for the pistol that was still gripped in Baresi's right hand. He prized it free. An image of the murdered Skoogs flashed in his brain and rage surged inside him. He almost pulled the trigger, but rationality won the day. If the mobster disappeared, Gentile would send someone else, and he'd be forever looking over his shoulder. No, he'd leave Baresi here. When he came to, he'd be much more interested in getting the money back to Chicago than tracing him.

Karlin pocketed the pistol and hurried back to the car. The night was still hushed and a mist was descending. Behind the hill, the sodium lights of Löderup glowed translucent in the haze. He was about to get into the Golf when he had a change of mind. He wasn't sure what the police knew, but there was always a chance that they might be aware of the car he'd been driving. He scurried back round to the basement door and made his way up to the kitchen. August always kept his keys there, hanging on a hook by the fridge. He found the one for the Volvo and within minutes, he was driving back along the track. Reaching the main road, he got a sudden jolt: a car was parked among the trees. With relief, he saw that it was empty and he realized that it must have been Baresi's.

Once on the open road, he made his final plans: get back to the hotel, keep out of sight and then board that Polish ferry!

CHAPTER 42

The mist had cleared almost as soon as he'd left Löderup, and there was very little traffic about as he approached Ystad along the tree-lined road from Nybrostrand. On his left, the sea, and on his right, countless holiday homes: wooden houses and chalets of various shapes and sizes scattered higgledy-piggledy among the trees. Even at a quarter past twelve, there were still lights on, and some hardier souls were sitting out drinking their nightcaps. Such images of peace and domesticity were in stark contrast to how Klas Karlin was feeling. His head was in a mess. He'd been so sure that this last trip would be easy. The fact that the brutal Salvatore Baresi had tracked him down had totally unnerved him. And if the Gentile mob could find him, so could the FBI. Then throw Anita Sundström and the local police into the mix, and Sweden was getting far too hot for him. He had to focus: twelve more hours and he'd be on that ferry. If they'd worked out his usual route in and out of Sweden, that would be the last place they'd look for him.

He drove into Ystad. The ferry port was deserted, as was the train station further along the road. The portico of the Harbour Hotel was still lit up. He was about to turn into the side street which led to the hotel car park when he slammed on the brakes and pulled into the kerb. A police car was parked just along from the hotel entrance, and two uniformed officers were standing by it. And there was another parked car just beyond. Then someone emerged from the hotel and came down the steps. Shit! In the light, he saw Anita Sundström. He might not have recognized her if he hadn't seen her photo in the newspaper. She walked up to the policemen and spoke to them. The two men nodded, got into the patrol car and drove off. The police were clearly onto him.

He had to get out of there. He turned into the side street and just carried on past the car park. He found himself driving through a network of back streets and alleyways, and it was only after several wrong turns that he managed to get onto a main thoroughfare. What was he to do? He had to remain out of sight until he could board the ferry. He made his way back onto the Nybrostrand road and crawled along it, looking for somewhere to hide. After a couple of kilometres, he spotted a deserted, sandy track which led to a small car park, beyond which was the beach. He could spend the next few hours here, but he'd have to make a move at some stage when the inevitable early-morning swimmers and walkers appeared. More worryingly, he'd have to go back to the hotel.

'Robert Olsen,' said McBride, holding up a passport. 'He's dyed his hair, but it's still the same slimeball.'

After discovering that the guest hadn't returned, Anita had dragged the manager from her bed and insisted upon her opening up his room. The manager had been reluctant until McBride bluntly explained that the guest in question was wanted for murder by the FBI.

They had already established that 'Robert Olsen' had left the hotel around ten o'clock. They couldn't fathom what he was up to going out at that time.

'Some sort of meet?' McBride had queried.

'Who does he know around here except the Skoogs?' Anita said as she took a cabin case and shoulder bag out of the wardrobe and put them on the bed. She unzipped the cabin bag and rummaged inside it. 'Well, we know why he came.'

McBride came over and glanced at the contents. Under a

thin layer of folded clothes were small bundles of dollars, neatly packaged. Anita picked up the shoulder bag and discovered similar bundles inside.

'I don't think this is from your drugs bust,' said Anita. 'This looks more like the money from the Q Guard robbery.'

'Agreed,' said McBride, taking out a bundle. 'He's been a busy boy.' She replaced the package and picked up a small, ornate crucifix. 'God, don't tell me he's caught religion!'

'OK. Let's put this stuff back. He's got to turn up sometime to collect these. I've told the patrol car to go. We need to keep out of sight so he thinks there's no danger.'

'I want to be the one to arrest him,' said McBride.

'Not without me!'

Karlin was restless. He'd tried to sit in the car and had even attempted a nap. It was impossible, so he ended up wandering along the beach. The Baltic lapped lazily close to his feet. In the moonlight, he could see the sand stretching into the distance. His mind drifted back to another beach further down the coast at *Skanör*. He'd walked along that beach with Anita Sundström before the trial, and they'd come to an understanding. That understanding had enabled him to escape and start afresh. Yet in America, he'd messed his life up once again. How come he could never make the right choice? Each time he'd tried to go straight, temptations were put in his way. And he'd succumbed because he was weak. All that illegal money he'd acquired over the years: it had been so easy. But at what cost? And what was it all for? A lifestyle that wasn't really him? Or had it been to impress Gudrun Skoog? She'd been so pleased when he'd first visited Löderup shortly after their move south. He was in a good security job and she'd been proud of him. It hadn't occurred to her to question how a man like him, who'd served a prison sentence only a short time before, had got such a job. And then again, she'd been so delighted when he reappeared last month, now a successful businessman. More subterfuge, more lies. He felt sick at the thought. He kicked at some stray seaweed. He'd not only deceived the only woman who'd ever cared about him, he was directly responsible for her murder.

CHAPTER 43

Anita yawned and glanced at the car clock. 07:14. She rubbed her eyes. She must have dozed off. Next to her, McBride was wide awake. She was more used to stakeouts than Anita. They were parked next to an enormous SUV in a corner of the hotel car park. Grahn and another officer were parked round the front within sight of the hotel entrance. Klas Karlin had failed to return. Where the hell was he? It was a question that she and McBride had batted around in the early hours of the morning. Perhaps he'd been scared off and had gone. With that in mind, Anita had alerted the officials at the Öresund Bridge and the Helsingborg ferry terminal.

As the night had slowly progressed, McBride had become increasingly uptight. Anita found it understandable. After months of hunting, she was now within touching distance of her quarry. She could at last tie a ribbon round the case file. Her reputation would not only be restored but enhanced – Paige McBride always gets her man.

'Coffee? Something to eat?' Anita asked.

'Coffee. No food.'

Anita got out of the car. In a weird way, she'd miss McBride. They'd started to connect on the Copenhagen trip yesterday, and during the interminable hours in the car park, they'd really talked. The conversations had established that they didn't have that much in common, other than their marriages hitting the rocks, but at least they were finding it easy to communicate, and Anita had felt herself becoming closer to the agent. Like her, McBride had made a mark in a male-dominated profession. More power to her elbow.

Anita headed off down Österleden. The traffic was starting to build. The Pressbyrån store in the square opposite the station would have what she wanted. She was really hungry, not having eaten much since lunch yesterday. The sun was already up and it was going to be another hot Scanian day. The 7.30 train to Malmö was waiting patiently in the station for the Monday-morning commuters. On the same side of the road, she could see Grahn's car. She didn't go across to speak to him, but he gave her a tired wave, which indicated that there was nothing to report. As she was about to enter the store, her phone began to buzz. She whipped it out. It was Hakim.

'Anything happening?'

'No. He hasn't appeared. Been missing all night.'

'He might still be in or around Löderup. We've just had a call from the guy at the local garage. He spotted the Golf again. Yesterday, around two. Fitted our timeline.'

'Yeah. By the time I sent Joel Grahn, he was obviously long gone. He came back to Ystad and booked into the Harbour and then went out again at around ten. But he's got to come back for his passport and the money, surely.'

'What money?'

'Sorry, Hakim. Of course, you don't know. We found some dollars from Q Guard in his room.'

'Really? That puts him well in the frame. Should we come across?'

'Yes. Come with Klara. Get Pontus and Bea to check for any sightings of the Golf.'

'Will do.'

Ten minutes later, Anita returned to the car with two coffees, a sandwich and two bars of Marabou chocolate.

'We know he went to Löderup yesterday afternoon,' she said to McBride as she got back into the car. 'That was before he checked in here.'

McBride just grunted, took the coffee and declined the chocolate.

Hakim and Wallen arrived just after half past eight and got into the back of the car. Anita gave them a quick update. She was interrupted by a call from Grahn.

'Have you seen him?' Anita asked animatedly.

'No, nothing like that. But I've just had a call from a resident on Örumsvägen – the road north of Löderup. She was out walking her dog last night and thought she saw the Golf. She's not a hundred percent sure, as it was dark, although there was some moonlight. That's why she's taken until now to ring in.'

'OK, thanks Joel.' She turned to McBride: 'Did you get that?'

'Yep.'

'Has he spent the night there?' suggested Wallen.

'Look, I think I'd better take a look. Hakim, we'll go in your car and check it out. Do you want to come, Paige?'

'I'll stick around here.'

'Fine. Klara, you can stay with Paige in case Karlin turns up here and she needs backup.'

Half an hour later, Anita and Hakim were driving along the track to the Skoogs' home.

'There's the Golf,' Anita pointed out as Hakim brought his vehicle to a standstill. They both got out and Anita drew her pistol. Hakim followed suit.

'Let's take it nice and easy. We don't know if he's armed.'

Anita peered in the window of the Golf. On the back seat was a bottle of whisky and a wilting bunch of flowers.

'The Volvo's gone,' remarked Hakim.

'Changed cars?'

It didn't stop them remaining vigilant as they approached

the house. The front door was locked. Stealthily, they made their way round the back. The door into the workshop was open and there was broken glass on the floor. The light inside was on.

'He must have broken in last night,' observed Hakim. 'What was he after? The money?'

'Don't think so. He must have had it with him when he booked into the hotel.'

They searched the house and found nothing, though a kitchen chair had been moved opposite the door.

'If the money has been hidden here all these years, it wasn't in the house,' muttered Anita.

'Forensics were thorough and so were we,' confirmed Hakim.

'It had to be somewhere.'

'Outside? Have we missed something?'

They made their way into the garden. 'Karlin's certainly not around now.'

'Look,' said Hakim. 'The grass has been trampled there.' Through the uncut lawn, there was a clear trodden path heading towards the trees. Once in the wood, they had no idea what they were looking for, so they split up. Then, suddenly, Hakim shouted, 'Over here!' Anita rushed to the spot. There, next to a pile of branches and brushwood, was the exposed concrete top of an old, disused septic tank. A metal manhole cover had been pulled back. Hakim switched on the torch on his mobile phone, got on his knees and peered inside.

'All I can see is an old bit of tarpaulin.' His voice echoed in the void.

'Someone was here.'

When Hakim raised his head to look, Anita pointed to a patch of dried blood on the concrete surface.

'A fight?' Hakim suggested.

'With whom? Maybe he just cut himself when he was

getting the money, if that's what he was doing.'

'Do you think this is where the Q Guard money has been all this time?'

Anita sighed. 'If it *was* here, it's gone now.'

According to his Rolex, it was five minutes and thirty-three seconds past ten o'clock. Wearing an old cap of August's he'd found in the car, Karlin had been walking for an hour, keeping as close as he could to the treeline so he wouldn't be seen by passing traffic. He was relieved that he hadn't noticed any cop cars. After a fitful night, he had decided to abandon August's Volvo in case they were looking for it. It was no use to him now, anyway. Besides, there had been a lot of morning activity along the track leading to the beach. Too many people.

He was approaching the outskirts of the town. He crossed the railway line that ran from Ystad to Simrishamn. He had to stick to the pavements now. He felt conspicuous and exposed, though no one paid him the slightest attention. He was nearing the centre. Somehow, he was going to have to sneak into the hotel and extract his belongings. It was further up the road on the right. As he got closer, he pretended to watch the activity in the port. The Unity ferry was already in. He was tempted to try and board it now, as he had the ticket on his smartphone. But there was nearly a million dollars sitting in his hotel room, along with his false passport – he would need that for ID. It was worth the risk this one last time.

Then he spied the car. Unmarked, but he could spot cops a mile off. They were watching the entrance. He'd have to slip in the back through the car park and hope there was no one around.

CHAPTER 44

Anita and Hakim got back to Ystad and left the car round the corner from the hotel. No one had rung in, so Klas Karlin hadn't yet appeared. Maybe he really had taken fright and fled. The car park was now emptying: guests were leaving or going out for the day. Anita's car was still in the corner and the enormous SUV parked next to it hadn't moved. She opened the door; there was Klara Wallen, but no sign of McBride.

'Where's Paige?'

'She's gone inside.'

'When?'

'A few minutes ago. She thought she saw Karlin go in by that fire door over there.'

'Why didn't you go with her?' Anita said heatedly. She could see the fire door was slightly ajar.

'She told me not to. Said she wasn't sure it was him and she was just checking. She said if it was him, she'd call me in.'

Anita didn't like the sound of this.

'All right, come on.' Hakim and Wallen followed Anita through the fire door into a back corridor. Ahead of them was a glass door that led into the public areas that Anita knew ran through to the reception. To their right was a back stairway.

'You two stay down here and see if there's any sign of McBride or Karlin.'

Anita then nipped up the back stairs and came out on the landing where Karlin's room was situated. She remembered it was 216 and faced onto the harbour. She walked along the landing and round the dog leg that took her to the front-facing bedrooms. 216 was one from the end. As she sneaked close to the door, she could hear voices from inside the room. If Karlin *was* in there, surely McBride hadn't gone in after him without support. The mad bloody woman! Anita drew her pistol, took a breath and threw the door open.

Agent McBride was standing in the middle of the room with her gun raised. It was pointed at the man Anita had known as Willi Hirdwall. He looked panic-stricken.

'What the hell are you doing, Paige?' The agent didn't seem pleased to see her.

'I said I'd make the arrest.'

'You haven't got the authority here.'

'Just shut the door!' There was something ominous in McBride's tone. There was no ambiguity in the next command. 'And drop your weapon.' McBride was now waving hers directly at Anita.

'What do you—'

'Drop it!'

Anita laid down her pistol on the floor and closed the door.

'You can't take the law into your own hands. We have procedures.'

'She's going to have to kill us both,' said Karlin.

'What?'

'I'm afraid Micky's right. You shouldn't have come barging in like that.'

'What are you talking about?'

'It's all Micky's fault. He disappeared with the money. I was just asking him what he'd done with my three million dollars.'

Even in Anita's befuddled state, the fog was starting to clear.

'You and him?'

'Partners. Except he did a runner.'

'Because you fucking killed Matteo!' Karlin said bitterly.

'Collateral damage.'

'Christ. You're a piece of work, Paige. Take that money there,' Karlin said, nodding towards the cabin case and shoulder bag he'd been getting out of the wardrobe when McBride had walked in. 'Let her live. Your beef is with me.'

'Can't do that. Too late now. When I call in help, they'll find that Micky Mosten grabbed my gun and shot the chief inspector. I managed to wrest the weapon from him and he got killed in the ensuing struggle.'

'Is that the shit you came out with after you blew away Matteo?'

'Don't do this, Paige,' Anita said hoarsely, desperately trying to stay as unruffled as possible. 'Hakim and Klara will be here any minute now.'

'I'd better be quick then.' McBride stood back and aimed her gun at Anita. Instinctively, Anita turned her head and closed her eyes. She heard the blast but felt nothing. She opened them again and saw blood splattered all over the wall and McBride sinking to the ground, an expression of mystification on her face. It was Klas Karlin who had fired the shot.

'Oh my God!' Anita couldn't move. Was he going to kill *her* now?

'Sorry, Anita.' She was now facing the barrel of his pistol. In the distance, she could hear shouts. Hakim and Wallen had been alerted by the shot.

'Honestly, you don't want to do this,' she said.

'You saved my life once. Remember? Just returning the favour.'

Then he flipped the pistol round so the grip was facing her.

CHAPTER 45

Two days later.

Klas Karlin – AKA Willie Hirdwall, Micky Mosten and lately, Robert Olsen – greeted Anita with a half-smile. He realized that this was the day of reckoning. He'd decided he would unburden himself and come clean about his multiple identities – and he was thankful for the opportunity. His days of deceit had caught up with him. The life he'd been planning for so long had been within tantalizing reach; those few weeks in Alicante were a taste of what could have been. Yet, deep down, he knew he could never really be at ease: he would always be looking over his shoulder, wondering if the next person he met would be the one to kill him. He'd broken people's trust so often that he trusted no one himself. It had been like that ever since the Q Guard robbery had gone wrong. Innocent people had lost their lives – Måns Wallström, and August and Gudrun Skoog. All three had meant something to him, yet his actions had caused their deaths.

Klara Wallen came in with three coffees. It promised to be a long session.

'You may remember Detective Klara Wallen,' Anita said, introducing her colleague. 'She was involved in the original robbery investigation.'

A flash of recognition flitted across his face. 'Yeah. You came down to the safe house in Skanör.'

Wallen nodded as she put the coffees on the table.

'OK,' said Anita. 'Let's get started.'

She went through the formalities for the tape; the interview was also being filmed. She knew that this first part was going to be painful: it would expose the mistakes made by the team back in 2006 and, in particular, her role in that process. Willi Hirdwall had fooled them over the robbery and had literally got away with murder. And it was she, Anita, who had sent him off to his new life.

'Firstly, for the purposes of the interview, we will refer to you as Klas Karlin.'

'Well, that *is* my real name.'

'Let's clear up your background. When did Klas morph into Willi Hirdwall?'

He shook his head slowly. 'Way, way back. My parents died in a car crash when I was four. I went into various foster homes in Kalmar. When I was thirteen, I was lucky enough to be taken into the home of Gudrun and August Skoog. But I was pretty wild by then. I suppose some shrink would say I was lashing out at the world. Despite being a nightmare to live with, all I ever got from Gudrun and August was kindness and attention. And that's where I met Willi Hirdwall. He was a couple of years older than me and had been with the Skoogs for a year. We knocked around together. We both loved football and handball. He kept a brotherly eye on me at school, as I tended to gravitate towards the bad crowd. I looked up to Willi – he was the person I wanted to be, but couldn't. I suppose I prove the point that nurture doesn't always win over nature.

'After we'd left the Skoogs, Willi got steady jobs, and I drifted through endless dead-end ones and fell into dubious company. Petty crime at first. Low-level theft. Then I got nabbed for stealing cars for a Polish gang. Finally, I got more ambitious. I was involved in a supermarket raid that went haywire. We'd already robbed a couple of shops, but at this one the manager got badly beaten up – nearly died. Not by me, but I was part of the gang. I ended up in prison. Willi came to visit and tried to persuade me to get my life sorted out. He promised to help when I got out, which he did. I stayed at his place and got the odd job. Ended up working in a local hotel kitchen. It was while I was there that Willi went missing: a sailing accident. His body was never found. I was devastated by the news. Willi had no family, of course, and I was living in his rented apartment with all his things. His death made me determined to turn over a new leaf. And what better way than to reinvent myself and become Willi? I officially changed my name to his – as you know, that's not a problem here in Sweden. I had access to all his stuff, so I took over his identity as well. And to give the new Willi Hirdwall a fresh start, I moved to Borås and got into security. Willi's last job had been doing something similar at a factory complex, so it looked as though I had some experience. Turned out I was quite good at it.'

'Come on,' Anita scoffed. 'Your clean sheet also had the advantage of obliterating your criminal record. Easier to get a job, especially in that line of work.'

'That might have played a small part,' Karlin grudgingly conceded. 'Anyway, I was glad to leave Kalmar. By the way, it was true what I told you about the broken heart. She hated the people I was mixing with at the time. Sensible girl.' For a moment, he seemed lost in thought. 'Then I moved to Malmö. After I'd been here for a while, the Skoogs retired to the place outside Löderup. August originated from round there.'

'OK. So you're now in Malmö. What happened next?'

'I settled down, behaved myself and started going to Malmö matches. Willi had always been a fan of The Blues for some reason. I moved to the Q Guard job three years before the robbery. It was a good one, too. The work wasn't fantastic, but it paid all right. I liked my workmates… particularly Måns,' he added wistfully. 'Then I suppose I just started thinking about all that money. It wasn't like guarding some ordinary warehouse or stopping thieves robbing a store or chucking drunks out of a nightclub. This was different. That huge amount of cash seemed obscene, and it was just sitting there. It started to play with my mind. I began to imagine what sort of life I could have with even a small bit of it. Then I found myself working out how to steal it. Bad habits die hard, you see. I was the one who'd planned the supermarket robberies back in Kalmar.'

He took a long drink of his coffee.

'My problem was that I needed to recruit a team. And mounting such an operation would take a lot of dosh, which I didn't have. I had to find a criminal sugar daddy. Then fate intervened. As it happened, I occasionally used the Bran Fitness gym in town and after a while, it became obvious that the place wasn't all it seemed. Being in security, you notice things, and I noticed some fishy activity: some of the clients having little packets slipped into their kit bags, money changing hands... stuff like that. So I made a few discreet enquiries and found out about Branislav Bilić. And that decided me to make a trip to Stockholm and make my case. Just like a business presentation.' He smirked at the memory. 'I was proud of the way I handled it, though I have to say it was a bit disconcerting knowing the guys you're talking to are a bunch of thugs who would either listen to your proposition or just as likely attach you to a big boulder and drop you in the Baltic. But they went with it, and Milan Subotić became my go-between. I made sure that when the gang was assembled, no one would know about me other than Subotić. His job was to recruit the team: Kolarov, the explosives guy, was one of their own – too specialized for the local scene – and I got Subotić to draft in Rickardsson and Alm. I didn't know those two personally, only by reputation. The thing is, in the security business, a number of guys are ex-cops and they often chat about the villains they've come across. That's how I got the info on Rickardsson and Alm. So the team was assembled and all set to go. But I needed an inside man to do the staff door. And if things went wrong, a fall guy would be useful. Kasper was ideal. I knew he was having financial problems and I got Subotić to work on him.'

'Except it went more wrong than you thought.'

'Måns? Yeah. I still get nightmares about that. He wasn't meant to be out there. The plan was to tie us all up. When I came out of the toilet and was met by Subotić, I asked where Måns was. When he told me what had happened, I knew we had a serious problem. It turned everything on its head. I had to think quickly while I switched off the alarm: I'd planned for Subotić to do it from Kasper's instructions but there was no point as Måns wasn't there. I knew I had to distance myself from the robbery in case it all unravelled. If I got shot, you were unlikely to suspect me. So I got Subotić to shoot me in the upper arm. He thought I was mad, but he was happy to do it: saved time tying me up. As far as the other three were concerned, I'd been shot trying to be a hero. When Rickardsson came in to do the CCTV, and Kolarov blasted the monitors, they assumed I was dead, or at least out of it.'

'Did Rickardsson take off his balaclava?'

'He did, actually. Silly fat bugger.'

'At least we got that right,' Anita said ruefully.

'Thanks to me.'

Anita thoughtfully twiddled with her empty coffee cup.

'You played us all along, didn't you?'

'Yes!' exclaimed Wallen. 'I remember in the hospital, you hinted at Jensen's financial problems and his behaviour in the run up to the robbery.'

'Well, I had to get you started. Then, when you were stuck on the others, I fed you Rickardsson. It was a stroke of luck he took off his balaclava. It was thinking about that that gave me the idea that I could take the gang out of the picture, with your help, of course. And I knew once you had Rickardsson, you'd make the connection to Alm.'

'And Kolarov?' added Anita. 'Seeing him and Subotić casing the site?'

Karlin waved a hand dismissively.

'I made that up. It was the only way I could tie in Kolarov for you. I didn't want him hanging around when I tried to make off with the cash. Besides, the way I told it, it was Måns who talked to them, and he couldn't exactly refute my story.'

Anita reflected bitterly on how easily she'd been manipulated by this man, whom she had taken pity on, befriended, and even entertained over Christmas.

'So when did you decide to make off with the money?'

Karlin pursed his lips. 'That plan started to form while I was lying in the hospital bed, before you came to interview me. I realized that you lot were going to be crawling all over the investigation like a rash: it was now murder as well as robbery. There was a good chance I'd get dragged in. From my point of view, Subotić was the weak link because he was the only one of the group who knew I was involved. And, to be honest, I didn't trust Bilić not to do the dirty on me.'

'So you decided to move the cash from the Sturup farmhouse? All along we assumed that Bilić had it.'

'That's what I figured you'd think once you made the link between Subotić and Bilić. Which meant you wouldn't be looking for it down in Skåne. The original plan was to leave it for a fortnight to let things settle down before Bilić had it collected. That gave me time. When I got out of the hospital, I contacted Subotić and told him that Bilić had ordered everything to be moved to a safer location. As I was in charge of the operation, he agreed without any objections. I told him we'd do it ourselves, as Bilić didn't want the others involved. Loose tongues and all that. I'd visited the Skoogs a number of times since they'd retired – they still knew me as Klas – and I knew about the disused septic tank among the trees at the back of the house. So, we transferred the money there. I got Subotić to do the driving and the carrying because of my arm.' He suddenly pointed at the two detectives. 'Gudrun and August knew nothing about it, by the way. Totally innocent.' His eyes began to moisten at the mention of their names. Then he pulled himself upright in his chair. 'All along, I knew I'd have to get rid of Subotić. I didn't like the man: a nasty, dangerous bastard. And he clearly didn't give a damn about what had happened to Måns. After we got back to Malmö and dumped the van, I told him I'd get rid of his pistol. I said the police would be examining the bullet they took out of the wall, so we'd better make sure the weapon was never found. He'd hidden it in his basement. Perfect for me. Quiet and virtually soundproof with all that junk stashed down there. I shat myself doing it. I'd never killed anyone before – and I haven't since. Well, I don't count Paige.'

'But your arm?' interjected Wallen.

'It wasn't as bad as I made out. Besides, I'm left-handed. I made Subotić shoot my right arm.'

'All right. So, Subotić is out of the way,' continued Anita. 'And we're helping you by rounding up the others. What about Bilić? He wasn't going to sit idly by.'

'You know he didn't: he sent those two morons down to grab me. You saved me that night, Anita. Sorry, Chief Inspector,' he said, glancing over to the camera.

'We couldn't understand how Bilić had worked out so quickly who you were and where you lived.'

'Nor could I. I knew he'd discover the money was missing when the fortnight was up. I thought that might give me some time. Someone must have tipped him off that I was cooperating with the police.' Anita's mind flitted back to the heated discussions the team had had after the attempt on Willi Hirdwall's life, and she remembered how unusually quiet Karl Westermark had been. Could he have let something slip? Given his later activities, she wouldn't have put it past him.

'We assumed Bilić just wanted to kill you so there would be no link to the gang, or witness at a trial,' Anita said.

'No. They were trying to abduct me to find out where the money had been moved to. You may have heard us arguing about it before I was shoved out into the garden. Once I'd divulged the hiding place, I'd have been kaput. As I say, someone must have tipped them off. Add that to Subotić suddenly disappearing... You didn't name him in the press, so Bilić might have thought he'd done a runner – and he obviously got someone to check out the farm. Probably my night visitors.'

'So what was your plan?'

'I would take some of the money out and piss off to Spain or somewhere. And then come back and collect more if and when I needed it. Except I never got the chance. You had me in that safe house for weeks, though I was quite happy to bide my time. With Alm making his confession, you had your star witness. All I was doing was helping to put Rickardsson away. Alm would get all the attention. And after the trial, I would slip away, take the money and be gone.'

'But Alm was murdered.'

'Precisely. That changed everything. Now I was your only hope. It put me in an impossible position. I remember our talk on the beach at Skanör. I had no choice but to cooperate. It would have looked suspicious if I hadn't. Then I realized the only way out was witness protection and a new life. Stay here and I wouldn't have lasted long. Besides, I couldn't get far enough away without a passport. I didn't have one, either as Willi or Klas. You, Chief Inspector, kindly provided me with a new passport and identity,' he added with a thin smile. That was something else she didn't want to be reminded about. 'So I never got near the money. It's spent the last sixteen years hidden away in the trees behind the Skoogs' house.'

'But it's not there now.'

'Isn't it?' he said in mock innocence. 'I only took the euros and then, this last time, the dollars. You found them when you and Paige came bursting into my hotel room.'

'I realize why you left the kronor, but the septic tank has been cleaned out. And we found blood. It's being tested at the moment.'

'Not mine.'

'So whose is it?'

'A charming American gentleman called Salvatore Baresi. He cut himself.'

'We know about Baresi. We think he's left the country. A private plane with a passenger matching his description took off from near Stockholm yesterday afternoon.'

Was that relief on Karlin's face?

'And where did the Makarov pistol you shot Agent McBride with come from?'

'Salvatore had it.'

'And he just gave it to you?'

'In a manner of speaking.'

'So, are we to take it that Baresi has absconded with the rest of the money?'

'Looks like it.'

'Right. We'll take a break.'

CHAPTER 46

'Let's revisit your more recent misdemeanours. America.'

'I did go straight for a while. I did various jobs when I got to Minneapolis. Worked in a factory, a garden centre and even the American Swedish Institute.' He switched on an American accent: 'There's a whole mess of Swedes in Minnesota.' He grinned. 'I even discovered that some distant family had made it out there in the 1890s. And it was at an event at the Institute that I met Paige McBride. Actually, her mother first, then Paige through her. She was a cop at the time. Going through a bad time with her hubby. So Paige and I started seeing each other a bit. One thing led to another, but nothing serious. Then she had the chance to transfer to another force and she saw it as a way of escaping her home town and a broken marriage. She ended up in Chicago and, as we were still in touch, she suggested there might be more going for me in a bigger city. By that time, she'd joined the FBI. I got back into security and got a job at a nightclub. Anyway, it turned out the club was owned by Giuseppe Gentile. His son-in-law, Matteo, was a regular. He was a conceited cretin, Matteo. Thought he was a tough guy because he'd married into a mob family. Big mouth on him which usually led to trouble. I got him out of a couple of scrapes at the club, which impressed him enough to recommend me to the old man. Gentile began to give me the odd task, like being around when extortion money was being collected. And once I'd proved myself, over time I graduated to his main bagman. Then one thing led to another and I just got more and more involved. But then one day, I woke up and thought: I want out of this. Except you don't just walk out on Giuseppe Gentile.' Karlin gave a mirthless cackle. 'You need money to do that: to get away and never be found. Besides, I still had the millions stashed away over here which I hadn't been able to get my hands on. That was partly your fault,' he said with a sham admonishing glance at Anita.

'Your choice.'

'So when I decided to quit the mob in America, coming back here to Sweden to pick up the Q Guard money seemed like a no brainer. The only problem was Bilić and his boys. But then I heard through the criminal grapevine that Bilić was dead and that Dragan Mitrović was behind bars, so I thought it would be safe enough for a few quick visits. 'Course, I hadn't taken into account the Italians' persistence – or Paige coming after me. Bit naïve, I suppose. And I hadn't reckoned on you lot either.'

'So how did Paige McBride get involved?'

'We'd lost touch for a while: both busy, I suppose. Then she suddenly contacted me and we went for a drink. I told her I was working at the club. Of course, it didn't take her long to join the dots between me and the Gentile family. A month or so later, I did my first cash-for-cocaine exchange with Gentile's new Columbian supplier, accompanying Matteo and Salvatore Baresi. The op was nice and smooth. But it was then that I realized I was getting sucked in too deep and there was going to be no way out. And Matteo wasn't the best person to be hooked up with – too flaky. And it was about this time I started to drink too much. Mind, I always avoided the drugs. That was Matteo's thing, which made him even more of a liability. Anyway, I had another night out with Paige and she could see I was troubled. Blurted out more than I should have – the drink, you see. I told her about getting mixed up with the drugs stuff and that it was all too heavy for me. I'd tangled with organized crime before; should've learned my lesson. Then a week later, Paige came to my apartment. She said she was working on a couple of narcotics cases, and she knew how I could extricate myself from the Gentile family. If I let her know when and where the next exchange was taking place, the FBI would raid it and she'd make sure I escaped. But, whoa! That sounded way too dangerous. I remember I told you once I wasn't a coward, but I wasn't crazy either. Then my *friend*, and sometime lover, suddenly turned nasty. She said she'd been doing some digging and that she couldn't find any record of a Mikael Mosten in Sweden that matched my profile. She knew there must be a reason for that, and she'd worked out I was either on the run or under witness protection. Either way, there were probably interested parties who'd like to know where I was. I couldn't believe she was threatening me, but she left me no alternative. When I reluctantly agreed to give her the information she wanted, she became all nicey nicey again. She said she'd arrange it that not only would I get away, but I'd get away with the money from the drugs, too. More than enough to start a new life. Again! Of course, there was a catch – she wanted over half the haul! We sealed the deal by going to bed.'

'Are you expecting us to believe that it was McBride who cooked up this idea and not you, like you did with Bilić? It's easy to blame her now she's dead.'

'It's the truth.' He took a sip of water. 'But it doesn't really make a blind bit of difference whether it was her or me. The point is it happened.'

'Fine. So you were in it together. How did Matteo get killed and how did you get the blame?'

'Yeah, that,' Karlin muttered. 'Everything was set up. As luck would have it, Giuseppe Gentile had another job for Baresi that night, and it was just going to be me and Matteo. Showed how much faith he had in me by that time. The exchange was to take place at a warehouse down on the Calumet River. I'd checked out the location the day before and found a door that I could slip out through when the Feds burst in. The door led to an inner room, and from there I could get out through a fire exit. It was my job to carry the money; Matteo was the one who was tooled up. Anyhow, around midnight, we met up with a couple of frightening Columbian goons. Right on cue, the Feds came charging in, and chaos ensued. I made it out through my door, with Paige making it look like she's chasing me – we'd already arranged where to meet to split the cash before I hightailed it out of Chicago. So we're in the room with the fire exit and I'm just about to split when in stumbles Matteo. How the hell he escaped from the Feds, I don't know. 'Course, when he saw us – Paige, me and the money – stupid though he was, he started putting two and two together.' Karlin's mind flashed back to that moment:

'What the fuck's going on?' Matteo's face was all confusion and he was waving his gun around. 'Micky?'

Paige already had her weapon drawn and trained on Matteo.

'Put the gun down!' she ordered.

The weapon dropped from his hand and he looked imploringly at me. 'Micky, what ya doin'?'

I picked up the gun and handed it to Paige. In the background, I could hear shouts. The other agents would be here in seconds.

'Beat it!' she ordered.

'Micky! Don't leave me!'

I picked up the bag and fled through the fire door. As I ran across the alleyway I heard a couple of shots.

As he related the story, Karlin shook his head as though he still couldn't quite believe it. 'I knew exactly what Paige had done. But she had to do it: Matteo would have given the game away. So now I had my freedom and my money. But at what a price! It didn't take me long to work out that with Matteo dead and the money gone, the Gentile family would be after my blood. And then an even greater realization hit me with the force of Thor's hammer. What if Paige had killed Matteo with his own weapon? My prints were all over it!'

'That was the case,' Anita confirmed. 'She claimed that she found Matteo's body and that you'd dropped the gun in your panic while getting away with the money.'

'Yeah, I reckoned she might do the dirty on me.'

'So, what did you do next?'

'I ended up in a bar and had a couple of whiskies to calm me down. I just had to weigh things up. It was like the robbery all over again. Someone got killed that wasn't meant to and I had to think on the hoof. Gentile was awaiting a call to say the exchange was done. When he heard nothing, he would come looking for me and Matteo. It would soon be apparent that something wasn't right. I rushed back to my apartment and picked up my passport and a couple of things. As I was leaving, I saw one of Gentile's guys drawing up in front of my building. I got out the back just in time. I went straight to the airport and caught the first flight I could get. Took me to New York. The next day I flew on to Berlin. Then I boarded a train to Paris. I didn't want to leave a trail, and you can move around the EU by land without having to show any documentation. I'd decided on Spain as my ultimate destination, but I reckoned that now was the time to make Mikael Mosten disappear for good. I needed a new identity.'

'So you got to Spain?

'Yeah. I used my drug money to set up in Alicante and got a forged passport under the name Robert Olsen. I'm obviously Scandinavian, so I decided to be Danish to slightly distance myself from being connected to Sweden. Easy enough down there if you've got the money. Then I decided to head back to Sweden to pick up the Q Guard stash. I'd spent years thinking about it just sitting there at the Skoogs' place. In an unguarded moment, while drinking with Paige after we'd agreed on shafting Gentile, I'd inadvertently blabbed that I had a substantial wad of cash to pick up in Sweden. Not that I told her where it came from.'

'That explains why she seemed so sure you'd turn up here.'

'She had a way of getting stuff out of me. Which is ironic, as I was ultra cautious coming back to Skåne. Always used trains so I didn't have to put the passport to the test at airports. Trains also made it harder for anybody sniffing around to trace my movements.'

'You were seen at Copenhagen Central Station.'

Karlin shrugged. 'The best laid plans... Anyway, you pretty much know the rest. I borrowed Kasper Jensen's old car so that I'd go undetected. Used the ferries to avoid the Bridge. Kasper was grateful for the money, poor bugger. It was the least I could do for him. Gudrun and August were delighted when I turned up again. On my first visit, I discovered that Gudrun had cancer and didn't have that long to live. I was going to leave August enough to see him right after she died. But I never got the chance – other than a measly four thousand euros,' he added bitterly.

'That's how we knew the Q Guard cash had turned up.'

'Charity has its drawbacks. I knew it'd take a few trips back and forth to retrieve all the money safely. The Skoogs thought I was travelling on business. That's why I had that expensive suit to look the part. God, if I hadn't gone back for the bloody thing!' He glanced towards the window, regret written all over his face. 'They were proud of my supposed success, would you believe? All that time I'd been doing crap jobs in America when in reality, I was wealthy beyond my wildest dreams.'

'It wasn't your money, Klas.'

'Suppose not,' he said ruefully. 'But when I was living in those dumps in Minneapolis, it became more and more mine. Q Guard would have been insured. It was no loss to them in the grand scheme of things.'

'What about August and Gudrun Skoog?'

'That was horrible.' His eyes began to water.

'Who killed them?'

'Salvatore Baresi,' he said with anguish. 'He tracked them down by talking to their old neighbours in Kalmar.'

'The Beijers,' said Wallen.

'Yeah, I remember them. Oskar was a miserable bugger. Anyway, Baresi traced the connection and came to Löderup thinking it was somewhere I might turn up. He was right.'

'You know he beat them up?' Anita could see she'd hit a raw nerve. 'I assume he was trying to find out where you were.'

'I know they tried to protect me. He couldn't afford to let them live afterwards.' Karlin was now choking back tears.

'He nearly got away with it by making it look like suicide.'

He took a deep breath and tried to compose himself. 'The terrible irony was that all that money was just behind the house.'

'You realize we'll probably never be able to bring him to justice. We've got no real proof.'

'Don't worry. He'll get his comeuppance.'

CHAPTER 47

'He's made a full statement. Came clean about everything.'

Anita was reporting back to Commissioner Falk. He was sitting behind his desk, with the window blinds half drawn to stop the sun reflecting off his computer screen.

'Well done, Anita,' he beamed.

'Not really. We made a pig's ear of the original robbery investigation. When you watch the interview, you'll realize how gullible I was.'

'I'm sure it's not as bad as that.' Falk stood up and came round to her side of the desk. 'The point is, we've now got the murderer of Milan Subotić, and the brains behind the Q Guard armed robbery.'

'We should have done that in 2006. And the money was sitting in a septic tank in Skåne all along,' she groaned.

'Forget the money. Irrelevant now. We've also uncovered a corrupt FBI agent, albeit deceased. The Company were very interested in that. Maybe they can pick up the Italian who murdered the Skoog couple.'

'Salvatore Baresi.'

'Baresi. That's right.'

'Except we have no actual evidence that he killed them. We only know that from Hirdwall… sorry, Karlin. I've a nasty feeling that Baresi is going to get away scot free.'

'Well, we'll see what we can do, and the Americans will do what they can.' Falk perched on the corner of his desk. 'So, what's happening with Karlin now?'

'Well, because he's confessed to his Swedish-based crimes, Prosecutor Blom reckons we can go to court very quickly. Won't have to go through all the rigmarole of endless requests for keeping him detained.'

'Good. The sooner we can tie it up, the better. Then all the press coverage will die down and we can move on.'

'They're going to have a field day when our incompetence comes to light. Imagine the fun they'll have when it emerges that the police went to all the expense of providing witness protection for the very man who'd planned the job in the first place – and then that same man killed the leader of the gang. For God's sake, I helped instigate the whole thing!'

'Our press office knows how to handle damage limitation.'

'They'll have their work cut out with this one. But even the papers aren't immune. Poor old Martin Glimhall will have to rewrite his book.' Anita sighed. 'All I can say is, thank goodness Erik Moberg and Henrik Nordlund aren't around to see it.'

A week later, a police van drew up in front of the District Courthouse on Kalendegatan in the shadow of Sankt Petri Church. The press were out in force: on the pavement outside, there was already a crush of journalists and photographers, desperate to get a glimpse of the man behind the fabled Q Guard armed robbery of 2006. And the story was even juicier than they had dared to hope – the man was also being accused of two murders! It would be headline news for days. Behind the phalanx of TV cameras and the media scrum, a throng of inquisitive passers-by had gathered. It was a sizeable crowd that greeted a handcuffed Klas Karlin as he stepped out of the van with three uniformed officers. He blinked at the sunlight and explosion of camera flashes. Anita, Wallen and Hakim were waiting to accompany Karlin into the courthouse. He had made it clear that he would plead guilty on all counts. It had taken sixteen years, but the case was coming to a close at last, reflected Anita. But there was no sense of triumph – more the ache of regret for missed opportunities, and for her foolishness and ingenuousness.

Karlin's route into the building had been cordoned off but, in their unbridled enthusiasm, some of the journalists had broken through the barrier. As the pressmen closed in, shouting out questions that Anita had no intention of answering until after the proceedings, she had to push her way through the crowd. Then, in the corner of her eye, she glimpsed a squat figure that was making an extra effort to get to the front. There was something vaguely familiar about the face. The pockmarked features raised a prickle of alarm. Suddenly, the man burst past her and the nearest officer to the prisoner, and before Anita or any of the others could react, he was next to Karlin. There was a cry of pain. Anita tried to pull out her pistol, but there were too many people around her to allow free movement. She forced her way forward but she was too late. Karlin was on his knees, as if in prayer. Then, very slowly, he sank to the ground, his white shirt crimson with blood. His assailant was now forcing his way back through the shocked journalists and bystanders while the startled police were also trying to get through the crowd. Then, as people realized the severity of what had just happened, Anita was deafened by shouts of pandemoniac incredulity.

Dragan Mitrović, large earphones clamped to his head, was nodding in time to the music.

A fellow prisoner knocked on his open door. Mitrović didn't hear him. The man tentatively entered the cell and gently tapped him on the shoulder. Mitrović swung round, grabbed him viciously by the wrist and started to twist it.

'Aaargh!' the man cried until Mitrović saw who it was and let go. He took off his earphones.

'Don't do that again!'

'Sorry, Dragan,' said the man rubbing his wrist. 'It's just that I thought you'd like to hear. Your cousin's murder has been avenged.'

Mitrović's eyes blazed. 'Milan's killer is dead?'

'An hour ago. Stabbed, and died on the way to hospital.'

'This is a good day. And was it Kolarov?'

The man nodded.

'Have they got him?'

'Not yet. There's a manhunt going on.'

'My people will get him away. He will be well rewarded.'

The man retreated to the safety of the door. 'It was all caught on camera. You can watch it on the news tonight. Enjoy.'

EPILOGUE

The bank manager watched as the four men entered the vault with their large metal suitcases and placed them next to the long table. Salvatore Baresi nodded at the other three, who silently left the room.

'A large deposit,' the bank manager commented. It wasn't unusual, and Mr Gentile had been one of his more cash-consistent customers over the years. Mr Gentile appreciated the friendly, personal and discreet service the bank offered, though this was the first time that so many suitcases had appeared all at once.

Salvatore Baresi was a regular visitor and he looked mightily pleased with himself. He had good reason. His Swedish trip had presented him with an opportunity within The Family, and he had grasped it eagerly. So the old couple had had to go, but who would miss them? He regarded them as collateral damage. He was proud of his professionalism: the job had gone smoothly and he hadn't been caught. And there was that extra kudos: he'd come away with twice what the Swede had stolen. The money he'd retrieved from the tank in the woods not only covered the amount stolen from Gentile but it would also cover what the Boss had had to pay out to the Columbians for their lost cocaine, thereby placating the suppliers. And that was after he'd skimmed his own nice cool million off the top. And then there was the cherry on the parfait – the demise of Micky Mosten. He'd had to admit to Gentile that he, personally, hadn't been able to kill Mosten because the cops had got to him first. It was a lie, but Gentile had bought it. Besides, it didn't matter now

– some lunatic had knifed the sneaky shit on his way to court. The Boss was so delighted with the outcome that he'd been promoted to the Gentile top table. He was being handed real power within the organization. Life couldn't get much better.

Baresi hauled one of the suitcases up onto the table and clicked it open.

'There's about ten million dollars in this lot.' The bank manager managed to retain his stoical expression. 'It's in Swedish kronor.'

'The krona? That's not a currency that Mr Gentile normally does business in.' He knew that it was best not to ask how the money had been obtained.

'No. Unusual circumstances. He wants this changed into dollars.'

The bank manager peered into the case. Baresi reached in, picked out a bundle of hundred-krona notes and passed them over. The manager took the batch and stared at the face on the top note.

'Excuse me, Mr Baresi, but do you have any five-hundreds?'

'Sure.' Baresi picked up another case and placed it on the table next to the first. Out of this he took another fistful of notes.

Again, the bank manager scrutinized the top note before flicking through the rest of the bundle like an experienced card sharp. His features furrowed as his expression changed. He looked troubled.

'Where did you get these from?'

'Well, Sweden, of course.'

'Yes, yes. But when? How recently?'

'In the last month.'

The bank manager blinked. Baresi didn't like the man's puzzled air.

'These five-hundred-krona notes have the image of King Carl XI.'

'So what?'

'They should have an image of the opera singer Birgit Nilsson. Those hundreds… should be Greta Garbo, not Carl von Linne.'

'Greta fucking Garbo. What are you on about?'

The bank manager lifted a third case onto the table and opened it himself. It was full of thousand-krona notes. He shook his head sadly.

'What's up?' asked Baresi, who was now feeling decidedly edgy.

'These should be Dag Hammerskjöld.'

'Who the hell is Dag whatshisname?'

'Bad news, Mr Baresi. I'm afraid all these notes are out of date.'

'Out of date? Cash doesn't date. We can still use a hundred-year-old dollar bill, for Chrissake!'

'It may apply here in the United States, but not elsewhere. Sweden changed all their notes and coins around 2015 and 2016. These predate the new notes.'

'What does that mean?' Baresi squeaked in horror.

'Sad to say, all this,' the manager said with a sweep of his arm, 'isn't worth a red cent.'

NOTES

Bank robberies in Sweden

At the beginning of the book, there is an armed robbery of a cash-handling facility in Malmö. It was only when I began researching the subject that I realized how many similar crimes had been perpetrated in Sweden in recent years. There were some particularly big heists in 2005 and 2006, and over a hundred and fifty in 2008 alone (*source: Swedish National Council of Crime Prevention*). In 2005, the country saw more violent robberies of cash transport vehicles per head of population than anywhere in Europe apart from the UK, Ireland and Malta. All the robberies that Anita refers to in Chapter 7 were real events.

Of course, one of the most famous Swedish heists is the one that gave us 'Stockholm Syndrome'. Kreditbanken on Norrmalmstorg was held up by gunman Jan-Erik Olsson in August 1973. Olsson entered the bank wearing makeup, a woman's wig and sunglasses. He ripped out a submachine gun, fired a round into the ceiling and shouted 'The party starts!' He took four hostages and demanded that his friend, the notorious criminal Clark Olofsson (*now the subject of a Netflix drama series*), be brought to him from prison, along with the equivalent of four million dollars. Amazingly, the authorities handed Olofsson over. Six days later, when the police rushed in with tear gas, the perpetrators gave themselves up. Interestingly, the police were able to film much of what happened in the bank during the time the hostages were being held, and they were able to listen in on the remarkable conversations between the hostages and their captors, and hear how their relationships developed and empathies were formed.

In 2009, the G4S cash security depot in Västberga in southern Stockholm was the target for one of the most daring and audacious robberies of more recent times. A helicopter was landed on the roof. The gang smashed their way through a reinforced glass window with a sledgehammer, took the equivalent of ten million euros and flew off!

Change in currency

The official reason why Sweden changed its cash in the mid 2010s, according to the Riksbank (Sweden's central bank), was to prevent counterfeiting. Another incentive to introduce new currency may have been as a result of research by Oxford University in 2013, which found that Sweden's bank notes were the second filthiest in Europe (Denmark's were the first), containing an average of 39,600 bacteria per note.

The new currency was introduced in two separate waves and all the old krona notes, from 20 to 1,000, became invalid after June 30th, 2017. However, the old bills were still accepted in banks until June 30th, 2018.

Since then, Sweden has headed towards a cashless society, and bank robberies are becoming a thing of the past. In 2020, there were only five – three of them armed. This, however, didn't stop author, Fredrik Backman, adopting a more modern-day approach to the age-old concept in his amusing, witty and bittersweet book *Anxious People*, which is about the failed robbery of a cashless bank and the subsequent taking hostage of eight people innocently viewing an apartment for sale.

Yugoslavian connections

Historically, Sweden has always been a country that has taken in those seeking sanctuary from war, famine or political persecution. Serbs are no exception, though the first significant wave during the 1960s and 1970s was welcomed for economic reasons, when agreements were signed with Yugoslavia, among other countries, to help overcome severe labour shortages. More migrants, this time Bosnian and Croatian Serbs, came to Sweden as a result of the Balkan Wars in the 1990s. These communities have produced many successful Serbian Swedes, particularly in the fields of sport and entertainment.

The influx also spawned what is known as the 'Yugo Mafia'. In the slipstream of migrant workers moving to parts of Western Europe came many of the criminals that had been emptied out of prisons by Socialist Yugoslavia. Criminal gangs were created in Germany, Austria, Denmark and Sweden. Under Željko 'Arkan' Ražnatović, a number of armed robberies were carried out around Sweden in the 1970s. After Arkan fled the country, his childhood friend Dragan 'Jokso' Joksović took over his organization, broadening its activities to include cigarette smuggling and extortion. Jokso also owned several upmarket Stockholm restaurants, which were frequented by the rich and famous. Despite being indicted several times, Jokso was never convicted for his crimes. He was eventually murdered by a Finnish hitman in 1998.

Jokso's successor was shot dead in the centre of Stockholm in 2003 and *his* successor was his son-in-law, Milan Ševo. Ševo survived several assassination attempts before leaving Stockholm for Belgrade in 2005. From there he is believed by the Swedish and Serbian authorities to have organized the 2009 Västberga helicopter heist.

Migration to America

Swedes have always had strong links with America. At the turn of the 20th century, the city with the second-largest Swedish population after Stockholm wasn't in Scandinavia – it was Chicago. It is estimated that 1.3 million Swedes emigrated to the USA between 1850 and 1930: about 35% of the population at the time. The reason for such an exodus was that Sweden was predominantly a rural country and life was economically hard. Others left for political and religious reasons. The first immigrants sought a rural lifestyle in Illinois, Kansas, Wisconsin, Nebraska and Minnesota. Later immigrants headed for the burgeoning cities for work. Some didn't find the better life they were looking for and a fifth of those who crossed the Atlantic in the mass migration period returned home.

In the 2000 Census, four million Americans said they had Swedish ancestry. Minnesota is the state with the highest proportion of inhabitants of Swedish descent – 7.3% of the population in 2020. And Swedish Americans have left their mark in every sphere of the country's life. Click on Wikipedia, and you'll find the list of high-achieving Swedish Americans is very long indeed.

Paige McBride mentioned Swedish-American newspapers in the story. Many of the Swedish immigrants who entered the USA in the 19th century came into the country with high degrees of literacy (due to the church's strong emphasis on being able to read, and compulsory basic schooling from 1842 onwards). It was therefore little wonder that a large number of Swedish-language publications sprang up in their communities. At their height, it is believed there were between 600 and 1,000 newspapers (mainly weeklies). The centre of this press activity was, unsurprisingly, Chicago where, according to one estimate, 187 Swedish-language periodicals were published.

ABOUT THE AUTHOR

Torquil MacLeod was born in Edinburgh, Scotland. After a brief career as a teacher and an even briefer one in insurance, in which he didn't manage to sell a single policy, he worked as a copywriter in advertising agencies in Birmingham, Glasgow and Newcastle before turning freelance. He lives in north-west England with his wife, Susan. The idea for a Scandinavian crime series came from his frequent trips to Malmö and southern Sweden to visit his elder son. He now has four grandchildren, equally spread between Sweden and Essex.

Also by Torquil MacLeod:

The Malmö Mysteries
(in order)
Meet me in Malmö
Murder in Malmö
Missing in Malmö
Midnight in Malmö
A Malmö Midwinter (novella)
Menace in Malmö
Malice in Malmö
Mourning in Malmö
Mammon in Malmö

ACKNOWLEDGEMENTS

Firstly, I'd like to thank my good friend Nick Pugh for doing another great book cover despite me mucking him around. I hope our convivial lunches make his frustrations easier to bear.

Over in Sweden, I am ever grateful to Fraser and Paula for their observations of day-to-day life in Skåne. And, of course, our good friend, Karin Geistrand continues to be a font of knowledge on police and other matters, even if she doesn't recognize what I've done with the information. I'd also like to thank reader Maria Fridefors from Malmö, who provided me with some fascinating insights into why many Swedes change their surnames. Still in Malmö, many thanks go to Catherine and Karren at the marvellous Taste of Britain shop on Engelbrektsgatan, who have done so much to promote my books in the city. I heartily recommend a visit if you're ever in the vicinity.

I called on my neighbour Mark Reading's wide military experience to give me a crash-course in firearms. It was worth the six-month wait for him to get back to me.

Thanks also to Andy and Caroline at McNidder & Grace for everything they've done. And to Paula Beaton for her careful scrutiny.

I'd like to thank Susan for all her hard work knocking the many rough edges off the manuscript. And, fortunately for the readers, she won most of the battles that ensued in that process.

My gratitude also goes to the readers who have contacted me with interesting and supportive emails. They are highlights that brighten the solitary working day.

Finally, I want to mention Bill Foster, who formed half of my medical brains trust with his wife Justine. We'd known each other since we were toddlers in Durham, and he went on to become a well-respected doctor and beloved father and grandfather. He was a great friend, and his passing last year has left a gap in so many lives. This book is dedicated to him.

OTHER TITLES IN THE SERIES

Meet Me in Malmö
ISBN 9780857161130

Murder in Malmö
ISBN 9780857161147

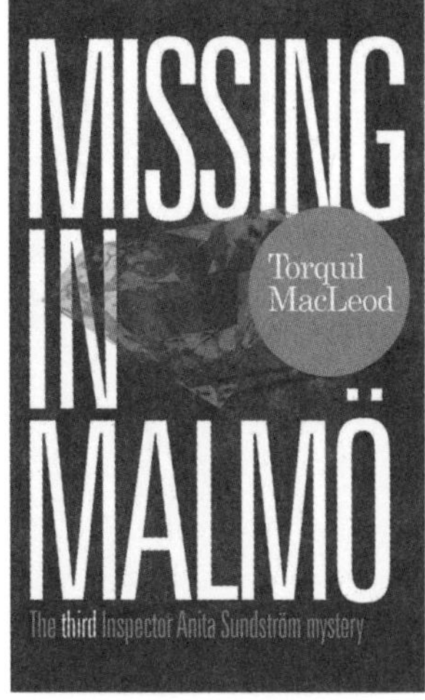

Missing in Malmö
ISBN 9780857161154

Midnight in Malmö
ISBN 9780857161307

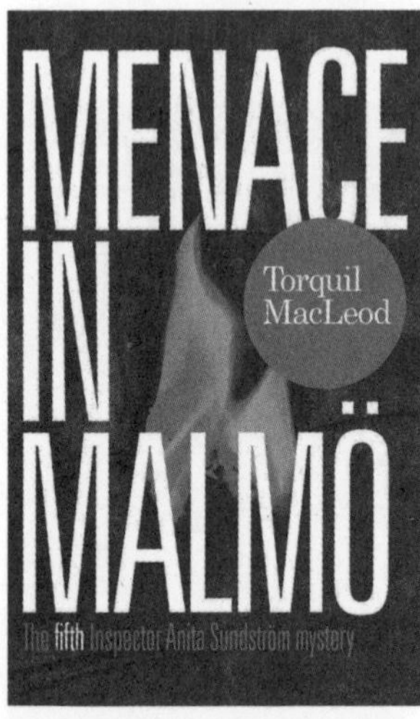

Menace in Malmö
ISBN 9780857161734

Malice in Malmö
ISBN 9780857161871

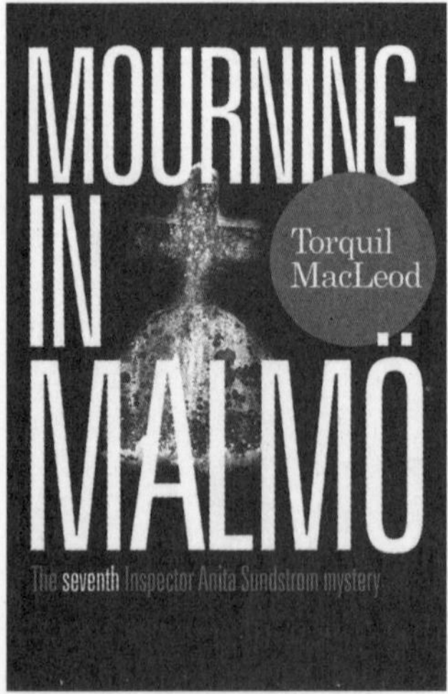

Mourning in Malmö
ISBN 9780857162076

Mammon in Malmö
ISBN 9780857162106